Praise for *A Good Day for Chardonnay*

"Entertaining . . . fans of zanier mysteries will welcome Sunshine's further adventures."
—*Publishers Weekly*

"A hilarious amalgam of mystery, Can't wait for the next episode."

Praise for *A Bad Day for Sunshine*

"Provides plenty of action. Recommended for fans of Linda Castillo and J. A. Jance."
—*Library Journal*

"Jones has a real talent for balancing suspense with laugh-out-loud humor, never losing the tension from either."
—*BookPage*

"*A Bad Day for Sunshine* is a great day for the rest of us—captivating characters, great writing, pace, humor, and suspense."
—Lee Child, *New York Times* bestselling author

"Fans of Jones's bestselling Charley Davidson series and Janet Evanovich's romps will devour this steamy series launch, which introduces both an irresistible pair of crime-busting Gilmore Girls and a quirky, mysterious setting."
—*Booklist*

"Compelling characters and a sexy, angst-filled bunch of mysteries add up to a winning series debut."
—*Kirkus Reviews*

"*A Bad Day for Sunshine* is everything you want from Darynda Jones . . . and more! Laugh-out-loud funny, intensely suspenseful, page-turning fun with a sassy new heroine you will love. Prepare to be hooked by this witty, sexy, and thrilling new series from one of my favorite authors!"
—Allison Brennan, *New York Times* bestselling author

ALSO BY DARYNDA JONES

Sunshine Vicram

A Bad Day for Sunshine

Charley Davidson

Summoned to Thirteenth Grave

The Trouble with Twelfth Grave

Eleventh Grave in Moonlight

The Curse of Tenth Grave

The Dirt on Ninth Grave

Eighth Grave After Dark

Seventh Grave and No Body

Sixth Grave on the Edge

Fifth Grave Past the Light

Fourth Grave Beneath My Feet

Third Grave Dead Ahead

Second Grave on the Left

First Grave on the Right

Death and the Girl He Loves

Death, Doom, and Detention

Death and the Girl Next Door

A
GOOD DAY
FOR
CHARDONNAY

Darynda Jones

ST. MARTIN'S
GRIFFIN
NEW YORK

Published in the United States by St. Martin's Griffin, an imprint of St. Martin's Publishing Group.

www.stmartins.com

Designed by Omar Chapa

The Library of Congress has cataloged the hardcover edition as follows:

Names: Jones, Darynda, author.
Title: A good day for chardonnay / Darynda Jones.
Description: First Edition. | New York : St. Martin's Press, 2021. |
    Series: Sunshine Vicram series ; 2
Identifiers: LCCN 2021006926 | ISBN 9781250233110 (hardcover) |
    ISBN 9781250233134 (ebook)
Subjects: GSAFD: Suspense fiction. | Mystery fiction.
Classification: LCC PS3610.O6236 G66 2021 | DDC 813/.6—dc23
LC record available at https://lccn.loc.gov/2021006926

ISBN 978-1-250-23312-7 (trade paperback)

Our books may be purchased in bulk for promotional, educational, or business use. Please contact your local bookseller or the Macmillan Corporate and Premium Sales Department at 1-800-221-7945, extension 5442, or by email at MacmillanSpecialMarkets@macmillan.com.

First St. Martin's Griffin Edition: 2022

10 9 8 7 6 5 4 3 2 1

For Jeffe Kennedy:
the author,
the princess,
THE LEGEND
(For realsies, thank you!)

1

Welcome to Del Sol,
Home of Something . . .
Or Somebody Famous . . .
Someday . . .
Maybe . . .

Sunshine stared into her cup of coffee as though it were a witch's cauldron, a window revealing all the ways she could kill her parents. Their deaths would be slow and methodical and painful. Much like the date she was on now.

She looked across the table at said date—the third one her parents had set her up with in as many weeks—and feigned interest by lifting a brow in dire need of professional attention.

"There's a lot more to pest control than people realize."

She'd tried to wax her own brows once.

"Our work can get pretty dangerous."

Ripping out one's facial hair took nerve.

"Last year I was attacked by a swarm of carnivorous beetles."

And painkillers.

"Another time, I thought I'd been bitten by a copperhead and fell down three flights of stairs."

And possibly a blood coagulant.

"Turns out I was just electrocuted."

If Sun were totally honest with herself—

"I will never stick my hand inside an RV's plumbing system again."

—and she liked to think she was—

"I don't care what the literature says."

—Carver wasn't the worst date she'd ever had.

"Then there was the time I tried to tame a jellyfish."

His height alone was enough to turn heads.

"Its name was Loki."

And he'd been graced with thick muddy curls.

"He glowed in the dark."

Ashen-gray eyes.

"Not that Loki had anything to do with my job."

And a sharp angular face.

"It's just, in case you've ever wondered—"

On a scale of one to Ferrari, Carver was a solid Ford Explorer.

"—jellyfish *cannot* be domesticated."

He'd make some lucky girl a fine ex-husband one day.

"I have the doctor's bills to prove it."

Still, there was something off about him.

"They don't have brains."

Something Sun couldn't quite put her finger on.

"Jellyfish. Not doctors."

He was handsome but not in a charming way.

"Insects do, though."

Smart but not in a clever way.

"Did you know there are over five million species of insects in the world?"

Nice but not in a genuine way.

"And thirty-five thousand species of spiders."

In a word, he was not Levi Ravinder.

"Thankfully, they rarely bother humans."

But so few men were.

"Even ones as pretty as you."

True, Carver paled in comparison to Levi, but so did every other man Sun had ever met. The fact that she'd been in love with the guy since she was a kid didn't help. No one stood a chance against the bad boy from a crime-ridden family who'd done good.

And now, instead of being with the man of her dreams, she was stuck with bug guy. She could only hope her parents'd had the foresight to buy side-by-side burial plots before setting her up.

"Is that your phone?"

Sunshine snapped out of her musings and dug through her bag for her phone like it was a life preserver on the *Titanic*. "Hello?" she said, sounding more desperate than she'd intended. She cleared her throat and began again. "Sheriff Vicram."

A male voice eerily resembling her BFF's spoke in hushed tones. "You told me to call if he came back."

Sun froze. Her sidekick since kindergarten, who also happened to be her chief deputy, sounded panicked. Though he did seem to panic more often than most men, Sun fought a wave of anxiety.

"Randy," he added.

"He didn't."

"Did too," he said defensively.

"Okay, look, stay calm, Quince."

Quincy Cooper had been her bestie since she'd throat-punched Peter Bailey for knocking him down on the playground. Quince had grown since then. Now he looked roughly like an industrial freezer with a grin that could melt the panties off a comatose nun.

Peter Bailey eventually got throat cancer, but Sun liked to think it had less to do with her throat punch and more to do with his three-pack-a-day habit.

"Stay calm?" he mimicked, incredulous. "You stay calm. Have you seen the size of this guy?"

"Quince, we've got this." She grabbed her bag and stood. "Call for backup. Everyone. Get Zee and Salazar there ay-sap. I'll be there in five. By the way, who's Randy?"

He released an annoyed sigh, drawing it out as though he were competing for Miss Drama Queen, USA. "The raccoon."

She stopped, slammed her eyes shut, and spun to face away

from her date. When she spoke, she spoke softly so Carver the pest-preneur wouldn't overhear. "You called me about a raccoon?"

"Yes, I called you about a raccoon. You told me to. He's wreaking havoc all over town."

"All over town as in *your house.*"

"There, too."

She took a deep breath and turned back to Carver. "I'm so sorry. I've been called in. Power outages on the other side of town. People running into walls. It's utter chaos."

He shot out of his chair. "Oh, no, that's okay. I mean, you are the *sheriff.*"

There.

That odd niggling at the back of her neck.

It was the way he said *sheriff.* As though her holding such a position was preposterous. Never mind her master's degree in criminal justice. Or her ten years on the Santa Fe police force, seven of which she served as a detective. To him, she was a curvy blonde. End of story. She'd sensed it the moment his gaze landed on her.

And her breasts.

Mostly her breasts.

Curse her ability to read people like the ingredients label on a bottle of water.

Most people, anyway. Levi Ravinder? Not so much.

When she started to walk away, Carver called out to her. "Do you want me to get this?"

She stopped again, stunned. After a moment, she took a deep, calming breath. As slowly and methodically as she'd been planning her parents' deaths, she pivoted around to him. "Not at all." She walked back, took out a ten, and dropped it onto the table.

"Oh, yours was only a couple of bucks."

She knew exactly how much her cup of coffee was. It was a freaking cup of coffee. With a nod, she gestured toward his triple espresso caramel soy macchiato with a dash of cinnamon and extra nondairy whip, and said, "It's on me."

He beamed at her, clearly impressed. "Well, thank you, Sunshine. Most women don't take that kind of initiative."

And she'd moisturized for this.

"I'd love to see you again."

Wedging a smile between the hard lines that had marbleized her face, she turned and headed out the door. Not that she'd actually expected him to pay for her coffee. Going dutch was always best in these situations. But, seriously, it was a dollar fifty.

One.

Dollar.

Fifty.

A buck and a half.

Twelve bits.

She couldn't rush off to her power outage fast enough. The fact that she'd lied about it was entirely beside the point.

She unlocked her cruiser and settled inside, thankful she hadn't dressed so much to the nines as to the five-and-dimes. Sixes at best. Sure, she'd applied makeup, a rarity these days, but she wore a peach summery sweater, faded jeans, and pretty suede boots with just enough of a heel to make her a danger to herself and anyone within a ten-foot radius.

Making a quick U-turn out of the parking lot, she headed toward Quince's house. She almost felt bad about abandoning her half-date soy latte with a splash of objectification and extra nondairy whipped misogyny. Carver was new in town, the owner and operator of the Four Cs, a.k.a. the Creepy Crawler Critter Control. And he—

Wait. She stepped on the brakes and frowned in thought. How did someone get an RV up three flights of stairs?

Sun had to make the arduous drive through the town of Del Sol to get to Quincy's cabin. So, like, five minutes. Caffeine-Wah had opened the outdoor area beside their coffee shop. Both locals and tourists sat around a blazing firepit despite the sultry night, listening to an acoustic guitarist and drinking cappuccinos spiked with either Irish cream or Dark River Shine, Del Sol's homegrown corn whiskey.

Even the newlyweds, Ike and Ida Madrid, were there, with their prize rooster, Puff Daddy, on a leash, much to the delight of the other patrons. Four months ago, those two had been mortal enemies, and yet marriage became them. Surely there was hope for the rest of humanity. And Sun. Eventually.

She glanced over at a couple of the locals as she passed, only mildly curious where one might obtain a leash for a rooster. Bernadette, the owner of Swirls-n-Curls, and Juana, the owner of Sun's favorite Mexican restaurant, Tia Juana's, sat at a high table having way too much fun for there to only be coffee in their cups.

The two women were Del Sol natives, born and raised, thus Sun's mind meandered to the question that had been plaguing her since moving back. She'd been encouraged—a.k.a. blackmailed— into looking into a local myth that had been around for decades about the Dangerous Daughters, a group of women who, according to legend, secretly ran the town.

Because of that, she looked at every woman who'd been born and raised in the small hamlet as a potential Daughter. But she just couldn't see Bernadette running a town. A bingo parlor maybe, or a speakeasy, but not a town.

Juana, however, was another story. That woman could run a battalion.

Sun took a right at the town square and spotted Doug, their local flasher, walking toward the illuminated park. Painfully thin and wearing his usual trench coat, thick glasses, and a headband with a feather in it, he made a U-turn when he saw her cruiser and headed down a dark alley. She'd clearly foiled his plans for the evening. Served him right. That man was a menace.

Feeling good about the fact that she'd saved an innocent pedestrian from a flashing that could never be unseen, Sun drove out to Del Sol Lake and parked down the street from Quincy's cabin. Mostly because she had no choice. He'd taken her quite literally when she said to call in everyone.

Two deputies' vehicles sat on one side of the narrow road leading to his house along with several vehicles whose owners Sun could only speculate. Though one did look hauntingly familiar. White Buick Encore. Cracked taillight. Sign that read HONK IF YOU LIKE THE TACO. Which did not mean what her mother thought it meant.

Sun spared a moment to pinch the bridge of her nose when a hand shot out of a bush and pulled her behind it. Thankfully, the hand was attached to a body. A body named Quincy Lynn Cooper.

Wearing a pair of night-vision goggles that covered the upper half of his face, he dragged her around the cabin and yanked her behind yet another bush, before shushing her with an index finger over his mouth and pointing to his back porch.

"I didn't say anything," she whispered, slapping at his hand, annoyed at being yanked while having to navigate the rough terrain in heels.

"He's there," Quince said, his whisper much softer than hers. It was then that Sun realized he was wearing full tactical gear to go with the goggles and comm set. It took everything in her not to react, and she fought a strong urge to pinch the bridge of her nose again.

Instead, she looked through the foliage and saw nothing. "Where?"

"There." He pointed toward the shadows of his back porch. "Somewhere. I heard him, but the coward is too afraid to show his face when I'm around."

Sun frowned. Stakeouts were not a favorite pastime, and who knew how long it would be before the masked bandit emerged from the home he'd invaded. The same home he'd been invading repeatedly for weeks, according to the behemoth beside her.

Quincy's small cabin sat on the banks of the Pecos River, and she let the sound of rushing water wash over her. She could even smell it. Fresh and clear. His cabin had previously been a rental for tourists and resembled four others just like it, but they were far enough apart to offer a nice bit of privacy thanks to some strategically placed vegetation.

Maroon paint, in bad need of a fresh coat, framed the exposed pine exterior and wraparound porch that ran the length of the abode. Sun loved little more than sitting on that porch with Quincy, sipping on a glass of chardonnay and watching the setting sun glisten over the Pecos like diamonds and ambers and amethysts. But the sun had set an hour earlier, hence the goggles.

When he handed her a pair along with a comm set and a quick, "Here," Sun fought a giggle. He'd gone all out. For a raccoon. She took the equipment and feigned a fit of coughs to cover her amusement.

He didn't buy it. He pressed his mouth together and ignored her as she struggled to untangle a blond lock of hair from a branch, then slipped the headset onto her head.

"Quince," she said, letting her eyes adjust to the green glow behind the goggles to focus on figure after figure stalking through the forested area, "when I said to call everyone in, I didn't mean, you know, *everyone.*"

"Well then, you shouldn't have said everyone. Besides, I needed help from on high."

"God?" she asked, fitting the earpiece he handed her into her left ear.

"No, sniper. Zee is on top of Mr. Chavez's barn."

A hushed female voice came over the radio. "You look great, boss."

Then another. Deputy Tricia Salazar, a curvy twentysomething with doe eyes and chipmunk cheeks, was learning to be Zee's spotter. "I agree. You should wear your civvies more often, boss."

Sun turned and, even though she couldn't actually see the deputies atop the rickety barn, flashed them her best supermodel smile. She could only imagine what that looked like with the alien tactical gear on her face. "Thank you, guys." She tossed her hair over a shoulder. "At least someone noticed."

"Oh, yeah," Quincy said, keeping a weather eye on his back porch. "How'd the date go?"

"Well enough to justify a plea of temporary insanity when I kill my parents. Why are you risking my deputies' lives for a rodent?"

He snorted. "They'll be fine. Even if they fall, it's not a tall barn. They'll shake it off."

"Like when you fell off your grandfather's barn and cried for two hours?"

"I was six. What did this one do for a living?"

"You mean after my last blind date, the breatharian life coach?"

"Yeah." He scratched his chin. "I wouldn't have figured your mother as one to set you up with a man living out of his van. Clearly, you're depreciating with age."

"Clearly. Mom said he was still finding himself."

"How old was he?"

"Early seventies. Thankfully, tonight's victim was more age-appropriate. And he had a job! Pest control. Or at least I think it was pest control. I wasn't really paying attention." When he ripped off the goggles and turned to gape at her, his eyes glowing green through her lenses, she asked, "What?"

"Let me get this straight," he said, ironically straightening to his full height of six feet, four inches, with shoulders spanning a similar distance. "You were on a date with a *pest control* guy when I called with a *pest control* issue, and you left him at the café?"

She stabbed him with the best glare in her arsenal, number 12.2—she'd recently upgraded—even though its genius was wasted behind the goggles. "Of course I left him at the café. Can you imagine what he would've charged for an after-hours emergency?"

"Budget issues?"

She snorted. "That's an understatement. My left pinky is bigger than our budget."

He gave her a surprised once-over. "As opposed to your right one?"

"I know right? I have weird fingers."

"Please. You should see my toes."

"I want to see them," Zee said over the comm.

"Never, sis. My toes are very private."

Quincy and Zee had decided they were twins separated at birth when they met four months ago. Since Quince was a blond-haired, blue-eyed wreck with few worthwhile talents—because the ability to sleep standing up didn't count—and Zee was a tall, gorgeous Black woman who could shoot the wings off a fruit fly at a hundred yards, Sun highly doubted the validity of their claim. Also, neither was adopted. So there was that.

"Okay, Quince, I have a random, off-the-cuff question," Sun said randomly and off-the-cuff.

"Shoot."

"What in the name of God is my mother doing here?" Sun watched as her mother tiptoed through the sultry night air, easing closer to Quincy's back porch. She'd pulled her graying blond hair into a ponytail that always made her look younger than her fifty-five years. A gauze tunic hung loosely over her slim frame.

"You said to call for backup."

"And you called my mother?" she asked, her voice rising a notch.

"No. I called her book club. Those ladies are fierce." The grin he wore made it impossible to be annoyed. He had a point, after all.

Sun scanned the area, now littered with women who'd run out of fucks to give decades ago, and focused on two in particular. They carried butterfly nets, one as though it were an assault rifle, the other as though it were a missile launcher.

"Just two more quick questions," she said.

He pulled the goggles back into position, and said, "Hit me."

"Why the hell do they have butterfly nets and where did they get them on such short notice?"

He chuckled and gestured toward a wily, five-foot firecracker in full camouflage regalia and neon pink crocs that were so blinding through the goggles Sun had to look away. Wanda also happened to be the one carrying her butterfly net like a missile launcher, which fit her personality to a tee.

"I think every time the men in white coats come for Wanda, she steals their nets and runs away."

The deputies laughed softly through the comm, Zee's an alluring, husky thing, and Deputy Salazar's a bubbly giggle like champagne. Or denture-cleaning tablets.

"That wouldn't surprise me," Sun said, wondering in the back of her mind if any of her mother's book club mates could be associated with the Dangerous Daughters. If it were even real. "It would also not surprise me if she brought the butterfly net more for you than for the raccoon."

He laughed again, but quickly changed his mind. Concern flashed across the part of his boyishly handsome face that she could see. "You're joking, right?"

Sun shrugged. Wanda had always had a thing for the intrepid deputy. Sadly, the intrepid deputy had always had a thing for Sun's mother, which would explain his calling in her book club more than his lame-ass excuse.

She used to think Quincy's crush was just a post-pubescent schoolboy thing, but since she'd moved back to Del Sol four months ago, Quince constantly asked about her mom, the lovely Elaine Freyr. How was she? What she was up to? Had she ever had an affair with a younger, freakishly comely man?

It was weird. And getting weirder every day. So much so, in fact, that Sun had caught onto his ruse about a month in. He was deflecting. Straight up. He was in love with someone else, and he didn't want her to know. *Her.* Sunshine Vicram. His best friend since the sandbox.

Sun vowed to find out who he was rounding the bases and sliding into home with if it were the last thing she did on this Earth. To date, she'd narrowed it down to thirty-seven women (and two men, just in case). She was so close she could taste victory. Or wishful thinking. Emotional figures of speech tasted startlingly similar.

Her phone dinged with a text from her date asking if everything was okay.

Before she could answer, Quincy whispered so loudly he probably scared off the masked bandit. "There he is!"

Sun glanced at the porch and, sure enough, the little guy was climbing out of a tiny hole in the ceiling of Quincy's porch as though being poured out of it, his fur fluffing up to three times his actual size. It reminded Sun she needed to cut back on the carbs.

Quince slid his goggles down and raised his dart gun, a non-lethal tranquilizer launcher that looked like a combination of an Uzi and a water gun.

"Please don't tranq my mother," Sun said, cringing as she stood beside him and watched the critter through her goggles.

Before he could get a clear shot, however, Wanda ran forward, her net at the ready. "I'll get 'im!"

"Shit," Quince said. Abandoning his cover, he vaulted around the bush toward the melee of vigilant women.

Sun fought off the branch again and followed, trying not to twist her ankle. She watched as Wanda, her mother, and Darlene Tapia, another member of the infamous Book Babes Book Club, ascended the stairs to the porch and rushed the panicked, screeching creature.

Poor little guy. Sun would've screeched, too. Those women were alarmingly fast runners.

"Don't get near it!" Quincy shouted.

"It's okay, handsome." Wanda took a swipe at the ball of fur, just missing it by several tenths of a mile. "I was vaccinated for rabies when I was a kid. I'm immune."

Sun's heart jumped into her throat as Wanda got closer. The rabies angle had yet to occur to her. "I'm not sure it works that way, Wanda!"

"I can't see anything," Elaine Freyr said, now watching from a safe-ish distance on the porch as her friends advanced. She spun in a complete circle, searching the shadows of the porch. "Where'd it go?"

Darlene Tapia followed suit. All three women were in the dizzying midst of full-on adrenaline rushes, screaming and recoiling with the slightest movement, Wanda swinging wildly as the raccoon scurried about trying to escape. Wanda was either going to kill the raccoon or concuss someone else.

Quincy took up position about ten feet out and raised the rifle again.

"Don't you dare," Sun said, glaring at him as she ran past. She hiked up the stairs, ducked another swipe from Wanda's net, and slid to a stop beside her mother, her gaze darting about.

"Son of a bitch," Quincy said with more whine than all of southern France. "He got away."

"And whose fault would that be?" she asked him over her shoulder. She turned back to the maniac who'd birthed her. "Mom, it's okay. We've got this." When Elaine didn't move, Sun put a hand on her arm. "Mom?"

Her mother stood frozen, staring up into a darkened corner of the porch. Sun pivoted slowly and came face-to-face with a very angry raccoon, their noses only inches apart.

It sat hunchbacked on a high windowsill, a slow hiss leaking from between its exposed teeth, as it gazed at her with wide, feral eyes. Eyes that glowed like they belonged to a creature possessed by a powerful evil. One so ancient, so primordial, it predated human language.

Then she realized she was still wearing the goggles and the ominous metaphor lost its ardor. Much like Sun's hopes to go her entire life without wrestling a raccoon in the dark with a gang of bookworms cheering her on. But stranger things had happened.

Before she could react, she heard the thud of compressed air. Quincy had taken a shot with her barely inches from the terrified animal. What the actual hell?

He'd just moved up a notch on her hit list, overtaking Ryan Spalding, a boy who'd claimed she'd given him a hand job under the bleachers in high school, when she realized it was a misfire.

The gun. Not the hand job. She'd never touched Ryan's penis, much to his chagrin.

Quincy let loose a dozen expletives followed by a sheepishly meek, "Misfire."

She wanted to roll her eyes but didn't dare take them off the rodent. They were locked in a stare-down of legendary proportions. "Zee," she said softly into her comm set, staying as still as she possibly could, "you wanna help me out here?"

Zee's smooth voice came back to her. "Will do, boss." Her calm tone spoke volumes. Like elevator music. Or an acid trip. She was already in the zone and probably had the creature in her crosshairs. "One inch to the left."

Sun eased to her left a microsecond before a dart whizzed past her ear.

It hit home just as the raccoon catapulted off the sill and onto her goggle-covered face. She screamed and sank her fingers in its fur to rip it off, but it held on for dear life, anchoring its razor-sharp claws in her scalp. She stumbled back and tripped on something hard and short. Probably her own indignation.

Her mother screamed but it barely registered before Sun found herself falling. No. Not just falling. Tumbling, suddenly weightless. She'd done a backflip over the wooden porch railing and seemed to be plummeting headfirst toward certain death.

A familiar set of arms caught her in midair before all three— the owner of said arms, the facehugger, and Sun herself—slammed onto the rocky earth beneath them. Air whooshed out of her lungs and, even with the insulation of her rescuer, the hard landing sent a jolt of pain through body parts that, until that moment, she was unaware existed.

It also dislodged the raccoon. The furball shot into the darkness and landed a few feet away with a soft thud.

She rolled off her rescuer and lay on her back, gazing up at the stars and gasping to force air into lungs that had seized up, when her mother's head popped into her line of sight.

"Honey, are you okay?" she asked, concern lining her pretty, upside-down face.

"Peachy, Mom," Sun said, her voice strained. "Thanks for asking." Her gaze slid past the woman who birthed her and back up to the stars again, hoping for a glimpse of the Little Dipper, wishing she could pluck it from the heavens and beat her chief deputy with it. "Deputy Cooper?"

"Yeah, boss?" he replied, panting close by.

"Are you conscious?"

"Yes."

"Can you give me one good reason why I shouldn't beat you to death with a feather duster?"

"I made you bacon the other day."

Damn it.

2

If you don't talk to your cat about catnip, who will?
—SIGN AT DEL SOL VETERINARY CLINIC

"You know this is all your fault."

Sun gaped at her chief deputy as he followed her through the bullpen toward her office at the station, caged raccoon in hand.

"If you would've just let me shoot him . . ."

Sun knew better than that. If anything, she'd saved him weeks of guilt. He didn't have the stomach for such things. She waved a hand at him. "I know, Quince, but there was no need to kill the little guy," she said to let him off the hook. "We'll get him checked out, then take him out to Dover Pass and release him."

He stopped and the look he gave her would've broke her heart if it weren't so funny. "We're just going to dump him? Leave him out there all alone and defenseless?"

"He's a wild animal. Completely untamed. And possibly rabid."

He lifted the cage onto her desk and studied the hapless creature snoozing away. "That never stopped your parents from caring for you."

Ouch. "Touché. But that doesn't take away from the fact that you can't keep him."

His shoulders deflated. They'd dealt with wildlife before, but Quincy had clearly grown attached to the menace and their cat-and-mouse game of tag over the last few weeks.

Sun opened a cabinet and looked at herself in the mirror. Only minor cuts and a tiny bruise on her jaw. Not bad. Her hair, however . . . She combed through it with her fingers, then gave up, closed the door, and popped a coffee pod into the maker. "I was having such a great hair day."

Quince chuckled. "Sometimes I forget you're a girl."

"Please. Like you don't have bad hair days."

"True. Remember our senior pictures?"

She stopped and stared dreamily into the vast oblivion. "How could I forget the greatest memory of my life?"

"And it's forever commemorated in our yearbook."

"I'm a little disappointed no one calls you SpongeBob anymore."

He stuck his fingers through the cage and petted their unconscious guest. "If we did keep him—"

"Quincy," she warned.

"—and I'm not saying we will, but if we did—"

"Quince." She knew he would do this.

"—he could be our mascot." He raised a hopeful gaze. "I've always wanted a raccoon to assist me with petty crimes."

Sun struggled to hide her amusement and joined him in admiring the fluffy furball. "He *is* adorable."

"Right?"

She looked at Quince, then back at the raccoon. "He's kind of like your spirit animal."

"What if he has rabies, though?"

"Then he would be *exactly* like your spirit animal."

Sun's newest recruit walked in then, Poetry Rojas, freshly graduated from the police academy and looking spiffy in his pressed black uniform.

"Hey, Rojas," she said.

He handed her a file. "Boss, can I ask you something?"

"Of course." She grabbed her cup and took a long, scalding draw.

"Did you hire me because you feel sorry for me?"

She choked, not sure if it was due to the scalding liquid burning the back of her throat or Rojas's question. Most likely a combination of the two.

"I'm not a charity case," he continued. "I want to earn this position on my own merit."

She tossed in a few last-minute coughs, then asked, "Seriously?"

"No." He grinned, an enchanting lopsided thing. Never mind that underneath the uniform lay enough ink to print *The New York Times* for a month. He was a good officer. "It just makes me sound like a better person when I say shit like that."

She tapped her temple and looked at Quince. "Always thinking, this one."

"I think," he said, defensively.

"Mm-hm." She glanced over the report Rojas had brought in. "I want you to pay attention to this, Quince. Rojas knows how to write up a report."

"I write reports."

"Listen," she said before reading aloud. "'Single-handedly and with zero safety incidents, updated the communication and output device that utilizes and produces vital information while simultaneously sharing critical data with coworkers and creating a more efficient and productive work environment.'"

After taking a moment to let the sentence sink in, Quince frowned at Rojas and asked, "What does that even mean?"

The glib smirk the new deputy offered her BFF was too much. "I changed the ink cartridge in the printer."

Sun nodded. "I like the way you think, Rojas."

"Thanks, boss." He bent to check out the caged menace snoring away. "How'd it go?"

"I had a raccoon's crotch in my face for what seemed like hours."

He arched a brow. "I didn't know you were into that sort of thing."

She picked up her cup and took another sip. "I have many sides, Rojas."

After a quick glance over his shoulder at Quince, he straightened and started to leave, but Sun could tell there was something more lingering just below the surface. He had questions. And doubts. She knew he would.

"Quince, can you give us a sec?"

"Sure thing." He gave Rojas a challenging stare, one that warmed Sun's heart. She'd known they would get along when she hired Rojas, and Quincy's ribbing was proof that she'd been right.

She sat at her desk and motioned for him to sit across from her.

The situation with Poetry Rojas was one that she would never have believed if it hadn't happened on her watch. Four months ago, U.S. Marshals had descended upon the town of Del Sol searching for an escaped convict named Ramses Rojas, Poetry's twin brother. What she figured out during the manhunt was that Ramses was actually Poetry. He'd gone to prison in his brother's stead.

How he had pulled it off, she would never quite understand, but it was important to Poetry. He'd implied once that he'd owed his brother, so when the cops mistakenly arrested him, he didn't correct them. In Sun's opinion, unless Ramses had given up a kidney for him, Poetry got the short end of the stick. Three years inside for a crime he didn't commit was asking a lot.

While there, however, Poetry had earned a bachelor's in Criminal Justice and was actively working to get his case—his brother's case—overturned. Getting caught in the middle of a jailbreak hadn't been his plan. Sun had seen the footage from the van the prisoners had escaped from. He'd had no choice but to go along. Luckily for her, because she would never have found him otherwise.

"How are you doing, Rojas?"

He leaned back in the chair, still a tad untrusting of the situation, and possibly of her, and said evasively, "I'm good."

"Your scores were excellent at the academy." Like she knew they would be.

"Thanks."

"No, thank you. It makes me look good."

He nodded and she realized getting past the barriers he'd built in prison for a crime he didn't commit would take some time. That was okay. She just happened to have some extra time.

"Do you have any questions? Complaints? Concerns?"

He lifted a shoulder. "I do have one concern, if you're asking."

She took another sip. "I'm asking."

He took a moment to consider his words, then said, "I think you got the wrong guy."

"I doubt it. I haven't arrested anyone in days," she teased. The statement didn't surprise her. Rojas had been questioning her decision to blackmail him into joining the team since she'd first done it four months earlier.

He sat up straighter in agitation. "What happens if I can't solve a case or if someone gets away on my watch or if I make a mistake and someone dies because of it?" He dropped his gaze to study his hands. "What if I fail?"

His misgivings only strengthened Sun's conviction that she'd made the right decision. She would've been worried were he not questioning his ability to do the job. "You *will* fail."

He fixed her with a guarded stare.

"You *will* make mistakes." She leaned forward and spoke softly. "You will regret decisions you made because hindsight is twenty-twenty. But you'll learn from them and do better next time."

"You don't make mistakes."

"Trust me, I do. On a daily basis."

He shook his head. "I've read your clearance rate from when you were a detective in Santa Fe. Ninety-seven percent. That's almost unheard of. If you do make mistakes, you don't make many."

"Maybe I'm just really good at fixing them before they become an issue," she offered, but she had the feeling he was referring to something a little more specific. Maybe something he'd done in the past that made him question his position. When he asked his next question, she was sure of it.

"Do any of them haunt you?"

"Yes."

Too much of a gentleman to ask her which ones, he nodded but kept silent, so she explained. He needed to know she was far from perfect. Everyone was. "My very first case as a detective."

He leaned onto his elbows, his interest piqued.

"Missing boy. The father on trial for securities fraud. The mother a puddle of nerves."

"What happened?"

The tightening in her chest proved she was still not over it. Over him. A five-year-old boy with huge brown eyes and a nuclear smile. He'd haunted her dreams for seven years. "He . . . we never found him."

"I'm sorry."

"Thank you. Just know, Rojas, we can't win them all. We do the best with what we have and try to make it home to our loved ones every night." When he only nodded, unconvinced, she added, "And I chose you for a reason. Never doubt that. But if you need to talk about anything, you know where I live."

"Thanks, boss."

Zee walked into the station, dart gun in hand, and Rojas almost broke his neck to get a clear view.

He nodded a hello as she walked past the office door, then said, "That girl can shoot."

"Yes, she can."

"Remind me not to piss her off."

"Don't piss her off." Sun motioned Quincy back into the office when he questioned her with a wave. "I think we both need to stay on the straight and narrow where Zee is concerned."

"She would never shoot me," Quincy said as he walked in to hand her a form that needed her signature. "What with us being twins and all."

Rojas scoffed. "You've clearly never had a real sibling."

Quincy scratched his brow with his middle finger as Sun studied the form.

Rojas chuckled.

Oh yeah, they were going to get along great.

"Is raccoon chow even a real thing?" she asked when she looked over the new expenditures Quince was trying to sneak through.

Before he could answer, Salazar walked into the office and spotted the sleeping prisoner. "Oooooh," she cooed, rushing forward and poking her finger through the bars. Sun made a mental note to schedule wildlife training ASAP. "He's so cute."

"I call dibs on partner-in-petty-crimes," Quince said.

Salazar pouted, her baby face appearing even younger. "I'm never going to get a partner-in-petty-crimes. I even wished for one on a shooting star when I was a kid."

How sweet.

He draped an arm over her shoulders. "It'll happen. Someday when you least expect it, *bam*. Your soulmate will appear. Your spirit animal. Your partner-in-petty-crimes. It's kismet."

"You think so?"

He turned her to face him and bent until they were eye-to-eye. Thus, a lot. "I know so. You can't give up hope, Salazar."

The young deputy rewarded him with a sheepish grin. "Thanks, Chief Cooper."

Sun laughed softly and grabbed her bag. "I'm heading home. You guys need to do the same. Big day tomorrow. Huge." She opened her arms wide to demonstrate. "Massive day."

Everyone stopped and gave her their full attention.

"What's tomorrow?" Quince asked.

"Sunday."

"And?"

"My day off."

"That constitutes a big day?"

"It does when I haven't had a day off in four months."

"That's not true." He held up an index finger. "You took a day off when you chased Doug under Cargita Bridge and knocked yourself out."

Doug had decided to flash his greatest assets to Mrs. Papadeaux one time too many. Sun wasn't chasing Doug so much as Mrs. Papadeaux. She was trying to kill him with a melon baller. Sun thought Doug would've learned his lesson the last time Mrs. Papadeaux chased him out in traffic and caused a pileup in their tiny town. Alas, he did not.

Sun still had nightmares about the woman's plans for Doug and how the melon baller fit in. "There was a snake," she said defensively from over her shoulder. "It startled me. And that was half a day. It doesn't count if you're unconscious."

"Really? Then I haven't had a day off in years. I demand back pay!" he called out to her as she exited the station.

Her phone rang. She checked the ID. Auri. Her auburn-haired juvenile delinquent. Her reason for living and trying really hard not to go to prison for murder.

She tapped the screen. "Hey, bug bite."

"How bad is it?" Auri asked in a hushed voice.

"He attacked me but I'm okay."

"Mom!" she said, ditching the whole covert thing. "He attacked you?"

"Hopefully I won't get rabies. Rabies suck. Or sucks. Is rabies plural? Can one acquire a single raby?"

"What the crap?"

"Language."

"Why did he attack you?"

"Probably because we were trying to tranquilize him and stuff him into a cage."

"Oh, my God! Grandma and Grandpa are never setting you up again."

This was far too much fun not to continue. "I agree. This has to stop. I decided about halfway through the date your grandparents have to die."

"You can't kill Grandma and Grandpa. We've discussed this."

"Can too. You need to dig out your mourning clothes."

"You'll go to jail."

"At least six months' worth."

"You know what happens to cops in jail."

"Think layers."

"Besides, people don't wear mourning clothes anymore."

"All black."

"Wait, really? I love black. Can I paint my nails black, too?"

"I encourage it. You can be Del Sol's only goth."

"Clearly you haven't been to high school lately. Also, no killing Grandma and Grandpa."

"You're sucking the joy out of my life right now."

"I'm a teenager. Isn't that, like, my job?"

Sun chuckled. "I'm on my way home."

"Grandma made brussels sprout casserole."

"So, pizza?"

"Yes, please. With extra pepperoni."

"You got it, kid."

Twenty minutes later, Sun dropped the pizza box on the counter, peeled off her boots, and practically ripped off her bra—without removing her sweater, of course—wiggling out of it before making a beeline for the fridge. There was a bottle of wine in there calling her name. Or calling her names. She could've sworn she heard the word *lush* coming from that general vicinity.

After filling her glass to the rim, she took out her phone to text Auri about the pizza, when it rang. The caller ID IDed the caller, as was its sole purpose in life. She answered Quincy's summons with a resounding, brook-no-arguments, "No."

"You want to hear this."

She took a sip, then shook her head. "No, I don't. I have a full thirty-six hours off. I'm squeezing every possible second out of them so I can come back refreshed and invigorated and less desirous to kill randomly."

"That's probably a good idea, what with you being the sheriff and all. I'll just tell the ambulance driver parked outside The

Roadhouse to take Ravinder straight to the hospital. You can in-terview him about the near-fatal stabbing at his bar on Monday when you're refreshed and—"

She'd sucked in a breath mid-sip and cut him off with a round of loud, hacking coughs. "I'll be there in five," she said, her voice strained.

After almost leaving without her boots, she jammed her feet back into them, zipped them up, then sprinted out the door, for-getting her bra draped over the back of her sofa. Gawd, she was good at this sheriff thing.

Skidding her cruiser to a stop like a professional drifter three-point-five minutes later outside The Roadhouse Bar and Grill, she sent dirt flying over Quincy's cruiser. And Quincy. The station received its fair share of calls pertaining to the rather seedy es-tablishment, but never a stabbing. At least none that she knew of.

The way Sun understood it, the bar was owned by the Ravin-der family as a whole, but mostly run by Levi's uncle Clay and a couple of Ravinder cousins with Levi holding a controlling in-terest. Or so she'd been told. He seemed to have final say in how things were run. A good thing, since he and his sister were the only levelheaded ones out of the bunch.

Lights bounced off everything around Sun as she jumped out of her cruiser and ducked under a strip of yellow tape, something she'd seen used only one other time during her four-month stint as sheriff of the sleepy tourist town, and that involved a truck, a herd of chickens, and a pallet of warming lubricant.

An ambulance and a fire truck sat in the lot along with two of her deputies' cars, lights blazing in the darkness from all four first-responder vehicles.

Salazar was already taking statements while Zee held off a small crowd of inebriated gawkers, several of whom were women who *just wanted to make sure Levi was okay*. Sun didn't realize her former—and admittedly current—crush had such a dedicated following. Not that it surprised her.

She hurried past just as Quincy closed the door to the ambulance. He banged on it to give the go-ahead, then brushed himself off as it sped away.

Her heart sputtered and stumbled before restarting again. Her fingers tingled and she curled them into fists, pressing her nails into her palms. Apprehension had taken a stranglehold. She uncurled the fists. Slid her hands down her hips. Forced herself to calm.

"Is he okay?" she asked Quince, the thought of Levi seriously injured darkening the edges of her vision.

"Don't know." He shook his head. "It doesn't look good."

It took every ounce of strength she had to not run back to her cruiser and chase after the ambulance. She'd wanted to see him before they took him away. If it were really that bad, she might not get a chance to talk to him before the medical center had to airlift him to Albuquerque.

Even if she did go to see him at this juncture, she'd only be in the way. She needed to let the professionals do their jobs and, more importantly, she needed to do hers.

She compelled herself to take a beat, to fill her lungs before asking, "What happened here?"

Quincy pointed to another taped-off area between two vehicles. A taped-off area drowning in blood. Huge dark shadows pooled between the tires of the vehicles and streaks of it painted the light-colored cars like graffiti. She bit down so hard her jaw hurt and tears stung the backs of her eyes.

"From what we can tell," Quince said, leading her closer, "three men jumped a Roadhouse patron and Ravinder came out to help."

She closed her lids. Of course, he did. When she lifted them again, Quince had turned around and was gesturing toward the road.

"He paid the price, too. There's security footage. We'll know more once we get a good look, but from what we've learned so far, he's damned lucky to be alive. According to the breakfast club over there," he said, pointing to the witnesses, "that pickup hit him dead on."

Sun stilled. "Pickup?"

"They backed up and tried to run him over again. Apparently, your guy has the reflexes of a mountain lion. Their words."

"I . . . I thought it was a stabbing."

"Right. The victim was beaten and stabbed multiple times. He also has some pretty serious defensive wounds." He turned back to the blood-soaked crime scene.

"The victim?" she asked, now frowning in confusion.

Quincy frowned, too. Then realization dawned and a knowing grin emerged. He took her chin and lifted her gaze to his. "Your guy's okay, Sunbeam. Toby has him by Big Red."

Sun spun around so fast the world tilted. Big Red was the pet name for the only legit fire truck Del Sol had. Also, it was yellow. Not a speck of red paint on her anywhere.

She looked back at Quincy. "He wasn't stabbed?"

"No."

"You said he was stabbed."

"No, I said there was a stabbing and Ravinder was injured."

She gaped at him.

"Two separate statements."

She continued to gape, a pastime she'd been partaking in remarkably often since moving back to Del Sol.

"Okeydokey." He gestured toward Big Red. "So, your guy was trying to stop the men who stabbed our victim. Apparently, those particular men didn't want to be stopped." He glanced back at the nightmare on Main Street. "Ravinder fought them but they managed to get into their vehicle and drive off. That was when the genius decided to pick a fight with"—he brought out his notepad—"a white Toyota Tundra with Texas plates." He looked at the fire truck, indicating the surreal creature commonly known as Levi Ravinder hidden behind it. "And here I thought Ravinder was the smart one of the bunch. Seems he didn't escape the worst of the Ravinder genes after all."

She nodded absently, trying her best to use her X-ray vision to see through the emergency vehicle for a glimpse of the fairest Ravinder of them all before remembering she didn't have X-ray vision. Damn her inability to see through solid objects.

"We had another ambulance en route, but Einstein over there is refusing to go to the hospital. Maybe you can talk some sense into him."

"Right. Sure. Okay, well, I'll try."

"Your confidence gives me hope," he said, his voice full of humor. A laugh a minute, that one.

Sun rubbed her palms together and walked toward the fire truck. She steeled herself, lifted her chin, and cornered Big Red with a quiet resolve. A resolve that evaporated the minute her gaze landed on the dusty, bloodied figure of Levi Ravinder.

She gritted her teeth at the sight of him to keep herself from shouting his name in horror. Her lungs stopped working and she walked through tunnel vision toward him. She'd only had two sips of wine. All of this lightheadedness couldn't have been the alcohol.

He sat on a step against the truck, clutching a baseball cap. His tan T-shirt, now dirty and soaked in blood, was ripped across the front showing just enough skin to make Sun's pulse quicken despite everything. The knuckles on his large hands and his sinewy forearms were covered in scrapes, bruises, and patches of blood, and his swollen left eye showed early signs of blackening.

His uncle Clay hovered nearby, arms crossed over a barrel chest, a nasty scowl lining his puffy face, and Rojas stood at Levi's side with questions of his own.

"JX?" he asked.

"Yeah," Levi said, twisting the cap in his hands. "That's all I got."

One corner of Rojas's mouth lifted. "You're lucky you got that much. I've never been hit by a truck, but I don't think I would've been trying to memorize the license plate while it was happening."

Sun's pride swelled just a little. She'd had a good feeling

when she blackmailed Poetry Rojas into joining the team. She knew he'd make a great deputy, and so far he had yet to prove her wrong. He was observant, sharp, and good with people.

She unclasped her hands—thankful she wasn't in uniform and tainting the professionalism of the station with her actions. She stepped close enough to notice the subconjunctival hemorrhage in his left eye, the blood trapped beneath the clear surface already spreading and encircling his whiskey-colored iris.

Alarm shot through her again. She cleared her throat and addressed the EMT. "He could have a concussion."

All heads turned her direction, including *his*. He didn't seem surprised to see her, which, why would he be? Then again, Levi had a perpetual poker face. He wasn't the easiest person to read.

"Sheriff." The EMT stood and offered his hand. "I've told him that very thing. I really think he should go in for a couple of X-rays."

Levi looked up at her, studying her for a solid minute before dropping his gaze. "I'm fine," he said, the sharpness in his tone impossible to miss. "If I weren't, you, Sheriff Vicram, would be the first to know."

Sun tried not to read too much into that statement. She failed. A million interpretations sprang to mind when he was obviously being sarcastic.

Rojas raised a questioning brow toward her.

"Thank you, Toby," she said to the EMT. "They're right, Levi. You need to be checked out by a doctor."

He bit down, his stoic façade cracking. "I need to be on the road chasing down that fucking truck. And I would be"—he gave his uncle a lethal glare—"if someone hadn't hidden my keys."

Surprised, Sun offered the stocky brunette watching from the sidelines a look of bemusement. Clay Ravinder was the last of Levi's uncles still in the area, and he was about as warm and caring as a pit viper. If he was keeping Levi from going after the truck, he had a reason, and it had nothing to do with Levi's well-being.

"Thank you," she said to him regardless, curious as to what he would say.

He said nothing. Instead, he sucked on a toothpick and let his gaze rake over her.

Nice. She turned back to the frustrated man sitting before her. Stepped closer. Lowered her voice. "I could arrest you."

Not one to let a foe seize the upper ground, he released an exasperated sigh and stood to his full height of *sexy* feet, *AF* inches. "For what exactly?" His voice, as deep and rich as the dark auburn in his hair, flooded her nether regions with warmth.

Holy hell, she had to get a grip. She swallowed, then said, "For being a stubborn asshat."

He let a mouthwatering smirk soften his battered face. "Is that a misdemeanor or a felony?"

"Does it matter?"

"I'm trying to decide if it's worth the jail time."

Sun's stomach did a somersault. It wasn't until he gave her an inspection as lackadaisical as a summer night that she remembered she wasn't wearing a bra. She brushed a lock of hair back as an excuse to raise her arm and cover her nigh-exposed assets. Surely, he couldn't tell with the summery sweater she wore, yet his eyes lingered in that general area for far too long, suggesting she could've been mistaken about the sweater's camouflage capabilities.

"Well," he said, seeming to recover when his gaze traveled back to hers, "while we're on the subject, you need to do a drug tox."

She laughed nervously. "I only had two sips."

"Keith Seabright is former special ops. He's a survivalist and the best hand-to-hand combat fighter I've ever met."

"Good for him," she said with an appreciative nod. "I always hoped he'd do well. Who's Keith again?"

One scythe-shaped brow inched up. "The man who was almost stabbed to death?"

She snapped back to attention, struggling to get a grip. She hadn't seen him for months, so Levi Ravinder up close and personal was like a hit of heroin.

"Right. Right." She grabbed a confused Rojas's pen and note-pad and started taking notes. Notes that her deputies probably already had. "Keith Seabright. Where do you know him from?"

"Here and there."

Great. She was going to get cryptic Levi. Out of all of his personalities, cryptic was not her favorite. She much preferred flirty Levi. Or lusty Levi, though she'd only seen it once in her life. Twice if one were to count their last encounter in his bed-room, but he'd been beyond exhausted. Hardly in his right mind.

Then again, the first time he'd been drunk, so . . .

She pretended to write down his statement. "Here and there. Okay, how long have you known him?"

"Longer than most. Not as long as others."

"Right. Longer than most. Not as long as—"

"Are we done?"

She looked up at him. "In a hurry?"

"I need to find those men."

She lowered the pen. "This is an investigation, Mr. Ravinder. You need to go to the hospital and let us do our jobs. Why do you want me to run a tox screen on your friend?"

He huffed out a breath and looked away, annoyed at being detained. "Because he was stabbed. Multiple times."

"From what I understand, three men with knives will do that."

He stepped closer. "You don't get it. There could've been ten and he would've taken them without breaking a sweat. He's what they call an elite. No way in hell three scrawny punks can take him down. They had to have drugged him. Put something in his beer or tranqed him somehow."

"Levi," Sun began, but he stopped her with another scowl.

"He wasn't moving right when he came out of the bar. And he was fighting back but it was like he was drunk."

"Hence his exit from a bar."

"Where he drank one beer. Seabright doesn't drink enough to become inebriated. Not when he's on a job. He's a soldier through-and-through."

"He was on a job?"

He raked his free hand through his hair and turned away from her. "I don't know. He seemed edgy. Hypervigilant. Like when he's working."

While that was interesting as hell—how would Levi know what Keith Seabright looked like while he was working and what exactly did the man do for a living?—it could wait until he was looked after. If Levi was right, however, this wasn't just a random bar fight. This was a premeditated attempted murder.

Quincy walked up then. "I might be able to explain your friend's behavior."

Levi turned back, tightening his grip on the cap impatiently.

"According to a couple of witnesses, he got into an argument with a man at the Quick-Mart this afternoon. They said it got pretty heated."

Levi frowned. "He didn't say anything about that."

"Why did he come outside?" Sun asked. "Was he leaving?"

"I need to go," Levi said.

Quincy stayed him by showing a palm. "Mr. Walden was working the Quick-Mart, if that's where you're wanting to go. We've already contacted him. He didn't see anything."

Levi looked toward the heavens as though begging for patience. "Then who were the witnesses at the store?" He scanned the small crowd. "I'll talk to them."

Sun had enough. "Give me your wrists," she said, her voice razor-sharp.

He spun around to her. "What?"

"Your wrists." She demonstrated by pointing to one of her own. "I'm placing you under arrest."

If rage had a name at that exact moment in time, it was Levi Ravinder.

3

Do we serve drunken, sarcastic assholes?
Find out next week on We Think the Fuck Not.

—SIGN AT THE ROADHOUSE BAR AND GRILL

"I mean it." She unclipped a pair of plastic wrist cuffs off Quincy's belt. It was either arrest him and force him to go to the hospital or release the floodgates and beg him to go, hoping her tears would sway him. First, they would not. Second, no one needed to see that. By officially arresting him, the sheriff's office would be obligated to take him to urgent care whether he wanted to go or not.

He bent closer and spoke through clenched teeth. "You can't be serious."

She wanted nothing more than to cup her hands around his jaw. To pull him to her. To place tiny kisses on his sculpted mouth and whisper promises of an inappropriate nature if he would just go to the medical center. But they had a crowd of onlookers, not to mention the fact that her deputies might lose the teensiest amount of respect for her if she tried to seduce an injured victim in the middle of a criminal investigation.

Then again . . .

She leaned closer, breathed in the hint of subtle cologne he wore, and whispered, "I couldn't be more serious if you paid me."

Careful not to hurt him, not that he would feel it on his current adrenaline high, she slipped the cuffs over his battered hands, baseball cap and all, and tightened them just enough so they wouldn't fall off.

"Don't do this, Vicram."

Her chest tightened around her heart. "You were defending a friend in battle and then got hit by a truck, Levi. Just get a couple of X-rays and then Quincy will release you."

"Me?" Quince asked, surprised.

Levi let out a frustrated sigh. "They'll be out of the state by then."

"We don't know that. Zee called it in. Every trooper in New Mexico is looking for that truck." She took his arm and led him toward Quincy's cruiser, a little surprised he didn't resist. "You do this and I'll go talk to Mr. Walden." Mr. Walden, the owner of the Quick-Mart, would not appreciate her late-night invasion, but at that point, she really didn't care.

"Walden saw something," Levi said. "He's just too much of a weasel to get involved."

"I can handle Walden." Levi wasn't wrong. The man was a bit of a weasel.

He stopped and the look on his face told her more than any words could have. Whoever Keith Seabright was, he meant more to Levi than most of his family members did. Not that that was saying much.

"Let me come with you." It wasn't a request. "I've been deputized. It would be legit."

How could she forget? "We can discuss it after the X-rays." The hemorrhage in his eye was getting worse. The entire white was now blood red and the swelling around his orbital socket was darkening to a startling array of purples and burgundies and blacks.

He bit down in frustration. As though a last resort, he said, "One of them is already dead."

"What?"

He pressed his mouth together, clearly reluctant to say anything. After a moment, he repeated, "One of the assailants is already dead. I wrested his knife away and severed his femoral artery. He will have bled out in minutes, so they'll have to dump his body. They headed north on 25, so odds are they'll pull off the highway and dump it, then get back on. That gives us time to find them."

The fact that everything he said shocked her to the core had to show on her face. She stood speechless a solid minute as Rojas and Zee moved closer, flanking Quincy. They must have overheard.

"It's what Seabright would have done had he not been drugged. They'd all be dead. Not just one. They'll have to burn the truck, too, but that can wait until they get to Denver."

Sun held up a hand to slow him down, then said, "First, are you sure you got his femoral?" When he only deadpanned her, she asked, "Okay, how do you know they went north? They could have gone either way once they got to the on-ramps."

"They went north," he insisted.

"How do you know?"

He bit down, his jaw flexing, before repeating himself. "They went north."

Sun wanted to curse. Or arrest him for real for obstruction, which was well within her rights. He was the most stubborn . . . "We're on the same side, Levi."

He lowered his head and studied her from beneath a set of impossibly thick lashes. "These cuffs say otherwise."

She didn't argue.

"Uncuff me and let me go get them."

Frustration ripped through her gut, but she wasn't about to give him the satisfaction of that knowledge. "Call it in, Quince. Make sure the state troopers know one of them is seriously injured. We need to call all the hospitals within a hundred-mile radius."

"They won't go to a hospital. He was dead before they hit the interstate."

She opened the back door of Quincy's cruiser, but he stood his ground. "Uncuff me, Vicram."

She looked past him, and asked Quincy, "You still have that dart gun?"

An evil grin spread across his face. He was about to answer when a tiny voice drifted toward them. "Levi?"

They all turned to see the very fruit of Sun's loins planted smack-dab in the middle of their crime scene. The auburn-haired beauty stood panting with round eyes and wet cheeks.

"Auri," Sun said, rushing to her. "What are you doing here?" She spotted the abandoned bike Auri had ridden over and cupped the girl's face in her hands. "Sweetheart, what is it?"

Auri had yet to tear her gaze off Levi, her lashes spiked with wetness, her bottom lip trembling. "I heard on the scanner."

Behind her Cyrus Freyr's SUV skidded to a halt and both he and his wife Elaine, aka Sun's parents, bolted out and hurried over, their journey coming to a sudden stop thanks to the crime scene tape. They waited on the other side of it.

"I'm sorry, Sun," her dad said, out of breath. "We heard that a male had been stabbed multiple times, and then Ravinder's name came up and she was out the door before we could stop her." He looked at Levi with a grin. "It seems the rumors of your demise have been greatly exaggerated." He gave him a once-over and corrected his statement. "Or at least mildly exaggerated."

Levi offered him a cursory nod before returning his attention to Auri. "I'm okay, Red."

"I thought . . ." Her voice broke and she swallowed hard.

With the gentlest of nods, he beckoned her toward him.

Auri ran and threw her arms around him. Sun didn't miss the wince. Despite being in obvious pain, he lifted his cuffed hands over her head and hugged her to him.

"I'm okay."

"I thought you were stabbed," she said between sobs.

Once again, the strong connection between her daughter and the man Sun had been in love with since the beginning of time hit her square in the chest. Even the fact that he was covered in

the blood of, quite possibly, three men didn't convince her to separate them.

Her chest tightened again, this time for a different reason.
Levi Ravinder seemed to grow more enigmatic by the hour. The
fact that he'd saved her daughter's life when she was seven only
added to his thundering appeal.

Sun's parents stood watching, as well, with the most endearing expressions on their sweet faces. For reasons unknown to
Sun, they seemed to love Levi. Sun had figured that out a while
ago. But even after everything, there were still so many questions
Sun had about his past. Or, more to the point, her past and his
involvement in it.

She'd been abducted when she was seventeen. Held for five
days. Violated, or so the evidence would suggest since nine months
later she gave birth to a squalling copper-headed ball of fire appropriately named Aurora Dawn.

Fifteen years after that, on Sun's second day on the job, they
found the decomposed body of one of Levi's uncles near where
Sun had been held. He'd been stabbed once through the chest and
left there for over a decade. The timing fit perfectly with Sun's
abduction, and after Levi's sister confessed to killing their uncle,
Levi confessed as well. Then one of Levi's cousins confessed. His
plant manager. His barber. Hell, even Doug, the town flasher, confessed.

Thus far, eleven people had confessed to killing Kubrick "The
Brick" Ravinder.

But the man's denim jacket had been soaked with blood that
was not his own. He'd hurt his opponent. Bad. And Sun had
Levi's DNA. She'd sent it in and was still waiting, four months
later, for the results.

She understood. A cold case was hardly high priority, but she
knew people. She could've rushed the job. So why hadn't she?

She walked over to Levi and Auri.

"Why is he in handcuffs?" her daughter asked, then looked
at Levi. "Why are you in handcuffs?"

"You'll have to ask your mother."

"Mom!" she said in that spitfire way of hers. She stepped toward Sun and asked under her breath, "Why do you have Levi in handcuffs?"

"Because I'm arresting him," Sun whispered back.

"What?" She jammed her fists on her narrow hips. "Why?"

"Because he won't go to the hospital."

"So you're arresting him?" she asked, her voice rising an octave.

Sun smiled inwardly with the knowledge that she was about to win this particular argument. It didn't happen often and she took her victories where she could get them.

"First, he thwarted an attempted murder. Then he fought off the three knife-wielding assailants unarmed. And then he got hit by a Toyota Tundra when he tried to stop the knife-wielding assailants from getting away because, apparently, he thinks he can stop a half-ton truck with his two-hundred-pound body. So now we know two things." Sun raised an index finger. "One, he's bad at math." Her middle finger joined the first one to form a V. "And two, he most likely has internal injuries and is bleeding to death on the inside."

Auri dropped her jaw and shifted her outrage to the man standing beside her.

Sun fought the urge to pump her fist in triumph. "I just want some X-rays to be safe," she said instead. "And Levi is not only refusing to go to the hospital, he is insisting on going after the assailants. Alone."

"You are *so* under arrest," Auri said, pointing to the inside of Quincy's cruiser.

A sly grin spread across his face. "Traitor."

She pointed harder. "In."

He leaned down, kissed her cheek, then did as he was told.

It was Sun's turn to drop her jaw. If she'd known that was all it would take, she would have called Auri to the crime scene half an hour ago.

He climbed inside the SUV and sat back, but Auri wasn't finished. She jumped onto the step and kissed his stubbled cheek. "Thank you."

The look he gave her, the adoration in his eyes, took Sun's breath away.

Auri stepped down and offered her mom an apologetic hug. "I'm sorry, Mom. I didn't mean to contaminate your crime scene."

"It's okay, bug," she said, even though in some places she could lose her job for such an indiscretion. She looked at her parents. "You have my permission to duct tape her to a chair and lock her in the basement."

Her dad chuckled, but her mom was still looking on dreamily, so enamored with Levi Ravinder, Sun fought a knee-jerk reaction to stake her claim. Mostly because she had none.

They'd certainly never been a couple. The one time they almost hooked up, they were just kids and he was half-drunk on his family's moonshine, a recipe he'd legitimized and grown into a very successful business. He owned one of the most famous corn whiskey distilleries in the world, Dark River Shine.

But she'd been back four months and, apart from her first week on the job in which he helped with a missing persons case, she'd only seen him a handful of times. And most of those were from a distance. Auri visited his nephew, Jimmy, but even when Jimmy came over to their house, Levi was never the one to pick him up.

Sun helped her dad put Auri's bike in the back of his SUV, then watched as they drove off. Quincy was talking to one of the onlookers, so Sun turned back to the cruiser and walked over to Levi.

He'd laid his head back and closed his lids, but he still sensed her presence. "You're not forgiven," he said without opening his eyes.

She crossed her arms over her chest and leaned against the door. "I didn't ask to be."

His face, so impossibly handsome, looked tired. He was

three years older than her, but he somehow looked younger at that moment. More vulnerable.

She watched him a while, reveling in just being so close, then said, "I saw the wince."

Confusion flashed across his face but he caught on quickly. "What wince?"

"When Auri hugged you."

"*Wince* is a strong word."

"What would you call it?"

"Flinch."

"And how is flinch better than wince?"

"A wince is a facial expression. I've spent years perfecting my poker face. I don't wince."

"Fine. Why'd you flinch?"

"I'm sore."

"Because you have internal injuries."

"Mm, I don't think so."

"You were hit by a truck."

"You hit harder."

That stopped her. She paused a moment to take him in, then asked, "Do I?"

"And it hurts worse."

"If you two are finished," Quince said from behind her, "I'll get him to the medical center. You know, since he could die from massive internal bleeding any second now."

Sun took one more lingering look at his powerful profile, then stepped back. "Thanks, Quincy. I'm going to talk to Walden. Surely, he saw something if that argument at his store was as bad as everyone said." She looked around, spotted her target, and called out to Salazar.

Salazar excused herself from questioning the fan club and hurried over. "Yeah, boss?"

"If you have everyone's names and contact info, you can let them go. The forensic team from Albuquerque will be here soon. Hang out and make sure they go wide. I want every speck of trash collected and photos of everything, no matter how small. I'll be back as soon as I can."

"You got it."

"Thank you, Deputy," she said, before yelling over her shoulder at Quincy.

He was just climbing into his cruiser.

"Make sure he stays there, Quince! I want at least five X-rays, three blood tests, and a sonogram!"

"You got it, boss!" He closed his door and eased onto Main toward the Del Sol Urgent Care Center.

Sun was busy fighting the urge to glance at Levi as Quince drove past when she heard gravel crunching behind her followed by a feminine voice. "Sheriff," the woman said, trying to get Sun's attention. "Sheriff Vicram?"

Sun turned to her. A disheveled brunette with a skintight miniskirt and a puffy pink jacket hurried up to her, which was a feat in those heels. And here Sun thought she'd had it bad.

"Sheriff, I saw the whole thing," she said breathlessly, probably due to her jaunt in the six-inch heels.

"Did you give your statement to one of my deputies?"

"What?" She came to a wobbly stop and glanced around, wild-eyed. "Oh, yes. Of course. Tricia asked me to come in tomorrow and give an official statement. We went to school together. But you need to know he didn't stab that man. Levi Ravinder? He—"

"We know, Miss . . . ?"

One of her ankles gave way and she veered to the side. Sun bolted forward to catch her, but she recovered like a pro, and said, "Crystal. Crystal Meth." When Sun's lids rounded in surprise, she said, "I know. My parents are hilarious. Which is why I'm having it legally changed. Getting a job is a bitch. I usually go by Crys."

How could she not know there was a woman in town named Crystal Meth? Sun was starting to like the girl despite herself.

"He was trying to help his friend. Levi. He didn't do anything."

"We know. He's not in any trouble."

"Oh. I just thought . . . I mean, you arrested him, didn't you? I just wanted you to know he didn't do it. I saw the men who did."

Sun gave the girl her full attention. "Can you ID them?"

"No. Probably not. I'm sorry. I couldn't really see their faces. The one who did the stabbing wore a baseball cap and the other two wore beanies. Jeans. Dark T-shirts. The only thing I can tell you is that they were all in their late twenties, early thirties? All white with fairly dark hair."

Wondering if she should bring her in for an interview immediately before her memory faded as the alcohol evaporated from her system, Sun looked around for Zee.

"He'd said goodbye to him, you know? The guy. And then—"

"Wait, who said goodbye to whom?"

"Levi. We were, um, talking and the guy, his friend, he came outside and said, 'Later, Rav,' and a few seconds after that we hear a scuffle."

Rav? She let that marinate on her tongue a minute. Savored it. She'd never heard anyone call him that.

"We look over and these men are beating the guy to a pulp and they have him on the ground kicking him. Levi takes off like a rocket toward them, but before he can get there, one of them pulls out a knife." Her eyes glazed over. "It happened so fast. They stabbed that guy over and over in a matter of seconds."

Sun put a hand on her arm to steady her. "What happened next?"

"Levi tackled the guy with the knife and the others joined in. I can't believe he didn't get stabbed." She focused on Sun, pleading with her to understand. "He was so fast, Sheriff."

"The man with the knife?"

"No, Levi. So adept. Like the soldiers you see in movies? I've never seen anything like it. He took them down like it was nothing even though they got in some good swings and one landed a kick to his face."

Every muscle in Sun's body tensed at the thought of someone kicking Levi in the face. Or anywhere else for that matter.

"He disarmed two of them and got up, but they were already running for their truck. He caught one, though, and he must've really hurt him, because the guy screamed and crumpled to the ground. That's when they hit Levi with the truck." She squeezed her eyes shut as the memory washed over her. "He got to the driver's side door and tried to open it, but the guy locked it, so Levi hit the window." Her gaze drifted back to Sun. "With his fist. He shattered it. He was just so . . . so determined. So angry. So . . ." Her gaze turned wistful. "So powerful."

Sun understood the infatuation all too well. The fact that the girl was outside with Levi and they were, *um, talking*, didn't surprise her. Crys was a beauty despite her unfortunate name. Levi would be crazy not to hook up with her.

She forced the green-eyed goblin back to its corner. She had no right to be jealous. With his looks, she could only imagine all the women he'd been with over the years. All the women who'd thrown themselves at him. Jealousy was such a useless emotion. Despite that fact, she was, and it irked her to no end.

Another ankle gave way. That time Sun caught her. "How about we sit down?"

"I'm okay. I only had one drink and I sipped on it all night. It's these stupid shoes." She wiped at her eyes, her hands shaking visibly, and Sun realized she wasn't so much drunk as in shock. Who wouldn't be after witnessing a brutal attack like that?

Knowing the girl's memory would be fine, Sun called out for Toby, the EMT. The guy was packing up. He tossed a bag into Big Red and hurried over.

"Can you get her to urgent care, Toby?"

"I'm okay," she repeated a microsecond before her left leg collapsed. Sun caught her again and righted her the best that she could. It was like trying to hold up a tower of Jell-O.

"You are two seconds away from breaking an ankle."

When she swayed again, the young EMT catching her that time, Sun insisted. "Urgent care, please, Toby."

He nodded and took the girl by the arm to lead her to the fire truck. His partner rushed over to help him. Sun figured his concern had more to do with the miniskirt than his occupation, but whatever it took to get the job done.

"Wait a minute," Sun said, stopping them.

They turned back to her.

"One of the assailants wore a baseball cap?"

The girl looked up in thought and nodded. "Yes. Blue or black, I think, with red on it? Maybe orange? It was dark, so I can't be certain."

Sun gritted her teeth. "Oh, I can. That son of a bitch."

"I'm sorry?" she said, but Sun whirled around and stalked toward her cruiser.

She should have known Levi was clutching that baseball cap a little too tightly. In all of their years of acquaintance, she had never once seen him wear a baseball cap. Not even as a kid.

No wonder he knew they were going north. It was a Denver Broncos cap. The assailants were clever enough to drive a truck, probably stolen, with Texas plates, but not clever enough to ditch the one identifying piece of evidence that could lead the authorities in their general direction?

Of course, the cap could have been planted to throw law enforcement off the trail as well, but for some reason, Levi knew it wasn't, and she wanted to know why.

She climbed into her cruiser and called Quincy.

He picked up and said only two words. "He's gone."

She slammed her lids closed. Son of a bitch. "Put a BOLO on his ass."

"You got it."

"He'll be heading north on 25."

"Okay."

"And extend an invitation to whoever finds him to use a Taser."

A knock sounded on her window. She lowered the phone and turned to see Deputy Salazar, bright-eyed and flushed-faced. "Boss!"

She rolled down her window.

"Las Vegas PD called," she said, handing her a note. "They were supposed to get this to you earlier today, but someone dropped the ball. Sounds important."

Sun opened the note. Blinked. Read it again. Thought about it. And read it a third time, just to make sure she wasn't seeing things.

At one time, Levi Ravinder had four uncles. All of them, along with his father, were members of the infamous Southern Mafia. Levi's father, for all intents and purposes, died in a car accident, and his uncles splintered. One was murdered—or killed in self-defense, the jury was still out—on a mountaintop fifteen years ago. One died of cancer. And one, Clay, was alive and well, unfortunately, and living at the Ravinder compound a few miles outside of town.

The fourth one took an extended vacation courtesy of the Arizona correctional system. Specifically, Arizona State Prison Complex in Florence, about an hour south of Phoenix.

It would seem that same uncle, Wynn Ravinder, wanted Sun to come to Arizona immediately. *He's dying,* the note said, *and has pertinent information about your abduction.*

Her abduction. Information about her abduction. Those words were like a sucker punch to her gut. She read them three more times before looking back at the crime scene.

Still no word on the victim, Keith Seabright's, condition. The forensic team would be there soon, and she would only be in their way if she stayed. Rojas could go talk to Mr. Walden about the argument Seabright got into that afternoon and gather any surveillance footage the man had. The state police were on the lookout for the assailants. As was Levi himself, most likely.

Nothing was stopping her. If she left now, she could be in Florence by morning. That familiar desire—or blind obsession, as her parents would say—to know more about those five days cinched her stomach tight. A stomach that was suddenly filled with shards of glass.

Could Levi's uncle Wynn really know what happened? Was Brick Ravinder really her abductor or was his murder in that vicinity coincidence? And what, if anything, did Levi have to do with it?

Because of a head injury she'd suffered at the time, Sun could remember very little of those five days or several weeks prior to her abduction. She had glimpses. A patchwork of visions and scents and sounds, but nothing coherent. Nothing cohesive enough for her to stitch the images together.

And then there was the surveillance footage from the hospital in Santa Fe. Someone had brought her in and left before the nurses could get a name. That someone, tall and slim, clutched his side where a dark stain slowly spread across his hoodie. Whoever brought her to the hospital had been seriously injured at some point, and Sun had about twelve thousand questions as to why.

She woke up a month later in that same hospital with no memory of what had happened. Two months after that she realized, to her utter horror, that intake had dropped the ball at the hospital. She was pregnant. The monster who took her had violated her.

Looking back now, it was almost inconceivable how something so precious, so wonderful, could come from such tragedy. But Auri was all of that and more.

Sun heard Quincy's voice and realized she was still on the phone. "What's going on, boss?"

She snapped out of her musings and lifted the phone to her ear. "You're not going to believe this."

"I don't know. I'm pretty gullible, apparently."

Realizing she might need someone to take turns at the wheel of the sixteen-hour round trip, she said, "Pack your toothbrush. We're going to Florence."

"Italy?"

"Arizona."

"So close."

4

Makeup fades. Tacos are forever.
—SIGN AT TIA JUANA'S FINE MEXICAN CUISINE

Sun eased open the door to Auri's darkened room and crept inside. Even though the center of her universe had just turned fifteen, and their house was mere inches away from Sun's parents' back door, Auri had a permanent room at her grandparents' house. If Sun wasn't home by nine, Auri had to come to Freyr House and stay until Sun got her. Usually when Sun worked that late, however, she just left Auri there until morning—a necessary evil that was becoming a habit of late.

She'd written her a love note and had planned to leave it on her nightstand, but Auri turned onto her back and raised a hand to shield her hazel eyes from the light streaming in from the hall.

"Hey, bug bite," Sun said. She set the note on the nightstand and climbed onto the bed, duty weapon, work boots, and all.

"Hey, Mom," Auri said, as Sun reclined against the headboard beside her.

She'd showered and put on her uniform for the trip, packing only the basic essentials. Toothbrush. Deodorant. A can of tuna because of that one trip that ended so badly.

She brushed a lock of her daughter's hair back. "You okay?"

Auri nestled against her and put her fiery head on Sun's shoulder. "No."

Sun had noticed. Auri's swollen, red-rimmed eyes said it all. "I'm so sorry, sweetheart. I hate that you saw Levi like that."

"I hate that he was like that at all." Her breath hitched, crushing Sun. "Why does he have to be so brave? He could've been killed."

"I don't know. He's Levi, for one thing, and the man who was attacked was a good friend of his."

"He didn't even take us into account."

"Us?" Sun asked.

"Yes. What would happen to us if he'd been killed? Did he think of that? No. Of course not. And do you know why?"

It was apparently a rhetorical question; Auri continued before Sun could guess.

"Because he's a guy. With a penis. Penises are stupid."

Sun tried not to giggle. "Yes, they are. Penises are very stupid. I don't want you to ever forget that."

"I won't. Don't you worry."

Sun had to wonder what Auri's crush, Cruz, had done to cause such penis-aversion. She'd have to thank him. He probably bought her at least another year before her daughter experimented with the opposite sex.

"I have to make a quick trip to a prison near Phoenix, bug. I'll be back tomorrow night."

"Can I come?"

"No," she said with a soft laugh. "You need to get some rest. We'll talk about your impromptu trip to an active crime scene when I get back."

"I can't fall asleep." She propped herself up onto an elbow to give Sun the full effect of the pout she'd perfected by the time she was two. "Pot's just not doing it for me anymore. I'm going to have to try heroin."

Masterful deflection. Then again, she did learn from the best. "Now, Auri, we've talked about this. Heroin is a gateway drug. Try cutting back on the coke, first, okay?"

"Mom," she whined and threw herself back onto the bed.

"I mean it. Two lines a day. Three at the most."

"Fine. I'll cut back." She rolled back up and batted her dark lashes. "Then we can discuss heroin?"

Sun tucked a strand of glistening hair behind her ear. "I promise."

"Thanks, Mom. You're the best." She threw her arms around her, then said, "Safe journey."

"Thank you, sweet pea. Now get some sleep."

Auri snuggled beneath the covers. Sun kissed the top of the hellion's head, then stood to find her mother hovering in the doorway, frowning, with her arms crossed over her chest.

"What's wrong, Mom?"

"Heroin?" she asked, her tone admonishing.

She brushed past the older woman, and said, "Better heroin than angel dust, if you ask me."

"Everything I touch turns delinquent."

"Don't touch my bills, then." Sun headed to the living room to find her dad raiding the fridge in his pajamas.

He looked past the bright light he'd been bathed in. "Hey, sweet pea."

"Hey, Dad. I'll be back by tomorrow night."

He gave the room a furtive glance, leaned close, and said softly, "Okay, but try to get back early."

Guilt twisted her gut into a knot. She had been relying on her parents a lot lately. Too much. "Of course. I'm sorry, Dad. This whole sheriff gig . . . the hours are longer than I expected. So much paperwork."

"Please." He snorted and waved away her misgivings. "You know we love having the dumpling here. It's just that tomorrow night is date night—"

She pressed a palm to her heart. "That's so sweet."

"—and your mother has discovered gay manga."

"Oh, my God."

"I don't know what that is, but our love life has never been better. I'd hate for the little redhead to catch onto the fact that her grandparents still have sex, but I can only hold the woman off for so long."

"I can't believe I grew up for this."

He took her hand into his. "How is he?"

The hand he held shook involuntarily, so she pulled it back. "He'll be okay. I think. I don't know. He escaped before we could find out for sure."

He pulled her into a hug. "He's something else, that one."

Understatement of the century. "Yes, he is. Don't let Mom touch my bills while I'm gone. Auri would die if our internet got shut off for a late payment."

"You got it, kid."

"Also," she said as her mother walked in, "could you guys check in on Auri for the next hour or so. I know it's late, but—"

"Of course, we can," her mom said. "She was so upset, Sunny."

"I know. And that's partly why I want you to keep an eye on her."

"Partly?" her dad asked.

"Yes. I mostly want you to check in on her because she has a boy in her room."

The gasp that overtook her mother was a long, drawn-out thing that almost had Sun doubling over. When her mother turned to rush into Auri's room, Sun grabbed her hand. "It's okay, Mom. Tonight, she needs a shoulder to cry on. I get that. And I trust Cruz. I do, but if you could just make sure he, you know, leaves in the next little bit? That would be great."

Her dad sank onto a stool at the snack bar. "Were we this oblivious when you were growing up?"

Sun snorted. "Dad, you were in military intelligence. I was lucky to make eye contact with a boy without you noticing."

"So, I'm just losing it in my old age."

"No," she said adamantly. She sat beside him and rubbed his back, planting her chin on his shoulder. "I like to call what you are suffering from Aurora Dawn Blindness."

Her mother shook her head haplessly.

"It's a nontransferable medical condition," Sun continued. "I think it has something to do with her coloring. It's so bright, it's hard to see past it. Also, she has you both wrapped around her finger so tight, you're lucky you can breathe."

"Apparently," Elaine said.

Sun hopped up and grabbed her bag.

Cyrus followed her. "What if he doesn't leave of his own accord?"

She didn't think of that. "In that case, a little encouragement might not hurt."

He chuckled to himself and Sun could only imagine what he had planned.

Auri breathed a sigh of relief as her mother left her grandparents' house. Nothing got past that woman, and on any other day, Auri was certain the fact that she had a boy in her room would not have escaped her mother's notice. But today, with Levi injured, her mom was frazzled.

She rolled over to the other side of her bed and looked down at the boy lying faceup on the floor, ankles crossed, arms tucked under his head like he hadn't a care in the world. Then again, he didn't know her mother as well as she did.

"Penises are stupid?" he asked.

After stifling a giggle with her hand, she said, "They are. Boys do stupid things."

"Oh, yeah? Like what?"

"Have you ever asked someone to hit you in the stomach as hard as they can?"

"Guilty."

"There ya go."

His full mouth widened across his face. A face that had taken her breath away the first time she saw it. "I can't argue with that."

Auri officially met Cruz the first day of school, but of course she'd noticed him sooner. Though she'd grown up in Albuquerque while her mom was in college, and Santa Fe when her mom was an officer then a detective for the Santa Fe Police Department, Auri had spent every summer since she was two with her grandparents. That meant getting to know many of the locals.

She thought she'd first noticed him at the lake when they were about ten, but thinking back, she realized she'd had an encounter with him when she was younger. She doubted he remembered it, but she would never forget even though it took her a while to realize he was the boy who very likely saved her life. A man in a white van offered her a ride. He tried to coax her closer. Then a boy on a bike skidded to a stop between them and the guy took off.

That would mark the second time she'd had her life saved. She'd wanted to ask him if he remembered the incident since she'd put two-and-two together last week, but she kind of didn't want him to. She'd been stupid when the man said her grandmother was looking for her and he offered to take Auri to her. Cruz didn't need to know the depths of her gullibility.

But she would never forget that boy on the lime-green bike. Dark hair. Rich, brown eyes. Fearless. Absolutely, utterly fearless. If not, Auri might not be here today.

"You good?" he asked, gazing up at her.

"I'm better. Thank you for coming over. You didn't have to."

He shrugged a shoulder. "'Course, I did." He took a hand from behind his head, reached up, and captured one of hers.

She let him. Let him entwine her fingers with his. Let him rub a thumb across her palm. Let him pull that very same hand down so he could place a soft kiss on the back of it.

There was something so gracious about him. So gentlemanly. He completely respected her for who she was. Her ideas and opinions and dreams mattered to him. And when he kissed her, his affection carried that same hint of respect, but there was something else there, too. Like he wanted to do more but held himself back to let her take it further if she wished to.

Every time they were together, everywhere they went, it was like he had to touch her. He put his hand on the small of her back when they went through a door. He tugged on a strand of hair when he sat behind her in class. He rubbed his shoulder to hers when they were talking to kids at school. Never suffocating. Never possessive. Just . . . there.

If she didn't know better, she'd swear he had ESP. His touches were warm and reassuring and perfect. Exactly what she needed at any given time, as though he could sense her every desire. Which was a distressing thought.

"I'm sorry about Mr. Ravinder," he said softly, brushing a thumb over her knuckles. "And I get why you're so upset seeing him like that, but who is he to you? I mean . . ." He groaned and covered his eyes, then started over. "That came out wrong. I just meant—"

"It's okay," she said, letting him off the hook, though watching him squirm was fun. "He's just really special. He . . . he helped me when I was a kid. And he's always been there for me."

His brows slid together. "How did he help you?"

She pulled back her hand and tucked it under her chin. She remembered it so clearly. The time she'd decided to take her own life. When she stood on the cliff over Del Sol Lake with that very intention.

Just one step. One tiny step and the product of all her mother's woes, the product of her mother's rape, would be gone and her mom could get on with her life. She could live and be happy and fall in love without the burden of an unwanted child dragging her down. But Levi and his nephew Jimmy showed up and started talking to her about the most everyday things. They didn't try to stop her so much as just listen.

She'd only recently admitted the truth of that day to her mother. The conversation that followed healed years of misery and self-doubt, and she now knew that her mother wanted her no matter what. That her mother loved her. Had always loved her.

Cruz had overheard a conversation about that day she'd had with Jimmy, so he knew that much. He did not know what Levi did for her though.

She lifted a shoulder instead and whispered, "The time I considered jumping off the cliff at the lake."

He looked away. Based on past experience, the subject upset him. A lot. If she remembered correctly, the words *fuck* and *you* popped up during that conversation.

"He stopped you?" he asked, snapping her out of her musings.

She tilted her head, appreciating his profile. "Let's just say he was the first person to ever save my life."

He refocused, training his powerful gaze on her. "The first person?"

She nodded but didn't elaborate.

A lock of her hair fell over the side of the bed. He took it and let it slide through his fingers as though fascinated. Auri just liked watching his biceps bunch up with the movement. She wondered how much he worked out because, even as a freshman, he was more sculpted than most seniors. Including the athletes.

"How many times has your life been saved?"

She squinted in thought. "A few, most likely. But two to be certain."

"Ah. So I have Mr. Ravinder to thank for keeping the enigmatic Auri Vicram alive and kicking."

"Enigmatic?" She snorted softly. "Have you looked in the mirror?"

"Me? Hardly. What you see is what you get."

And what a sight it was. "So, for real? You?"

He frowned in confusion.

"What I see is what I get? I see you."

He stilled, his eyes shimmering in the low light. "I'm all yours."

A soft knock sounded at the door. "Auri, sweetheart?"

Auri rolled over sleepily and raised a hand to shield her eyes again like she had with her mom. Making sure to add a grogginess to her voice, she said, "Hey, Grandma. Hey, Grandpa."

They eased into the room. "Your mom said you were having trouble sleeping. We brought some hot chocolate."

"Laced with barbiturates?"

Her grandma stopped and cast a hapless expression on her husband. "Everything I touch."

Auri scooted to the other side of her bed, leaned against the headboard, and took the piping hot cup. "Thanks, Grandpa."

"Are you feeling better, pigeon?"

"A little. How is Levi's friend?"

"He's still in surgery."

"I hope he makes it. Levi was really upset."

"Yes, he was. But he was glad to see you."

She lifted a shoulder. "I hope so."

Her grandma sat beside her on the bed while her grandfather sat on the end.

"We were going to clean out the attic tomorrow if you're up for it," her grandma said. "It's supposed to be cool. A perfect time to climb up there before summer sets in."

She took a sip and nodded from behind the cup. "I'm totally up for it."

"Good."

"Thanks for the hot chocolate."

"You're welcome," Grandma said. "I hope it's helping."

"It is. I'm already getting sleepy."

She smiled, leaned in, and kissed her cheek. "Okay, well, sleep tight, peanut. We'll come check on you again in, oh, say, thirty—"

"Twenty," Grandpa said.

"—twenty minutes. Just to make sure the hot chocolate did the trick."

Auri felt herself deflate. She groaned aloud, and said, "Mom knew, didn't she?"

Grandpa practically cackled. "How do you think we found out?" He leaned over the other side of the bed. "Hey, Cruz."

She heard a sheepish, "Hey, Mr. Freyr."

"Twenty minutes."

"I'll be gone in ten, sir."

"I knew you were a good kid."

Auri had put a hand over her eyes as humiliation burned through her. She looked through her fingers and watched as a hand rose from the horizon of her mattress and gave her grandpa a thumbs-up.

The couple chuckled and headed for the door, but not before her grandpa turned back with a final warning. "I'm going to hold you to that ten minutes."

Cruz climbed to his feet and waved sheepishly before they padded down the hall. "Well, that was a disaster."

Auri looked up the length of him, straight and tall and star-tlingly handsome, and said, "Not really. My mom could've arrested you. She's apparently really into that sort of thing."

He rested an endearing expression on her. "It's good she's the sheriff, then. If she just went around randomly arresting people without the badge to back it up, she'd have to be committed. I had an uncle who used to do that."

He started for the window, and Auri practically jumped out of bed. "You still have nine minutes."

"Yeah, I don't want to push my luck."

"You can go out the front door."

"And ruin the vibe? No way."

He lifted the window and vaulted out easily. She loved watching him do that, his lithe body like an athlete's. Or a panther's.

She went to the window as he got on his bike. "You could come back tomorrow. My grandparents could probably use the help."

He played with a pedal, bouncing a foot on it. "I have to help my dad tomorrow."

"Oh. Okay, well I'll see you at school Monday, then." When he didn't answer, she said, "Cruz?"

He turned away from her, looking into the darkness when he spoke again. "I'm kind of in love with you, Auri."

Her lips parted in surprise. He started to take off when she blurted, "I'm kind of in love with you, too, Cruz."

He nodded and took off into the darkness, but all Auri saw was a sparkling luminous soul. He kind of loved her. She was good with that.

5

Caller reported a man wearing a
T-shirt that read, Who needs drugs?
Underneath that in a smaller font it read,
No seriously. I have drugs.
Man arrested on charges of drug possession.
Deputy Salazar was grateful for the heads-up.

—DEL SOL POLICE BLOTTER

"Seabright got to Pres safely," Rojas said when Sun entered the station, referring to Presbyterian Hospital in Albuquerque. She needed to tie up a couple of things before they headed out, but Pres was on the way. They could stop and check in on him.

Quincy was en route. Hopefully. That guy took longer showers than she did, and she had to shave her legs.

She'd also texted Levi Ravinder about a thousand times. She was going to kill him. If he didn't die from internal bleeding first.

"Good," she said, dropping her bag on Quincy's desk. "Any word on his condition?"

He spun his chair around to her. "Other than he's alive? Not yet. There's some lady waiting in your office, though."

She checked her watch. "At midnight on a Saturday night?"

"I told her you were stopping by here before heading to Arizona. She seems upset."

"She *is* upset." The female voice of Mayor Donna Lomas

echoed across the station, sounding alarmingly similar to the mating call of a barn owl.

"Oh, sorry, ma'am," Rojas said. He spun back to his desk and pretended to be working diligently instead of updating his status.

Sun ignored her and asked Rojas, "The forensics team?"

"They just got there. Zee and Salazar cleared everyone out."

"Perfect. Thank you."

He frowned in thought. "It's odd that we never found any of the knives."

Yep. He was going to be a great addition. "I agree." She couldn't help but wonder if Levi still had the knife he'd used on one of the assailants. Maybe hidden in that cap. She should have frisked him when she had the chance.

The mayor strolled out of Sun's office just as she was texting Levi for the tenth time. She wouldn't hesitate to arrest him for obstruction if he took that knife with him. The mere thought twisted her gut. Removing evidence from a crime scene could rack up some serious charges.

"Why didn't you call me?" she asked.

Sun glanced up surprised. "Because you told me to stop."

Only a couple years older than Sun, the beauty known as Donna Lomas wore a bouncy blond bob, square wire-framed glasses, and a tailored navy pantsuit that accentuated her curves and made her look like a businesswoman from New York.

Her bob swished when she shook her head in frustration. How could the woman look like she'd just stepped out of a salon at this hour? "I told you to stop calling me for every little non-catastrophic event. This was a stabbing. In my town. And no one called me."

After propping a fist on her hip, Sun said, "First you tell me to call you any time there is an incident. Then you tell me not to call you. Now you're telling me to call you?" When the mayor only glared, Sun added, "I just want to get this right."

"You were calling every time someone got a paper cut."

Sun frowned and looked at her finger. "It was really deep."

Admittedly, Sun may have taken it a tad far, especially with the 3:00 a.m. paper-cut emergency, but she found a bizarre sense of pleasure in razzing the woman. If she didn't want to be called for everything, she shouldn't have told Sun to do that very thing. She needed to learn to choose her words more carefully.

The mayor did a one-eighty and stood staring into Sun's office, supposedly to get a grip on her anger, but Sun figured it had more to do with her own decorating prowess and the mayor's inherent need to imitate her. If she saw a single Sheriff Hopper Christmas ornament the next time she went into the mayor's office, Sun was crying foul.

After a few moments, the woman asked, "Why do you have an empty dog crate on your desk?"

Alarm shot through her. She hurried past the prickly mayor and stopped just before entering the small room. Sure enough, the furball had escaped. The crate sat askew on top of a stack of papers, the gate hanging open on its hinges.

"I'm using it as a paperweight," she said, her gaze darting around like the ball in a pinball machine.

Rojas came up behind her and put a hand on her arm, sending her skyrocketing toward the ceiling in an embarrassing display of unprofessionalism. She put a hand over her heart and glared at him.

"Sorry, boss," he said, easing past her.

Since he was going in first, she forgave him instantly. She just did not need another face-crotch experience. "No, no, it's okay." She leaned inside, scanning every inch before tiptoeing past the threshold. No idea why. "Do you see him?"

He'd bent to check under her desk. "Nope."

"See who?" the mayor asked, growing wary.

"The ghost haunting my office. He's tried to kill me twice."

"You are not taking care of business," the mayor said, giving up with a huff of air and brushing past her.

Sun thought about warning her, but why be amicable now?

Rojas shrugged. "I don't see him, boss."

"Okay." She cleared her throat and straightened her spine, both physically and metaphorically. "Thank you, Deputy. You might, you know, look around."

He nodded and left just as the mayor whirled on Sun. "You have to fill that position."

She set the cage on the floor beside her desk. "You came here at midnight on a Saturday night to tell me that I need to fill the lieutenant's position?" Her former lieutenant, Bo Britton, had passed away before she'd taken up her post, and she had yet to fill the revered man's spot.

"No," she said, gazing at Sun's autographed poster of Sheriff Hopper. "That's not the only reason I came."

Sun fought a desire to rip the poster off the wall and cradle Hopper's face to her breast. Hopper was hers.

"I just figured, while I'm here, we could examine the status quo."

"I have to go to Arizona."

"See, that's what I mean." She whirled back to her. "You aren't taking care of business here."

Sun bit down. She'd been meaning to talk to Quincy about the position, rifle through his thoughts on the subject, but it just hadn't come up yet. However, that didn't mean she couldn't throw the man under the bus. "I'm waiting for my chief deputy's recommendation. He has yet to give me one."

"Then insist on one," the mayor said. "Give him a deadline, then move on. We need to fill the spot."

Sun dragged in a lungful of air. "Anything else we need to discuss now that could easily wait until Monday?"

"The Ravinder case. You have yet to make an arrest."

"I have yet to hear back from the lab."

"Still? It's been months."

"It's a cold case. I guess they aren't in any rush."

"Naturally. They hardly care about us out here in the boonies. Do I need to make some calls?"

"No," Sun said, resigning herself to the fact that it would have to be done. "I'll do it."

"Fine. See that you do."

Sun wanted more than anything to say, "You're not the boss of me." But she'd been actively trying to keep her inner six-year-old at bay. Instead, she said, "You got it." Mostly because Mayor Lomas could make things difficult for her if she chose to.

The woman had threatened to look into Sun's election campaign. The one Sun had known nothing about until she was actually elected. Her parents had somehow snared the position for her without her knowledge.

On the bright side, she now knew there was nothing her parents couldn't do, nothing they weren't capable of, so the next time they came to her for help with their computer, she would not fall for it. They were like the Illuminati. Or the KGB. Or Cirque du Soleil.

But election tampering, if getting her elected without her knowledge fell under that umbrella, was a serious offense. Her parents could be arrested. And not in a funny, *let's teach them a lesson* way like when she and Quincy threatened to arrest them for harboring a fugitive that time they hid Auri from her after the kid scratched Sun's cruiser with her bike. She'd even handcuffed her exasperated mother.

Good times.

"What about the other thing?"

"The other thing?" Sun asked, knowing exactly to what she referred.

The mayor put a hand on her hip, not falling for it. "The Dangerous Daughters?"

"Ah. Right. The mythical beings who secretly run the town behind everyone's back, including the city council's."

Sun had heard rumors of the infamous group of women who'd come together to run the town at a time when only men were allowed to sit on the council. It all seemed pretty farfetched. Even if they had existed, surely they didn't now. That was decades ago.

The mayor seemed obsessed with them, however, and part of the woman's condition to stay out of the mountain of dirt that constituted Sun's past was for Sun to uncover the members of the clandestine group. Their negotiations and dealings and general goings-on.

"Exactly," she said. "I was afraid you'd forgotten about that part of the bargain."

Ultimatum was more like it. "Like I told you, Mayor, the Dangerous Daughters are just rumor and innuendo. How would a group of women from the fifties secretly run the town? And where would they do it from? Their rest homes?"

The mayor pinned her with a rather evil—and sexy if Sun did say so herself—smirk. "That was the deal, Sheriff. You find out who they are. Or were. Either way, I want the lowdown on that group."

Sun narrowed her lashes. "Why?"

She snorted. A very unladylike thing to do for such a prominent figure. "This town is considered freakish enough without stories of the Dangerous Daughters getting out."

"Right. Because that would taint our eccentric reputation."

The scowl the mayor leveled on her would have melted the face off a lesser sheriff. "You aren't even pretending to take this seriously."

"Of course, I am," she lied. She was throwing all of her acting skills at this.

Though, admittedly, she'd asked around. She even asked her parents. Nada, and they knew everything about the town. No one could tell her anything other than the rumors she'd already heard. Short of scouring old newspaper clippings and police blotters—which she had zero time or inclination to do—she was out of luck.

The mayor lifted her chin a notch. "Maybe I should follow my own advice."

"That would be new."

"Maybe I should give you a deadline."

"A dead what?"

"Give you a little motivation."

"Motivation is not the problem."

"Light a fire, so to speak."

"Does this have anything to do with that glass cliff you mentioned my first day on the job? Because I'm not taking the fall for anyone. If funds have been misappropriated—"

She arched a perfectly coiffed brow. "You know they haven't."

Sun frowned, remembering her own brow conundrum. "How do you know I know?"

"Because you've looked into every transaction this town has made over the past decade. That's how I know."

"How do you know I've . . ." Sun gave up with a frustrated shrug. The woman was right. She'd gone over the town's records with a fine-toothed machete. "Then what was all of that about? And why do you want to know about the Dangerous Daughters?"

"Strategy."

"Strategy?"

"You left." She studied her polished nails. "You've barely set foot in this town for fifteen years, then you come back here and think you can just pick up where you left off? You can just take over like you own the place?"

"Wait a minute. You played me?" Sun asked, appalled. And a tad impressed. "You wanted me to comb through those records."

"And now you're up-to-date. You know the issues. How each council member votes. Who is in whose pocket."

Damned if she wasn't right. Sun had noticed a disturbing trend with a couple of the city council members. A tendency to favor some of the more prominent business members, including one of the new winemakers in town who was getting his way an awful lot.

"Okay. Fine. I'm up-to-date. It worked."

"Naturally," she said, her pretty mouth curling up at one corner. "On to the Dangerous Daughters. You have one week."

"What?" Sun bolted to her feet. "You're actually giving me a deadline?"

"Like I said, I'm following my own advice."

"What is it, *exactly,* you want uncovered?"

"I told you. I want names. I want to know who established it and how. And I want to know what they've been up to recently."

"Mayor," Sun said from between clenched teeth, "I have a county law enforcement facility to run. Tracking down an elderly group of women who probably aren't even with us any longer—if they ever existed at all—is hardly a priority. Especially right now."

She leaned over the desk and said softly, "Then make it one." Sun bit back her reply as the mayor pivoted on her heels and strode out of the station, saying over her shoulder, "And keep me updated on the stabbing victim."

Sinking into her chair, Sun stewed all of thirty seconds, then grabbed her phone to text her chief deputy. How long could it take to shower and grab a toothbrush?

Rojas poked his head in just as she hit SEND. "There is a Jimmy Ravinder who would like a word with you before you head out, boss. He said you know him and it's important."

"Jimmy?" She rose and looked across the station to the darkened lobby out front. Sure enough, Levi's nephew, Jimmy Ravinder, was sitting in one of the chairs, twisting his hands. "Why is everyone coming to the station at this hour? Did Zee put up that neon sign we confiscated from the madam again?"

Madam Magdalena, the local cat lady, was nothing if not creative when she had a neon sign made that read CAT HOUSE and put in her window. She insisted it was because she loved cats. And she did, if her nineteen-and-counting feline zoo was any indication. Still, wouldn't that pastime cost her a bit of business? Surely, some of her would-be patrons were allergic.

He chuckled. "No idea, boss."

"Thanks, Rojas." She journeyed through the bullpen to let

Jimmy in herself, but when she opened the door, he remained sitting. "Hey, Jimmy. You want to come back?"

He looked so young. His dark blond hair, perpetually cursed with a bout of bed head, stuck up in the back and his spiffy new black-framed glasses fit snug against his face thanks to a band that ran from earpiece to earpiece.

She realized he seemed agitated.

"You arrested my uncle," he said without looking at her.

"No, Jimmy, I didn't. Why don't you come back?"

He stood, but kept his gaze on the floor. "Oh, I thought you arrested him because you think he killed Uncle Brick."

"Nope. No arrests on that, yet."

"Okay. Good, because he didn't do it."

She stilled, trying to decide how to proceed and how unethical it would be to interview him without his mother present. Even though she'd secretly become friends with the local wildcat known as Hailey Ravinder, the woman would kill Sun first and ask questions later if she did anything to hurt her son. Though the boy did come in on his own accord, he was barely seventeen. And on the spectrum, a fact that would play heavily into Hailey's decision to kill her, Sun was certain.

"How about we go to my office."

He shrugged, so she led him to her office and offered him a seat. "Do you want a soda?"

He shook his head, too busy taking in the surroundings. She could hardly blame him. She was quite the decorator.

She sat at her desk and asked as nonchalantly as possible, "So, do you know who did? Do you know who killed your uncle Kubrick?"

"Yes," he said, matter-of-fact.

She heard Quincy come into the station. They really needed to hit the road, but the temptation to learn more about Kubrick's death was simply too irresistible.

"Could you tell me, then? Could you tell me who killed your

uncle?" Her heart raced. Despite her desire to uncover the truth about that night no matter the cost, she wasn't sure she was ready for the truth, the whole truth, and nothing but the truth.

"Yes." He leaned closer for a better look at a figurine on her desk. If this were any other person, she'd think he was playing her when he didn't elaborate, but this was Jimmy Ravinder. He was innocent and genuine and incapable of playing anyone.

"Okay," she said, trying not to laugh. "*Would* you tell me?"

"Yes." Just when she thought he was going to stop there again, he added, "Me."

She gazed at him a moment, then leaned back. "You killed your uncle Brick?"

He petted the mountain lion figurine with an index finger. "Yes."

"Sweetheart, you were two."

"I know. It was an accident, but my mom *freaked out!*" He shouted the last words, his seriousness adorable, but he never took his gaze off the lion. "She told me not to tell anyone. Ever."

Maybe not too innocent to make up stories? The fact that he couldn't possibly have done it made his confession all the more adorable. But she wanted to know why. Why were so many people confessing? "Jimmy, did someone put you up to this?"

"Can I use your restroom?" he asked, shifting in his seat.

"Of course." She stood and pointed the way, then looked past him to Rojas and Quincy talking in the bullpen.

Rojas leaned against Quincy's desk. "I just lost, Chief."

"Your virginity?"

"You lost, too. I think that kid just confessed."

"No way."

Quincy deflated before her very eyes. He'd been in first place to win the pool, but with another confession added to the growing list, his potential winnings of forty-nine dollars and a pan of Salazar's homemade enchiladas dwindled by the second.

"I really wanted those enchiladas."

"My *tia* is making some for dinner after church tomorrow. You should come by."

"You're killing me, Rojas. I have to go to Arizona. Think the boss would buy it if I called in with Ebola?"

"Since she's looking right at you, I'd say no."

They both straightened as Jimmy walked past her and took his seat again.

She sat across from him and grinned. "Okay, let's say you did kill your uncle."

"Accidentally, because I was two."

"Accidentally, because you were two, and your mom told you never to tell anyone, why are you telling me now?" If someone was putting the people in Levi's circle up to confessing, it wouldn't have been Levi himself. His pride would never allow it, especially since he'd been insisting he had killed Kubrick for months. But why else would people just randomly keep confessing if it weren't a concentrated effort?

"Because I thought you arrested Uncle Levi for killing my great-uncle Brick, so I had to, but since you aren't, I'd like to take it back now."

"Your confession?"

"Yes."

"Yes!" Quincy raised his fists into the air. "He's retracting his confession. I'm still on top."

Rojas shook his head. "I don't think it works like that, Chief. He already confessed. It still counts as a bona fide confession."

"Those aren't the rules."

"I think they are."

Sun shot both deputies a thinly veiled glare to silence them just as Jimmy stood to leave. "Thank you for coming in, Jimmy."

He dropped his gaze. "Okay, thank you. I should go."

"Okay." She led him to the door. "I appreciate your trying to help your uncle Levi."

"I know."

She wanted more than anything to give him a hug, but

according to her daughter, only Auri, Levi, and Jimmy's mother were allowed to hug him. And very briefly at that.

"I'm going to have Deputy Rojas take you home, okay?" Poor kid probably walked into town and they lived miles outside of it.

"I guess, but I don't know him."

"Can I vouch for him?"

"Yes."

Rojas walked up and held out his hand. "Hey, kid. I'm Deputy Rojas. Is it okay if I take you home?"

That didn't sound creepy at all.

"I guess, but I have to call my mom and tell her so if you kill me and leave me in a ditch she will know who did it."

He chuckled. "Deal." The deputy led him out the door to his cruiser.

Sun went to grab the phone off her desk.

"What the hell, boss?"

She turned back to Quincy, who'd poked his head into the room only to stop and stare at the empty cage on the floor.

The epitome of dejection, he looked up at her. "You let him go?"

She grabbed her phone and walked over to stare at the cage alongside him. "He escaped."

"He escaped?" He asked the question as though it were a personal affront to him. As though the raccoon had rejected his offer to live a life of petty crime with him.

"I told you to lock it."

"I clicked it closed."

"You clicked it?" When he nodded, she said, "They have opposable thumbs."

He leaned against the doorframe, no longer able to hold the weight of his own disappointment. "Wait," he said, suddenly wary. He straightened and looked around. "Does that mean he's loose somewhere in the station?"

"It does indeed." She scooped her bag off his desk and headed for the exit sign. "And guess who gets to hunt him down when we get back."

"Why me?"

"Are you seriously asking me that?"

"Apparently."

Two minutes later, after they had settled into her cruiser, Sun said, "Auri had a boy in her room."

"What?" His belief that Auri was the very angel who hung the moon in the heavens just received a hairline fracture. "You kicked him out, right?"

"No."

The look of astonishment he shot her was almost comical.

"I sicced the grandparents on him." She headed toward the interstate. "They'll keep an eye on the situation."

"Oh. Okay. So, um—"

"Mom is still great. Just like she was three hours ago when you last saw her. Thanks for asking."

"What? I can't check to see how your parents are doing?"

"Of course you can, but you never check to see how my parents are doing. You check to see how my mother is doing. There's a difference."

He turned to look out a window. "She's always been really cool to me, that's all."

She turned onto the interstate and set her cruiser to seventy-five. It was going to be a long night. "I know what this is."

"You do?"

"Yep."

"And?"

"You're seeing someone and you don't want me to know about it."

After he stared at her a solid ninety seconds like she'd grown another head, he said, "Excuse me?"

"You keep asking about my mother because you're seeing someone and you don't want me to know who, so you're distracting me with your longtime crush."

He stared again, only not as long this time. "Came up with that one all on your own, did you?"

"And I'm fairly certain it didn't take you an hour to shower and grab your toothbrush. You went to see her."

He snorted. "Honey, if I went to see my girl on the side, I would've been gone a lot longer than an hour."

"Touché, but how do you explain Friday afternoon when you said you were out patrolling?"

"I *was* out patrolling."

"That's a federal offense, you know. Getting nooky on the government's dime."

"Did you really just use the word *nooky*?"

"At the very least, you could be fired."

"No one says nooky anymore."

She turned to him. "You're really not going to own up to this when I've caught you red-handed?"

"Sunny, the only thing you've caught red-handed is your own paranoia."

"Then why won't you tell me where you were Friday afternoon? Because you were with *her*. She wants you to leave, doesn't she? She wants you to take her away from all this and start a new life in Californ-eye-ay."

"Wow, you've really thought this through."

Sun's insecurities were getting the better of her. She truly felt Quincy had been pulling away. Or, at the very least, keeping secrets. Not that she had any room to talk. Maybe he was tired of the small-town life. Maybe he wanted more and didn't know how to tell her.

She grew serious. "You know you can tell me anything." It would be her luck that the moment she ended up back in Del Sol, albeit kicking and screaming, her best friend on the planet would leave. Again, not that she could blame him. She'd done the same thing to him fifteen years ago.

She banged her forehead against the steering wheel. But only once. And not, like, hard. "I did something and you don't know how to tell me, so you're avoiding me and we will eventually grow apart, and you'll want to see other people and"—she turned a surprised expression on him—"you have a new bestie, don't you?"

"Did you sample the confiscated LSD while I was gone?"

"You aren't going to tell me, are you?"

"Acid trips are a bitch."

"You aren't even going to talk about it?"

"Says the person who refused to talk about the abduction for fifteen years."

Classic defense mechanism. "I didn't talk about it because I didn't remember anything."

He nodded.

"Okay," she said, making a decision. "I'm dropping this for now."

"About time."

"But I'm giving you two days to tell me what's going on, or I'm finding a new best friend."

"You can't do that."

"Watch me."

"No, I mean you literally can't do that. No one wants to be friends with you."

She speared him with a look of indignant astonishment. It was one of her best looks. "I have tons of friends."

"You have tons of acquaintances. Huge difference."

"I can assure you, one of my acquaintances is about to inherit the mantle of Sunshine Vicram's BFF, and you're going to have no one except that floozy you're seeing on the side."

"Good luck with that."

"I'll need the tiara back."

"I'm not giving the tiara back." With his arms still crossed, he scooted down in his seat, laid back his head, and closed his eyes. "Or the sash. Wake me in two."

She didn't answer. She'd drop it for now, but he was holding something back, and the curiosity incinerating her chest was giving her heartburn.

6

*Did you accidentally go shopping on an empty stomach
and are now the proud owner of aisle 4?
We can help!*

—SIGN AT DEL SOL FITNESS & MORE

The muscular purr of a big engine block hummed through the frigid night. Soothed her when she just wanted to sleep. She was warm at last. Safe at last.

"Stay awake, Shine," he said, his voice deep and rich and youthful. She knew who it belonged to but couldn't quite place its owner.

Everything inside her hurt. Everything around her spun. And her stomach wanted nothing more than to empty its contents onto the floorboard.

She felt a firm hand wrap around to the back of her skull, lifting her slightly. Her lips parted as the hard plastic of a water bottle pressed against them. Cool water filled her burning mouth. She tried to swallow but it scorched her throat. She ended up choking and spitting it all back up. Her stomach contracted painfully, doubling her over. When she vomited, a metallic taste flooded her mouth. She felt bad but the guy's hoodie was ruined anyway. It was covered in blood. She just didn't know whose.

"You okay, boss?"

Sun jerked awake and tried to open her eyes, but a white so

bright it blinded her convinced her to keep them shut. At least until she figured out where she was.

She felt a tug on a wayward strand of hair.

After a moment, she opened her eyes just enough to check the clock on her phone. 7:58.

In the morning?

She bolted upright and squinted through the pain. The landscape, while beautiful and similar to parts of New Mexico, was definitely not.

"We aren't in Kansas anymore," the man beside her said.

"I thought we were taking two-hour shifts?" She stifled a yawn, then winced at a jolt of pain in her neck.

"We are," Quincy said. "I just took several in a row. You have some drool." He pointed to the side of his mouth.

Sun wiped at her mouth and glowered at him. "Why didn't you wake me? I need to call the prison to give them a heads-up."

"Anita did that for us."

Anita Escobar was their administrative assistant who moonlighted as dispatch and, honestly, the woman worked more than Sun did.

"She's already in?"

"Daylight savings time." He tapped his watch. "She got to the station an hour ago. Also, you snore."

Her clock had changed from Mountain to Pacific while she slept. Arizona was one of the few states that didn't honor daylight savings time. A perk that Sun had prayed for since childhood. She hated *spring forward* with the fiery passion of a thousand suns.

"Keith Seabright?" she asked, inquiring about their stabbing victim.

"Out of surgery. Critical but stable."

"Oh, thank goodness. I really don't want any murders on my watch."

"But multiple stabbings are okay?"

"The jury's still out."

"You know it'll happen, Sunbeam."

"Bite your tongue. Levi?"

He shook his head. "Nothing. The guy's a ghost. And nothing on our assailants, either."

"True. They won't find Levi until he wants to be found, but I was really hoping to get a hit on that Tundra. No dead bodies along the interstate?"

"Have you been cleaning out your closet again?"

She grinned just as her stomach growled. Taking his reply as a no, she switched her focus and said one word. "Sustenance."

"I'm not sure what this town has to offer, but I figured breakfast would be in order. We can't get into the prison until after the nine o'clock headcount anyway."

"An actual sit-down breakfast? Hell yes. Or I have a can of tuna in my bag."

"Oh, yeah." He thought back. "From that time with the thing and the man."

"Exactly."

"Sweet, but I don't think we'll need it. Anita found us a café close to the prison."

"Is there anything that woman can't do?"

"Not that I know of. Maybe pee standing up. Or hot yoga on account of her vertigo. You can tell me all about that dream you had while we eat."

Startled, she looked over at him. The dream came back to her in a rush. So vivid and gut-wrenching and surreal. She'd had similar dreams before, but this time it rang truer, as though more a memory than a figment of her brain's hypervigilant imagination.

There was something about the voice. And the hands. If only she could see the man's face. Either way, she wasn't sure she wanted to share just yet. Maybe it was only a dream even though it felt real. Dreams did that. They all felt real at the time. But like all of the flashbacks from that period of her life, it was grainy and distorted and more emotion than substance.

Maybe she could use it as a bargaining tool. "I'll tell you

everything about my dream, Chief Deputy Cooper. Right after you tell me what you're hiding."

He nodded. "Breakfast in absolute silence, it is."

Damn. So close.

She brought out her phone to check up on her little pasta primavera, which was a nickname Auri hated. Not that her loathing stopped Sun from using it. Auri would need *something* to tell her therapist.

After texting the same word seven times and discovering autocorrect changed it to something different each time only after she hit SEND—seriously, how does one go from *pumpernickel* to *colonoscopy*—and having her daughter type back things like, *Mom, stop,* and *This is getting painful,* and, *Mom, really, stop,* Sun gave up and called her.

"What the heck, Mom?" she said.

"Sorry. Freaking autocorrect."

"It's not autocorrect when you can't spell."

"Pumpernickel is a hard word. Now knock-knock."

"I already know this one."

"Not this one. It's new. And you're on speakerphone. We have to entertain Quincy."

"Hi, Quincy!" she shouted.

"Speaker. Phone. You don't have to yell."

"Sorry!" she yelled to spite her.

"Hey, bean sprout," he said with a chuckle.

Sun only bristled a little that he got a *hi* and she got a *what the heck.* "Knock-knock."

Auri exhaled. It was a long, drawn-out ode to every tragedy Shakespeare ever wrote. "Who's there?"

"Pumpernickel."

"Pumpernickel who?"

"If I had a pumpernickel for every time I found a boy in your room—"

"Oh, my God, Mom! Did you tell Quincy?"

"Tell me what?" Quincy asked, the smirk on his face manifesting in his voice.

"Nothing," she said.

"Bean Sprout Vicram," he teased, "did you have a boy in your room?"

"No."

Sun made a strangling sound, trying to suppress a giggle. "I'm going to assume your grandparents made sure Cruz left you with your virtue intact."

"Mother."

Sun's brows shot up at the formality their relationship had sunk to, and she had a full-on scuffle with the giggle fighting tooth and nail to escape. The kid had a boy in her room. She had to know there would be consequences.

"My virtue is right where you left it."

"In the laundry room?"

"Are you guys there yet?" she asked, wisely changing the subject.

"Just about. We're going to grab some breakfast, then hit the prison. I can get some numbers in case you want to invite any more boys into your room once they get paroled."

"Mother," she said again. "I'm going to start recording our conversations so I'll have something to present to the judge during my emaciation hearing."

When Quincy tossed her a questioning look, she covered the phone and whispered, "Emancipation."

"Ah."

"She's been threatening it for years, but I figure as long as she can't pronounce it, no judge in the state will know what she's asking for."

He nodded and tapped his temple.

"Stellar idea, honey," she said into the phone.

"Did you find him?" Auri asked, doing a one-eighty.

Because Auri's tone held a sadness that hadn't been there a

moment earlier, Sun knew exactly who she was talking about. "Not yet, sweetheart. I don't think Levi will be found until Levi wants to be found."

"What if he's really hurt? He could be lying dead somewhere."

Sun had worried about that very thing. "We'll find him, bug. Maybe you should ask Jimmy if they've heard anything." A long shot since she'd just spoken to Jimmy, but Levi could've gone home last night.

"Okay. I'll text him now."

"Let me know. Are you helping your grandparents with the attic?"

"About to. Grandma made pancakes and Sybil is coming over."

"Awesome. You guys have fun. And keep me updated."

"Be careful, Mom. You know—"

"Yes," she interrupted. "I know what they do to cops in jail. You tell me in minute detail every time I threaten to kill your grandparents. Love your face."

"Love yours, too. Bye, Quincy!"

"Bye, sprout." He chuckled softly when Sun hung up. "Emaciation? That's hilarious."

"Which is why I never correct her when she mispronounces anything. One, it's adorable. And, two, my need to be entertained supersedes her need to cinch a full ride to Harvard."

"I don't know, Sunbeam. I think the kid has a shot at the Ivies."

"She does, doesn't she?"

"If she doesn't get pregnant first."

Sun slammed her lids shut. "That child's virtue had better be right where I left it when I get back."

"Good luck with that," he said, his laugh a little too jovial as he turned into the parking lot of the Florence Café.

Breakfast turned out to be a pancake lover's dream. Unfortunately, Sun had decided to cut back on the carbs, so she had bacon and eggs while living vicariously through her BFF, trying not to drool as he cut into a huge stack of fluffy goodness and refused to answer any of her questions on the subject of whatever he was hiding from her. It didn't happen often, so the curiosity was eating her alive.

"Oh," he said, steering the conversation away from the topic at hand again, "Anita wants us to stop by the St. Anthony's Monastery and pick her up some olive oil."

"Odd request." She checked the seven texts Carver, her blind date, had sent her. She had no idea the guy was going to be so obnoxious. She would have to let him down easy, but not over text. She'd meet him for coffee when things calmed down. After firing off a quick text telling him she was out of town, then texting Levi for the 275th time, she asked, "Olive oil? Is that a secret code for something?"

"She swears the monastery has some of the best cold-pressed olive oil in the world."

"Oh. That settles it then. I've always wanted to see St. Anthony's anyway."

Florence, Arizona, a pretty town sprinkled with palm trees and saguaro cacti, sat surrounded by miles of desert, a gorgeous vineyard, and a world-famous olive orchard. It boasted a population of over 26,000, but about 17,000 of those were residents of the massive Arizona State Prison Complex.

An hour after arriving in the town, Sun and Quincy drove through the first set of gates the prison had to offer. The guard told them where to go and roughly how to get there, but once inside, his directions seemed convoluted. The place was a maze.

"It's like a small town in here," Quincy said, leading Sun this direction and that with an index finger. She decided to rename him the Pathfinder. Mostly because he got them totally lost.

"I think we're lost," she said. "We may have to make a run for it."

"If we do, I'm using you for cover." He pointed to an armed guard in a watchtower looking down at them, sunglasses in place, rifle at the ready.

"At least we'll go out in a blaze of glory."

"Well, a blaze at least. I thought New Mexico was hot. This is like the seventh level of hell."

New Mexico *was* hot, they just happened to live in one of the cooler areas. Which, while still hot, was not Southern Arizona hot.

They retraced their steps and followed the guard's directions again. This time they ended up at the level three facility. Precisely where they needed to be. Concrete gray buildings formed the prison units with huge, hangarlike structures surrounding a massive yard. Chain-link and razor wire completed the décor, adding an industrial feel to the already military-like establishment.

The inmates were starting to file out, so the count was over.

"I like it," Quincy said, scanning the area. "It's homey."

Sun threw the cruiser into park. "I agree. A few curtains, a good desk lamp, I'd live here."

"You seem nervous," he said.

She lifted a shoulder. "More curious than nervous. But, yeah, nervous, too."

"Because of the venue?"

"Nah. I'm just anxious about what Wynn knows. Or, more likely, doesn't know."

They got out and walked up to the speaker, their IDs at the ready.

"I've never met Wynn Ravinder," he said.

"You and I were in middle school when he went inside the first time."

"What's he in for?"

With all the sleeping on the road and lack of small talk over breakfast, they hadn't really discussed the particulars of Wynn or their expectations.

"Murder," she said. "Though he swears he didn't do it."

"Don't they all. Still, he's in level three. Must be a model prisoner."

"Let's hope so. If he's anything like his brother Clay, we are packing up and heading home. I'm not putting up with any shit."

"Agreed."

She pushed the button and began the process of entry anew, the sweltering heat and her anxiety making her light-headed.

Half an hour later, they'd secured their sidearms and were shown to a small interview room. Gray with a steel door and a metal table bolted to the floor, the barren space offered nothing a prisoner could use as a makeshift weapon. A guard stood in the open doorway while they waited.

"What do you know about this guy?" he asked them.

The kid looked too young to be a prison guard. Too chubby and fresh-faced, but he was built like a sumo wrestler, minus a hundred pounds or so. Sun had little doubt he knew how to handle himself.

"Ravinder?" she asked. "Just that he's served eleven years of a life sentence without the possibility of parole for first-degree murder, and yet he's managed to earn his way into a level-three facility." Most inmates with more than thirty years left on their sentence were in a maximum facility. Level four or five, depending on the prison.

"Exactly." The guard nodded while checking his phone. "Be careful." He looked up at them. "To the untrained eye, Ravinder's a model prisoner. Well-liked, even by the guards. He's also an electrician, which helped get him bumped to level three. But just so you know, he's the shot caller."

"A shot caller?" she asked, surprised.

Judging by Quincy's expression, he concurred. Inmates doing time for murder who'd earned the title of shot caller didn't often fall into the *model-prisoner* category.

"Let me reiterate," the guard said. "He's *the* shot caller."

Sun had done her research, but criminal records rarely listed little things like the fact that a prisoner might be a shot caller. Or, apparently, *the* shot caller. She'd need to see his prison jacket for information like that.

The fact that Wynn held such a lofty position meant the other inmates either respected or feared him. Most likely both. That kind of role was rarely earned through niceties and good manners. Wynn Ravinder could be ruthlessly violent when he needed to be and probably had a cruel streak.

Having never been to prison, Sun couldn't blame the guy for doing anything to survive in such a hostile environment, but rising to the position of a shot caller in a prison of over 17,000 inmates took a lot more than just surviving.

She leaned closer to Quince and spoke quietly. "He's starting to look more and more like his brother Clay than I'd hoped."

"You think this is bullshit?"

"It's starting to look that way, but first, what does he want? And second, if he's dying, why aren't we in the medical ward?"

"Well, fuck," Quincy whispered. "He played us."

"Maybe. Let's see what he has to say and try to get a peek at his jacket."

"Until then . . ." Quincy looked at the guard. "I want a stab vest for the sheriff."

"What?" she said. "Don't be ridiculous, Quince. It's not like we're going out into the yard."

He bent closer. "Sunny, maybe he's called you here to find out what *you* know about your abduction. Not the other way around. Do you know how easily a shot caller can get to you in here? He'll have hundreds below him. Possibly thousands if he truly is top dog. All waiting to do his bidding just to get noticed."

She looked at the guard and held up two fingers as though ordering drinks at a pub. "We'll take two."

Ten minutes after they'd strapped into the hard body armor, a single guard led a handcuffed man into the room. If he were truly violent, he would have had two escorts. The fact that he only had one eased her mind, though just barely. Still, when they started to uncuff him, Sun held up her hand. "He's fine just like he is."

The guard looked at Wynn as though gauging his reaction.

When Wynn only smiled at Sun, the guard nodded and left the room. That exchange depleted what little confidence she had that they'd make it out alive.

Wynn Ravinder, a startlingly handsome muddy blond in his late forties, watched her like a hawk watches its prey. He was tall and slim, rock hard, and covered in tattoos from the looks of his forearms and neck, though thankfully she saw no Aryan tattoos.

He was attractive in the same way Levi was, as though chiseled by the gods, yet they looked nothing alike. Besides the lean, solid bodies and razor-sharp jawlines, the resemblance ended there. Since Levi was most likely not blood related to Wynn— rumors abounded that Levi's mother had strayed and that his real father was part Native American—their lack of resemblance was no surprise.

But like Levi, Wynn looked as though he would be equally as comfortable in Armani gray as prison orange. His striking features and obsidian-sharp gaze answered her questions as to how he became such an elevated shot caller.

Unfazed about the cuffs, he lifted the pant legs of his orange uniform and folded himself into the chair across from them. Sun took out a pen and notepad and waited. After studying her a solid minute, he eased back in the chair and eyed her from underneath his lashes.

"You came," he said at last.

"You called," she countered. "I doubt we have much time, what with you dying and all."

"You worried about me?" He gestured toward the rigid stab vests they both wore, which only *looked* like Kevlar. They were a hard, almost impenetrable plastic. Kind of like wearing a cutting board.

"They insisted we wear these," she lied.

He nodded. "They do that. You look like your mother."

Sun felt Quincy tense.

"Mr. Ravinder," she said, ready to get out of there, "you said you had information about my abduction."

"I do."

"You also said you were dying, yet you look like the healthiest person in this place. Guards included."

He lifted a shoulder. "I work out."

"You aren't dying."

"No."

"Okay, let's go," she said to Quince, even though the disappointment crushed her.

She started to rise, when Wynn stayed her with, "But I do have information."

She leveled a dubious look on him.

"I didn't lie about that."

After weighing the pros and cons, she sat back down and gave him a slow once-over to establish some semblance of dominance. She doubted it worked. "What information?"

"First, you should probably know, I killed my brother Kubrick fifteen years ago."

Auri sat in the same spot for two hours, scouring the newspaper clippings her grandparents had saved about a series of old missing persons cases in Del Sol. They had clippings on several other cases as well, but this one spoke to her.

Multiple people went missing over the span of a decade in the late fifties and early sixties, and the cases were never solved. A steelworker. A businessman. A young woman whose relations seemed more worried about a necklace she was wearing at the time of her disappearance than the girl herself. And more. Then one day the disappearances suddenly stopped.

"Did you see this?" Sybil asked, leaning toward her with a police report.

Sybil St. Aubin had been Auri's best friend since moving to Del Sol. Maybe that was why the missing persons cases spoke to her so loudly. Just over four months ago, Sybil was one of them. She'd gone missing and her captor held her for days, waiting until her birthday to kill her. He'd wanted revenge on Sybil's mother, which was just messed up.

Thankfully, Auri's mom was on the case. As well as the best tracker in the state, Levi Ravinder. They found Sybil but lost her again when the kidnapper tried a second time. If not for Zee and her remarkable sharpshooting abilities, both Sybil and Auri's mom would be dead.

The thought crushed Auri. Her mom was one thing. She didn't know if she would survive losing her. But the thought of losing Sybil was almost as bad. She glanced up at her friend and marveled once again at their similarities. Red hair and, well, red hair. That was pretty much their only similarity other than their interests and hobbies and general outlook on life. And boys. Mostly boys.

Sybil's hair was a light auburn while Auri's was an embarrassingly bright copper. People stopped her in the street and asked if they could touch it. Not creepy at all. And Sybil had a light sprinkling of freckles that Auri envied. They were so cute. Auri had a darker complexion and no freckles to speak of. Also, no round-rimmed glasses like the ones that made Sybil look book-nerd adorable.

When she'd met Sybil at the lake on New Year's Eve, Auri's first thought was that she looked like an American Girl doll she'd had when she was little. The one her grandparents bought her because it had red hair, and who looked more like a schoolmarm than a little girl.

Her opinion had yet to change.

They sat cross-legged on the attic floor.

"They may have caught the killer, after all," Sybil said, referencing the police report, "but it never went to trial, so they never knew for certain."

Auri took the report but held it so Sybil could read with her. A musty police blotter with faded ink on yellowed paper described an incident at the county jail that happened on August 12, 1965. "Oh, my God," Auri said. "They killed him."

"Yes." Sybil flipped to the second page. "A drifter named Hercules Holmes. He escaped and disappeared, but they found his body a couple of weeks later. Someone killed him before he could go to trial."

"That's awful," Auri said.

Her grandmother weaved toward them through boxes and furniture. "The Holmes case?"

They looked up and nodded.

"What do you know about it, Grandma?"

She sat in a dusty rocking chair and put her elbows on her knees. "Just what's in that box, I'm afraid."

Auri looked at the piles of clippings around her. "Why do you have this stuff anyway?"

"History," her grandfather said, panting from the climb up. He'd brought strawberry sparkling water and handed them each an ice-cold can.

"Thanks, Grandpa."

"Thank you, sir," Sybil said.

"Sybil, if you don't start calling me Cyrus, I'm kicking you out. For good this time."

She grinned and popped the top on her can. "Okay."

They had a fan going, but it was getting hot fast. Auri's grandfather fanned himself and took in all the work they had yet to do. "We're going to have to pick this up when it cools down in the evening."

"Oh," Auri said, jumping up. "Well, I'm okay. Do you mind if I keep looking?" She didn't miss the knowing glances they exchanged.

"Of course not, peanut."

"You saved all of this, all of these cases, for history?" Auri asked.

"Sure." He sat on an old trunk next to his wife. "We're actually working on opening a Del Sol history museum, and those old newspapers are gold."

"But these are just clippings from old, unsolved cases. Except maybe the missing persons cases. They apparently caught that guy."

"Do you believe they did?" her grandmother asked.

Auri and Sybil exchanged glances, too, testing each other's reaction. "I guess," Auri ventured. "I mean, it says that they caught this drifter named Hercules Holmes with one of the missing persons' wallets."

"So that makes him guilty?" her grandmother asked. "That makes him unworthy of a fair trial?"

"No," she said adamantly. "Never." She knew enough about the law from watching her mother scour over cases for years to know things were rarely that simple. She put the report down and looked at them. "You think he was innocent."

Auri's grandmother held up her palms. "I'm just asking what you think."

She pressed her mouth together and thought about it. "The way I see it, he was either guilty and so he escaped or innocent and someone helped him escape."

Cyrus narrowed his lashes at her, and if Auri didn't know better, she'd say there was a sparkle of pride in his eyes. "What do you mean?" he asked, coaxing her to go deeper. He did that a lot.

"Well, he magically escapes a heavily guarded jail cell and then ends up dead two weeks later? According to the report"— she bent and read aloud—"he died from a single gunshot wound to the head shortly after escaping." She looked back at him. "That doesn't mean he didn't somehow manage to get himself killed, but right after his magical escape? It seems more than a little suspect to me."

Both he and her grandmother nodded in agreement.

"And he was a drifter passing through town," she added. "These cases went back years. Where was he then?"

"Go on," her grandmother encouraged.

"And what about the boardinghouse?"

"What boardinghouse?" Sybil asked, combing through the clippings for more.

Auri handed her a clipping from just before the drifter was killed. "According to the sheriff's investigation, at least five of the missing victims were travelers who stayed at the same boarding-house." She rummaged around until she found another report. "The Fairborn House." She stopped and thought about it. "The Fairborn House? As in Mrs. Fairborn? That sweet old lady who confesses to all of the crimes in Del Sol?"

"Really?" Sybil asked her.

"Yep. She's been doing it for years. Every time a crime happens in Del Sol, she confesses to it. She even confessed to Kubrick Ravinder's murder."

The girl's mouth formed a perfect O. "Did she do it?"

Auri giggled. "Of course not, silly. Can you find anything else on the boardinghouse?"

"I'll try."

By the time they looked up again an hour later, her grand-parents were gone.

"Sybil, I may have spoken too soon. Maybe she did kill Kubrick after all. I think Mrs. Fairborn was a serial killer before they even called them serial killers."

"Wow," Sybil said, just as intrigued. "Wait, what did they call serial killers before that?"

Auri shrugged. "Maybe pancake killers? Bacon-and-egg killers?"

They devolved into a fit of giggles and only sobered when a thought hit Auri like a line drive at a major-league game. "I think we need to investigate," she said.

"Really? Can we do that?"

"Sure. My mom does it every day. How hard can it be?"

7

Sprinkles are for cupcakes, not toilets.

—SIGN IN BATHROOM AT THE SUGAR SHACK

Sun didn't hide her disbelief. She frowned at the man sitting across from her. "If I had a nickel for every time someone confessed to killing Kubrick Ravinder . . ."

Quincy agreed. "He's the most popular dead guy since Edward Cullen."

Wynn shrugged and leaned back in his chair. "What do you want to know?"

She took the pen in hand to start taking notes should she need to. "How did he die?"

"Painfully."

"Does that mean you strangled him slowly?"

A knowing grin slid across his face. "I did, apple blossom. But that's not what killed him."

"Sheriff Vicram," she corrected, only mildly curious as to why he'd referred to her as the flower of an apple tree. She was more interested in his knowledge about Kubrick's death. While his larynx had been crushed, that was not how the man died.

"Much to my elder brother's dismay, I put a knee on his throat, slid a knife into his chest, and watched with glee as the life drained out of him."

It wasn't often that she heard a hardened criminal use the

word *glee*. There was something primal about the man. Something sharp and commanding and ruthless. The whole shot-caller thing made perfect sense now. His dark blond hair, although slicked back, hung to his shoulders in the choppy style of a man who didn't concern himself overly much with his daily coif. Then again, what inmate did? His scruffy jaw only added to the look.

"So you and Kubrick didn't get along?" Quincy asked.

"We took our sibling rivalries like we took our corn whiskey. Very seriously."

It was no wonder. Moonshine was, after all, how his family had made a living for decades. But anyone could have found out how Kubrick was killed. That didn't tell her a thing. "How long—?"

"Twelve seconds." When she paused, he added, "It took twelve seconds for him to die. I counted."

She began again. "How long was the blade?"

"Long enough to get the job done."

"How many inches?"

He released a lungful of air and examined his fingernails, as though their questions were growing tedious. But he'd called her. Not the other way around.

"I didn't measure," he said, offering his hawkish gaze again. "But if I were to use a body part as reference, I'd say about eight inches. Give or take."

Close enough.

"And he just lay there?" Quincy asked. "Let you crush his larynx and plunge a knife into his chest?"

"Don't be ridiculous. We fought." He speared him with his glistening gray eyes. "I won."

Sun feigned boredom. "Then that was your blood all over Kubrick's T-shirt."

Another knowing grin crept into the corners of his mouth. "You mean all over his denim jacket and that flannel shirt he wore every fucking day of his miserable fucking life?"

Two for two. He was the first confessor to get this far. Besides Levi, of course, but she hadn't questioned him this extensively.

"Unless," he continued, "you're talking about the filthy wife-beater underneath."

Sun's knee-jerk reaction to the derogatory term for an A-line tank top bucked inside her. Regardless, she didn't move a muscle. Didn't flinch. Yet he knew.

"I'm sorry." He tilted his head to study her. "Did that offend your delicate sensibilities?"

"The only thing offending my delicate sensibilities, Mr. Ravinder, is the fact that you think we came here for tea and scones. You haven't proven anything."

He shrugged. "Then check the blood on Brick's jacket. My DNA's in the system. I'm assuming you sent in a sample." He leaned forward. "You wouldn't have a reason to hold off on that, would you?"

Sun's façade slipped for a split second. It was all a predator like him needed. She'd just showed her hand, but he couldn't possibly know how long she'd waited before sending the evidence in to the lab in Santa Fe along with Levi's DNA. Not without having some fantastic connections.

Quincy cast a curious glance her way before returning his attention to their host.

She hadn't told him she'd kept Levi's DNA sample in her desk drawer far longer than she had a right to. And part of her wasn't really sure why. Other than the fact that, if it was a match, he could go to prison. If it came out that she'd withheld evidence, even for a short time, in a murder investigation, she could lose her job.

The unfortunate fact that evidence in general tended to get lost or contaminated when surfing through the channels of justice could work in her favor should it come to that, but no one could prove that she took the sample on any given day. Besides Levi himself, and she could hardly see him turning her in.

Wynn leaned closer to Sun and lowered his voice. "What do you say we ditch Captain America over there and continue this conversation alone?"

"Over my dead body," Quincy said.

He shook his head and tsked. "That is the wrong thing to say in this place, junior."

"Why are you confessing?" she asked him.

"Why do you care?" he countered. "You'll have your man. You'll have solved the case. You'll probably get a medal. Isn't that all you badges care about?"

After a long thoughtful moment, she said quietly, "Chief Deputy Cooper, can you leave us alone for a minute?"

He tried to hide his astonishment when he looked at her. He failed. After a long, tense moment, he recovered, cleared his throat, and said, "No, ma'am."

She gave him her full attention and said softly, "Deputy, that's an order."

He stared at her for what seemed like an hour. She could practically see his mind racing with all the scenarios of how this could end badly. But she didn't like showing her vulnerabilities. It would be hard enough asking what she wanted to ask Wynn without having Quincy in the room. Besides, statistically, men were much more apt to open up to a woman.

"They frisked him," she assured her partner. "They're right outside the door. I'll be fine."

Wynn sat back in his chair, clearly amused when Quincy unfolded his large frame, tossed him a quick glare, and headed toward the door. With a single knock, it opened and Quince was shown outside.

When it closed again, she said, "I don't believe you."

"Then get over it, because it doesn't matter. You'll have your killer."

"It matters."

"No, apple blossom," he said, leaning forward again. "It doesn't. The investigation will be closed. The case will be solved. And all of those people breathing down your neck can go fuck themselves."

Her mind churned with questions. There was so much she wanted to know, but to trust a convicted felon would make her all kinds of stupid.

Still, a part of her wanted him to be the killer, because there was no denying the most damning piece of evidence of all. The ID bracelet Kubrick had clutched in his hands, even after fifteen years of animal mauling and decomposition. The ID bracelet with Levi's name on it.

She decided to play along with Wynn for now. Curiosity won out every time. "Were you in it with him?" When he didn't answer, she clarified. "Did you help him abduct me?"

The look he gave her, part concern and part sympathy, almost convinced her he cared. Almost. "No, Sunshine. I found out later. After he'd taken you."

"That's when you joined his cause?" When he only deadpanned her, she added, "It was a lot of money. Who could blame you?"

"And here I thought we were becoming friends."

"Walk me through it. You found out Kubrick abducted me and then what? You came to my rescue out of the kindness of your heart?"

He kept his gaze trained on her face. In fact, besides an initial sizing up, he hadn't ogled her or objectified her in any way. Hell, even the guards had done that when she and Quince had walked in. Did that imply a level of respect? Or was he simply that cunning?

"There isn't much kindness left in my heart, apple blossom. But at the time? Sure. Why not."

She nodded and decided to delve deeper. "How did you find out where he was keeping me?"

"It wasn't difficult. Brick was a creature of habit."

"He'd taken other women there?"

"You weren't a woman," Wynn said, suddenly serious. "You were a kid."

"I was seventeen."

"Exactly. Either way, no. Brick was not in the habit of abducting women. He used that shed as a hunting cabin."

"Okay. You figured out he was keeping me there and then what?"

"And then nothing. He busted me trying to get you out. We fought. The rest is history."

She nodded, deep in thought. "Who took me to the hospital?"

He spread his cuffed hands, indicating himself.

Her chest tightened so hard, so fast, it felt like it was going to explode. Wynn Ravinder was certainly the right build. The person in the hospital surveillance video seemed younger, but even now, in his forties, Wynn was lithe and agile.

"What did you give me? In the truck?"

"Besides a ride?"

He didn't know. Then again, it was a long time ago and he was bleeding profusely. How could anyone remember every minute detail? Maybe he really did forget.

She studied him and decided that was not likely. Quincy was right. He was playing her. Though he did seem fairly certain the lab results would prove his DNA was on Kubrick's clothes. But even that could be explained. He could've been a part of her abduction with Kubrick. They could've argued about the two-million ransom they were demanding. Came to blows. None of this proved he came to her rescue.

There was just something off about all of it. Why so many confessions? Was someone trying to muddy the waters? And even though Wynn had the right build, she couldn't help but doubt his claims. Especially when taking the ID bracelet into account.

Sun had always had a sixth sense about people, and Wynn just didn't fit. Putting him at the scene that night, fighting Brick, giving her water, taking her to the hospital. Not that Wynn wouldn't have done all of that. After meeting him, she had little doubt there was a part of him that was noble. She just didn't think he *did* do it. Envisioning him at the scene was like trying to force a square peg into a round hole. It didn't fit without some pretty serious manipulation.

Just when she'd dismissed his claims completely, he added, "Unless you mean the water I poured down your throat."

Her lungs stopped working.

"You remember that? Right before you threw up all over me? And my truck, I might add." He eased forward, and whispered, "Ingrate."

Her world spun. Nobody could know that except the person who took her to the hospital. No one possibly could. She'd only started getting flashes of that night in the last few months and she hadn't told a soul about the pickup or the water or the vomit. Mostly because she didn't know if it was real or simply a product of her drug-induced imagination.

Unable to sit any longer, she stood and walked to the postage-stamp window Quincy was dogging her through. He was mad. She needed to see his face regardless. He stood on the other side of the door like an anchor. Always there for her.

She turned back to Wynn. "Why are you doing this? Baring your soul. Why now?"

"I have conditions."

Ah. And so it begins. "You mean demands."

He lifted a shoulder. "If you want a signed confession, I have three."

"And you think you have enough to bargain with?"

"What? I still haven't convinced you?" he asked, seemingly surprised.

She shrugged. "You don't fit."

He tilted his head in a shruglike gesture. "I usually don't."

"Again, why now? Why not ten years ago?"

"You weren't the sheriff ten years ago."

"Why not four months ago, then? When I was first elected."

"I only recently heard you found his body."

"Your own brother's remains were found on a mountain four months ago and no one told you?"

He spread his hands as far as the cuffs would allow. "I'm all but forgotten."

"If your blood is really on Brick's clothes, I won't need your confession."

"Ah, but there's so much more, apple blossom." He swiveled

around in the chair to face her more fully. "A lot you don't remember about the time leading up to the abduction. About the days you spent in that shed. About that night. You're right about one thing. Kubrick didn't do it alone."

She felt her eyes round and cursed inwardly. If she were interviewing a suspect, she would never give away the game so easily. She would never reveal her thoughts. Show emotion. Give him the upper hand. With this case—her case—she seemed incapable of doing anything but.

"I'll tell you everything," he said, very aware of the fact that he was winning.

"Then you lied."

"I lie all the time. Can you be more specific?"

"If you know everything, you and Kubrick were definitely in it together."

"Not hardly. The man liked to brag. As did his partner in crime."

"Whose name is . . . ?"

"Nah-ah, apple blossom. When my . . . *demands* are met, we can talk."

"I'm the sheriff of a small county in New Mexico. I have exactly zero pull here, but feel free to demand away."

"Don't worry. They're simple."

"Sure. What is it exactly you think I can do for you?"

"I'm in here for the rest of my life, apple. I don't have a whole lot to look forward to, and I want to be closer to my family so they can come visit me more than once a decade. I want to be transferred to Santa Fe."

The look of astonishment she planted on him said everything he needed to know about her ability to pull that off.

"It's called a transport order."

"I know what it's called. But getting a prisoner transferred across state lines is kind of a big deal. I just don't think it can happen."

"Why not? I have vital information about an ongoing murder

investigation and am willing to testify to certain . . . atrocities that were committed in said case. I can even lead the authorities to the weapon I used to defend myself, which will have my fingerprints on it."

"You have the knife?" she asked in surprise.

"I know where it is. In return, I'm transferred to the state where the case occurred and will be available to testify once I name my brother's accomplice. Et cetera, et cetera. It can be done."

"You came prepared," she said, walking back to the table.

"Always."

She sat across from him again. "And two?"

"I want you to look into my case."

"Oh, right. I forgot, you're innocent."

"Hell, no," he said with a snort. "There's not a single innocent person in this place. But I am innocent of the crime they put me in here for, and I've heard you are *just* savvy enough to figure that out and prove it for me."

Wow, was he ever wrong about a person. Then again, she'd been wrong about him. "Who do I have to thank for spreading false rumors about me?"

He relaxed against the chair, the metal cuffs jingling with each movement, and refused to answer once again. After giving her enough time to form her own flawed opinions, he said, "My lawyer is sending over the case files. Everything we have."

"Wonderful. Is there a magic wand in there, too? I'm going to need one."

He laughed softly. "I think that's in my other case file."

"Of course it is. And three?"

He waited a beat. Studied her. Sized her up just long enough to make a layer of sweat appear on her palms. She suddenly desperately wanted him to be telling the truth. His claims would exonerate Levi.

After another moment, he straightened in the chair, and said, "I wanna see the girl."

Disturbing. "Look, I know it's been a while for you—"

"Not as long as you might think."

Okay. She didn't need to know that. "—but smuggling women into prison is not one of my talents. And, believe me, I have many."

"So I've been told."

The more they spoke, the more she wondered who was out there talking her up to a convicted murderer. Because she wanted a word. "What girl?"

"*Your* girl."

Sun stopped tapping the pen on the pad and tilted her head. "I'm sorry?"

"When I get back to New Mexico, I want you to bring your daughter to see me."

Emotions Sun didn't know she possessed rushed through her like a lightning strike. Sharp and hot and desperate, they blinded her for a few seconds. Why would a convicted killer want to see her daughter? How did he even know she had a daughter? Levi could've told him if they were still in contact, but why would he? Why would the conversation turn toward her?

All semblance of professionalism abandoned her. All of her training, all of her skills with de-escalation and negotiation disappeared within the span of a heartbeat. She became someone else. Someone willing to risk her career. Someone willing to kill.

She leaned forward. "What the hell did you just say to me?"

"I get to see the girl or no deal."

Sun was drowning in apprehension so thick she could hardly see straight. She'd been on the force for almost ten years and this man reduced her to an unstable powder keg in a matter of seconds.

Tears seared the backs of her eyes as she looked into the dark depths of gray in his.

"Apple," he began, but reconsidered when her glare turned murderous. "Sheriff, it's not what you think."

Something hit the door. Or, more precisely, someone. It opened and Quincy was by her side at once, trying to ease her away from

Wynn. She held the pen in her fist like she was going to use it to shank the man across from her.

"Get back, Ravinder," Quincy said, coaxing Sun to do the same.

"I understand," he said, ignoring Quincy. "You need to sleep on it."

"The only thing I need to sleep on is how to make sure you never make it out of prison alive."

"I didn't hear that," Quincy said to Wynn. He looked at a guard that had hurried in, quickly followed by a second. "You didn't hear that."

One corner of Wynn's mouth rose. "He was right about you. You're amazing." Before she could comment, he added, "I'm willing to take you on your word. You meet the first two conditions, I'll sign a confession and tell you everything on the contingency that I'll get to see your daughter at some point in the next year."

She felt a tear slip past her lashes as question upon question ran rampant through her brain. She settled on the most predominant. "What makes you think I would ever agree to such a demand?"

Wynn shrugged. "I just thought maybe she'd like to know who her father is."

The breath in her lungs couldn't have fled any faster if he'd punched her in the gut.

A guard leaned down until he was between them. He focused on Sun and said, "You two need to back down or this interview is over."

Quincy planted her ass back in her chair with a firm push, and Wynn eased into his. Satisfied, the guard straightened but didn't dare leave the room.

Sun forced herself to calm. To unclench her teeth. "Fine. I'll bring my daughter to see you."

"What?" The question was from Quincy who stared at her, appalled.

"I'll bring her to see you as soon as you tell me why."

Quincy sat beside her, but he wasn't happy about the direction the conversation had taken in his absence.

A sadness seemed to come over Wynn when he said, "I've been told she resembles her grandmother."

Sun knew instinctively he was not referring to the carefree creature known as Elaine Freyr. "You don't get to play with my daughter's life. To use her as a pawn. I'll make it my life's mission to see that you rot in here until you die first."

It was his turn to let his emotions overtake him. He stood and turned his back on her.

The two guards tensed. One of them put a hand on his arm as though to subdue him if need be, but he remained calm.

"Can I speak to you alone?" he asked. When he turned back to her, his expression had changed. A vulnerability shone through. A vulnerability Sun didn't believe existed in a man like him. He was a good actor, she'd give him that.

Still, that curiosity burned too hot and too bright for her to ignore. "Quincy?" she asked.

He hesitated but decided not to push the point. The guards followed him out, only they didn't close the door this time. They did, however, give the two some semblance of privacy by walking a few feet away. Quincy crossed his arms over his chest and stood closer, refusing to give the man too much space.

"Ask yourself this, Sunshine. Why would I want my conviction overturned if I'm about to confess to killing my own brother? I'm going to rot in a cell either way."

"You just said you were rescuing me. You probably wouldn't get any time for defending yourself and saving my life. I doubt the DA would even pursue it."

He nodded and dropped his gaze. "I didn't think of it that way."

She didn't believe him. He was far too smart not to have thought of that angle.

"They were friends of mine," he said after a moment. "The couple I was convicted of killing. They were friends and I've spent almost a dozen years in prison while the person who really killed them has walked around free. They deserve better."

He was good. "Do you know who did it?"

He sat down and wiped at some imaginary dirt on his palm. "Yes."

"Did you tell your lawyer?"

"No. I didn't know then. I know now."

"Why not just have him *taken care of*?"

"Too easy. I want him inside. I want him to be in fear for his life every single day for as long as he lives."

"Like you are?"

He scoffed. "Not hardly, but that's not the point. Most people don't thrive in here like I have."

"Are you her father?"

The question slipped out before she could stop it. She didn't know what to believe at this point. Even if he did know everything he was claiming, he could still have been involved in her abduction. Maybe the plan went south and he and Kubrick fought. It made a lot more sense than his galloping to her rescue.

He cast her a sideways glance. If her question surprised him, he didn't show it. "No," he said softly.

Not that he would tell her if he were. "Tell me who is and you have my word I'll do everything in my power to get your conviction overturned."

"'Fraid I can't do that, apple blossom. I have to have something to bargain with."

"You mean something to hold over my head."

"Po-tay-to, po-tah-to."

"Even if it were possible, even if I found the evidence needed to get the case reopened, it would take years to get your conviction overturned."

"I told you, I have complete faith in you."

Sun watched as he scrubbed the palm of his hand with a thumb, the clinking of the metal cuffs not unlike the sound of the metal chains she wore for five days when she was seventeen.

Her chains were heavier. The sound deeper. They'd echoed on the walls of the dark shed. But somehow the sound was still similar.

She shook out of the memory and decided on one more test. "Whose knife was it?"

"I'm sorry?"

"The knife you killed Kubrick with. Whose was it?"

"Mine."

"That's how you cut my ropes?"

He took a moment to study her, probably catching onto the fact that she was testing him again, and said, "I don't remember. But I'll give it to you the minute I'm transferred. Even more incentive to get me moved."

He must not have known about the ID bracelet. She did wonder how he would explain Kubrick's clutching a bracelet with Levi's name on it, but that little piece of evidence was not common knowledge and she didn't want to tip him off.

She could only think of one more test. One more piece of evidence that could prove he was indeed her rescuer. She stood, walked around the table, and leaned against it in front of him.

Wynn angled away from her warily. "It's been a long time since I've had a body like yours this close to me, apple blossom."

"May I look at your hands?"

After a moment, he gave her the barest hint of a nod.

She reached down and lifted his right hand to examine the palm he'd been rubbing. The cuffs that were anchored to the belt around his waist only allowed her to lift it so far, but she could see his wrist.

She didn't remember much about that night, but she did remember the blood oozing out of a deep wound on her rescuer's wrist as he tilted the bottle of water to her mouth. The dark stream was thick and pulsing and his hand shook as though a vein had been nicked during the struggle.

"You think those guards can keep you safe?" he asked, admonishing her with a soft warning.

Ignoring the empty threat, she ran her fingers over the inside of first his right wrist, then his left. Nothing. Only a small scar higher up on the inside of his forearm.

Either she remembered wrong or Wynn Ravinder was indeed lying. But if he were, how did he know so much about her abduction? About that night? About her rescue?

She needed to stop with all the questions and just check the DNA. That would give her a definitive answer and a lot more to work with. Still, the Kubrick brothers were not exactly altruistic. Why would he confess to a crime he didn't commit and in the next breath want to be exonerated from another crime he swore he didn't do?

There was no way in hell she would take Auri to prison to have a tête-à-tête with a convicted felon, but that was a bridge she could cross when she got to it.

"I'll be in touch," she said, dropping his hands.

8

Big girls don't cry.
They pop a couple Xanax,
wash them down with vodka,
and set a car on fire.
If you are this girl, we can help.

—SIGN AT DALE SAUL, ATTORNEY-AT-LAW

"Well?" Quincy said when they got back to the cruiser. "Is he your guy?"

Sun backed out and entered the prison maze once again. She rolled her eyes at her phone and put it away after seeing three texts from Carver the pest-preneur. "I wish I knew."

"What's your gut telling you?"

"It's conflicted."

He grinned. "It usually is."

"Why would he confess to this?"

"I think the bigger question is, why does he want to meet the bean sprout?"

Her conflicted gut clenched in response.

They stopped at the guard shack and waited while the officer searched the cruiser.

"You're good to go, Sheriff," he said after a few, closing the hatchback.

She waved a thank-you and pulled onto East Butte Avenue. "What if he really knows who her biological father is?"

"Sun," he said, growing serious, "I have little doubt that he does, if he knows who Kubrick Ravinder's partner was. But is that information that you need?"

"What do you mean?"

"I mean, who cares? Let's get this guy, sure, but who cares who her biological father is? Will it help Auri? Knowing who violated her mother and got her pregnant?"

"That was why I never wanted her to find out," she said, her gut twisting painfully now.

"I have to confess something, Sunbeam."

She cast a nervous glance his way as she pulled onto 79 toward the monastery. "That doesn't sound reassuring."

"What happens in the cruiser, right?" he asked, making sure whatever was said between them stayed between them.

"Always."

"When we find out who he is, he will pay for what he did one way or another."

"I'm going to pretend I didn't hear that."

"You disagree?"

"No," she admitted. "But if we start taking the law into our own hands, we are no better than the criminals we put away."

"Is that your official stance?"

"It is. Unofficially, however, you will do nothing of the sort, because I get first dibs. I have Auri's DNA in the system. Have had for years, hoping for a hit."

"If that's the case, and Wynn Ravinder's DNA is in the system already, wouldn't you have gotten a hit by now? Even if Auri's biological father were only related to him?"

"It depends on when Wynn's DNA was entered into CODIS. I haven't run it in a while, but he's been in prison for eleven years. Surely it was entered then."

"Then that would mean her biological father isn't related to Wynn."

Sun's mind raced with all the possibilities the new information could bring. Could she finally find out the truth after all these years? It all hinged on the account of one convicted murderer.

"What do you think the odds are that this is going to work? Will we be able to get Wynn transferred?" she asked.

"That depends on your connections, I'd say. Maybe we should talk to Womack."

"Royce? Good idea." Royce Womack had been the Del Sol County sheriff way back when Sun was in middle and high school. He was the first one at the hospital after her abduction, so she'd been told. He'd beat her parents there by a hairsbreadth. Sun liked to think it had more to do with his fondness for her than his connections in law enforcement, but it was hard to say for certain. "I'll see if he'll meet us for coffee when we get into town. In the meantime, my gut is telling me something else."

"And that is?" he asked.

"That Wynn Ravinder isn't as bad a guy as one might suppose."

"And you're certain your gut doesn't need therapy?"

She gave him a knowing glance.

"Fine. Let's say you're right. He's still a Ravinder. He could be a domestic terrorist and rise above the fold."

The guy had a point if they were talking only about the brothers. But Levi and Hailey were a different story. With Levi becoming a wildly successful distiller and Hailey turning her life around when her son, Jimmy, was born, they were outliers in the Ravinder clan. Hailey now worked for Levi in the office of Dark River Shine and was going to school at night to get a degree in business. Not to mention the fact that she was secretly reporting Clay Ravinder's comings and goings to Sun. An activity that was infinitely more dangerous than either of them were admitting.

Speaking of secrets . . . "Who are you seeing?" she asked Quince.

He turned an astonished expression on her. "This again?"

"This again."

He put on his sunglasses and turned away. "I'm not seeing anyone."

"Is she married?"

"No."

"Is that why you won't tell me?"

"No."

"That's why you won't tell me."

"No, it's not."

"You're coveting thy neighbor's wife."

"I'm doing no such thing."

"C'mon," Sun said, turning into the lot of St. Anthony's Greek Orthodox Monastery. "I tell you everything."

He snorted.

"Dude, who did I call first when I got my period?"

"Christ on a cracker." He covered his ears.

"My mom? My dad? No. I called you. My best friend on planet Earth."

"Which goes to show there is such a thing as TMI."

"You're really not going to tell me?"

"That I'm not seeing anyone? I just did."

"Then what are you hiding?"

"Oh, that. Well, if I told you, I wouldn't be hiding it anymore. That makes zero sense, Sunbeam. How can I hide something if I tell you?"

She groaned and put the cruiser in park.

"We have no lives," she said, suddenly depressed. "We're young-ish, oddly attractive human beings."

"Speak for yourself."

"What's wrong with us?" She looked at him.

"I don't know." He seemed to deflate, as though he felt her words on a deeper level than she'd expected.

"Quincy?" She put a hand on his arm.

He turned back to her. "We really are pathetic, aren't we?"

"Hey," she said, trying to be offended. She failed. "We are. We're losers. Also, if I guess right will you tell me?"

"I'm not seeing anyone."

"Then you're pining for someone."

"I'm not pining for anyone, either."

"Besides my mother?"

"Besides your mother." They sat contemplating their circumstances when he seemed to come to an important decision. "You know what? Enough is enough."

"I agree. Completely. One hundred percent. What are we talking about?"

"Us." He gestured, indicating the two of them. "And our general pathetic-ness."

"Oh, then I absolutely agree."

"We need to stop pining after something we can't, for whatever reason, have and take a look at what's in front of us."

After some thought, she concurred with a nod. "Absolutely. What's in front of us?"

He paused a long moment, then said, "Us."

She tilted her head in confusion. "Us?"

"You and me."

He turned in his seat to better face her and removed his shades. This must be serious. "Think about it. How long have we been friends?"

"Forever."

"And who do you love more than anyone?"

"Auri."

"Okay, besides her."

"My parents."

"No, I mean, I know that," he said, getting flustered. "Besides your family."

"Levi," she said, trying not to grin.

He rolled his eyes. "Besides Levi. Wait." He puffed out his lower lip. "You love Levi more than me?"

"Hmm," she said, having to think about it. "Not more. Just differently."

"And where has that gotten you?"

"Nowhere fast?"

"Exactly. Maybe that's our problem. Maybe deep down we're attracted to each other."

Sun couldn't help the look of horror on her face. "Really deep down."

"And we just need to work out our true feelings for one another."

"Way, way deep down."

"And maybe once we do that we can move on."

"Like almost nonexistent deep down."

"I get it," he said, holding up a palm in frustration. "Your feelings are really deep. Look, what do you want in a relationship?"

She lifted a shoulder. "The usual. Someone I can share my life with who'll leave me alone most of the time."

"See? We are so much alike. What if we're perfect for each other, we've just never given us a chance?"

"You mean sex?"

"No." He started to scrub his face but stopped and looked at her from over his fingertips. "Well, yeah."

"So, like friends with benefits?"

"No. Yes. Maybe."

The romantic sensibilities in this guy bordered on legendary. And he was still single. Whodathunk? Sun gazed into the clear depths of blue in his eyes.

He took her hands into his as an orchestra played romantic music in the background.

Without looking, she reached over and turned off the radio, then re-clasped their hands.

"Why didn't we think of this before?" he asked.

"Because we've been besties since kindergarten and having sex would very likely ruin a lifelong friendship?"

"Maybe. But maybe not." He scratched his adorably scruffy chin. "I like to believe we've simply been in denial about our true feelings."

She squinted in thought. "I don't think so. But I'm willing to give it a shot if you are."

At that point, she'd be willing to do anything to lessen the constant longing—a.k.a., obsession—for Levi Ravinder she'd had since she realized boy and girl parts differed greatly. And he was a big part of that discovery.

"So"—he grew serious with a heaping side of wicked if the impish slant of his mouth were any indication—"date night soon?"

Butterflies stormed her belly much like a battalion of soldiers storming a beach. If she didn't have those kinds of feelings for Quincy somewhere deep down—way, way deep down—why would butterflies attack? Maybe he was right.

Having made her decision, she lifted her chin in a gesture of finality. "You know what? Let's do this."

He extended his fist. "Let's do this."

They fist-bumped to seal the deal, then sat stewing in one of the most uncomfortable silences she'd ever endured, giving her a chance to take in the grounds around them. The lot was surrounded by foliage and palm trees. A white Santorini-style church sat atop a hill in front of them.

Quince scanned the oasis surrounding them as well. "I feel like having this conversation in the parking lot of a monastery is wrong."

"Having this conversation is wrong period. But who knows? Maybe you're right." She gave him a good appraisal. He was beyond attractive. She'd never questioned that. And she did love him more than just about anything or anyone on Earth. Who knew? Maybe he was onto something.

They got out of the cruiser and headed toward an adobe-style entrance that sat on their right. A beautiful red chapel nestled in greenery sat beyond that, but they headed toward the bookstore first to gain entrance.

The monastery was a lovely combination of chapels, elaborate gardens, and scenic walkways dotted with gazebos and Spanish fountains. They toured the grounds as quickly as possible, considering it was already thirty minutes out of their way, and bought several bottles of olive oil from the monks.

"I suddenly want to sauté something," Quincy said when they got back to the car.

"Don't do it in the cruiser. I'll never get the smell out."

The trip back was filled with small talk that gave their upcoming date a wide berth. Neither wanted to dwell on it, though Sun's thoughts did steer in that general direction when Quincy sat snoring in her passenger seat.

Quincy? Quincy Cooper? She prayed she wasn't making the biggest mistake of her life.

To take her mind off the linebacker next to her, she called Royce Womack. The former sheriff agreed to meet them for coffee later.

He'd become an invaluable asset to her. He'd helped her on a case her first day on the job when the U.S. Marshals were in town hunting for an escaped convict.

"Where are we?" her new beau asked. He stretched and threw in a yawn any lion would be proud of.

"A little over halfway." The sun had started its descent a few hours earlier and now hung low on the horizon.

"Shit. How long have I been out?"

"Not quite five hours."

He scowled at her. "I thought we were taking two-hour shifts."

"That's so weird. I thought the same thing last night. You hungry?"

"Always."

"Then you woke up just in time."

Sun pulled into Gordo's, one of her favorite restaurants in Gallup, put her cruiser in park, then answered yet another text from Carver asking when he'd get another coffee date.

So she could pay ten dollars for a cup of coffee? No, thank you. She typed, "Out of town. Official business."

He texted immediately asking when she would return. She groaned and handed the phone to Quince. "You're my undersheriff. You take care of this."

A sly brow raised as though questioning her sanity. She snatched back her phone. There was no telling what Quince would say to him. She shot off a quick reply about getting home late, then climbed out into the unforgiving New Mexico sun.

Apparently giving up on the low-carb lifestyle, she and Quincy both ordered beef enchiladas smothered in green chile with beans, rice, and pepitas. To top it off, they shared a sopapilla since Quincy *swore* he couldn't fit anything else into his stomach. Of course, he said that right before he ate four-fifths of the fluffy, honey-filled pillow.

Sun hadn't had carbs in days. He was lucky he didn't lose a hand.

Two hours later, after several rousing renditions of "Fancy" by Reba McEntire, they were having coffee in the Presbyterian Hospital cafeteria in Albuquerque with Royce Womack. He was in town picking up a new recruit to RISE, his rehabilitation program. He'd agreed to meet Sun and Quincy there so they could check up on their stabbing victim, Keith Seabright.

"What are our odds?" she asked him after explaining the Wynn Ravinder situation. She'd never had an inmate transferred across state lines, though she knew it happened all the time. But in most of those cases, it was for prosecutorial reasons and the inmate faced new charges once they arrived in-state.

"It can be done," he said, though he hardly seemed confident. He took a long draw of his coffee. "As long as there's no extradition with all the legalities that entails, the approval can happen in a matter of hours. You'll have to convince the DA, of course, and then he'll have to convince a friendly judge to issue a warrant, but it can be done. I can talk to Gowan. She'd probably do it."

As judges went, Gowan wasn't Sun's biggest fan, but she and Royce always got along. "So what's the problem?" she asked.

"The problem is a matter of timing. You seem to want this done—"

"Yesterday," she said a little too enthusiastically.

He scrubbed his face, his scruffy beard the stuff of legend. "She's on vacation in Sedona."

"So, tomorrow?"

He chuckled. "You're killing me, Vicram. Even if I can get a hold of her, you know how the justice system works."

"I also know how you work."

"The judge owes me one," he said. "But even if she signs it tomorrow, it could take weeks to actually get Wynn here."

"Which is why you're going to make a few calls to your friends in transportation."

"Sunny girl, Sunny girl, Sunny girl. If only the world revolved around you."

"Wait, it doesn't?"

"The soonest I could get him up here, and that is if everything else falls into place, would be Friday. Thursday at the absolute earliest, and that's if I can convince the guys at transportation."

"So call them now. Prepare them."

"You're going to have to get that paperwork through ay-sap. How confident are you this will get done?"

"Ninety-eight percent." She thought about it, then said, "Ninety-seven at the least." The new DA out of Las Vegas, who served as DA for Del Sol County as well, was not her biggest fan, either, but surely he'd agree this needed to be done. He'd been on her for an update on Kubrick Ravinder's case. He was about to get one.

"The guys in transport are going to kill me," Royce said, scrubbing his face again.

"It's a road trip. Who doesn't like road trips?"

"The guys in transport."

"Maybe they should have thought of that before taking a job in transport."

His expression flatlined.

"Not helpful. Noted. Two words," she said, leaning in as though she had a juicy secret. "Audio books."

A charming grin widened his mouth. "I'm pretty sure that's one word."

"Tell them I'll throw in a weekend stay at a picturesque cabin with a small but manageable raccoon infestation right on the Pecos River."

Quincy choked on his coffee. "You're bribing transportation with my cabin?"

"What? It's not like I have one to offer. You can stay with me if they ever take us up on it."

"I feel violated."

"I could've offered you, instead," she said with a wink.

Royce laughed softly. "How's your victim?"

Quincy and Sun had spoken with Keith Seabright's doctor before meeting Royce, and she finally got a look at their victim. Seabright had scruffy dark hair, a strong jaw, and smooth, sun-kissed skin. Thankfully he was young and healthy.

She looked over her notes and shook her head. "He's stabilizing. They're hopeful, but my witness was right. Tox screen showed an almost lethal dose of fentanyl in his system. Levi swears he's a health nut to an obsessive degree. Has never touched drugs."

Quincy nodded. "That entire event was set up to make it look like it was a bar fight gone wrong."

"Someone wanted him dead," Sun agreed. "And I want to know who." She looked at Royce. "Thank you so much for meeting us here on your day off."

Apparently, he was supposed to be fishing when he got a call about a recruit detoxing and had to hightail it back to civilization. "You know how those go, I'm sure."

"I do, indeed," she said forlornly.

They said their goodbyes, then went to speak briefly to the charge nurse on Seabright's ward. Sun started to give her a card, but thought better of it. The middle-aged woman could hardly take her eyes off Quince, so she reached into his pocket and slid her his card instead.

"Will you call Quincy, I mean Chief Deputy Cooper, if there are any changes? Anything at all."

The woman's face lit up like she'd just won the lottery. "Of course."

Quincy questioned her on the way down in the elevator. "First my cabin? Now me? I didn't realize you were my pimp."

"I could totally be your pimp. I'd be the best pimp ever." She turned to him, wild with excitement. "Think about it, Quince. We could make so much money."

He offered her a grin straight out of *The Gentleman's Guide to Wickedness and Evil.* "We could, couldn't we?"

Such a charmer.

Her phone dinged and her jaw unhinged when she saw it was Carver yet again asking her if she'd made it back to town. "What the actual hell?" she asked as the elevator doors opened. An elderly woman glared at her for her outburst. She stepped out, offering a sheepish nod of apology.

Quince read the text over her shoulder. "You're going to have to do something about that guy."

"Think Zee needs some live target practice? He could even do that zigzag thing. Make her work for it."

9

*If you refer to your librarian as your dealer, this is the place
for you.*

—SIGN AT DEL SOL PUBLIC LIBRARY

The more Auri dug, the more convinced she became that sweet
little Mrs. Fairborn was indeed a raging, maniacal serial killer. But
proving it could be sticky. Her mom would never let her investigate
a cold case, especially when one of the pillars of the community
was involved, albeit an old and crumbling pillar. So she'd been
racking her brain to figure out how to prove the imposter's guilt.

It took her all day, but she figured out how she could investigate Mrs. Fairborn without her mother finding out. It wasn't
like she could walk up to the woman and ask her if she killed
all those people. Auri needed evidence. And there was only one
place to get it: Mrs. Fairborn's house.

She had no choice. She had to break in and find the evidence
to nail the wily woman. Of course, she'd feel a lot better about it if
Mrs. F. weren't so danged adorable. Auri just needed to run it by
Cruz and Sybil first, but Cruz wasn't picking up and Sybil's mom
made her turn off her phone to do homework.

If Auri didn't need a lookout, she would never involve Sybil.
And if she didn't need someone to do the breaking part of break-
ing and entering—a.k.a. picking locks—she would never involve
Cruz. It was simply too dangerous. She could only hope they would

make it out of the killer's lair alive and relatively unmaimed. Then again, the woman had to be in her eighties. How much maiming could she do?

Auri waited for her grandparents to go on their date. Who knew old people dated? Or married people, for that matter? Then she headed off into the evening glow of an orange sun. She needed a car. She was getting her learner's permit soon, but tonight, she'd have to put foot to bike pedal once more.

After flipping a coin, she rode her bike to Sybil's first. The sun was setting fast and she figured she had about an hour before her grandparents got home. Although she did leave a note telling them she went to her and her mother's house to take a shower. That would buy her another twenty minutes, hopefully, because the ride all the way out to the St. Aubin mansion took her twelve.

She dumped her turquoise bike in the tree line that separated their property and the forest beyond.

Ever since Sybil's abduction and attempted murder, the St. Aubins had ramped up their security. The White House had nothing on them. There were, however, a couple of very slim blind spots Auri could squeeze through. The two girls had mapped them out by having Sybil watch the cameras and Auri walk the perimeter. It worked. They now had access to come and go as they pleased, but they weren't exactly rebels, so they had yet to use their sneaky escape route to actually escape. It did come in handy, however, when all communication had been cut off.

Auri took out a handful of almonds from her front pocket. Much safer than rocks, as they'd learned a couple of months ago. Explaining the broken glass took imagination and finesse, but Sybil had pulled it off. After all, who would question her heartbreak when a bird flew through her window. There were tears and everything, and Mrs. St. Aubin only cared about consoling her grieving daughter, so she never asked to see the rock-shaped bird.

The girl could act.

Sybil came to her window, a huge smile lighting her face. She checked over her shoulder then motioned Auri up.

Auri had become a master of the trellis. A trellis master. A trellis aficionado. She climbed the thick wooden lattice and eased across the pitched eve to Sybil's window.

"What are you doing here?" Sybil said after a quick hug, a bubbly giggle turning her voice into musical notes.

Auri clung to the windowsill for dear life, but didn't dare go inside. It took too long for her to scramble back out the window should she need to flee to a safe distance. "I figured it out."

"At last! I'm so glad for you, Auri." She pushed her round glasses up her nose with her index finger, and asked, "What were you trying to figure out again?"

Auri laughed softly. "How we can prove that Mrs. Fairborn is a cold-blooded serial killer."

Sybil pursed her lips. "It's always the unassuming ones."

"Right? So, a lot of the victims' families describe various items their loved ones had with them at the time of their disappearance."

"Oh, yeah. I read about a couple of them."

"I found a complete inventory someone compiled. I figure Mrs. Fairborn must still have some of those items stashed in her house."

"Makes sense."

"If we find them, we catch the killer."

Sybil grinned maniacally. It was a thing of mischievous beauty. No one would suspect the mild-mannered Sybil St. Aubin to have such an adventurous streak. In fact, if they were caught, no one would believe for a minute Sybil had colluded in their shenanigans. Everyone would blame the whole thing on Auri, as they should, which was one reason Auri decided to bring her in. Sybil and her guileless ways would be safe.

But she also couldn't bring her into this completely clueless to the ramifications should they get caught. "I want you to think about this before you decide," Auri said. "It could be dangerous, and we'll only have a short window to get in and get out. But timing is of the essence."

"Why?"

"Because Mrs. Fairborn confesses to every single crime committed in Del Sol."

"Oh . . . kay."

"And there was a crime last night."

Sybil frowned. "Yeah, but that was a stabbing."

"Exactly."

"By three males."

"Yes."

"There were witnesses."

"Yep."

"And she'll still confess."

"Absolutely."

"Hold on." She held up a palm, calling for a time out. "Tiny, meek Mrs. Fairborn will confess to stabbing a man and running over Mr. Ravinder with a truck even though several witnesses saw exactly who did it?"

Auri twirled a finger around her ear. "I'm telling you, she'll probably be in the station first thing tomorrow morning. And a crime like that will take her a while. She confesses in great detail."

"How will we know she's actually in there?"

It was Auri's turn to grin maniacally. "I have an inside man." Sybil gasped. "Is it Quincy? Should we coordinate with him? Go over the plan? Synchronize our watches?"

She frowned in confusion. "I guess, but why would we want to?"

Sybil blinked at her like she'd lost her mind.

Auri blinked back. "So, you're in?" she asked after an awkward thirty seconds.

That grin Auri knew and loved reappeared. "I am *so* in."

They shook hands to seal the deal, then hugged through the window. "See you tomorrow. Remember, wear something breaky-and-entery."

"You got it. Should I bring my lockpicking kit?"

Auri ogled her. "You can pick locks?"

After a flash of panic raced across her face, she said softly, as though embarrassed, "No."

"Oh. Darn. Well, that's okay. Bring it anyway. Maybe Cruz can use it."

Sybil nodded in excitement.

Auri gave her another quick hug, then walked the narrow strip where the cameras wouldn't catch her. The sky was beginning to darken and she took a wrong step about halfway. While the camera probably didn't catch it, light flooded the manicured lawn.

She froze for all of five seconds, then ran for it. Sybil giggled at the window as Auri jumped onto her bike and rode around the perimeter to the drive, her pulse drumming in her ears, half expecting to hear sirens.

She rode as fast as she could for a solid two minutes before slowing down. No sirens. Always a good sign. Now onto her second target, the enigmatic Cruz De los Santos.

Cruz lived much closer to Auri, thankfully, but it still took her exactly ten minutes to make it down the mountain and back into town to his house.

She'd never snuck to Cruz's house, but she knew his room was in the southwest corner around back. She leaned her bike against a tree and tiptoed around the house. Cruz's light was on, so she hurried past the dark window of his dad's room and crept up to his window.

Sheer curtains made it impossible to see clearly inside, but they were just barely open down the center creating a slit that she could see through. That was the exact moment she realized what a god must look like.

Cruz stood at his dresser with a towel around his waist. His dark hair and muscular shoulders glistened in the low light of his room as he searched for an item of clothing. Probably underwear, she realized. Heat spread up her neck. What was she doing?

She stood back and pretended not to have seen him when she knocked softly. He walked over, his blurred image getting closer and closer. She could still run. It wasn't too late.

Then the curtains were open and his smile hit her like a nuclear bomb.

He raised the window, crossed his arms over his bare chest, and leaned against the frame. "If it isn't Aurora Dawn Vicram. What brings you to the boonies?"

A grin she couldn't have stopped with a restraining order spread across her face. "I have a proposition."

He covered his incredible pecs with his hands, and asked, "Are you here to take advantage of me?"

She snorted. "No. Another kind of proposition."

"Oh, well, come in anyway." He gestured her inside, and while climbing into a window seemed great in theory, it was anything but.

He had to reach out and lift her over the sill as it dug into her shins. Her arms wrapped around his neck and he slid her inside where they fell back onto his bed, her on top.

She stilled and waited, making sure his dad didn't come in.

"You know my dad can't hear us," he said, his voice hushed regardless and oddly strained.

Cruz's dad was deaf, not that he let that stop him.

They waited a moment longer and Auri got to study Cruz's strong features up close and personal. His eyes shimmered under spiked lashes, but they were red.

She giggled softly and asked, "How long were you in the shower?"

"Not long, why?"

"Your eyes are red."

He turned his head and squeezed them with a thumb and index finger, then sniffed and said, "Allergies."

"Are you sure? Your voice seems a bit scratchy." She lifted a hand to his forehead.

He flashed her a nuclear smile, but it came on the heels of a momentary frown, almost as if he were hiding something. "I'm good. Better now."

She'd been so focused on herself and her own silly life, she hadn't picked up on the fact that Cruz did seem a bit different lately. Quieter. More reserved than usual. Which, for Cruz, was saying a lot.

"Cruz, is something going on?"

"You mean besides the hottie lying on top of me getting wet?"

"Hottie?" she asked, stunned. When he only grinned, his gaze traveling over her face, his words sank in. "Oh, right, sorry." She started to squirm off, but he put a hand on her butt and held her to him.

"Hold on a sec. Don't move just yet."

Something powerful washed over her when his hand caressed her ass. A warmth spread throughout her body and pooled in her lower abdomen. "Why?"

"Well, I didn't want to alarm you, but do you remember when I was helping you inside and we fell on the bed?"

"So, like, thirty seconds ago?"

"Yeah, my towel fell off."

She went completely still, afraid to move. "You mean you're . . . you're naked?"

He nodded.

"Underneath me?"

He nodded again.

"What do we do?" she whispered, and the corners of his mouth formed the most breathtaking grin she'd ever seen. Part humor and part sensuality.

"I figure we have two options."

"Okay," she said, her pulse quickening with each sweep of his gaze across her face. Like she was beautiful. Like she could complement the likes of him.

"You can take off your clothes and join me—"

She sucked in a soft breath.

"—or you can close your eyes and roll off me. I promise to get dressed quickly."

Without the slightest hint of hesitation, she squeezed her eyes shut and rolled.

He laughed and rose off the bed.

She heard him rummage through his dresser, then walk to his closet where a soft swoosh of material echoed in the room.

"Okay," he said.

She sat up, lowered her hands, and lifted her lashes to find him in a pair of black gym shorts and an army-green T-shirt.

"Is that what you sleep in?" she asked.

"Depends on what's clean." He sat beside her. Close beside her. His warmth seeped into her skin. "So, what's on your mind?"

"Oh, right." She'd almost forgotten. "When we were helping my grandparents today, Sybil and I found clippings and reports from an old case with multiple missing persons right here in Del Sol."

He lifted a strand of her hair and studied it. "Okay."

"Long story short, we're pretty sure Mrs. Fairborn is a serial killer."

Surprise took hold of him. "Mrs. Fairborn?"

She nodded.

"*The* Mrs. Fairborn?"

She nodded again.

"The same Mrs. Fairborn who just celebrated her eightieth birthday?"

"Yep. And we need help breaking and entering into Mrs. Fairborn's house tomorrow while she's at the station confessing to stabbing that man at The Roadhouse and hitting Levi with a Toyota Tundra even though she can't drive and has no car."

"Okay." He said it so nonchalantly, Auri tried to figure out how to make him understand.

"You'll be doing the breaking."

"Okay."

"It's illegal."

A dimple creased one corner of his mouth. "Did you expect me to try to talk you out of it?"

"No. Well, maybe. A little."

"The way I see it, if I get caught breaking into a house with the sheriff's kid, my part in all of it will get swept under the rug."

"You think my mother would sweep a third-degree felony under the rug?"

"Yes, I do. You're her daughter."

She scoffed. "You don't know my mother very well."

"I'm not saying you won't get in trouble. I'm saying *I* won't. Because you compelled me." He tucked the strand of hair behind her ear. "I'd be under your spell. That's something your mom will understand. I promise. Also, she likes me."

Auri tilted her head. "She does, doesn't she?"

"She let me stay in your room when she could've arrested me."

"That says a lot." Something dinged on Cruz's small desk and Auri looked over at the clock perched atop it, the red digits forming the numbers eight zero zero.

"Oh, my God." She catapulted to her feet. "Is that the time?"

"Did you sneak out again?"

"I'm so sorry." She twirled around, looking for her things even though she didn't have any. "I have to go."

"I thought you were going to cut back."

"My grandparents went out on a date. They'll be back any second. Is that really the time?"

"Yes," he said, casting her a sideways smirk.

"I'm dead. I am so dead." She ran to the window and practically fell out of it. "Oh," she said, turning back to him once she gained her footing, "wear comfortable clothes tomorrow and shoes you can sprint in, just in case we have to run from my mom."

"Okay," he said, watching her from the window.

Auri jumped on her bike and sped off. A light came on in the kitchen as she rode past and blind panic spurred her faster. She could only hope she didn't get Cruz into trouble.

10

Forecast for tonight:
Alcohol, low standards, and poor decisions.
> —SIGN AT THE ROADHOUSE BAR AND GRILL

It wasn't that late when Sun and Quincy got back. Part of her felt bad considering her parents had wanted a date night. But another part, a bigger part, didn't feel the least bit concerned. It was their fault she was sheriff.

After checking in at the station and finding out they'd recaptured Randy the raccoon, rescuing him from inside a vending machine, Sun headed home for a much-needed shower and a glass of wine. She would have made it, too, had her fuel light not come on.

She pulled into the Quick-Mart and parked beside her favorite gas pump: number three. Humble. Nondescript. Unassuming. But because the credit card machine still wasn't working on pump number three, she had to go inside to pay.

She stepped into the small convenience store and slammed into a brick wall. When she bounced back, she looked up into the face of the brick wall. A wall named Levi Ravinder. For some reason, her hand immediately went to her gun. Thankfully she had the wherewithal to leave it holstered, but he'd tracked the involuntary movement with his caramel-colored irises before refocusing on her face.

She did the same to him. The bruising had only gotten worse.

His left eye was swollen with dark, puffy splotches. His jaw was a combination of several shades of blue under the scruff, yet somehow the damage only added to his appeal.

When he questioned her with a minuscule lift of a single brow, she dropped both her hand and her gaze. The latter landed on the items he'd just bought: a large coffee and a giant bottle of painkillers.

Concern rocketed through her, but she slipped into her best poker face and stared him down. Or up, as the case may be. "I see you're still alive."

"Disappointed?"

"Did you ever get checked out?"

"I checked him out," the cashier said, a twenty-something named Lottie, who stood staring at Levi like he'd just saved the world from an alien invasion. Lottie was the younger sister of a classmate and had been destined for stardom. The fact that she was working at the Quick-Mart for Mr. Walden was a little depressing.

Sun didn't respond to her. Instead, she waited for Levi to answer.

"I've been busy," he said at last.

"Right." She nodded, unconvinced. "Did you find them?"

"I found where they aren't."

"That's one way of looking at it." She glanced over her shoulder toward the parking lot. "No wonder we haven't picked you up yet. You switched trucks." She recognized the only other vehicle on the premises, a dark gray F-150. It belonged to Levi's distillery, Dark River Shine, but she'd never seen him drive it.

"Don't bother," he said when she made a mental note of the truck. "I won't be driving it much longer."

"No, you won't." She turned back to him. "Because I'm taking you in."

He graced her with a pitying curve to his mouth. "No can do, Sheriff. I'm still looking for the men who attacked Seabright."

"As are we."

"And how far have you gotten?"

"About as far as you have from the looks of it."

After a lengthy stare-down during which she tried to assess the damage to his left eye, the hemorrhage alarmingly dark, he started around her. "I'll be on my way."

She blocked him with a sidestep and her palm once again landed on her duty weapon. The reflex spoke more to her years of service than to any question about how dangerous Levi Ravinder was. He was very dangerous, just not to her.

Or so she'd thought until he closed the distance between them and glared down at her. "Are you really going to try to stop me?" he asked, his voice deep and even.

"Only if you make me." Her mind raced through the plethora of offensive moves she could use to subdue the man, the same man who stood a head above her, but the last thing she wanted to do was hurt him any further. Still, if he forced her hand, she would have no choice. "I'm taking you in, Levi. And then I'm taking you to urgent care."

She reached for a plastic tie on her belt, hoping it wouldn't come to that, when a loud crash reverberated from behind the counter. Sun looked over and jumped the barrier. Lottie was having a seizure, her dark head thrown back, her arms stiff, her back arched.

"Call 911!" she shouted to Levi as she cleared the immediate area of anything Lottie could hurt herself on. Then she pressed the TALK button on her mic when she realized Levi hadn't answered her.

She rose onto her feet. Both man and truck were gone. When she looked back, Lottie was coming out of it. She scooted against the liquor case, her knees drawn, hands cradling her forehead.

Sun squelched the dubious scowl threatening to break free. "Stay put. I'll call an ambulance."

Lottie's eyes widened, but she recovered quickly. "Oh, no. I just need some water. I'm much better now."

Sun leaned closer and let the barest hint of the scowl she'd been holding back float to the surface. "Oh, I insist."

The sheepish air that came over Lottie's entire demeanor spoke volumes as Sun depressed the talk button on her mic. Lottie was going to urgent care and she'd have every test known to man run on her before the day was done if Sun had anything to do with it. Or she could charge her with obstruction. So many choices, so few hours in the day.

The lights were out at the Freyr house, thus Sun headed straight for her own humble abode and the magnificent shower ensconced within. No need to wake Auri.

Thirty minutes later, squeaky clean and slightly annoyed that Carver had texted her yet again, she'd settled on her sofa in a knee-length nightshirt, beige slouch socks, and an overfilled glass of chardonnay. She opened her laptop to do some research on Keith Seabright when a knock sounded at the door. She froze. Surely he wouldn't. Surely he didn't know where she lived.

She took a huge gulp of wine, then stood and walked to the door, fully prepared to confront Carver and inform him that their one date was also going to be their only date. Honestly, the nerve of the guy.

She did a quick scan of the room. All of her strategically placed décor that served as lethal weapons should she or Auri ever need them were in place. A metal arrangement with razor-sharp, detachable leaves. An umbrella in a stand that harbored a short sword. A tissue box with a Taser underneath.

The first thing she did every time she entered the house was lock up her gun. The wall safe sat just inside the front door. Having seen too many crime scenes, she quickly entered the combination and let the door crack open on its hinges.

"It's just me," Quincy said outside the door. "No need to unlock the safe."

She looked through the fish-eye lens at her bestie's handsome face, then relocked the safe before opening the door. "What are you doing here?"

"Date night."

She looked down at her oversized nightshirt and the thick knit socks bunched around her ankles. She'd pulled her wet hair into a ponytail and applied a mask that was, thankfully, invisible to the naked eye, besides giving her an unnatural shine. "So soon?"

"No time like the present." He lifted a box of wine.

"I had no idea boxed wine was a real thing," she lied, opening the door wider.

"Yeah, it's all I had." He'd showered, too. The scent of soap and warm cologne filled the air as he walked inside. "I prefer the term *cardboardeaux*."

"Okay, then," she said, fighting a grin and questioning their decision. Was this really happening? With her best friend? With Quincy? After closing the door, it hit her. What was really going on. She crossed her arms over her chest. "You just want to get laid."

He put the wine on her snack bar and turned back to her. "Well, yeah."

Fair enough. "Yeah, me too." Sun walked to her still-full glass of wine and downed it in five massive gulps before coming up for air.

The edges of his mouth slid into a humorous smile. "Nervous?"

She coughed then walked up to him, holding the glass out for more. He refilled it before pouring himself one, and they went to town on a boxed red with subtle hints of fruit. Like, really subtle.

"Is that prunes?" she asked, smacking her lips.

He shrugged and downed another glass, apparently as nervous as she was. And they had to get back to work in ten hours.

The wine hit her instantly. She walked to the sofa and sat down before it and the world got pulled out from under her.

He joined her there.

"We need to set some ground rules," she said, a strong buzz already taking hold.

"Agreed. You come first."

She choked on the sip she'd been in the middle of taking and decided a slower approach to the wine thing would be best for all involved. "What? No. Why? What about you?"

"Honey, don't worry about me. I can come inside of three seconds."

"It takes a big man to admit that."

He sobered and studied her, before admitting, "You aren't like the other women in my life."

"Inflatable?"

"They had their reasons for being with me. I just . . . I want this to be good for you." His statement was almost sad.

"Okay." Possibly more aroused than she cared to admit after seeing Levi, she sat her wine down and attacked. It had been a long time. A very, very, very long time.

He lifted her onto his lap and she draped her arms over his wide shoulders before reality sank in. Kissing him was about as stimulating as kissing the back of her own hand. She turned her head, and said, "Oh, my God, wait."

"Okay," he said from behind a trail of kisses from her mouth to her ear.

It was enough to make her forget where she put her senses again. To throw caution to the wind. For the protest that had formed on the tip of her tongue to vanish.

He stopped and licked his lips, his expression similar to when Sun ate Lemonheads. "What is on your face?"

"Oh, yeah, that's a mask. You don't want to lick that."

Her mouth covered his again.

He was everything a girl could want. Insanely handsome. Amazing body. Fantastic personality. A girl would be crazy not to desire him, which had her questioning her sanity when she broke off the kiss again.

But she pulled back at the same time he did. They looked at each other, the hopelessness of the situation sinking in.

Then a thought hit her. "Maybe we need to be naked."

"Of course!" He knocked a palm against his head. "That's exactly what we need."

They kissed all the way to her bedroom, ripping off clothes as they went, bumping into this table and that dresser. She may have heard a crash or two, but she couldn't be certain. He broke off the kiss to lift his shirt over his head in that way men do and, admittedly, her knees weakened just a little. His pecs were the stuff of legend.

Before Sun knew it, her skin was brushing across his and he felt good. She had to admit it, and yet . . .

They stopped again, naked in each other's arms, their breaths coming in short, agitated gulps.

The look in his eyes, although resigned, was filled with admiration. "You are so beautiful, Sunny."

She ran her hands over his biceps. "So are you, handsome." She gestured toward the bed. "How about we take a break."

She crawled into bed as Quincy went to refill their glasses of prune-flavored wine. A part of her adored him even more now. And she didn't doubt that another part of her did love him in that way. They'd just been friends for so long.

When he came back to the bedroom, he was wearing his underwear. Charcoal-gray boxer briefs. He handed her a glass, then slid his legs under the covers with her and leaned back against the headboard.

"Now we know," he said, almost sadly.

"Now we know." She ran her fingers along the rim of her glass. "Who are you trying to forget?"

"What?" he asked, coming out of a trance he'd been in.

"Who are you pining after?"

He shook his head. "It doesn't matter."

"Quincy." She put a hand on his jaw and turned him toward her. "Of course it does. Is it Zee?"

There had been an instant attraction between the two, but as far as Sun knew, neither had acted upon it.

"No, Sunbeam. She's all kinds of gorgeous, but . . ."

"But you gave your heart to someone else."

"You might say that."

"When?"

He lifted a shoulder. "You've been gone a long time."

"Wait, it's not really my mother is it?"

He laughed. "No, though I have to admit, if not for your father, I would've proposed to that woman years ago."

"Can I ask you something?"

"Always."

"When did you get a bacon tattoo?"

He glanced down. On the left side of his impressive abs sat two slices of bacon. "Told you. You've been gone a long time."

"You got a bacon tattoo and didn't tell me?"

"'Parently."

"It's like I don't even know you anymore."

"I'm like a wild stallion, Sunburn."

She tried not to snort. She failed. After taking one more sip, she put her glass on the nightstand, and scooted down beneath the covers.

He did the same, turning to face her. "It's really too bad."

"What is?"

"That you're missing out. I could've made the heavens open up and the angels sing."

"You're that good, huh?"

"I would've made you question everything you know about the S-word."

"Syphilis?"

"You'd never be the same again."

A languorous sigh escaped him as the Sandman lured her closer and closer to oblivion. It had been a long two days. Then again, who was she kidding? It had been a long four months, and she didn't know what she would've done without Quincy by her side. "I *am* in love with you, you know."

He ran the pad of his thumb over her bottom lip. "I'm in love with you, too, Sunburn. In so many ways." He leaned forward and kissed her again, his mouth warm and pliant against hers.

When he leaned back, she grinned at him. "Kissing you is like kissing my brother."

One sexy corner of his mouth lifted playfully. "You don't have a brother."

"Which makes it even weirder."

"Yeah, well you drooled in the car while you were sleeping."

"Shit," she said even though she already knew. "Was that the deal-breaker?"

He laughed softly, his eyes drifting shut. "Honey, if my standards were that high, I would never date at all."

"Who is she?" she asked him one last time before letting the darkness overtake her. She thought she heard a name whispered on his breath but couldn't be certain.

She dreamed of rain. It pelted the metal around them, but they were safe inside. The space was cramped, but she didn't care. That just meant he had to be that much closer to her.

Hands caressed her back. Slid over her ass. Cupped her breasts. Hands she'd wanted to be caressed by for so long she could hardly believe it was actually happening.

Sitting astride him, she leaned back and gazed into the whiskey-colored irises of Levi Ravinder. So exquisitely real. But he was younger. She was younger. They took refuge from the downpour inside his old truck. Where some would see a pile of junk, she saw a classic. It fit him perfectly. The sensual shape. The warm colors. The growl it made when he'd cruised into the parking lot that night at school. He'd graduated already, but he'd come back for the big game, and Sun's world toppled all over again.

Lightning flashed bright and hot to reveal his heavy-lidded gaze as it slid over her. She sat straddled atop his lap and he pulled her down to him. Pressed her mouth to his. Pushed his fingers between her legs.

She'd never felt anything like it. Heat flooded her nether regions like a tidal wave of molten lava. It pooled in her abdomen and throbbed with a sensation so exquisite, she bit her lip to keep from gasping aloud. Then his hands were at the waistband of her jeans. The button. The zipper.

Cool air rushed over her when he peeled them off only to be replaced by the warmth of his palms. Long fingers spread her apart and pressed inside, and that familiar pressure formed in the distance. Each time he brushed his thumb over her clit, the pressure grew, coming closer and closer. He bent his head and drew a nipple into his mouth.

A knock sounded on the window. She tried to look, but he kissed her again. Pushed deeper. Rubbed faster. She sucked in his warm breath, and he laid her back on the seat, parting her legs with the expanse of his shoulders. Then his tongue, like liquid fire, slid over her clit. She grabbed handfuls of hair, unable to keep the climax from rocketing toward her.

The knock sounded again.

"Mom?"

Sun jerked awake and regretted it instantly. Pain exploded in her head, making her dizzy and nauseous. The bed dipped as her daughter sat beside her. Sun scooted back to give her more room, only to run into something beneath the covers. Something large and warm snored softly beside her, and since she didn't own a dog, she could only guess who was still in her bed.

She fought the urge to slam a hand over her face. Instead, she fluffed up her bedspread to camouflage the lump, pried open her eyes, and looked up into the adorable, angelic face of her child.

"You're going to be late for work," Auri said, still in her pajamas. "But if you have a minute, can I talk to you?"

"Of course," Sun croaked.

"When did you learn Klingon?" the child asked. Hilarious. Then she giggled and the sound burst inside the cavernous recesses of Sun's mind like a claymore.

Sun raised a finger to her lips and patted the tiny creature's face.

Auri giggled again. "Here." She led Sun's hand to something cool and round. A glass.

Sun pushed it away until she heard two plops and a fizz. God bless her.

"When will you learn not to mix red and white?" the little minx asked her.

"How do you know—"

"Can we talk girl to girl?"

Sun struggled onto an elbow and took a sip of the bubbly liquid. Then she remembered once again who was under the covers with her and the adrenaline rush churned her stomach.

She had to be cool. Maybe her one-and-only offspring couldn't make out the huge lump in her bed. He was on his stomach, so he was semi-flat against the mattress.

"How did you know you were pregnant?"

Sun's lids flew open and a loud gasp echoed in the room.

Auri laughed so hard she fell back on the bed beside Sun.

"Aurora Dawn," Sun croaked. "You are evil."

"Duh. I inherited my evil ways from you." Then, as nonchalantly as if Auri were reaching over to pluck a grape off a vine, she lifted the covers and peered at Sun's bedmate.

"Hi, Quincy," she said.

Sun saw a set of long fingers wave from under the blanket. "Hey, bean sprout. This isn't what it looks like."

Auri tilted her head in doubt and leveled a calculating gaze on her mom. "I think now would be a good time to remind you what a great kid I am. And how I would never judge you for sleeping with your best friend."

"I didn't," Sun said.

"We didn't," Quincy concurred.

"Mm-hm." She leaned in, kissed Sun on the cheek, then bounced out, yelling back, "I get the first shower!"

Sun grabbed her head before it fell off, and sat up, horrified. "I'm going to kill her."

"You can't kill her for being a mini-Sunshine."

She looked at the lump beside her. "That child is nothing like me. I would never have done something that evil to my mother."

"Oh, please." He rolled over and sat up. "Ninth grade. Chainsaw. Ketchup. A package of hot dogs."

"No, no," she said, trying to sit up as well, but the world spun. "That was totally different."

"Your mother had nightmares for months."

He had a point. "I can't believe this happened."

"Which part?"

"All of it. And now Auri? She's totally going to tell my mom."

"I'm not a snitch, Mom!" Auri yelled from her room.

Sun grabbed her head again and fought the Earth tilting on its axis to look over at Quincy. "Are you okay?"

He shrugged a wide shoulder. "I have a great constitution. I can drink for days." The second the words left his mouth, he bent over the side of the bed and emptied the contents of his stomach into the trash can there.

That time, Sun did follow suit. Minus the trash can.

An hour later, Auri emerged from her room like a butterfly emerging from its cocoon as she headed for the coffeepot. "Is he gone?" she asked, perky as a Disney princess on Adderall.

The little shit looked stunning in a mint-green summer blouse and black leggings.

Sun squeezed her eyes shut. She had never even brought a man home to meet Auri. It was always just the two of them, no matter how serious she'd gotten. And now this?

Way to mom, Sunshine.

"Yes, he left, sweetheart," she said over her shoulder as she headed back to her room. That most magic of elixirs known as Alka-Seltzer had done the trick. That combined with a hot shower and a little black coffee, and Sun was as good as new. Almost. Most of the cobwebs had been shaken off, at least.

One thing the elixir didn't shake off was the dream she'd had about Levi. Her dreams had been so vivid lately, and this one was no exception.

Before she could ask Auri to come into her room—she had to explain—she heard the front door open. A scream quickly followed.

"Mom!"

Sun ran into the living room to see Auri stepping back, cowering from Elaine Freyr. She stepped around her daughter and gasped before grabbing Auri and folding her into her arms.

"What is wrong with you girls?" her mother asked. "Ruby Moore sent over a basket of muffins."

A huge basket. A basket that made the one they got four months ago look like a Barbie DreamHouse prop.

"I'm scared, Mom."

Sun smoothed her daughter's hair, and whispered, "Me too, hon. Me too."

Elaine glanced down and studied the basket in her hands, her expression suddenly wary. As it should've been. "Are you girls punking me?"

Auri giggled, giving up the game. "How do you even know what that means, Grandma?" She tiptoed over for a kiss from the woman.

Sun headed for the microwave to reheat her coffee before heading out.

"Ruby said to make sure you two got a few before that husband of mine finishes them off, so I thought I was doing you a favor."

"Don't do me any more," Sun said.

"She's so nice," Auri said. "I wonder what horrible thing is going to happen, though."

Elaine took a look at her surroundings. The overturned table. The broken glass. The bra on the back of the sofa. She chose to ignore them. "What do you mean?"

"Mom," Sun said, dubious. "You have to know Ruby's muffins are cursed. The whole town knows."

Elaine sighed. "You cannot honestly believe that ridiculous rumor."

"Yes, we can," Sun and Auri said at the same time.

"Because they *are* cursed, Grandma. Chastity Bertram's mother slipped a disc after she got one. And Beatrice Morales's cousin broke both her legs and both her arms exactly twenty-seven minutes after one showed up on her doorstep." Auri picked up her backpack, then thought again. "Of course, that only happened because she and her little brother were fighting over it and he pushed her down the stairs."

"Good heavens." She set the basket on the snack bar. "Why was Quincy's cruiser parked in the drive so early this morning?"

Sun sucked in a soft breath mid-sip and spent the next three minutes coughing up a spleen.

"I would tell you, Grandma," Auri said, heading out the door. "But snitches get stitches and wind up in ditches."

Elaine looked at Sun. "What does that even mean?"

"It means," Sun said, her voice strained, "I raised my daughter right." She gave her mother a quick peck on the cheek, then left the woman standing in her kitchen, shaking her head. That happened a lot.

"How are things going?" Sun asked Auri as she drove her to school. It was a short trip, so she didn't have a lot of time.

"Okay," she said with a shrug. "Team Lynelle still talks behind my back."

That fact sliced through Sun's heart every time she thought about it. "Honey, don't worry about people who talk behind your back. They're behind you for a reason."

Auri's mouth fell open. "That's really good. Did you just make that up?"

"No. Fortune cookie."

"Ah."

"Honey—"

"I know what you're going to say." She held up a hand to stop her. "It's okay, Mom. According to the girls at school, Quincy's a major hottie."

She couldn't argue that. "Want to talk about it?"

"About you and Quincy?" she asked with a snort.

Sun pulled into the drop-off area and waited to move forward. "I know how it looked, hon."

"It looked to me like you have no room to talk," Auri said, a satisfied smirk on her face.

That got Sun's attention. "Really? In what way?"

"You had a boy in your room. I had a boy in my room. I say let bygones be bygones."

Sun turned to wave at Principal Jacobs, mostly to squelch a wayward grin. "I'd like to start by saying you have a very valid argument."

She crossed her arms over her chest. "Thank you."

"I'd *like* to say that," she corrected, "but I won't, because you don't."

Auri frowned. "Why? It seems logical to me. And Cruz and I weren't even naked."

Sun pinched the bridge of her nose. "Okay, first off, nothing happened."

"Nay-ked," she reiterated.

"I know." Sun lost points in that area, but she needed Auri to know the truth. She eased forward and was about to piss off a lot of other parents, because she had no intention of leaving Auri with the idea that she and Quincy had gone all the way.

Then again, that had been the original plan. She cringed at the thought. She risked the friendship of the most important man in her life besides her dad. She wasn't including Levi since he wasn't actually in her life. But seriously, how stupid could she be? "I just want to make sure you understand nothing happened."

"Exactly! We're on the same page here, Mom. I can get out here."

"Oh, no you don't."

"So close," Auri said, collapsing dramatically against the door.

"Now that you think you're old enough to have boys in your room—"

"One boy, Mom. One."

"—I think we need to have the talk."

"We had the talk, Mom. We've actually had the talk several times throughout my life and it never gets any less uncomfortable."

"This one is different." The kid had a boy in her room. She had to know there'd be consequences.

Judging by her daughter's expression, panic was starting to take over. "You say that every time!"

"Since we're on the subject of you getting pregnant—"

"What?" Auri screeched. "We weren't on any subject."

"—I've realized I've been putting off this conversation long enough."

Auri paled. "You really haven't."

"I feel now is the right time."

"It really isn't."

"We need to discuss the devil's doorbell."

Auri paused and tilted her head to the side. "The devil's what?"

"You know. The button of bliss. The pushpin of pleasure."

"Oh. My. God."

"Satan's socket."

"I'm going to need so much therapy."

"Lucifer's little darling."

"Have you been reading those pamphlets again?"

"Now, for future reference, *you* can ring the devil's doorbell any time you want to, sweetheart."

"I could run away and join the circus."

"You, and only you."

"Or go into witness protection."

"Cruz De los Santos is not allowed to ring that bell."

She put her hands over her ears. "Mom, I can't hear this."

"Your button of bliss is off-limits to him and any boy until you're thirty-five."

Auri dropped her hands and glared at her. "There should be a test to find out how unstable your parents are."

"Hey. I'm totally stable."

"So is nitroglycerin until you shake it."

Someone honked behind her, so she turned on her emergency lights.

Auri's head fell into her hand. The final nail in the coffin.

"And for the record," Sun said, planting an angelic smile on her little kumquat, "the next time you have a boy in your room, I'm going to put bars on the windows. Got it?"

"Got it." She glanced out the window, her demeanor changing like the gentle shift of a breeze. "Is he okay, Mom?"

"I don't know. That wine did a number on both of us."

"Levi," she said.

Ah. Sun rubbed her daughter's shoulder. "He's fine. He's Levi."

"Cross your cold and bitter heart?"

"Cross my cold and bitter heart."

Auri leaned over and hugged her, taking Sun by surprise considering the doorbell thing. Then she hurried out without another word.

It would have ended there, except in her haste, she forgot her backpack.

Sun grabbed it and hurried after her.

"Sweetheart," she called, weaving through cliques of kids, following the auburn glow of her daughter's carrot top. "Aurora," she said a little louder.

Auri stopped and looked back at last. Sun caught up to her just inside the building and was surprised to see a wetness between her thick lashes.

"Oh, baby," she said, pulling her into a hug. "It's Levi. He'll be okay. He always is, right?"

She nodded.

Sun looked over Auri's head at a couple of girls pointing

at them and snickering. She recognized one of them as the girl who'd orchestrated a news program when Auri had first started school in Del Sol. They'd found out about Sun's abduction, about Auri's questionable parentage, and blasted it to the entire school before IT could shut it down.

It left Auri devastated, and Sun had wanted nothing more than to arrest them for obstruction of justice, since her case was ongoing. But certain people of influence wouldn't allow it. The families involved cried freedom of the press. Sun cried bullshit, but apparently money talks even in Del Sol.

Sun also knew the girl had made it her personal mission in life to make Auri's life a living hell. If not for Cruz and Sybil, Auri would be miserable at Del Sol High.

She was about to quote their favorite motto—What would Lisbeth Salander do?—when she rethought it. Somehow cutting a bitch seemed a bit harsh in this situation.

Until the girl looked straight at Sun, an adult in a sheriff's uniform, and unleashed a cheeky sneer.

Sun's irritation skyrocketed. "Did that girl just sneer at me?"

Auri looked over her shoulder. "That's Lynelle. She sneers at everyone."

Sun drew in a deep breath. She couldn't do anything that might get them both arrested. Thus, in lieu of doing jail time, she asked her daughter, "What would Hermione Granger do?"

Wearing a Cheshire grin, Auri turned toward Lynelle, lowered her head, and said softly, "She would leviosa a bitch."

"Damn straight she would."

They fist-bumped, but Auri's gaze didn't waver. She stared until Lynelle's sneer faltered and the girl turned away.

"See?" Auri said. "She's only as good as the sheep that follow her."

Sun hugged her again. "She's vindictive, though. Be careful with that one."

"Thanks, Mom. I'm off to Defense Against the Dark Arts."

11

As soon as Sun got back to her cruiser, she grabbed her phone, clicked on messages, and scrolled until she found Levi. This was no longer just about the case or even about his health. If he wasn't worried about the aftereffects of his being run down by a truck, she wasn't, either. But Auri was a different story.

She texted as fast as her fingers would let her. *Listen asshat, you can either text me back or call me. I don't care which, but if I don't hear from you within the hour, I swear to God I'm calling in the dogs and hunting your ass to the ends of the Earth. Auri is devastated and worried and heartbroken and you suck for doing that to her.*

She almost felt better as she headed toward the station. Her phone rang, sending her pulse through the roof. She looked at the caller ID. It wasn't Levi.

"Hey, Quincy," she said into the phone.

"Hey, boss. What are you doing?"

She pulled onto Main. "Praying my child's sass helps her become the CEO of a large company someday and not a shot caller in prison."

"Word. So, Randy escaped."

"Seriously?" She slapped a palm against the steering wheel. "Damn it. That's all we need. Put out a BOLO, coordinate road-blocks for both I-25 on-ramps, and call in everyone. *Everyone.* Who's Randy again?"

Quincy sighed. "My partner-in-petty-crimes. How can we partner up if he keeps escaping?" After a long silence in which Sun had no words of solace for him, he asked, "So, is everything okay?" The implications of that question were multifaceted, but now was not the time to go into their night of debauchery.

"I really had my heart set on waking up rich today. Other than that, everything's peachy. I'm pulling up to the office now."

"See you soon."

She walked into the building and headed straight into the bullpen. Besides Anita manning the front office, only Rojas and Quincy were in.

"How are you doing?" she asked Rojas. He was sitting at his desk, going over the surveillance tape from the looks of his screen.

"Occasionally, I have a shooting pain in my left elbow."

"On the case?"

"Nothing yet, but I just got started on this one."

"Anything from the state crime lab?"

"Not yet, but they said they probably wouldn't get started on it until this morning."

She nodded, then looked at Quincy. "Anything new on Seabright?"

"They're going to lower his meds today. Try to wake him up."

"Okay. Good. Stay on that." She headed into her office to get settled.

Quincy followed her and stood in the doorway. "We good, boss?"

"Wonderful. I had to put on my sunglasses just to open the refrigerator this morning. Other than that, it's all good." She swallowed a couple of painkillers, then dropped the bottle into her desk drawer.

"I mean, you know, concerning—"

"Quincy." She walked from behind her desk and stood in front of him. "Last night is on both of us. You were right. It was worth a shot."

He nodded. "I agree. And just for the record"—he glanced over his shoulder then turned back to her—"you look amazing naked."

She laughed and pressed a palm to her temple. "So do you, handsome."

Anita, Sun's admin and confidante, walked in from the front followed by one of Levi's cousins. All the Ravinder men, aside from Levi and, surprisingly, Wynn, were stocky with sallow complexions and muddy brown hair. Joshua was no exception.

"Joshua Ravinder would like to have a word with you," Anita said, "if that's okay, Sheriff."

He ripped off a faded baseball cap and stepped forward to shake her hand.

Sun ignored it, raised an index finger in warning, and said as firmly as possible, "No." Anita stopped short and blinked in surprise, but Sun rounded Quincy to come face-to-face with Joshua. "Absolutely not."

"What?" he asked, as confused as Anita.

"I refuse to hear anything you have to say."

"You don't have to listen." He handed her a handwritten note.

She scanned it, then glared at him. "No way."

"I'm sorry, Sheriff, but I—"

"No way do you have better handwriting than I do." It was perfect. The slant and loops all equal. The height a veritable straight line. Sun's chicken scratch barely qualified as a written language, and Joshua Ravinder's penmanship rivaled John Hancock's?

"Um," he said, taken aback.

She made a show of ripping the letter in half, then halved it again before handing it back.

"Hey." Disappointed, he tried to reconstruct it. "You have to take my confession."

"No, I don't." She turned and headed for her desk again, stopping short with his desperate plea.

"But I did it," he said, following her.

After he stepped into her office, she closed the door, pointed to the chair across from hers, and said, "Sit," before sitting herself. He obeyed instantly.

She gave him a lengthy inspection, then asked, "What is going on? Why is everyone confessing?"

"Everyone?" Either he was a really good actor, or he was genuinely surprised. "Who's everyone?"

It was her turn to be surprised. "You don't know?"

"Sheriff, I'm confessing because I did it. I killed my dad."

Sun hadn't realized until that moment that Kubrick was Joshua's dad. She softened under that knowledge, but tried not to show it. "No, you didn't. So why are you in here trying to convince me that you did?"

He lifted a shoulder and toyed with his cap like a child being scolded in the principal's office.

She leaned onto her elbows. "I could arrest you for submitting a false confession."

He lifted a shoulder again, and said meekly, "Not if I really did it."

Okay, fine. She'd go through the drill. "How was he killed?"

Amusingly, the guy perked up with the question. "Stab wound in the chest." He said it as though answering a question on a game show.

"What kind of knife was it?"

That tripped him up. He chewed a nail in thought, then said, "A Jimmy Lile split fourteen-tooth model FB Titanium Grey Cerakote with mirrored borders, a steel guard, and a green, nylon-wrapped handle."

Okay, that was specific. And pretty much the exact knife Rambo used in *First Blood*. "What was he wearing?"

"Oh!" He thought back. "Probably a denim jacket and a plaid shirt."

"What were his hands tied with?"

"Rope."

"We're done." She tossed a pen on her desk.

"But you didn't finish reading my letter. It was self-defense."

"Joshua, we're up to fourteen confessions now. I get it. You figure by claiming self-defense, you'll get off easy. You could even say you were rescuing me."

"You?" he asked, utterly lost if his expression were any indication. "I'm sorry, Sheriff, but what do you have to do with it?"

She leaned back. "I want to know why everyone from Levi's milkman to his pastor is filing a false confession."

He twisted the cap in his hands. "Ravinder's the best thing to happen to this family in a long time, Sheriff."

Her heart swelled. It always amazed her that Levi, the youngest of the Ravinder men, had become the head of the entire clan and had earned the title of *Ravinder*. As far as she could tell, the others were all called by their first names.

"The whole town, really," he continued. He was right. Levi's distillery employed dozens of Del Sol's finest.

"So, you're all protecting him?" She knew the answer, of course, but wanted to hear it from him. She also wanted to know who was behind it. Levi would never put his people up to something like this.

He studied the nail he'd chewed on earlier. "No, ma'am. Like I said, I did it."

"All right, then. Thank you, Joshua." She stood and opened her door, inviting him to leave. He started to follow her but turned and put the torn letter on her desk.

"Great!" Quincy yelled out in the bullpen. She looked over at him as she escorted Joshua out. "Just great. Randy ate my almonds."

When he threw an empty wrapper into his trash can, Sun couldn't help but notice Rojas, whose desk was next to Quincy's, cringe in guilt and turn away as he wiped salt off his mouth. Oh, yeah. He was going to fit right in.

She saw their latest blasphemer out, then locked herself in her office to make a call. To make *the* call.

After being transferred, put on hold, and transferred again, a female came onto the line with a short, to-the-point, "Danforth speaking."

"Yeah," Sun said, lowering her voice, "I was wondering if you're naked."

A high-pitched squeal nigh burst her eardrum. "Sunshine! Is it really you?"

"It is if you're naked."

"Oh, my God, how are you? How's the sticks? How's Auri? Is she willing to cut off her hair so I can make a wig out of it yet?"

Sun laughed. "Not yet, but I think I'm wearing her down."

"Holy shit, it's good to hear your voice."

Nancy Danforth was a hot mess who'd gotten Sun into more trouble than she had a right to back in the day. She'd started at the forensics lab at the New Mexico Department of Public Safety around the same time Sun started with Santa Fe PD. After a particularly brutal reaming they'd both received concerning a tainted blood sample—an incident that turned out to be neither of their faults—they'd bonded over a glass of wine and a case of Thin Mints.

Not a box. A case.

And they'd been close ever since.

"What did I do to finally warrant a call from you? I was beginning to think you'd lost your voice, what with all the texts I get."

Sun cringed. "I'm sorry, Nancy. Turns out, sheriffing is a full-time gig. Who knew?"

"I'm so proud of you, Sun."

"Thanks, love. But you and I both know I didn't do a thing." Nancy was one of the few people Sun had trusted enough to tell the truth about the election.

"Doesn't make it any less awesome. Oh!" she said before lowering her voice and asking, "Is this about the you-know-what?"

Sun took a swig of coffee for courage, and said, "Yes, it is. Have you had a chance—"

"I have."

Normally Sun's stomach was made of stouter stuff, but it lurched at the thought of what was about to be revealed. "And . . . was there a match?"

"There was."

Sun fought a wave of dizziness and chalked it up to her hangover when really it had more to do with the fact that Wynn was lying. He had to be. Somehow, he knew all—or most—of the sordid details of that night fifteen years ago, but the more Sun thought about it, the less she believed him.

If he really did know Kubrick's accomplice, he could've gotten everything from him. And with Levi's ID bracelet clutched in Kubrick Ravinder's hand, there was almost no way Levi was *not* involved. She just didn't know to what degree. Nor to what end.

Nancy rustled some papers, then asked, "Are you ready for this?"

"As I'll ever be." She held her breath as Nancy spoke.

"You were right. The blood on Kubrick Ravinder's jacket belonged to another Ravinder."

Sun's lids drifted shut.

"His brother. Wynn Ravinder."

Sun sat silent for a solid minute, blinking back the encroaching darkness. He hadn't been lying.

When she didn't respond, Nancy continued. "Seems he's an inmate in the Arizona State Pen. Do you know him?"

She sank against the back of her chair. "We've only recently become acquainted."

"Well, there's about a gallon of blood that places him at that crime scene."

"And . . . and you're sure?" Sun asked.

"Admittedly, DNA evidence is not as exact a science as the public would believe, but yeah. He's your guy, Sun. No doubt."

"Holy shit."

"Holy shit, indeed. I'll get this report to you today. When are you coming to see me?"

She fought through another wave of disbelief, then teased her with, "Call me when you're naked."

Nancy giggled and hung up.

Sun walked through a cloud of euphoria and into the bullpen.

"I'm winning!" Salazar said to her. "Confession number fourteen puts me on top."

Both Salazar and Zee had come in while she was on the phone. Zee cast them both a saucy grin, as though she knew something no one else in the station did.

That fact didn't faze Sun. Somehow she made it to Quincy's desk, but her BFF—whom she now knew every inch of—was watching Rojas as he walked to the front door to meet his tia Darlene.

Quincy depressed the TALK button on his radio and said, "Poetry is in motion. Repeat, Poetry is in motion." He chuckled and turned to Sun. "I've been waiting for days to say that." When he got a look at her, however, he sobered and jumped to his feet. "What's up, boss?"

Darlene Tapia, Poetry Rojas's honorary aunt, had brought a basket of homemade breakfast burritos for him and the gang. She handed it over, wrapped the uniformed deputy in her arms, and said, "I am so proud of you, *mijo*." She set him back, licked her fingers, and tried to tame a recalcitrant cowlick with her spit.

"Tia," he said, feigning embarrassment, but he loved it. He adored the woman. Even though she'd only been a neighbor, not a blood relation, she'd practically raised him and his twin brother.

"Boss?" Quincy repeated.

"They got a match."

His face morphed into a grim expression. "Ravinder?"

"Yes, but not the one we expected."

"No way."

She shook her head, still in disbelief. Why? Why would

Wynn Ravinder come to her rescue? Why would he kill his own brother trying to save her, if that was what really happened?

He sank back into his chair. "He was telling the truth."

"Looks like it."

Quincy stabbed her with a glare. "Then he was in on it. Your abduction. He had to be. Things went south and he and Kubrick fought. You can't tell me he went there to save you."

"I don't know, Quince. None of it makes any sense. There is a part of him that seems . . . almost noble."

"You keep saying that, but nobility in that family borders on psychopathic."

A knock on the front window sounded. Sun and Quincy looked over at Carver. The exterminator waved enthusiastically and pointed to his phone.

Sun lifted hers to read a text from him, inviting her to lunch. She groaned.

Quincy read it over his shoulder. "He's persistent."

She typed back, *Huge case. Rain check?* She hit SEND then waved back at him.

He read it and his manic expression faded. After texting her a thumbs-up, he waved goodbye, a sad, dejected thing.

Rojas walked up. "Want me to take him out?"

"Someone needs to," Quincy said. "He clearly hasn't gone out with anyone since the aughts. Is that how he dressed on your date?" he asked Sun.

"What? No. That's his uniform."

The guy had been wearing a pair of stained gray overalls with his signature four Cs on an embroidered patch and carrying an aluminum spray can and nozzle.

"What's up, Rojas?" she asked Poetry when he continued to linger.

"I've gone over the footage from the Quick-Mart and it's impossible to get an ID on the man our victim was arguing with.

"But there was definitely an argument?"

"Oh, yeah. A pretty heated one."

Zee walked up, holding a black-and-white printout of a screenshot from the altercation. She handed it to Sun and pointed. "That baseball cap? That's a Denver Broncos hat."

Sun looked at Quincy. "That's the cap Levi had at the scene. I'm sure of it."

"Then he stole evidence from a crime scene. Can I arrest him already?"

"If you can find him. Any of the employees hear anything?"

Rojas pointed to the store owner, who couldn't have been more than ten feet away from what looked like a very volatile argument. "Mr. Walden swears he didn't hear a thing." His expression deadpanned. "My ass. Said Seabright was a semi-regular customer. Always very pleasant. Always paid in cash. But somehow he didn't have a clue as to what the argument was about."

"How would he remember he always paid in cash?" Quincy asked.

"No clue, but I'm guessing Seabright was off the grid. Especially if he never used plastic."

Sun studied Seabright's profile. The guy was tall with striking features underneath a layer of scruff. "Interesting. Okay, I want to see the footage."

"You got it, boss." Zee went back to her desk to cue-up the video, but Rojas stayed put.

"What else you got?" she asked him after looking closer at the printout.

"This may be nothing."

She raised a brow. "That's what the Duke of Wellington's first officer said when he saw Napoleon coming."

"Really?"

"No, but he might have. What's going on?"

"There are some guys hanging out in town."

She crossed her arms over her chest. "Well, this is a tourist town. People tour."

He propped a hip onto his desk. "Yeah, but they're just hanging. They're not touring."

"Interesting. Are they locals?"

"No."

"You haven't been in Del Sol long."

"I know a local when I see one. And at least two of these men have been to prison."

That got her attention. "You can tell that by looking at them?"

"I can."

She didn't doubt him for a microsecond. "What do you think they're doing?"

"They're waiting."

"For?"

"Us."

That surprised both her and Quincy, who didn't seem to be questioning Rojas's judgment in the matter, either.

"For us to do what?" he asked him.

Rojas pointed at him. "That's the ten-million-dollar question."

Sun whistled. "Ten million. Geez, prices have gone up. Can you get some pictures?"

"Of course, boss."

"Thank you, and—"

Anita stuck her head into the bullpen. "The DA is on line two for you, boss. He sounds angry."

"Great," Sun said, embracing the adrenaline spike that shot needles into her heart. She'd need the extra boost to deal with the man. She looked at her deputies. "Wish me luck."

"Luck," Quincy said, knowing she didn't get along with the DA.

Still, convincing the man to transport Wynn Ravinder across state lines would not be the hardest thing she'd done that day. She'd had the talk with her daughter, after all.

12

If it turns out you're not an afternoon person, either, we can help!

—SIGN AT CAFFEINE-WAH

Sun hung up with the DA, scrubbed her face, then headed into the bullpen. "Rojas!" she shouted, even though he was only a few feet away from her. Her conversation with the surly DA had not gone well, but she finally convinced him to have Wynn Ravinder transported to Santa Fe. The fact that she had to resort to blackmail did not sit well with either of them, but the married father of two shouldn't have asked her out last year.

Zee had cued up the Quick-Mart video showing the argument between their victim, Keith Seabright, and one of his assailants, but that could wait. She needed to know more about these men casing the town. And Zee wasn't at her desk anyway.

Rojas jumped and turned to her, his burnished skin glowing healthily in the soft morning light. He looked good. Better than he had when she'd met him four months ago, before she sent him off to the police academy.

"Let's grab a cup."

He grinned, hopped up, and followed her to Del Sol's latest and greatest coffee shop, Caffeine-Wah.

The owners, Richard and Ricky, two of her best friends from Santa Fe, opened the establishment when Sun found out she'd been elected sheriff. They'd wanted to put a shop in Del Sol for a long time. Her win gave them the perfect excuse, as they wanted to remain close to Auri. Sun understood. They'd helped raise her, after all. Which would explain Auri's incredible taste in clothes. She sure didn't get that from her mother.

However, neither of her friends were in. The girl behind the counter said they had to run to one of their Santa Fe stores that morning, but they'd be back soon. She and Rojas ordered, then sat at a bistro table near the front window.

He pushed a few buttons on his phone and handed it to her.

"What's this?" she asked.

"The guys casing us."

She looked up in surprise. "You got pictures of them already?"

"I did. Do you recognize any of them?"

She scrolled through the shots, about ten each of three different men. Rojas was right. They were literally just standing around. Window-shopping or reading a paper or sipping tea on the veranda of the Del Sol Diner. "How did you already get pictures of them?"

"You were busy with the DA. He really seems to like you."

"Yeah," she said with a soft chuckle. "He's a peach. I don't recognize any of them. Do you?"

"Nah. Sorry, boss."

She noticed a couple had visible tattoos. "What about their ink?"

"That one," he said, scrolling back until he came to the stocky one with the tattoo of a scorpion on his hand, "is La Cosa Nostra."

She gaped at him. "Really?"

He laughed. "No."

"Rojas," she said, admonishing him while fighting to keep a straight face.

"But that's what's weird. None of their ink is local. A couple of their tattoos are exactly the same, so they're affiliated. I guarantee it. Just not with anyone around here."

"Around here as in Del Sol?"

"Around here as in the whole of New Mexico. If I had to guess, I'd say they're East Coast."

"Wonderful." Because that was what she needed. A crime war on her turf. His teasing about La Cosa Nostra may have not been that far off the mark. "Which ones have been to prison?"

He pointed out two of the three. The stocky one with the scorpion tattoo and a taller one wearing a black leather jacket from the seventies.

"The third one," he said, scrolling to an older gentleman with salt-and-pepper hair and a spray tan if Sun ever saw one. "I'm just not sure about him. If he did do time, he did it well. Probably a higher-up of some kind. I can run facial recognition when we get back, but I doubt we'll get a hit. We need someone with access to a federal database."

"I can ask my contact in the FBI." She looked out and studied the two men she could see from her vantage. "How do you know all of this? What's the giveaway?"

"It's in the eyes. The way they move. Their posture." He looked at her. "You ever notice how men in prison either hunch or stand ramrod straight with their chests puffed out?"

She thought back and nodded. "I do actually. It always seems to be one or the other."

"And therein lies the tell. The differences in the pecking order."

"What about the ones that do neither?" she asked, thinking of Wynn Ravinder. He didn't seem to feel the need to put on a show. As though he were just as relaxed in prison as Sun was at the spa.

A slow, calculating smile spread across Rojas's face. "Those are the ones with true power. Those are the ones to watch out for."

A wave of goose bumps raced over her skin. Maybe she was playing with fire by inviting Wynn back into the state, but she wanted to know everything. Especially the son of a bitch who violated her. What she would do with that information, she didn't know, but at least she would have it.

She looked out the window. "What about anyone else in town? Have you noticed—"

"Him."

She blinked. "That was fast. Who?"

Rojas pointed to a gray-haired gentleman walking toward the coffee shop. A man who just happened to be her father, Cyrus Freyr.

Sun propped her elbows on the table and faced him. "Have you been messing with me this whole time?"

"No way, boss. Why?"

"That man has never even spent a day in jail, much less prison."

He eyed the guy again. "Sorry, boss. That man has spent time inside, but from the looks of him, it was maybe a military prison? Or something similar?"

She snorted, then rethought her doubt and turned back to study the man in question. Had he been in jail and never told her?

Her father got a text, turned, and headed back to his SUV down the street.

Sun shook it off and asked, "Can you send those pics to me?"

"Already did. I also set Zee on surveillance until I could brief you. I'll take over in a few." He took a sip of his pink lemonade spritzer topped with whipped cream and a maraschino cherry, then pointed. A plainclothes Zee stood browsing the books the Book Nook employees were just now moving onto the sidewalk, her tall, lithe form doing anything but blending in. The girl was stunning, and one of the men they were watching had taken note. A fact that could play in their favor.

She looked back at Rojas's fruity drink. "It takes a confident man to order a drink like that."

He tilted his head and smiled in appreciation. "Thank you, boss."

She laughed and decided to take a second for an impromptu check-in. "Got any questions for me?"

"I have two, if you're asking."

She took another draw on her pinon coffee sweetened with hazelnut. "I'm asking," she said, echoing the conversation they'd had a couple of days before.

"First, why do you call the yellow fire truck Big Red?"

A surprised giggle bubbled out of her. She'd expected something a little more . . . official, but that worked. "When the town ordered Big Red, they threw a naming party. They were really excited. They chose the name before she was delivered, and while they'd ordered a red hook-and-ladder, she showed up yellow. Unfortunately, they'd already ordered a nameplate for her, so Big Red she is."

"This town is so weird."

She couldn't argue with that kind of solid, fact-based logic. "And second?"

He waited as though contemplating if he should ask. "I know it's none of my business, boss, and please don't feel obligated to answer, but what happened to you?"

"What do you mean?" she asked, suddenly self-conscious. "It was only a little box of wine and Quincy drank half of it."

When he fixed a patient smile on her, she caved.

Poetry Rojas was direct, she'd give him that. She liked it. "You want the long version or the CliffsNotes?"

"Whatever you're comfortable with?"

Great answer. She told him what happened to her when she was seventeen. How she was abducted and held for five days while the kidnapper demanded every penny her father had, only for her to end up dropped off at an emergency room in Santa Fe with a severe concussion and covered in blood, most of it her rescuer's.

Sure, she glossed over a few of the sticky points, but her story was out in the world anyway thanks to a few vindictive high school students. One only had to guess the sordid details, because nine months later, a fiery ginger with the lung capacity of a yeti clawed her way out of Sun's nether region and her world had never been the same.

She also skipped over the amnesia part. She only remembered bits and pieces of her ordeal and was missing almost an entire month beforehand.

"Now can I ask you a question?"

Rojas sat contemplating her story. He swam back to her and said, "Of course."

"Why did your mom name you Poetry? And how often were you beat up because of it?" she teased. "I love it. Don't get me wrong, but it's very unusual. I would think even more so for a boy."

He smiled as he thought back. "I don't think she did, in all honesty. She never admitted this, but I think she was going to name me Porter after a jazz musician she was in love with, but the woman entering the information at the hospital couldn't read my mom's writing and typed *Poetry* into the computer."

"Poetry fits you," she said. "At least she got your twin brother's name right. Ramses?"

He shook his head. "His name was supposed to be Ransom."

"Wow. Your mom was clearly very creative. Another jazz singer?"

"Blues." A sadness came over him. His parents had died when he and his brother were kids.

"Well, either your mother had horrible handwriting or that nurse needed glasses."

He looked out the window toward Zee for the fiftieth time in five minutes.

"I frown on office romances," she said to him, "but not for long. It causes wrinkles. No one needs to see that."

"What, Zee?" he asked with a scoff. "Never. She's so far out of my league it's like we're not even playing the same sport."

"Not true."

"No, for sure. It's like she's an Olympic skier and I play stickball with miniature horses."

"Is that a real thing?"

"I wouldn't stand a chance."

She disagreed. Rojas was a little younger than Zee, but only by a couple of years. He was incredibly intelligent, charming, and quite the looker. Zee could definitely do worse.

Then again, so could he. Zee was a goddess among mortals.

Sun wanted to ask him more about how he pulled it off. How he managed to do three years in the state pen in his brother's stead without being found out, but a nuisance she was going to have to deal with soon walked into the coffee shop.

"Sunshine," Carver said, strolling up to their table, his coveralls folded down to reveal a T-shirt underneath.

"Hey, Carver. What are you doing here?"

In the four months Sun had been back in Del Sol, she never once remembered seeing Carver Zuckerman. She could've just not noticed him, but for him to suddenly be there every time she turned around? Either he was stalking her or . . . Holy crap. She blinked up at him. He was stalking her. Even more reason to kill her parents.

"Just saw you come in here. Thought I'd come say hey."

"Oh. Well, hey back."

"Of course," he said, growing serious. "I meant what I said. We have a lot in common. I'm here if you need a shoulder."

What the hell did he think she went through on a daily basis that she needed a man's shoulder to cry on? Besides, she had Quincy for that.

"I know you have a big case," he continued. "How's that going?"

"I can't really discuss it, Carver."

"Right." He shook his head. "But I'm here if you need me. I see a lot more in this town than most."

"I'm sure you do."

"Well, I won't keep you." He stepped closer. "I'd love to see you again, though."

Was he really going to do this to her here? In front of her deputy?

"I really don't have time for a social life right now, but if that ever changes . . ."

"That's what your mom said. She's a looker, eh?" He elbowed Rojas's shoulder.

She rubbed her fingertips over her forehead, her hangover headache coming back with a vengeance.

Rojas watched him leave, and if looks could kill . . .

"What's up? Don't tell me Carver has been to prison?"

"No. He's too slick."

"Slick? Carver?"

"He's a sociopath, boss. Be careful."

She knew Rojas would be invaluable, but damn. "He lacks some social intelligence, but—"

"He's a sociopath," he repeated.

"Okay, then."

"And he gives me the creeps."

"Yeah, well, maybe he has nothing else to give, Rojas. Did you ever think of that? No. You only think of yourself."

"Just be careful," he said with nary a hint of a grin. And she'd tried hard.

She took another sip, contemplating everything she'd learned in the last half hour. Three things, to be precise. Rojas could look manly even with a pink drink in his hands. Carver was very likely stalking her. And the men who were casing the town, so to speak, were waiting for the sheriff's department to make a move. She just didn't know why. Or in which direction.

Oh, and lest she forget, her father had possibly been to prison. And her parents never told her.

"I should probably relieve Zee," he said. "They're only going to buy into her book browsing for so long before they catch on."

"You've clearly never gone to a bookstore with my mother."

He chuckled. "No, I haven't."

"If you do, take snacks." They stood to leave. "I'm going take a look at that surveillance footage and see if we can't get a ping on Levi Ravinder's phone."

Though, by that point, Sun had half a mind to kill the guy. If he wasn't already dead and lying in a ditch somewhere.

"But you *told* me to dress breaky-and-entery." Sybil glanced down. "Those were your exact words."

Auri studied Sybil's attire. Black turtleneck. Black yoga pants. Black beanie covering the top of her auburn head with two long braids hanging down to her elbows. She even had black sneakers on. The girl never wore sneakers.

Auri clamped her mouth shut to keep from giggling at her adorable accomplice. "Yes, but I meant understated breaky-and-entery. Unassuming. You're a walking advertisement."

Sybil dropped her head in shame. "I'm sorry. I'm so bad at breaking and entering."

That time Auri did giggle. "There are worse things to be bad at. Believe me."

After leaning closer, Sybil asked, "When are we doing this?"

Auri scanned the halls for the thousandth time, which were starting to empty as the students of Del Sol High filed into their respective classrooms. They were heading into second period, and Cruz was still a no-show. Maybe he'd changed his mind. Maybe he'd really wanted her to get naked with him.

The thought alone caused a warmth to blush across her face. Was he disappointed? The fact that she'd wanted to hold on to her V-card had never seemed to bother him before. He'd never pressured her. Not once.

Maybe it was the whole breaking and entering thing. That would put off anyone.

The bell was about to ring. They'd officially missed their opportunity to skip second. Just as she and Sybil started into class, they heard the metal doors at the back end of the school open.

They turned. Cruz stood holding the door open, waving them over as he kept watch.

Auri's heart soared. He hadn't abandoned her.

The two of them hurried toward him. He held it open as

they ducked under his arm, then eased it closed until a click that sounded like a thunder strike echoed around them. Auri cringed, hoping the sound didn't get anyone's attention.

"Where have you been?" she whispered.

He led them around the back of the main building and into a parking lot only a few faculty members used.

"Sorry. I woke up late."

The girls giggled. "Your dad didn't wake you?" Auri asked.

"No, he had to leave early."

They stopped at a jaw-dropping red Ford Raptor.

"You're driving your dad's truck?" Auri asked, surprised.

"Yeah. He let me since I was running so late."

"Then how did he leave early?"

He frowned in thought, then said, "Motorcycle."

"That's a nice truck," Sybil said, gazing in awe at the massive beast.

Auri agreed. "Can he be my dad, too?" she asked him.

"That would make us siblings, so, no."

The implications of his statement sent a flutter to Auri's stomach.

He lifted a sinewy arm and opened the passenger's door for them. They climbed—literally as the truck sat a thousand feet off the ground—into the cab. When Cruz got into the driver's seat, the truck fitting him like an Italian glove, he made the climb look effortless.

"I think I'm ready to tackle Mount Everest now," Auri said, teasing him.

He grinned at her and started the engine.

"You only have your permit," she said as the beast roared to life. "I can't believe he let you take his truck."

He grinned again, only this time the charm had fled and another emotion had taken its place. Apprehension? Sadness perhaps? "That's why I have this." He took a cap off the dash and pull it low over his brow.

Auri wanted to ask him about the emotion that flashed across his face, but not with an audience. That was a conversation best saved for another time. The display, however, was about the thirtieth she'd sensed in as many days. Last night, as Auri laid in bed dreaming about Cruz, she thought back to when it all started. He and his father had gone on a fishing trip near Chama in northern New Mexico for spring break. She didn't see him for over a week, and when she did, he seemed distracted.

Maybe he met another girl while on break. Maybe he didn't know how to tell her. Sure, he *said* he was kind of in love with her, but . . . no buts. She was a big girl. She could take it. What she couldn't take was being strung along, and she'd tell him that as soon as they were alone.

He put the truck into drive and they headed out of the lot before someone caught them skipping.

Both locals and tourists were already out and about, grabbing coffee and shopping with the resident artists. He pointed as they drove past the sheriff's station. Auri ducked her head. Sybil took a different approach. She undid her seatbelt and nose-dived for the floorboard, her gaze darting about like a cornered animal.

Auri fought yet another giggle, but the events of the next few seconds would teach her not to be so quick to judge. She looked past Cruz just in time to see her mother exiting Caffeine-Wah. The woman in full sheriff regalia stopped and watched as the huge truck drove by.

Cruz shrank back and lifted his shoulder to hide as much of his face as he could, but the movement brought Auri directly into her mother's line of sight. Their gazes locked for a split second before Auri dove for cover. Straight into Cruz's lap.

With her face firmly in Cruz's crotch, Auri asked, "Did she see me?"

"She's still looking," Cruz said, his voice suspiciously full of humor. "You'd better stay down there for a while."

Auri frowned. How long could it take to drive past a coffee shop?

Cruz shook as though laughing.

She raised up. "Cruz De los Santos."

A pair of dimples appeared on the sides of his full mouth and her ire—fake as it was—evaporated.

"Are you sure Mrs. Fairborn is at the station?" he asked, changing the subject.

"I have it on good authority."

He cast her a suspicious glance. "What kind of authority?"

"I have an inside man." Auri did everything but blow on her nails and polish them on her shirt.

"Can I ask who it is?"

She shook her head. "Sorry, Charlie. I could tell you, but I'd have to kill you. Then where would we be?" She looked down at Sybil, who sat hunkered on the floorboard still. "Sweetheart, you can get up now."

"Oh. Okay." She scrambled back onto the seat and pushed her glasses up with an index finger.

They pulled onto Mrs. Fairborn's street, but parked at the end of the block. After a nonchalant walk down a narrow alleyway, they hauled themselves over a wooden fence.

Well, Auri and Sybil did. Cruz walked through the gate and eyed them both like they were crazy. It happened. He also stopped to give Sybil's outfit a once-over as though just noticing her cat-burglar attire.

Much like Auri had, he suppressed a grin, turned, and strolled to Mrs. Fairborn's back door like he belonged there.

"See that?" Auri said to Sybil. "We need to act natural. Like we're supposed to be here."

"Right." Sybil, who seemed on the verge of hyperventilating, took a deep breath and nodded. "Act natural. I can do that. I can act natural."

Auri wanted to laugh, but she was right there with her.

"We're in," Cruz said. He'd been kneeling at the back door. He stood and opened it.

"Wow." Auri stopped, stunned. "You really did it."

"Isn't that what you wanted me to do?" he asked, his eyes crinkling with humor.

"Well, yeah. It's just . . ."

She crept forward, gazing into the abyss that was Mrs. Fairborn's large house—or what looked like a mudroom—keeping a watchful eye as though something was going to jump out at her. Now that it was really happening, she was having all kinds of second thoughts.

Panic took hold. Backing away, she looked between her two friends, and asked, "Who wants coffee?" right before she turned and hightailed it over the fence despite a wide-open back gate.

Zee started the video from where Keith Seabright entered the store. Since the Quick-Mart sat right across the street from the sheriff's station, the station was in the background of one of the four grainy panes. Unfortunately, all four surveillance angles formed four blocks on the single screen, and there was no way to get only one angle per screen as that was how it was recorded. It made deciphering the details even harder.

"Did Mr. Walden give you any trouble?"

Mr. Walden, the owner of the Quick-Mart, could be cantankerous when he wanted to be.

"No," Zee said with a shrug. "But he did ask me out."

"He's eighty!"

"If a day."

"Does he know you're a sniper?"

"He does now," she said with a smirk. "There." She pointed to the screen as a lean, fit brunette walked in wearing a T-shirt, a pair of army fatigues, and a few days' worth of scruff. He paid cash for his gas, looked over his shoulder, then left.

As he exited the store, another man, stockier and wearing a baseball cap, bumped into him. Seabright looked like he was going to ignore it, but he suddenly turned on him, the movement so fast it was impossible to make out, and shoved.

The man went flying against an outdoor ice cooler.

Seabright went after him. He dragged him to his feet by his collar, but the man raised his palms in surrender.

Seabright didn't let it go. He looked down at his shirt, or maybe his arm, then got in the man's face.

"He wasn't carrying anything, was he?" she asked Zee.

Quincy rolled his chair over to watch. "I've studied this tape a dozen times. Neither was carrying anything."

"I thought maybe the guy had spilled something on him."

"Exactly," Zee said. "Why would he get so upset?"

Quincy scooted closer. "From what Mr. Walden said, Seabright was the most easygoing guy he's ever met. Nothing fazed him."

"But look," Zee said, pointing again. "There's a stain on his shirt." She turned to Sun. "This may be crazy, boss, but I think he tried to stab Seabright and failed."

"Could be, sis," Quincy said. "Seabright is former Special Forces. He could've seen the knife from the corner of his eye and thwarted the attempt."

"And he clearly has lightning-quick reflexes," Sun said.

"Maybe the guy didn't know what he was getting himself into," Zee added. "Which was why, for their second attempt, they drugged him."

"Makes sense." Sun leaned closer. "Damn, I wish we had a better angle."

There were a few people in the store, and every one of them turned to see what was going on. When Seabright shoved the man one last time and headed for his truck, a dark-colored Dodge, several people went to the window to investigate.

The assailant went the opposite direction.

"There," Zee said, pointing to the taillight of a light-colored, late-model pickup. "He's getting into a Toyota Tundra."

Quincy looked at Sun. "Just like the one used to run your boyfriend down."

"No plates?" she asked.

"They stayed far enough out of camera range, like they'd cased the store beforehand."

"Maybe we need to check the footage over a few days."

"I can do that tonight, boss," Zee said. "If you'll buy me some hot wings."

"Oh, and beer," Quincy said, suddenly excited to help.

But Sun had spotted an oddity in the video. Sometimes it wasn't what people were doing, but what they weren't doing that caught one's attention.

"Run it back," she said, squinting at the lower left pane. The high angle showed the rear of the store and the cash registers in the background.

Zee rewound—metaphorically speaking—to when Seabright entered. He paid and headed out of the store, but while everyone inside looked toward the commotion up front, one kid did the exact opposite. He turned toward the rear of the store instead. Toward the camera.

He looked directly at it and raked a hand through his hair, as though purposely showing his face. As though signaling anyone who might be watching.

"What the hell?" Zee said. She leaned closer. "I didn't even catch that. How did I not catch that?"

"It's okay, Zee. It took me a moment, too. But watch Seabright." Sun pointed. "He looks right at the kid before he leaves. Can we zoom in?"

"Not with this program, boss. I can run it through an editor, but the quality is horrible. I doubt we'll get an ID."

"We may not need one." She leaned closer and studied him. A feeling of recognition that started in the back of Sun's mind hurtled forward. She hit the space bar just as he pulled back his hair. He was thin with dark locks in bad need of a trim, but it was the shape of his face. The bone structure. The nose. The eyes.

"You know this kid?" Quincy asked.

"Yes." The word came out airy as astonishment thundered

through her. Wetness stung the backs of her eyes as she tried to fill her lungs. She would know that kid anywhere. She still carried his picture to this day along with one that showed his age progression. She'd spent months memorizing every line of his face.

"Sun?" Quincy put a hand on her back.

"Unless I'm mistaken, his name is Elliot. Elliot Kent."

"Okay," he said, his tone wary. "And that's of vital interest because?"

She lowered her hands. "Because he's been dead for seven years."

13

At that awkward stage between birth and death?
We can help you through it!
—SIGN AT DEL SOL BROKERAGE AND PSYCHIC READINGS

Quincy handed Sun a fresh cup of coffee as she watched the video yet again.

"Sun, we can't know that the boy in that video is Elliot Kent."

"It's him. I'd know him anywhere." His face had been emblazoned into her mind's eye. She'd looked at a hundred pictures. Watched tons of videos. Spoken to dozens of people. She knew Elliot Kent almost as well as she knew her own daughter. "He was my very first case when I made detective and my very first failure. Among many, unfortunately."

"Your first case?" Quincy asked, thinking back. "That was what? About seven years ago? He couldn't have been more than—"

"Five."

Quincy studied the kid, not sure what to think, but Zee didn't question it.

"Why did you think he died?" she asked.

"We found bloody clothes near the house. We just—we didn't hold out much hope of finding him alive after that. And there was never a ransom demand, even though we initially thought the abduction was related to his father's illegal activities."

"What illegal activities?" Quince asked.

"Ponzi scheme of sorts. He cleaned out entire families. Left them devastated, even though he insisted he wasn't behind it. Said he was the fall guy. The government felt otherwise. He was on trial when all of this was happening."

"One of his victims?"

"We looked into that. Thought it could have been blackmail, but there was never a demand. We thought about revenge, but ruled that out when Elliot just vanished. The abductor would've wanted Mr. Kent to know what he'd done. And why."

"What about a ploy for leniency?"

"We considered that, too. Mr. Kent broke down repeatedly in court, especially after they found Elliot's clothes. Which," she said, looking over at him, "were found the same day the defense rested."

"Did that have any sway on the jurors?" Zee asked.

"I don't care how strong a case a prosecutor has, nothing beats the tears of a father, crocodile or not. You bet it did. He got acquitted on four of the five charges, but there was no denying that last charge of investment fraud." She took a sip. "Got fifteen years."

"And you really think this kid is his son?"

"Yes. Nothing added up, even then. There were just too many times I caught his mother with such a look of utter devastation. Utter hopelessness."

"As any parent would be."

"Not at all." She sat up straighter. "Parents are devastated, yes, but they always have hope, even when the last shred of evidence points in the opposite direction. They always justify it, at least in those first few weeks. Nothing will convince them their child is gone until we find a body. But Mrs. Kent, she was different. Her devastation was more . . . absolute."

Zee took a sip of her own coffee. "Like a parent who had something to do with a coverup?"

Sun pulled her lower lip between her teeth in thought, then said, "Yes and no. Parents who commit filicide, those parents who are abusive to begin with, go about their business afterward as though nothing happened. They get on with their lives. It's honestly the strangest thing. And it throws jurors off. It's so hard for a normal person to fathom their indifference, and sometimes they mistake their behavior for innocence. But Mrs. Kent was genuinely devastated."

"Maybe they accidentally killed him."

"I considered that, too, until about ten minutes ago." She looked back at the screen. "I'm telling you, guys. That's Elliot."

They watched as Elliot exited the store and climbed into the passenger's side of Seabright's truck.

Quincy was finally beginning to believe her. "Does anyone else find it odd that he got into a man's truck who ended up with multiple stab wounds a few hours later?"

Zee concurred. "It can't be a coincidence, boss."

"I agree. So what? Seabright kidnapped Elliot? It just doesn't seem like his MO."

"And your gut is telling you this?" Quince asked. "Because you've known him for so long?"

She scowled at him. "No, Levi's gut told me. The man I'm going to kill the minute I find."

"Might not want to lead with that."

"But Elliot signaled to us," Zee said. "Why now? He's been missing for over seven years. Is this the first opportunity he's had?"

"There's something else we need to seriously consider." Tired of fighting it, Sun gave the dread gnawing at her gut free rein. "This was taken a few hours before Seabright showed up to the bar alone. If Elliot is being held against his will, Seabright had plenty of time to take him back to wherever he is being held and lock him up again. And with his abductor in the hospital—"

"He could die," Quince finished for her.

She turned to Zee. "I need you to talk to Mr. Walden again. Try to find out if he's ever seen the boy with Seabright before. If he's been with him this whole time."

"I'm on it, boss."

"Quincy, I need an address on this guy. Anything in his name or even his parents' name. Get Anita on that. Then how about you and I go talk to Mrs. Kent?"

"Thought you'd never ask."

Sun's phone dinged just as Anita came into the bullpen. "Hey, boss. Mrs. Fairborn is here to confess to stabbing Keith Seabright Saturday night."

"Damn it," Sun said under her breath after reading the text. "I need to run an errand before we head out."

"I got Mrs. F.," Quincy said. "You go. I'll call in Salazar to babysit while Anita and I try to get an address on Seabright."

"Thanks, Quince."

"To be honest, boss, I'm looking forward to reading how an eighty-year-old woman with blue hair repeatedly stabbed a two-hundred-pound man in a knife fight outside the Ravinder's bar." They watched as Anita led her in. "I didn't know she had it in her."

"You realize if your mother finds us here, she's going to catch onto the fact that we're skipping," Cruz said once they were ensconced into a corner booth at Caffeine-Wah.

"She just left here. She won't be back for a while. It's all good."

Sybil nodded absently, her lids as round as the rims on their cappuccino cups. Poor thing. Auri should've never dragged her into this.

She got a text from her mom and checked the time. Her mom was very careful not to text during class. Sure enough, second period just let out. They were officially skipping two classes.

Her stomach gurgled from her nerves as she read the text.

Knock, knock.

Who's there?

Etch.

She laughed. *Mom, that one's older than the Pecos River.*

Etch.

Mom.

This is not Mom. This is Etch.

OMG! Fine. Etch who?

Gesundheit. Now have a good day.

Her mom only used the Etch joke when she was worried about something and couldn't come up with anything better.

Is everything okay?

I just needed to read your voice. I'll probably be home late.

Everything was definitely not okay.

I love you, Mom.

After a moment in which she was sure her mom covered her heart with a hand and sighed aloud, Auri had to laugh when her mom typed back, *It's hard to blame you, really. All things considered.*

Then she added an entire line of hearts and it was Auri's turn to sigh.

"Your mom's pretty great," Sybil said.

"She seems to think so." She looked at her cohorts. "I'm sorry I chickened out." She tightened her hands around her cup. "I think I'm ready now."

"It's okay," Cruz said. "Let's give it a minute. Mrs. Fairborn will be in the station for hours."

She nodded a little too enthusiastically. Cruz's penetrating gaze didn't help.

Seeming to sense her discomfort, he refocused it on Sybil. "So, do you know your new expiration date?" When she turned a confused expression on him, he added, "When you're going to die."

"Cruz!" Auri said.

Sybil had known her whole life she was going to die on her fifteenth birthday. She'd had a premonition as a kid and had dreamed about it since. Thankfully, Sunshine Vicram had something to say about that and Sybil survived a terror no kid should ever have to endure.

Cruz shrugged, oblivious, which was not like him. "It's just that Auri's mom stopped your premonition from happening, so I wondered if you knew your new expiration date."

"Oh," Sybil said, brightening. "I do, actually."

"For real?" Auri asked.

"Yep." She slid her glasses up her freckled nose. "As of this moment, I'm going to live until I'm eighty-three and die of congestive heart failure."

"Oh." Auri cringed inwardly. "That's good . . . I guess."

"Yeah. I'm shooting for ninety-three. I've decided to get more exercise and eat healthy." They all looked down at the pastry in her hand. "Right after this delicious chocolate croissant."

The bell dinged and the owners of the coffee shop came in through the front carrying boxes. Auri decided to take advantage of the opportunity given her.

"Here." She handed Cruz a butter knife. "Hold this to my throat and go with it."

"Okay, but if they stab me, I'm blaming you."

"Deal."

Auri and her mom had lived in a loft above Richard and Ricky's garage in Santa Fe for years. They were like family and Auri had been the flower girl at their wedding. But in all the years they'd lived there, the couple held one captivating secret over their tenants' heads: the eyeliner trick.

Ricky, a gorgeous Asian, wore the most perfect eyeliner Auri had ever seen. He applied it with surgical precision and Sun and Auri wanted to know how.

Now was her chance to find out.

She waited until they got closer, positioned herself to be at Cruz's mercy, then said, "Help me! He wants the eyeliner trick or he'll kill me."

Ricky set his box on a nearby table and looked at them, less than impressed. Richard, with his glorious mop of spiked, black hair, followed suit, only his expression held more humor than disinterest.

Sensing her inevitable defeat, she added, "And he'll get blood all over your porous Italian tile." Which, really, who put a porous tile in a coffee shop?

Ricky gasped. "Fine. Your chai latte is on the house."

She rolled her eyes. "My chai latte is always on the house. He knows that. You're not fooling him." She pointed at the kid holding a butter knife against her throat, rather limply much to her chagrin. "He's a criminal mastermind."

Ricky gave Cruz a dubious examination.

Richard winked playfully at him. "The redhead put you up to this?"

He lifted a shoulder.

Ricky leaned closer to her and whispered, "Better luck next time, squirt."

She deflated. So close.

She disentangled herself from her captor and stood to give them each a hug. "You just missed Mom."

"We have some fresh-baked pastries we'll take over in a bit. Aren't you supposed to be in school?"

"We're on a scavenger hunt!" Sybil shouted. Really loudly. She didn't handle panic well.

"Yeah," Auri said, going in for the save, "for history. We're finding different historical sites in town and taking pics of them."

"Nice," Ricky said. "You should take a picture of Richard. He's a historical site."

Richard glared at him. "I'm not that much older than you."

"Whatever helps you sleep at night, Grandpa."

Auri giggled, then sat down and scowled at Cruz. "We need to talk."

"Okay," he said, a telltale grin lifting one corner of his mouth.

"Your performance was underwhelming."

"Underwhelming?"

"Yes. Less than whelming, if you will. I was not whelmed. You're going to have to step it up if you want to fool those two."

He smiled behind his cup. "I'll remember that."

"All right, good." She took a deep breath to steady herself, then nailed Cruz with her best look of determination. "I'm ready to go all the way."

Cruz choked on his coffee about the same time Auri realized her double-entendre faux pas.

"No, inside." She patted Cruz's back. "Inside Mrs. Fairborn's house. Did you think I meant—?" When he gave her a hapless shrug, she asked, "Have you even met my mother? She knows about the devil's doorbell, Cruz."

"The devil's what?" he asked between coughs.

"She will know if it's been rung. We need a plan."

"Why would we ring her doorbell if we're breaking in?"

"No. The devil's— Never mind."

Sybil sat glued to the conversation, her gaze bouncing back and forth between the two from behind her massive mug.

"And we had a plan," Cruz said. "You chickened out."

Auri sank against the seatback. "I know. I'm sorry. Did I mention that I'm pretty certain Mrs. Fairborn killed her husband, too?"

Her two cohorts refocused on her. "No, you did not," Sybil said.

"He went missing around the same time and the sheriff never did a thing about it."

"That sweet old lady," Sybil said in awe. "A black widow. Whodathunk?"

"Okay. I'm ready now. For real this time. Let's do th—" She stopped and listened. "Do you hear that?"

Cruz and Sybil looked around.

"That's my mom."

Sunshine texted Auri as she hurried down the alley toward Caffeine-Wah. She typed, *I just needed to read your voice. I'll probably be home late.*

When her daughter typed back, *I love you, Mom,* her heart almost imploded.

She typed her usual smart-ass response, then entered the coffee shop through the back door.

Levi's sister, Hailey, had sent up the signal, a code word they used that meant she needed a meeting ASAP. They'd been investigating Clay Ravinder for a few months now. He was threatening to take everything away from Levi, everything his nephew had worked so hard to build, and use it as a bargaining tool to get back into the Southern Mafia. Or, at least, one syndicate of it.

Neither Sun nor Hailey could let that happen. In fact, Hailey had come to Sun when she was still a detective in Santa Fe. As soon as Sun got some hard evidence on Clay's less than aboveboard pursuits, thanks in no small part to Hailey's ability to eavesdrop, she'd turn the case over to the feds.

They could hardly arrest Clay for his plans to run Levi out of his own business. They had no physical evidence he was planning anything illegal. But according to Hailey, Clay was working with Sun's predecessor, a corrupt sheriff named Redding, and they were into everything from drugs to guns. Sun had a connection with ATF that could serve her well in this instance.

But Clay was getting restless. More volatile. More unpredictable. Sun might not be able to wait much longer. Still, she would have no case at all if not for Hailey.

Sun and Hailey's mutual animosity had been serving them well. No one, not even Levi, suspected they were working together, much less that they'd become good friends over the last few months. Hailey was intelligent and caring, something Sun had never suspected growing up. If she'd known what Hailey had gone through, Sun liked to think she wouldn't have been so quick to judge her. Then again, Hailey did steal her bike.

Sun ducked into the back of Caffeine-Wah and glanced around the storage room for her accomplice.

"Sunshine," Hailey said from a dark corner.

Sun rushed to her and wrapped her arms around her. "Are you okay, hon? What's going on?" She set her back.

Hailey wore that worried expression. The one Sun feared. If Clay ever found out his niece was helping the local sheriff bring him down, he would kill her. Plain and simple.

Her dark blond hair hung in tangles down her back and her red-rimmed eyes emphasized the depth of the circles underneath.

"What happened, Hailey?"

"Have you heard from Levi?"

Dread knotted her stomach. "I saw him this morning, but he escaped. Did he come home Saturday night?"

She shook her head. "He hasn't been home in days, but I'm hoping it's because you're looking for him. Right?"

"Yes, hon. We've been looking for him. He was hurt Saturday night at the bar, but at least we know he's alive."

"I know," she said with a nod. "Clay told me. It's just . . . I'm worried Clay has done something to him."

Sun's stomach spasmed painfully. "Why? Has something else happened?"

"Not that I know of, but he's exactly the kind of opportunist who would kill Levi and blame it on the injuries he sustained Saturday night."

"But you don't know that for sure, right?"

She sank onto a crate. "No, I don't. But Clay met with Redding yesterday."

Former sheriff Redding was getting to be a serious thorn in her side. He was as corrupt as they come and was not happy when Sun won the election against him.

"I couldn't hear what they were saying, but I did hear something about a Mr. Southern coming to see the plant." Her expression turned panicked. "Sun, he's offering the distillery to a higher-up in the syndicate. I know it. If we're going to do something, we need to do it now."

"Son of a bitch." Sun turned away from her in thought. "But I don't get it. What's in it for Redding?"

She shrugged. "He wants the badge back. And Clay wants him to have it. The position would give Redding the ability to smooth the way for the syndicate to come in and take over. Because of that, Clay has promised to get it for him."

Sun bit her lip in thought. "Do you know how?"

Hailey dropped her gaze. "I'm not certain, but they have a plan in place."

"Way to bury the lede, Hailey."

"Something about number three being their best option."

"Which is?"

"I don't know. I'm sorry, Sun. I've been so worried about Levi."

She turned back and knelt before Hailey. "No, I'm sorry. Have you texted him?"

"Over and over. He's . . . he's probably turned off his phone. Right?"

"Absolutely. He knows we can track him using his phone, and he was pretty dead set on finding those men who tried to kill his friend. Speaking of which, do you know Keith Seabright?"

Hailey shook her head. "Sounds familiar, but I don't think I've met him."

"Okay." Sun considered not mentioning her trip to Hailey, but the woman was literally putting her life on the line for her family. She deserved the truth. "I think you should know, Hailey, I went to see your uncle Wynn."

"Wynn?" she asked astonished. "He's out?"

"No. Quincy and I went to Arizona. He wants me to look into his conviction. Says he's innocent of the crime he's in jail for."

"Then he is," she said, adamant.

"You sound certain."

"Sun, Wynn is the most honorable person I know apart from Levi. If he'd done it, he would not try to weasel out of his sentence."

"You need to know, he also said he killed Kubrick."

Her blond brows slid together and she shook her head. "I think he's lying."

"Hailey, you just said your uncle is honorable."

"I said honorable. I didn't say he never lied. He would lie through his teeth, but he would do it for honorable reasons." She studied her nails and asked, "Are you going to look into his case?"

"I told him I would look at the file, but I can't make any promises."

Hailey took Sun's hands into hers. "Thank you."

Sun squeezed. "But you need to know, he had a set of conditions. I'm trying to get him transferred to Santa Fe."

Her face lit up like a sparkler. "He's coming here?"

"Maybe."

"Sun, if you can get him out, if you can prove him innocent, he'll help. He'll stop Clay."

"Hopefully, he won't have to." Sun sat back on her heels. "So, this is really happening. Clay is going to try to kill Levi, take over the distillery, and help Redding remove me from office."

"Yes. And from what I heard, it'll happen soon."

Wonderful. "Hailey, are you being very, very careful? If Clay finds out . . ."

"I know the risks, Sun. I knew them when I came to you." Hailey squeezed her hands. "I have to go. Please be careful."

"You, too, sweetheart."

They both stood just as Sun got a text.

She checked her phone. "Uh-oh. The wife needs me back at the office ay-sap."

"Quincy?" Hailey asked with a soft chuckle.

"Yep. Are you good?"

"I'm good."

"You know I can put you and Jimmy in protective custody."

Hailey shook her head. "It's okay. I'll be careful. And I'll let you know what else I find."

Sun turned to leave and came face-to-face with an irascible redhead, her eyes wide, her mouth slightly ajar. Since Auri—as well as everyone else in town—believed Sun and Hailey were mortal enemies, standing in a dark storeroom holding hands with her could look odd.

Richard and Ricky screeched to a halt behind her, their faces panicked. They didn't know who Hailey was or why she and Sun met in secret in their storeroom, but they knew no one could find out. Absolutely no one. Sun had stressed that ad nauseum when she set up the meets.

"Auri," Sun said, then she turned on Hailey. "And don't let

me catch you back here again, Ms. Ravinder, or I will have you arrested."

"You're the sheriff," Auri said, hardly biting.

"Right. I'll arrest you myself. Because I can." She nodded toward Auri. "Because I'm the sheriff."

"At least now I know where I get my acting prowess from," Auri said. She went in for a hug. "Hey, Ms. Ravinder."

Hailey wrapped her up. "Hey, beautiful. Your mom and I were just discussing—"

"Coffee!" Ricky said. "We just got a shipment in from Ethiopia. Best coffee ever."

Auri's expression turned dubious. "And you call yourself a thespian."

That did it. Ricky stood thoroughly offended. "This coming after that Academy Award–winning performance with your boyfriend."

Sun's phone dinged again. "I have to go. Quincy's lost without me." She put her hands on her daughter's shoulders and sobered. "You know how sometimes what I do is life or death?"

She nodded.

"This is one of those times, bug bite."

A knowing smile spread across her lovely face. She looked from Sun to Hailey then back. "Got it."

"Good girl. Now why aren't you in school?"

14

Arrested for holding hands in public
because they didn't know you and made a scene?
We can help!

—SIGN AT DALE SAUL, ATTORNEY-AT-LAW

Of all the crap she put on her daughter, now she had to entrust the girl with a secret certain members of society would kill for. She would talk to Auri about it later. Right now, Quincy was screaming at her. Metaphorically, as he'd used three exclamation points in his text.

"Are you okay?" he asked when she walked into the station a little worse for wear.

"Why? Don't I look okay? I did have a Thin Mint I found in my car that tasted sketchy."

He shook his head.

"What's so urgent?"

"That." He pointed to her office.

She stepped closer. Levi was inside, pacing back and forth like a caged animal. He stopped and turned toward her, his expression angrier than normal. As much as she hated to admit it, she didn't care if he was angry. Or why. Her heart skipped a beat with the knowledge that he was still alive.

"He seems agitated," she said to Quince.

"He is," Levi responded, waiting for her to come to him. Apparently, he wanted some alone time in her office.

A frail voice drifted toward her. "Howdy, Sunshine."

Mrs. Fairborn. Sun waved at the elderly woman who'd set up shop at Quincy's desk. "Hey, Mrs. Fairborn. How's the confession coming?"

"Fantastic. How do you spell *bloodcurdling*?"

"I'll help you with that, Mrs. F.," Anita said, scooting up a chair beside her.

Sun gave her another wave, then entered her office where she got a better view of Levi's battered face than she had that morning. It looked worse than she'd hoped it would. Not that he wasn't still ragingly handsome, but the deep blacks and blues around his left eye, not to mention his mouth, were troubling. Thankfully— and astoundingly—there wasn't much swelling, but the subconjunctival hemorrhage had completely discolored the white of his left eye, leaving it a bright blood red.

"Please tell me you had that checked out."

"Please tell me you found them."

"Can you answer my question?"

"As soon as you answer mine."

"You know, you're still under arrest."

"I've been under arrest for months. What makes today any different?"

He was right. She'd arrested him, unofficially, four months ago when he'd first confessed to killing his uncle Kubrick. At the time, she suspected he only confessed because Hailey had beat him to the punch. She was the first of many to confess. But he knew things about the killing that Hailey hadn't.

"Did you find them or not?" he asked.

"The assailants? No." She almost didn't want to ask the next question, but she needed to know. "Did you?"

He turned his back to her, clearly angry. "Are you even looking?"

"Hey," she said, offended. "You know we are. We've had some developments."

"Great. Because developments will help."

"I don't think I like your attitude, mister." She shoved her free hand onto her hip. "Which could only mean one thing. You're in a massive amount of pain." Even when she'd seen Levi at his angriest, he was rarely a straight-up asshole to her.

He turned to face her again. Her statement seemed to steal some of his thunder. "*Massive* is a strong word."

She stepped closer. "Quincy, can you close the door?"

"Sure, boss. Which side would you like me on?"

"This one. I need a witness."

He did as ordered and waited.

"A witness for what?" Levi asked.

She set her coffee on her desk. "Take off your shirt."

The intrigued brow that formed a questioning arch did nothing to slow her pulse. "You don't need a witness for that."

"I don't. You do." When he crossed his arms over his chest, refusing to cooperate—shocker—she said, "Look, either you let me do this or I'm arresting you and watching while Quincy strip searches you."

"For the love of God, Ravinder," Quincy said, "let her check you out."

Most likely, any internal bleeding from the hit-and-run would've manifested by now. He would hardly be standing. She hoped the danger had passed since he seemed strong as ever. But better safe than sorry.

Favoring one side of his body, he lifted his shirt over his head with a grunt. He could barely lift his left arm high enough, but he managed to get the shirt off and hold it firmly in a clenched fist. He was freshly showered and the woodsy scent of patchouli filled the room.

Along with the scrapes and bruises she'd expected to see was a massive, platter-sized bruise along his left ribcage with petechial hemorrhaging down that side of his torso.

Sporting her best poker face, she walked around him. His wide shoulders tapered down to a lean, muscular back that had not fared any better. It had deep gashes, probably from being dragged across the gravel, that needed to be looked after.

She walked around to face him again and lifted a hand to his bruised jaw, fighting the urge to send it all the way around his neck. To pull him closer. To lock him to her.

His shimmering gaze trailed from her eyes to her mouth where it lingered a long moment. "So, in your far-from-expert opinion, what's the prognosis?"

She dropped her hand. "First, you should be in a hospital."

"And second?"

"I don't believe for a minute you found nothing out there. I can't force you to tell me, Levi, but we should be working *with* each other, not against."

"That's convenient."

She crossed her arms over her chest. "Meaning?"

"Suddenly we're colleagues? You sure you don't want to arrest me again?"

"I'm still considering it," she said, stepping closer. "Don't push me."

He clenched his jaw and admitted, "I found the truck."

Why she would be surprised, Sun had no idea, but she was. She schooled her features. He was sharing. According to Auri, sharing was caring, but she only said that when Sun had ice cream.

"And the man you injured?"

"The man I killed?" he corrected. "Not in it, if that's what you mean. They burned it to the ground at an abandoned warehouse near Las Vegas."

"They didn't get far," she said, surprised no one called it in. Las Vegas, New Mexico, was only about forty-five minutes from Del Sol and fires were not taken lightly in the arid state.

"That means they had to dump the body somewhere between Del Sol and Las Vegas, but damned if I can find it."

"Do you think they buried it?"

"They wouldn't have taken the time. I got the VIN, but I doubt it belonged to any of the assailants."

"And you're sure there was no body?"

"I told you. He would have bled to death in a matter of seconds. They dumped the body, I just can't find where. And with all that blood, they had no choice but to burn the evidence."

She nodded. "I'm going to need that baseball cap."

"It's in my truck."

"Covered in your DNA."

He shrugged, completely remorseless.

"Quincy, do you mind?"

Without breaking eye contact, Levi fished his keys out of his pocket and tossed them to her chief deputy.

After he left, she held out her hand. "And the knife."

He dove into his other front pocket and brought out a foldable hunting knife. She reached over him, grabbed an evidence bag and opened it up. "Is there a reason you took this?"

He held it up to her. "Besides the initials and the intricate engraving? No."

"You were trying to trace it back to the engraver."

After he dropped it inside, he nodded. "Yes."

"And?"

"Denver artist. Sold it at a convention, but the initials were added later."

"Did he have a record of the transaction?"

"The guy paid cash."

"Damn it."

He dropped his gaze, and asked, "How's Red?"

She sealed the bag and reached around him again to put it on her desk, unwilling to give up her prime location just yet. "Worried about you."

He bit down, the muscles in his jaw working. "I'm sorry."

"She adores you."

His gaze bounced back to hers. "The feeling is mutual."

His admission caused a warmth to blossom in her chest. "Thank you."

He let appreciation soften his features.

"You know, even with the badge, I'm not a real threat to you, Levi. I never was."

He scoffed. "Shine, you are the only person on the planet I do feel threatened by." He spread his knees apart as though encouraging her to inch closer. "Nothing you do or say is going to change that. Extra points for effort, though."

Under the guise of concern, she reached up and ran her fingertips along the bruises on his cheek, down to his lean jaw, over to his full mouth.

"Just so you know," he said softly, "we have an audience."

Startled, Sun turned to see Zee, Salazar, Anita, and Mrs. Fairborn gaping at them through the wide-open door. "Oh, shit," she said, lunging away from him. She brushed herself off and straightened. "Thank you, Levi. I can't believe I tripped."

"They've been watching for, like, five minutes."

"Hey, Mrs. Fairborn. How's the confession coming?" she asked again, discomfort prickling along her nerve endings.

"Not as good as your interrogation," the spitfire said. She wiggled her brows.

Zee fought a grin as Salazar and Anita busied themselves with paperwork. Mrs. Fairborn gave her a thumbs-up.

Sun cleared her throat. "Way to sheriff, Sunshine. I need to call Las Vegas PD. Where was that truck exactly?"

"North of Airport Road off 25," Levi said. "I think it used to be a mobile-home construction facility or something."

"You can tell me later how you found it. For now, call your sister."

Levi acquiesced with a nod, carefully donned his shirt, and walked out.

She followed.

"How do you spell *massacre*?" Mrs. Fairborn asked Levi.

He chuckled as Quincy brought the cap into the bullpen, signed, sealed in an evidence bag, and delivered. Metaphorically speaking.

Sun nodded a thank you. "Let's get this to forensics."

"Sure thing, boss."

"I just called Pres," she said, referring to the hospital where they'd taken Keith Seabright.

Levi whirled around to her. "How is he?"

"He's alive. Critical but stable. You were right about the tox screen."

"I know."

She stepped closer. "Levi, how much do you know about him?"

"We've been friends for a few years, but he's very private. I just know he was in Special Forces and is now a survivalist living off-grid."

"Let me show you something." She led him to Zee's computer. After sitting in Zee's chair, she gestured for him to take Salazar's and showed him Elliot. "Do you know this kid?"

He scooted closer for a better look, then lifted a shoulder. "That's his nephew, Eli."

Her gaze darted to Quincy. "Elliot."

Quince walked over, his expression pensive.

"Who's Elliot?" Levi asked.

"Elliot Kent was abducted from his home in Santa Fe seven years ago. He would be twelve now." She gestured toward the screen. "And he would look exactly like that."

"Are you saying you think Seabright abducted a kid?"

"Do you have another explanation?"

He sat back in the chair, clearly angry. "Eli is Seabright's sister's kid. They live in Bisbee. He stays with him a lot in the summers and during hunting season."

"Levi, Keith Seabright had only one sister and she died when he was ten. She was fourteen. She never had a kid."

Levi looked like the air had been knocked out of his lungs. "You're wrong. He would never abduct a kid."

"We can figure that out later. But if Eli was abducted and Keith's in the hospital, that means Eli is alone and . . . and possibly imprisoned."

The look he gave her would've killed a lesser being. "You're wrong." He stood and stormed out.

She caught up to him and stopped him at the front entrance by throwing herself into his path, an act of desperation comparable to playing in oncoming traffic. She put a hand on his arm.

He speared her with a glare worthy of a king. "Move. I'm going to find Eli." He started around her, but she stepped into his path again.

"You know where he lives?"

He gave her a reluctant shake of his head. "No, but I have a good idea."

"Hold on." She took out her phone and called one of her favorite places on Earth.

"Who are you calling?"

"He's a kid," she said, putting the phone up to her ear. "What kid doesn't like pizza?"

"Adobe Oven," a male voice said.

"Hey, Ernie."

"Hey, Sunshine. Need a pie to go?" How he always recognized her voice when he got dozens of calls a day was beyond her.

"I'm actually calling on official business."

"Sounds serious."

"It is. And you can help save a kid's life," she said, priming him. He was well within his rights to refuse to answer her. Ernie had always liked her. She hoped that would help grease the wheels. "I know this is asking a lot, but can you give me the address of a customer you deliver to? A Keith Seabright?"

"I'm sorry, love. I can't."

Damn it. She was hoping to forgo the warrant talk. "Ernie, Keith is in the hospital and we need to find his nephew. It's urgent."

"No, I mean I literally can't. I don't have an address for them. One of them always meets us at Tinsley's Crossing."

"Oh." She glanced up at Levi. Tinsley's Crossing was about five miles north of town and led to any number of homesteads.

He nodded, so the information must've matched his notion of where they lived.

"Thanks, Ernie. Oh, wait. Can you tell me the last time they ordered?"

"Sure." She heard him punch some keys on a computer. "I know it's been at least a week. Yeah, here we go. They ordered sandwiches and a pie a week ago Friday."

Darn. "Okay, thanks, Ernie." She was hoping Eli had ordered something to eat in the last couple of days. That would imply he was simply on his own and not locked up somewhere.

"How is he?" Ernie asked. "Mr. Seabright?"

"He's still breathing."

"I'll pray it stays that way."

"Thank you." She hung up. "Is that the right area?"

"It is."

"Then I may know where they're staying." She looked toward the plate glass window and gestured to Quincy.

"I think I know, too. I should go out there alone."

"And why is that?"

"Seabright doesn't need a bunch of bumbling deputies trampling all over his place."

"No offense, Levi, but I don't give a rat's ass what Keith Seabright needs right now. My only concern is that boy." She crossed her arms. "I'm coming with you, and you don't have a say in the matter."

He mimicked her, crossing his arms, too. "No, you're not, and I think I do."

Quincy walked past them, carrying a tactical bag and a shotgun. "Quit being a dick, Ravinder. Let's go."

"Fine," Levi said to Sun through clenched teeth. "We'll take my truck"

"You and Zee follow," she said to Quincy, hurrying to Levi's truck.

She called Rojas as she hopped inside the dark cab to fill him in. "Keep an eye on our visitors. Watch what they do when we leave."

"You got it, boss."

She hung up and called Anita. "Call SFPD and find out if there have been any developments on the Elliot Kent case. Anything at all."

"Absolutely."

She heard Mrs. Fairborn in the background. "Does *Hennessy* have one N or two?"

"You don't know?" Anita asked.

"I just drink the stuff. I don't read the label."

Sun hung up and looked at Levi. "This town needs an observation deck."

"Are we doing it this time?" Cruz asked Auri.

She'd convinced her mom she had a study hour in preparation for upcoming exams, and their teacher had allowed them to go on a coffee run as long as they brought him one, too. Her mom must've really been off her game to fall for it. Probably the life-or-death thing with Hailey. Auri would get the rest of that story later. For now, she'd gotten away with skipping. She had to take full advantage.

She checked with her inside man. Mrs. F. was still confessing and, if history repeated itself, she'd be there all day. They'd make her tea and buy her lunch. She would fill out a detailed confession and then one of the deputies would drive her home.

Sadly, the former sheriff, Baldwin Redding, wouldn't put up with Mrs. Fairborn's confessions, so she'd had to get the mayor involved. He finally started letting her confess again, but he didn't like it.

Of course, if he was anything like his son, an upperclassman at Del Sol High, he didn't like much of anything unless it involved footballs, girls, and kegs.

"We're doing this," she said, determination driving her forward. Inch by inch.

"Okay, just one more step," Sybil said, urging her to put one foot in front of the other.

They were outside Mrs. Fairborn's back door again and had been there for the last ten minutes. It stood wide open, just waiting to swallow them whole.

"I can do this."

"Yes, you can," Sybil agreed.

It was crazy that Sybil was the one encouraging her to break the law.

She gave up. Her feet just wouldn't move any farther. "Maybe we should try again tomorrow."

Cruz tilted his head. "And you know about a crime tonight that she will be confessing to tomorrow?"

She bit her bottom lip. Before she could come up with another stall tactic—and her stall tactics were legendary according to her mother—Cruz hopped off the back porch, stalked forward, and threw her over his shoulder.

She squeaked as he carried her inside.

"We're in," he said, setting her on her feet, then closing the door.

A warmth spread over her when she realized he'd put his hand on her butt when he set her down.

He stood back but kept his hands on her shoulders until she'd steadied herself. "You good?"

She cleared her throat and nodded. "Yes. I'm good. Thanks."

He nodded and looked around. "I say we each take a room."

Mrs. Fairborn's house hadn't changed much since the old boardinghouse days. Auri had read all about it. It had seven rooms upstairs and three down, along with a living room, drawing room, whatever that was, dining room, and kitchen back when kitchens were hardly the focal point they were today.

"This is going to take forever," Sybil said, turning full circle.

Auri walked to a small bedroom off the kitchen. The housekeeper's quarters, according to the old floor plans she found. The door was locked. She turned to Cruz. "Maybe not."

He grinned and knelt to pick the lock. "You'll have to show me how to do that someday."

"And give up my position on the team? My lockpicking abilities are the only reason you brought me along, so not likely."

He opened the door and offered a regal bow, gesturing for her to go first.

Auri walked across the threshold and sucked in a soft breath. Entering that room was like stepping back in time. Newspaper clippings, the same ones Auri had been reading, papered one wall. A dresser sat weighted down with old perfume bottles, powder tins, shaving kits, and scented lotions. Dark wood furniture. Baby blue chenille bedspread. Lace doilies. A painted tin pitcher and water bowl. It was all so amazing. So reminiscent of a different era.

Yet everything had been cleaned recently. Not a speck of dust on anything.

"It's like an antique store in here," Auri said, her tone full of awe.

"But unless there are some kind of identifying marks on these items," Cruz said, "we can't connect them to any of the missing persons."

Sybil stood in awe, too. "Whatever you do, don't move a thing. If you pick something up, put it back the way you found it. This stuff is well cared for. Mrs. Fairborn will know if someone's been in here."

"Agreed."

They slowly started picking up items, one-by-one, to see if anything had a name etched into it. After twenty minutes, they found nothing but a fascination of all things old.

"This stuff is incredible."

"They really liked lavender," Sybil said, crinkling her nose. "And talcum powder."

Auri looked over. Cruz was going through the books on a nightstand. Naturally. He was a poet himself and wrote some of the most beautiful poems Auri had ever read.

He opened a book and waved her over. "There's a name, but I don't recognize it from the list of missing persons."

Auri took out her phone and snapped a shot of the name Virginia Bagwell. "I don't recognize it, either."

"It may be nothing," he said, closing the book and repositioning it.

"I'll look into the victims' relatives. You never know."

"I have a question, though," Sybil said, sniffing yet another bottle of perfume. "Where do you think she buried them?"

Simultaneously, as though the move were choreographed, they all dropped their gazes to the wooden floor beneath their feet.

Panic took hold of Sybil. She looked back at them a microsecond before she tore out of the house. A high-pitched shriek followed in her wake.

"Sybil wait," Auri said, trying to put a tobacco tin back where she found it.

Cruz took off after her. Finally satisfied, Auri followed, but just as she got to the door of the room, something shiny captured her attention. She skidded to a halt and looked at a handful of necklaces dangling from a hook by a chest of drawers. One necklace in particular, actually. She'd seen a picture of it. An antique cameo made from real ivory set in a heavy brass oval.

She remembered the article about the missing girl who'd worn it because in the interview, the girl was a poor relation of the family searching for her, the one that seemed more worried about the necklace than the girl. It broke Auri's heart.

She pulled her phone out of her pocket and snapped a shot of the necklace before racing out the back door straight into the welcoming arms of Deputy Poetry Rojas.

15

Man arrested for practicing karate on swans.
The swans won.

—DEL SOL POLICE BLOTTER

Anita texted as they headed out to Tinsley's Crossing. Other than a couple of reported sightings that never led anywhere, Santa Fe PD had no movement on the Elliot Kent case. Sun wondered if anyone even looked into the sightings. They certainly never told her about them since she'd become sheriff, and she had been lead detective.

She also got a text from her blind date from hell, which she ignored. Because that would make the problem go away. And a text from her former partner-in-crime and the queen of bad decision making, Nancy Danforth, asking her if she would be in town soon and suggesting they get a drink. Getting a drink with Nancy was never a good idea, yet Sun fairly drooled at the thought. She missed her. Simple as that.

Though no one could take Quincy's place in Sun's heart, Nancy came in at a close second. She'd been her only true girlfriend in the city and fun didn't begin to cover Nancy's list of admirable traits. Sadly, moderation was not one of them.

She texted her back. *Let's make a date, but you have to promise you won't lose your underwear again. Or hire male strippers.*

Her phone dinged almost instantly. *LMAO. Deal.*

Since the cab of Levi's truck was filled with a dark and impenetrable silence—he was sulking—Sun decided to stop glancing at his magnificent profile every few seconds and do some research on their stabbing victim. She didn't know how long she'd have enough of a signal to get internet.

There wasn't much on the elusive Mr. Seabright. Levi had been right. The guy was a ghost. Other than the fact that there were apparently a dozen Keith Seabrights in the state, after sifting through those, she managed to find a few mentions on various military enthusiast sites.

The only two pictures she found of him were grainy and could have been shots of her great-aunt Sally for all Sun knew. Then a post popped up on Facebook. A pregnant woman in El Paso, Texas, claimed an assailant in a ski mask had hijacked her car with her two-year-old son inside. He held a gun on her and had ordered her to drive out of the city.

They were at a stoplight when a soldier dressed in army fatigues, average height, dark hair, walked across the crosswalk. He looked inside the car and must've noticed how scared she was, but she thought he'd kept walking. A few seconds later, the passenger's side door opened and the man was ripped out.

The woman didn't hesitate. She floored it and drove straight to a police substation. The post went on to explain the Army had no knowledge of one of their soldiers intervening in a civilian altercation.

A link led to a news clip on the incident. A reporter held a microphone up to a by-the-book police chief. "The move was risky. He couldn't have known the gun wasn't loaded. It could've gone off and we would never authorize or condone the use of that kind of force." Another officer came onto the screen. "Let's call a tomato a tomato. The guy's a hero."

Nothing she read about the guy, if any of it was actually about him, led her to believe him capable of kidnapping. She was leaning farther and farther in Levi's direction and not just physically, because he was like gravity.

"As far as you could tell," she began, choosing her words carefully, "from the times you interacted with him, Seabright's nephew, Eli, was not being held against his will?"

After a sideways glance that held more glare than curiosity, he said, "Not at all."

"And you're sure he only has him in the summers?" If that were the case, where was Elliot Kent the rest of the year?

His left shoulder rose just enough to make him tighten in reaction to the pain the movement caused. "No," he said, his voice strained. "Sometimes Eli was with him. Sometimes he wasn't. That doesn't mean he snatched the kid."

He turned up a bumpy mountain road and winced. She pretended not to notice.

"You said he was hypervigilant Saturday night, like he was on a job. What exactly does Keith Seabright do?"

"Odd jobs here and there from what I could tell."

"So like handyman stuff?"

"Yeah."

"And that would require the need for hypervigilance? Because building a shelf over someone's toilet is so dangerous." When he didn't answer, she exhaled. Loudly. So he would know she'd done it and she meant every molecule of air that left her lungs, too. "Levi, you're still legally bound to this office. To the badge. You were deputized, a fact you only seem to remember when it benefits you."

Former sheriff Redding had been the first to deputize Levi long before Sun came along. Levi was not only a legit businessman despite his upbringing, he was an expert tracker due to his summers being spent with the man many considered to be his biological grandfather.

After another reluctant moment, he caved. "Seabright's been known to do a side job here and there for certain . . . government agencies."

"He's a mercenary?"

"Only when it's for a good cause. He left the do-as-you're-ordered life ten years ago."

"I've never met a mercenary."

"That you know of."

"True. So now he hunts and picks berries and uses gas-generated power to charge his cell?"

"He usually gets his berries from the farmer's market, but yeah. Pretty much."

The farther up the mountain they went, the rougher the road became. Sun looked in the rearview to make sure Quincy and Zee were still with them.

"You're thinking what I'm thinking. He's staying at Walden's old place."

"That would be my guess."

"You weren't kidding when you said he lived off-grid."

"Nope."

Walden had been living in town for the last few years, which worked better for him since he owned the only convenience-store-slash-gas-station in the area, but he'd once lived in a mobile home on his family's land. The home burned down, but the hook-ups were still there.

Sun thought back to how evasive Walden was when they'd questioned him. "I'm beginning to think Walden knows more about Seabright than he's letting on."

"It wouldn't surprise me."

"But if Seabright is so off-grid, will Eli be okay? What if he's out here alone?"

An unconcerned smile spread across his face. "That kid could weather a winter in the Siberian tundra. Seabright taught him everything he knows." He thought a moment, then asked, "Do you think the attempt on Seabright's life has anything to do with Eli?"

She'd wondered that, too. "I have no clue. We certainly can't rule it out, though what one has to do with the other is lost on me. How do you know him?"

"Seabright? He'd come into the bar sometimes and we got to talking. On top of everything else, he's a certified electrician and did a few odd jobs at the distillery for me. Got to know him a bit. He'd bring Eli around every so often."

She ticked off the man's attributes on her fingers. "So he was in Special Forces, is a certified electrician, lives off the land, and does odd jobs for distilleries and secret government agencies. A true jack-of-all-trades. How did Elliot even end up with him?"

Levi studied the road, if one could call it that, his expression a mixture of concern and contemplation.

"The fact that your friend is a mercenary does shed a new light on things. I just can't fathom how. Or why."

"I was thinking the same thing." The truck dipped as they traveled over a large pothole and Levi's jaw flexed in response.

"Can I do anything?" she asked.

He glanced over at her in surprise. "I think you're capable of just about anything."

A grin widened her mouth before she reined it in. "I meant to help. This is clearly painful for you."

"Ah. Open the glovebox."

She did, assuming there'd be a bottle of painkillers inside, but she only saw registration and maintenance papers and an insurance card.

"Underneath the manual."

She lifted the truck manual and felt around until she pulled out an envelope.

"You can take that home with you. Keep it safe. It would make me feel better."

"What is it?"

"My will."

The deadpan she graced him with only made him laugh. In turn, he winced again, much to her delight. "Hey, you asked."

"Are you planning on dying soon?"

"No, but plans change." He said it with such finality, it stopped her from probing further, and they rode in silence after that.

She folded the envelope in half and stuffed it in her bag. It made sense that he'd have a will. He was now worth a small fortune. And the fact that he didn't trust his family hardly surprised her, but why give it to her? Why not just leave it with his lawyer?

After a thousand years of solitude, Sun started singing "Oklahoma" in her head just to give it something else to do besides think about the man sitting next to her. The case—or cases, depending—gave her a headache. The possibilities were simply too vast, and until they dug deeper, there was no sense in speculating. She needed more solid evidence to form an official opinion.

They pulled up to a cabin Sun hadn't known existed. No sign of a burned-out mobile home in sight. Not that she knew all of the small hunting cabins in the area, but this one was actually pretty nice. The exterior well-maintained and any fire hazards kept far away from the main dwelling.

"Is this Walden's place?"

"Used to be. He built a hunting cabin but told me once he never used it and was thinking about selling. That was years ago. So either Seabright bought it from him or he's renting from whomever did."

After the team took up position, Quincy on the southeast corner and Zee on the northwest, Sun and Levi took the stairs to the porch. Sun stood to one side, and knocked. When they got no response, she knocked again. "Sheriff's office. We need to talk to Eli about his uncle. Is he in?"

Still nothing. She tested the doorknob. Despite having three dead bolts, the front door was unlocked. She glanced back at Levi in question.

He shook his head. "He'd never leave it unlocked."

A tingling sensation raced up her spine. She drew her weapon and eased inside. Small for a house but rather large for a hunting cabin, the interior was bright and airy with finished walls and a loft on one side. Large windows allowed for natural light to filter in through the trees when it could and solid furnishings graced a corner here and there.

"Eli?" Sun said, crisscrossing one foot in front of the other, her duty weapon in both hands at her side. "Your uncle Keith has been injured. We just want to make sure you're okay."

She came to a small room under the loft. It was filled with the usual plethora of weapons one would expect to find in a hunter's cabin, but it also had a TV and an Xbox that ran on a generator next to an outbuilding. There was also a small desk and a bookshelf lined with books. Fiction mostly, both kid and adult, but several textbooks as well on every subject from history and English to science and algebra.

"Has Seabright been homeschooling him?" Sun asked.

Levi's expression would suggest he was just as surprised.

One of the books sat open on the desk with a pencil and notebook beside it. Elliot, or Eli, seemed to be working his way through Algebra Two. "Not bad," Sun said, checking over his work.

Sun went to the back door and let Zee in. "Nothing, boss."

"Thank you." She turned to Quince as he entered.

He shook his head. "Not a sign of him."

They did a quick survey of the rest of the cabin, then holstered their duty weapons.

Quincy lifted a pan. "It looks like they haven't been here in days."

"That's a decoy," Levi said.

Quincy raised it to show him. "It's a pot of beans."

He grinned. "A pot of decoy beans. It's not real. It's meant to throw anyone who might be looking for them off their trail. He was here this morning."

Sun's heart raced into overdrive. After all this time, could she really be this close to finding Elliot Kent? "How do you know?" she asked him.

He grabbed a toothbrush out of a small medicine cabinet in the bathroom and tossed it to her.

"It's damp," she said to Quince.

Quince took out an evidence bag, and she dropped it in. If nothing else, they could test the DNA, make sure it was Elliot.

Levi tested a towel hanging on a rack. "I'd say he's only been gone a couple of hours."

"Seabright's good," Zee said, inspecting the corner of the cabin where Eli clearly slept.

Sun noticed it was nearest the pellet stove, the best place to be in the winter, but between two windows to catch the cooling breeze in the summer. "Good in what way?"

"You said Eli was from Bisbee?" Zee asked Levi.

He nodded.

"See this?" She lifted an ashtray with the word *Bisbee* displayed across it, and Levi smiled knowingly.

"A decoy?" Sun asked.

She nodded. "A decoy."

"How do you know?"

"Look at all of this stuff." She gestured to the multitude of cheap keepsakes. "You would only find these at a travel center off the highway. Have you ever been to Bisbee? Nobody who's actually from a town has this much dime-store crap on display. He's no more from Bisbee than I'm from Mars."

"I drove through there once," Quincy said, helpfully. "Bisbee. Not Mars." Again, helpful.

Sun was one step closer to finding the kid. Elliot Kent. She'd dreamed of him so often. Prayed he was okay even though statistically the odds were beyond astronomical.

"He could be watching us right now," Levi said.

"You think?" Sun walked to a window that looked out over the mountainside. "Levi, he sent us a signal in the Quick-Mart. A clear cry for help. Why would he do that if he weren't in danger?"

"If that were the case," Quincy said, "why not just go to the sheriff's station?"

Levi shook his head. "I don't know, but something spooked

him. He would never leave the door open." He looked at her. "I can track him. But he probably took off on his dirt bike."

"Thus, he's long gone."

"Right, but let's think about this. Seabright and the kid came back out here after the run-in at the store."

"Right," Sun said. "Maybe Seabright brought him out here to keep him safe? Then he went back into town to try to figure out what was going on? That man tried to stab him outside the store. He had to know it wasn't random."

Levi nodded. "That's why he was being so hypervigilant. He knew someone was after him."

"He knew there was a hit out on him," Quincy said.

Sun chewed her lower lip. "If that's true, why wasn't he carrying that night?"

"No firearms inside of any business that serves alcohol," Levi said, eyeing her like she'd lost her mind. "No exceptions. I thought you knew the law."

"I am well aware of the law, but then why go into the bar in the first place? If he couldn't carry a weapon inside?"

Levi dropped his gaze and cursed under his breath. "He needed to talk to me. Son of a bitch. If I'd known . . . I was outside . . . talking to another patron."

"Ah, yes. Crystal." Only according to Crystal, there wasn't a lot of talking going on.

He cast her a curious glance. "Yes. She was talking about her boyfriend. And she asked me for a job."

"Classic. So, you're a counselor, too?"

"All bartenders are counselors."

"In all the years your family has owned that bar, I have never once seen you tend bar."

"Because you've been in there so often," he said, his words dripping with sarcasm.

Quincy lifted a serrated hunting knife. "You said Seabright headed back to his truck before he got to talk to you?"

"Yes," Levi said. "He probably knew he'd been drugged."

She turned to her team. "I need to get to Santa Fe and talk to Elliot's mother personally." She looked at Levi. "Can you give them a lift and I'll take your cruiser, Quince?"

"I'll take you," Levi said.

Quince looked at her askance. She nodded in agreement, so he asked, "Should we call in a team to process this place?"

"Not just yet. Let's try to get Eli to come to us first." She sat at his desk, ripped a page out of his notebook, and began a letter. "But just to be safe, try to get some fingerprints and a DNA sample."

Zee hopped to it. "You got it, boss."

Once Sun had cell service again, she checked in with Anita. "How's it going with Mrs. Fairborn?"

"That woman has a very active imagination."

"Yeah?"

"Can we publish her confessions and make money off of them?"

"No."

"Boss," she said, pleading, "this one has aliens."

"No way." She cupped her hand over her phone. "Send it to me as soon as she's finished." Reading Mrs. Fairborn's confessions had become the highlight of their day. She'd once confessed to stealing a pool noodle and using it in a bank robbery that led to a night of debauchery with a male stripper named Chad. The problem was she never explained how the pool noodle played into the bank robbery.

Either way, the woman had missed her calling.

"You got it, boss," Anita said with a giggle. "Also, Las Vegas PD called. They found the truck and the owner. It was reported stolen from a hotel in Trinidad on Friday. The owner was traveling and slept through the whole thing."

"Surveillance?"

"All the hotel got was a black-clad male, medium build, who could steal a truck in under sixty seconds."

"They targeted it for the Texas plates to throw us off." She looked over at Levi. "Well, most of us."

He winked at her. *Winked!* She could only take so much of that man.

"Are you worried about him?" she asked Levi after she hung up.

"Which one?"

"Either, I guess. Both."

"Then yes."

They'd made it back to the main road, so his white-knuckled grip on the steering wheel eased a little.

"How are you to drive?"

"Fine."

"Are you certain?"

"Don't I look fine?"

He did indeed. "It's just, if you need to take something for the pain, I can take over."

"I don't need to take anything for the pain."

"I could've sworn I smelled whiskey earlier."

He smirked. "I could've sworn I smelled wine."

"Damn. Really? I've had a lot of coffee since last night." Her experiment with Quincy was the gift that kept on giving.

"Unless your coffee was made with fermented grapes, I'd say the wine is still in your system."

That was disturbing.

Just like she had with Hailey, Sun considered not telling Levi about her visit with Wynn, but part of her really wanted to see his reaction. To gauge it. She steeled herself and said, "I wasn't going to tell you this until I had more information, but I went to see your uncle Wynn yesterday."

He was so much better at the poker thing than she was. Instead of reacting at all, he stilled and kept his gaze laser-locked on the road. The only indication he even heard her was when the muscle in his jaw jumped under the pressure of his bite.

"He says he killed your uncle Kubrick."

Nothing.

"Which is funny, since you told me you did it."

Zip.

"Then again, half the town has confessed to that killing."

Zero.

"Including Jimmy."

That got him. He turned to her in surprise. "Jimmy?"

"Mind telling me why half the town is confessing to a fifteen-year-old murder?"

"My nephew, Jimmy?"

"The one and only."

He cursed and turned away from her. "They're all lying."

"Including Wynn? The DNA test came back with a match. Wynn Ravinder."

He looked down in confusion, then said, "That's not possible."

"DNA tests don't lie."

"But people do."

"You have another explanation?"

"I already gave it to you. I killed him." His tone was razor-sharp when he added, "He's playing you."

Sun looked out the window. "The evidence says otherwise. He's requested to be moved to Santa Fe. The DA is getting it done as we speak."

As though that answered everything, he leaned his head back, the barest hint of a smile lining his mouth. "Of course."

"He also says he knows who Kubrick's accomplice was," she added, her stomach clenching at the thought. "Auri's biological father."

The stunned expression he turned on her made her take a mental step back. "Is that what this is about?" His reaction was genuine. Nobody was that good.

"He's going to sign a full confession," she said, testing him further, "and tell me who the accomplice was in exchange for the move."

Her phone rang, the sound just sharp enough to cut through the tension.

"Hey, Quince," she said, thankful for the interruption.

"You aren't going to believe this."

She sat up straighter and put him on speakerphone. "Try me."

"Guess who got paroled a couple of weeks ago. And there's no way this is a coincidence, boss."

It took her a sec, but then it dawned on her. "No way."

"Yep. Matthew Kent. Elliot's father."

16

Caller reported a suspicious man carrying
duct tape, rope, and a shovel.
Chief Deputy Cooper responded.
It was the stock boy at Del Sol Hardware.

—DEL SOL POLICE BLOTTER

Mrs. Kent still lived in the same house she had during Mr. Kent's trial. The same house Elliot went missing from. As happened often in child abduction cases where the children were never found, she'd never moved. She even drove the same maroon minivan, now scarred and falling apart.

Sun knocked on the door, and the woman who answered was hardly recognizable. Her lids were lined with red, her nose pink from a fresh bout of tears.

"Mrs. Kent?" Sun said, stepping closer.

"My husband isn't home," she said. She started to close the door, but Sun showed her ID to stop her. It was only then that Mrs. Kent took a closer look.

"I'm Sunshine Vicram. I was the lead detective on Elliot's case."

The surprise that registered on her face was unmistakable. "Detective Vicram?" she said, as though unable to believe it.

"Sheriff now. But please call me Sunshine. How are you?"

Her demeanor did a one-eighty. Changed from surprise to

wariness. She looked over her shoulder, and said, "I'm okay. Is there—is everything all right? Have you heard anything?"

"May we come in?"

She hesitated, trying to come up with an excuse not to let them in. Apparently finding none, she reluctantly opened the door. She seemed healthy and yet there was a frailness to her. A nervousness.

When Levi stepped across the threshold, she gasped aloud. "Occupational hazard," he said to explain his general appearance.

"Are you going somewhere?" Sun asked. The entryway was lined with luggage.

A child, no more than six or seven by the sound of his voice, called out to her, "Mom, can I bring Harold?"

"Sure, honey." She looked back at Sun. "His turtle. I'm . . . we're going to my mother's house in Albuquerque for a few days." She kept them as close to the door as she could without being rude.

"Oh. Is your husband going, too?"

She bit down. "No. He's not. In fact, he'll be home any minute. Is there something you needed?"

"Yes. Do you know a man named Keith Seabright?"

Sun's poker face needed a little work done—a nip here, a tuck there—but Addison Kent's needed a complete transplant.

"No," she said after wresting her expression back into neutral.

Sun put a hand on her arm. "Addison, you know you can tell me anything."

Her nerves fried, she shook her head. "There's nothing to tell, Sunshine. Is that all you wanted? We need to get on the road."

A young boy ran into the entryway and plopped down a cage with a turtle in it. "Are you here for Daddy?" he asked.

Levi laughed softly.

"No, honey," Sun said. "Is this Harold?"

"The second. Harold the first escaped last year."

"Oh. Little scoundrel."

He laughed and took off again.

"Addison, are you in danger?"

"What?"

"Your husband just got out of prison and you're escaping to your mother's."

She released a breath she'd been holding. "No. We're fine. Matthew is just . . . working through some things."

"And it would be safer for you at your mother's," Sun said, finishing the thought for her.

"Something like that."

She handed her a card. "Please call me if you hear anything."

"Anything?" she asked, the wariness back in her voice.

"Anything you feel is important." Sun gave her a reassuring nod then left her standing in the entryway.

They climbed back into Levi's truck, but they didn't talk until he pulled onto St. Francis, heading toward I-25.

"That was interesting," he said.

"Yes, it was."

"What are you thinking?"

"I think this entire thing revolves around Elliot's father, Matthew Kent, and the money they never found."

"How much?"

"Fifty million, give or take, and that's the lower end of what the investigators speculated."

He whistled. "Even I would kill for that much."

"Really?"

"Depends on how much I like the person."

"Matthew swore he was simply the fall guy for the whole operation. Said the higher-ups took the money and ran, leaving him holding the empty bag, so to speak. And the FBI scoured the man's records. If he did hide it, he's a stone genius."

"You think now that he's out someone is coming after it?"

"It's a possibility."

"But how does Elliot play into all of this?"

"I don't know."

"She has to know he's alive. Clearly she knows Seabright."

"I'm shocked you would think that, after that stellar performance she gave in denying she knew him."

"That was painful to watch."

Sun laughed. "Poor thing. It all makes so much sense now. The Kents never really, I don't know, behaved appropriately? Does that sound bad?"

"Not as bad as their faking their own son's abduction. Who better to have abduct your child than a trained mercenary?"

She nodded. "A noble one who would give his life to keep him safe."

"My question is," he said, turning onto the northbound on-ramp, "was she in it with Seabright alone, or was the husband involved, too?"

"He was involved," she said, matter-of-fact.

"You sound certain."

"Twenty-twenty hindsight. No wonder Addison stayed in the area, so close to Santa Fe. Matthew was in prison there, sure, but she would never leave Elliot. She risked jail to keep him safe."

"But from what?"

"I think Matthew has some explaining to do."

Her phone rang. She grabbed it and said, "Hey, Quince. We're on our way back."

"You might want to hurry."

Great. "What's going on?" she asked, dread knotting her stomach.

"We caught a bandit red-handed."

"Like a shoplifter?"

"Something like that."

"And you need me there because?"

"I'm pretty sure she's related to you."

"She?" What did her mother do now?

"You know. Five feet nada. Red hair. Enough sass to peel the tarnish off a brass elephant."

After Sun took a long—very long—moment to let his words sink in, she said, "Auri shoplifted?"

"What?" Levi said from beside her. He reached over, grabbed the phone, put it on speakerphone, then repeated, "What?"

Quincy chuckled. "Chill. Auri didn't shoplift. She would never do that."

Relief flooded every cell in Sun's body.

"Shoplifting is so last year. She's more of a criminal master-mind now. She's been arrested for breaking and entering."

Sun finally knew what it felt like for the world to drop out from under her.

Sun couldn't get out of Levi's truck fast enough. She gritted her teeth as she went through the electronic doors and hurried to the bullpen.

Levi followed at a slower pace.

"Where is she?"

"Sun," Quincy said, patting the air with his palms, "first make sure you're calm."

Quincy had explained the bare minimum over the phone. All she knew was that her genius daughter and her two cohorts broke into Mrs. Fairborn's house, but they didn't know why as the little shit had lawyered up.

Lawyered up!

She gaped at Quincy. "Did you really just tell me to calm down?"

"He did, boss," Rojas said helpfully.

"I'm just saying you should probably take it down a notch."

"And now you're trying to de-notch me?"

"He is, boss."

"The St. Aubins picked up Sybil and Cruz's dad is out of town," Quincy said, moving past his comments. "We tried to call through a relay, but he had a bad connection, so we had to text. He said he'll be home first thing tomorrow."

"I took him home," Rojas said.

"The good news is," Quincy continued, "Mrs. Fairborn is not pressing charges."

"I took her home, too."

"Thank you, Rojas." She sank onto Quincy's chair. "What the actual hell?"

"You'll have to ask your offspring for the answer to that."

"Wait." She looked around. "Where is she?"

Quincy grinned. "She's in the holding cell."

"Good." She looked at Rojas. "What about the men casing the town? Any movement?"

"You were right. The minute you guys took off for Seabright's place, one of them followed."

"I didn't see anyone," Levi said.

"Oh, that's because I pulled him over for speeding." He handed Sun a printout of the guy's license.

"You were right," she said to him. "New Jersey. Now we have his info and his agenda."

"They're after Elliot," Levi said, reading over her shoulder. "I need to get out there. I'll do it a little stealthier this time. See if I can't catch him unaware."

"I'd appreciate that. Maybe I should go with you? After I see to my daughter, of course."

Sun opened the metal door to the holding cell, sad it wasn't actual bars that she could clang shut behind her to give her daughter a taste of her life to come. She did the next best thing and slammed it. The boom echoed throughout the station.

Auri sat on the edge of the stainless steel cot looking at her feet. A small trash can sat beside her half full of used tissues. Sun braced herself. Tears or no tears, the girl deserved a thrashing.

"Let me get this straight," she said, standing over her. "You convinced Cruz and Sybil to skip school with you so you could break into Mrs. Fairborn's house to prove she was once a serial killer."

Auri raised her head and looked at her like she was a mind reader. "How did you know?"

"I've seen the articles in your grandmother's attic. I thought the same thing when I was a kid."

"Why didn't you do anything about it?"

"Like break into her house?"

"Which shows initiative, right?"

"Auri, you broke the law. The very thing I stand for. You broke into an elderly woman's house. What if she'd been home?"

"She wasn't," she said between hiccups. "I made sure."

"And just how did you do that?"

"I have a guy on the inside."

Fury enveloped her. "Quincy."

"What?" Guilt consumed the redhead. "No. It . . . it wasn't him."

"He. Is. Dead."

"He didn't know why I was asking, Mom. It's not his fault."

"It never is."

She covered her face with her hands as sobs took over. "I'm getting everyone in trouble."

"What did you think would happen, Auri? The mayor is down my throat. The DA is watching every move I make. The former sheriff is looking for any excuse to get me removed from office."

Auri's tears began anew. "I'm sorry, Mom. But doesn't it matter that Mrs. Fairborn really did it?"

"So, what? You've already tried and convicted her?"

"No." She sobbed again.

"Sweetheart," she said, grappling for the strength to finish what needed to be done. She had to learn a lesson she'd never forget. "You're forgetting one important fact. Serial killers don't stop. Something or someone stops them. The stuff you found proves nothing other than Mrs. Fairborn is a collector."

"Of dead bodies!"

She sat beside the redhead. "Auri, even if you're right, there is a procedure. Mrs. Fairborn's rights need to be protected. You can't just break in looking for evidence."

"But I knew you wouldn't get me a search warrant."

She had to turn away, astonished at Auri's determination. She was dedicated to the cause, Sun would give her that.

"I have more work to do. I'll call your grandparents to come pick you up."

"Are you going to tell them?"

"Of course I am. You have to know there are consequences to your actions, Aurora."

A fresh flow of tears began, but she lifted her chin and nodded. "I'm sorry, Mom."

"And I'm sorry about today."

She blinked up at her. "Today?"

"With Hailey."

"I didn't know you and Jimmy's mom were friends."

"We are, but no one can know that. Not just yet. It has to be our secret."

"On account of Clay trying to take over Dark River Shine from Levi?"

Sun stumbled over her thoughts. "Who told you that?"

"Jimmy."

Shaking her head, she said, "That kid doesn't miss a thing."

"Nope. But I'm glad you're friends with his mom, now. I like her."

"I do, too."

"And she's teaching me how to make corn whiskey."

She pinched the bridge of her nose. "Of course, she is."

She left her daughter to suffer a few minutes more and walked out to the bullpen to a sea of expectant faces. This was the moment her deputies learned to respect or revile her.

"Arrest all three of them tomorrow."

Levi straightened as though ready to ride to Auri's defense, but Quincy beat him to the punch.

"Sorry, boss. I can't do that."

"Quince," she said, exasperated. "This is hard enough. I can't be that sheriff. I can't let my kid get away with murder."

"Sun, she hasn't killed anyone. Yet," he added. "That we know of."

"We didn't document anything anyway, boss," Rojas said.

"We just wanted to scare the crap out of them. I got the call. I made the decision. This isn't on you."

Quincy pointed to him in agreement. "Not to mention the fact that Mrs. Fairborn isn't pressing charges."

"Speaking of which." She stepped closer to Quince and glared up at him. "Did you, perhaps, wonder why my daughter wanted to know if Mrs. Fairborn was in the office giving her confession?"

He scrubbed his face with a hand. "She said she wanted to come in and talk to her about an old article she found."

"And if she asked you to store a box of old dynamite she found in an alley somewhere?"

"I would . . . seriously question her motives."

"Sure."

She heard her mother's voice echo across the station. "Sunshine!"

Anita had led her parents back. They rushed to her. "Where is that baby?" Elaine asked, her gaze darting about.

"Mom, that baby has committed a serious crime."

"Sunshine Blaze Vicram," she said, scolding her. For real? "She didn't do it on purpose."

"Mother, that is exactly what she did."

"Well, yes, but she had good intentions."

"I give up." She turned and nodded to Rojas.

He opened the holding cell and let loose the kraken. It ran across the bullpen and jumped into the open arms of the two most whipped people in all of Del Sol. Besides Sunshine herself. And, apparently, Levi.

Auri turned and gave him a hug, too. "I'm sorry, Levi."

"For what?"

"I just . . . I don't want to be a disappointment to you."

He set her back and lifted her chin. "That's not even possible."

She hugged him again and he kissed the top of her head. From there, she went from deputy to deputy giving out hugs and apologies like they were a politician's promises. The imp even hugged Rojas.

He stepped to Sun when her parents took her, and said, "She's good."

"I know. Damn it."

"Boss," Salazar said from her computer. She was so quiet, Sun hadn't even realized she was in. "I think I found something."

She walked to her desk and leaned down.

The young deputy was reviewing the footage from the store again. She froze the frame right after Elliot showed his face. "We were all so focused on his identity that I think we missed something." The others joined them. "Watch what he does before he walks out and gets into Seabright's pickup."

She rewound a few seconds and pressed play. Elliot returned a can to the shelf, then turned to the camera. "Sorry. A little farther back." She rewound again and played the footage. That time Elliot picked up the can and seemed to put something under it before he put it back and turned to the camera.

"Wait," Sun said. "Play that again."

She went back even farther. Elliot raised something to the camera, turned and placed it on the shelf, then put the can over it. The picture was so grainy, it was hard to tell what it was.

"Holy crap, Salazar. Good eye."

"Thanks, boss."

"Is that a note?" Levi asked.

She turned to him. "Let's find out."

Along with Levi and Quincy, Sun hurried over to the store. On the way, Levi asked, "Who's Carver?" He must've seen a text from the guy.

"Blind date." She shoved the glass door open and hurried inside.

"Hey, Sheriff," Lottie said.

"Hey, Lottie." Sun chose to forgive the girl for the seizure she'd faked so that Levi could get away. "Have you seen this kid in here tonight?" She showed her a printout of Elliot.

The girl pursed her lips in thought. "I don't think so."

"Thanks. Let me know if you do?"

"Sure thing, Sheriff." The girl turned to Levi and Quincy and changed the tone of her voice. "Hey, Mr. Ravinder. Hey, Quincy."

Sun rolled her eyes and went to the canned goods aisle. Sure enough, Elliot had stashed a note underneath a can of tuna. She put on a pair of gloves and opened it. There, written in a kid's scribble, was the word *Sorry*. She showed her cohorts the note.

"Sorry for what?" Levi asked.

Quincy shrugged. "Kids will sometimes take on the guilt for anything that goes wrong in their lives. Maybe he felt bad about Seabright being attacked."

She shook her head. "This was about the same time the guy tried to stab him, but Elliot couldn't have seen that from this vantage. And it was hours before Seabright was attacked at the bar."

"You're right," he said, frowning. "It's like he knew something bad was about to happen."

Levi scrubbed the non-banged-up side of his face and strode out the door.

What would a twelve-year-old kid who, for all intents and purposes, had been abducted years ago have to be sorry about? And why, if he'd been coming into town with Seabright all those years, would he signal them now? And in such an obscure way? How did he know they would be looking at the surveillance footage? Unless . . .

Unless he was somehow involved.

17

Many have eaten here. Few have died.

—SIGN IN THE KITCHEN OF SUNSHINE VICRAM

There were three reasons Auri adored her grandparents. Well, there were a million, but three main ones. One, they loved her. Two, that love was unconditional, no matter how bad she screwed up. And three, they made certain she felt that love to the marrow of her bones.

Even if she was never allowed to see Sybil again after introducing her to a life of crime and degradation. Even if Cruz never wanted to see her again after turning him into one of Del Sol's most wanted. Even if her mother lost her job and never spoke to her again and they ended up living on the streets of Del Sol, rifling through their neighbors' trash cans for food, she knew she would always have her grandparents. And that they would feed her.

"How about some pizza?" her grandpa asked after escorting her into the house.

"I don't deserve pizza," she said.

His expression turned pensive as he nodded. "You're right. How about I order it with extra pineapple as punishment."

She laughed and hugged them both before heading to her room, where she overheard him ordering. Pepperoni with extra pepperoni.

Oh, yeah. They loved her.

She texted Sybil, expecting a furious text from her mother ordering her to never go near her child again. Instead, Sybil texted back. *Auri! What happened? What did your mom do? Are you grounded for life? For all of eternity? Are we going to prison? Wait, let me call.*

She laughed and picked up mid-ring. "Hey."

"Hey, Auri. What's the verdict?"

"Still waiting on the sentence hearing, but so far it looks like prison will not be in our future. Mrs. Fairborn isn't going to press charges."

"Oh, thank God."

"You know what this means, right?"

After a minute, Sybil guessed, "We don't have to learn how to make weapons out of our toothbrushes?"

"No. Well, yes. But more importantly, it means Mrs. Fairborn is guilty."

"Holy crap, you're right! Why else wouldn't she press charges?"

"Exactly."

"We have to prove it."

"We will. I have to fix something first. I just wanted to check on you. Are you grounded?"

She let out a lengthy sigh. "No, but I would feel better if I were."

"Oh, no." Dread slid up Auri's spine like a snake. "What happened?"

"Can you imagine what it was like for my mother, getting a call about me from a sheriff's deputy after I almost died? Twice? She is so traumatized, Auri, she had to take a sleeping pill and go to bed."

Tears stung the backs of her eyes. She really knew how to leave a mark. "Sybil, I am so sorry."

"What? No. That's not what I was getting at," she said, her tone edgier than normal, "I am a big girl. It may not seem like it sometimes, but I can make my own decisions, and I chose to do this."

"Because of me."

"It was my decision. I am the one who has to live with what I just put my mother through. And my dad. He's downstairs drinking some of Mr. Ravinder's moonshine."

The guilt that swept over Auri made her feel nauseous. No matter what Sybil said, it was entirely, one hundred and ten percent, Auri's fault.

"Hold on," Sybil said. "What do you mean you have to fix something? Fix what?"

No way was she going to involve her best friend any more than she already had. "I'll tell you at school tomorrow."

"You realize we only have three weeks left," Sybil said, almost sadly.

A soft laugh escaped Auri. "You are the only person I know who gets sad when school lets out for the summer."

"I just like seeing you every day."

"And that has to change why?"

"We can still hang?"

"Sybil St. Aubin, we are going to have a blast this summer. You just wait. If I'm not in jail."

"You just said . . . why would you be in jail? Auri, what are you planning?"

"Nothing you need to worry your big brain about. See you tomorrow."

"Aurora!" she shouted as Auri hung up.

She knew she'd cave if Sybil pressed the issue. She needed to do this alone. She needed to fix her amateur mistake before she could go to her mother again. If she went to her mother again. Maybe, instead, she'd go to Quincy. He'd believe her.

Thing was, she adored Mrs. Fairborn. But did that mean she should just let her get away with murder? If she did, if she let her feelings influence her ability to do the right thing, to bring closure to those families who'd lost loved ones, what would that make her?

Cruz wasn't texting back and worry gnawed at her. She

could only hope his dad grounded him and nothing more. She'd screwed up before, but this was catastrophic on several levels. Levels she hadn't thought of before she decided to take the law into her own hands.

While she waited for word from him, she dug a little deeper into the origins of the necklace. It was so intricately carved, but even if it dated back to the Roman Empire, which that one didn't, it would still only be worth a few thousand dollars.

The way the family spoke in the interview they gave one reporter, that necklace was a family heirloom and worth more sentimentally than anything material they owned. They claimed the missing girl, Emily Press, was a poor relation and had stolen it when she'd come to visit.

She brought up the picture she'd snapped of the pendant and studied it again, enlarging it this way and that. The oval the cameo was set in wasn't even real gold. It was brass, bulky, and not particularly pretty, and it had patinaed with age.

"Pepperoni with extra pineapple," her grandma said as she brought Auri a slice.

Auri clicked out of the camera app and laughed as she looked at the plate. "That doesn't look like pineapple."

"Yeah, they forgot it. I could send it back."

"No!" Auri jumped up and grabbed the plate from her. She was starving. Apparently food in jail was not a given.

"Whatcha doin'?" her grandpa asked. He handed her a glass of sparkling water with cranberry.

"Thanks, Grandpa. Just some homework."

"If you want to talk about anything . . ."

"You mean how I ruined the lives of two of my best friends, may have gotten my mom fired, and disappointed everyone I know and love?"

"Yes," he said with a humorous grin. "But not everyone."

"You're not disappointed?"

"Please," her grandma said with a snort. "You have no idea what your mother put us through. You couldn't disappoint us any worse than she did that time she threw a party while we were out of town and invited an entire biker gang called the El Choppos, who used my bras to shoot water balloons at the neighbor's house."

"Oh," Auri said, genuinely concerned.

"Her defense was that she only let them use my old bras."

Her grandpa gave her a stern expression. "If you promise not to invite motorcycle clubs to our house, I think we'll be golden."

She giggled. "I promise."

"Then we're good, peanut."

"Always?"

"Always," he said.

After three slices of pizza, two glasses of sparkling water, and an hour and a half of research, Auri found a relation of Emily Press, the woman who went missing with the necklace.

From what Auri could tell, Billy Press, the owner of a car dealership in Amarillo, Texas, appeared to be in his early thirties. If her calculations were correct, he would be a great-grandson of Emily's uncle, which would make him her cousin, albeit distantly. She found him on Instagram and sent him a message with the shot of the necklace attached, telling him that she had been researching his cousin's case and asking if he recognized the pendant.

The message may have been jumping the gun a bit, but her family deserved to know what happened to Emily, and they deserved to get that necklace back.

But then what? Would sweet Mrs. Fairborn go to prison? Because of Auri? Because of her meddling? Her intrinsic need to set the world right? The families deserved to know the truth, but it had been decades. Maybe the truth could wait a little longer.

Still, she had pertinent information on a cold case. Could she be charged with obstructing justice if she didn't tell the truth?

With head spinning and stomach churning, Auri brushed her teeth and washed her face, then crawled into bed fully clothed. When her grandparents came in to check on her, she closed her eyes and deepened her breaths. They each took a turn kissing her head and her grandma tucked the covers tight before leaving.

Unfortunately, they didn't close her bedroom door all the way and closing it now would be a dead giveaway, so she would have to risk it. Deceiving her grandparents yet again was giving her heartburn, but she needed to know Cruz was okay. And, more importantly, she needed to apologize to him.

After waiting another half hour, she could hear her grandpa snoring and sprang into action. She hopped out of her window—or rather tumbled out of it—and eased her bike out of the drive.

Two cars passed her and her heart got stuck in her throat both times, praying her mom was still at work. Thankfully, both were false alarms.

Cruz's house was dark when she rode up, but his dad's truck was in the dirt driveway. Her heart sank. Had he come back early from his trip because Cruz had gotten into trouble?

She turned off her headlamp as she passed his dad's window and tripped twice as a result while sneaking up to Cruz's. She knocked lightly, but nothing happened, so she knocked again.

"You're going to kill yourself one of these days."

The high-pitched screech that erupted out of her throat would be talked about for generations to come. The night a velociraptor came to town and woke up the entire population of Del Sol. Some people confused it with the tornado sirens. Others, a newborn sperm whale.

Turning to the godlike creature stepping down from the truck, she clutched her chest and gasped. "You scared me."

"I never would've guessed."

"Is your dad back?"

He closed the door and dropped his gaze. "Not yet." After stuffing the keys into his pocket, he walked up to her. "What are you doing here?"

"You weren't answering your texts. I had to check on you."

Even in the darkness, Cruz's eyes shimmered when he

smiled. "It was my turn," he said, leading her to a bench on the front porch.

They sat, the only light radiating from a streetlamp a couple dozen feet away. "For what?"

"I was going to come check on you."

"Oh, well, my grandparents went to bed early."

He leaned back and crossed his arms over his chest. "Your mom's going to kill you. Then she'll kill your grandparents when she finds out how often you sneak out."

"Oh, they're already on her hit list. They keep setting her up on blind dates. I had to show you this." She scrolled through her phone until she came to the picture of the necklace.

He took it to get a closer look. "Is this from Mrs. Fairborn's house?"

"Yes. It's like the Hope Diamond of the missing persons cases. I read an interview with one of the victim's family members. An uncle, I think. It's like he didn't even care that his niece was missing. He seemed more worried about this old necklace."

She showed him the article with a picture of the necklace. "It's apparently really valuable, but from my research, it's only worth a few thousand dollars. Nothing that would trump his niece's safety."

"Where was it?"

"Hanging from a hook by the door. I grabbed a shot on the way out." She scooted closer. "This proves it, Cruz. Mrs. Fairborn is a serial killer."

"Holy shit." He looked at the picture and compared the two before handing her phone back. "You have to show that to your mom."

She raised her hand to chew on a nail. "I can't," she said from behind it. "What if Mrs. Fairborn goes to prison because of me?"

He reached over and pulled a fallen leaf out of her hair. Evidence of the tumble from her window. "If she goes to prison, it'll be because she most likely killed lots of people, but I get your point."

She sat mesmerized by the way his lashes cast a soft shadow on his cheeks for a few seconds, then looked past him at the truck. "Is everything okay?"

"What do you mean?"

She lowered her head and said softly, "I saw you. Deputy Rojas took our phones, but you pulled out another in the holding cell." Her gaze drifted back to his. "Were you texting Deputy Rojas pretending to be your father? Was that his phone?"

He pulled away from her. Just barely. Just enough for her to notice, and she only did that because a light breeze rushed over a part of her arm he'd been protecting.

"He doesn't actually know, yet, does he?" she asked, the realization startling. Why did he not only have his father's truck, but his phone as well?

"I'll tell him when he gets home."

"Tomorrow morning?"

When he offered her a barely perceptible nod, she decided to drop it. He was lying. She could tell.

"You'd tell me if something were wrong, right?"

A sad smile spread across a face so handsome it stole her breath. "Right."

Auri pedaled home more concerned than ever. In the last four months, Cruz's dad had only let his son drive his truck a few times, and only when he was with him. But now, all of a sudden, he gets to drive it all over town? And Cruz had his phone to boot?

She had to figure out a way to ask her mother about Chris De los Santos, Cruz's dad, without alerting her to the fact that something wasn't right. She thought back to the last time she'd seen him. It was before spring break at the end of March. She hadn't seen him since.

The Saviata Bridge was coming up, a narrow structure that bridged a shallow ravine. Having heard a vehicle approaching from behind her, Auri pulled to the side and waited with eyes

closed, praying it wasn't her mother. Or one of her mother's deputies. Or her grandparents.

A vision hit her of her grandparents going in to check on
her and finding her gone. They would panic. They would call her
mom, the FBI, and National Guard. And then they would bring
in the big guns. Her grandma's book club.

The car, a tricked-out Nissan with the bass turned up loud
enough to set off car alarms all over town, passed by without
incident. Or it would have if Auri had been paying attention to
her footing.

She was closer to the edge than she thought. Her foot slipped
out from under her as the car passed and she tumbled down the
ravine. Unfortunately, her bike followed.

Somewhere between doing the splits in midair and trying to
balance the bike on the balls of her feet to keep it from crushing
her head, she crash-landed on her back and slid the rest of the
way down the steep ravine.

She lay at the bottom, listening to the trickle of water that
bubbled mere inches from her head. After a moment, it became
clear that the person in the Nissan was not going to help. She
thought about calling out for help, but her rescuer could insist on
calling Emergency, then where would she be?

Pushing against the metal contraption she'd been trapped
under, she managed to move it a few inches before her foot slipped
and it crashed down on her again. Pain shot through her ankle and
shin. Her foot was somehow wedged between a metal bar and the
chain.

This was a job for Superman. Or Cruz. Same dif.

After some maneuvering, and a few stabs of pain that had
her seeing stars, she jammed her fingers into the slit in her jeans.
Her phone, which didn't quite fit all the way in her front pocket
anyway, must've flown out during her performance.

She groaned and looked around. Her headlamp, still on, par-
tially lit a small area off to her side. It picked up a flash of color in

the dark part of the ravine below the bridge. Surely that was her phone. How to get to it was the real question.

Nothing was broken. She was certain of it. Her foot had decided to jam itself through the metal frame at an odd angle, because that's what feet do. A car drove over the bridge, but the ravine was just steep enough to make it impossible for them to see her.

Leveraging her weight with her free arm, and wondering when she'd gained a hundred pounds because no way was she this weak, she huffed and puffed until she was a solid two inches closer to the flash of color. Reaching across the handlebars that were above her head, she angled the light for a clearer picture. It didn't help. She still couldn't tell what it was. Either way, it wasn't her phone.

She scanned the area around her and finally saw it a couple of feet up the side. The lamp reflected off it when she moved it in that direction. Now for the real challenge. She had to get her foot free. Then she could get to her phone and call for help if she needed it.

After another test, she gave up and found a stick instead. Careful not to move her foot, she used all the powers of elasticity she could muster from the universe and her body—mostly her body—and reached up to coax her phone closer. After eons of grunting and groaning and sticking her tongue out of the side of her mouth because for some reason that helped, it slid down the ravine straight into her outstretched hand.

It was like she had superpowers. She vowed to use them for good.

With the chain digging into her skin, she was just about to call Cruz when the object not ten feet from her piqued her curiosity again. It wasn't a usual shape like a bottle or a cup. It was ghostly in appearance and almost swan shaped.

In a last attempt to get a clearer image, she took a picture with her phone. But even with the night-vision mode, the image was grainy. She enlarged it until a shape formed. Something white and puffy. She enlarged the picture even more and just made out the shape of a hand, only it was swollen and disfigured.

Her stomach flip-flopped and clenched. She couldn't move. Just when she'd convinced herself it was probably a mannequin, the breeze shifted and the putrid scent of death hit her like a wrecking ball.

Her lungs seized and she went completely still, suddenly scared that whatever had happened to the person lying in the ravine could happen to her. She was, once again, smack-dab in the middle of a crime scene. A crime scene that had to be secured.

Glancing around, she lowered the brightness on her phone, now scared she would attract attention, and brought up her contacts. With shaking fingers, she dialed her mother's cell.

Her mom answered, her tone teasing. "It's late. And you are grounded from your phone for all eternity. This better be good."

"Mommy," she said, her voice as small as she could make it.

Auri could hear the alarm in her mom's voice when she said, "Sweetheart, what's wrong?"

"I—I think I found a dead body."

18

Despite the high cost of living, it remains popular.
Let us help you plan for your future!
—SIGN AT DEL SOL BROKERAGE AND PSYCHIC READINGS

Instead of accompanying Levi to the cabin to look for Elliot like she'd wanted, Sun spent the last few hours going over the case files and the trial records for Matthew Kent's conviction. Levi went without her. He promised to call the minute he knew something one way or another, but she didn't know if he had cell service. If he had a way to contact her.

Matthew Kent refused to name any of his accomplices, the people he said were actually pulling the strings, exclaiming to anyone who would listen that they would kill him. He played the fall-guy part for everything it was worth. And with Elliot's disappearance, he very nearly got away with it.

Investigators lost the money trail after it left a bank in the Caymans. Tens of millions of dollars. Money didn't just disappear. Someone had it, but by the looks of Addison Kent, it was not her or her husband.

In the pictures from the trial, Addison looked exhausted. Her dark hair unkempt. Her pale face hollow. She'd been through the wringer thanks to her husband. The fact that they were still married baffled Sun, but maybe Addison just didn't want to file for divorce while her husband was in prison.

She looked over at Rojas. He was still there, going through the footage from both the bar and the Quick-Mart, hoping to catch a glimpse of the men in the pickup. Without it, they had nothing.

"Rojas, I was impressed with you before I blackmailed you into joining the team. Go home. This can wait until tomorrow."

"What's your excuse then?" he asked. "You know, if it can wait." He stood and walked over to her. "You want me to make a fresh pot before I go?"

She smiled like he'd just offered her a little slice of heaven.

Headlights filtered through the front glass of the station. Levi pulled up and parked. He must not have found Elliot.

"I got it," Rojas said, going to let him in.

Her phone rang. She looked at the clock. Eleven thirty on a school night. Her daughter had better have a good excuse for staying up so late.

She clicked on the green button. "It's late. And you are grounded from your phone for all eternity. This better be good."

"Mommy," Auri said, her voice so soft she almost didn't hear her.

"Sweetheart, what's wrong?"

"I—I think I found a dead body."

Sun scrambled to her feet and followed Rojas out the front. "Where are you?"

"I fell."

She snapped her fingers at Rojas and signaled him to get to his cruiser. He nodded and took off toward his parked SUV while she commandeered Levi's vehicle. "Where, baby?" she asked.

Levi didn't hesitate. He climbed back into his pickup while Sun got into the passenger's side.

"You know that little bridge on Sunrise?"

"Saviata. Yes. I'm almost there."

Levi backed out and had her on Sunrise in less than two minutes. Rojas followed with his emergency flashers on.

They skidded to a halt and Levi was out the door faster than Sun could get unbuckled.

"Don't come down here!" Auri shouted.

Rojas brought out a flashlight and searched with the beam until it found her.

Levi started down the ravine.

"Don't come down here!" Auri shouted, giving it another shot. "It's a crime scene."

The smell hit Sun about that time and served only to spur her panic into hyperdrive. She followed Levi down.

"Crime! Scene!"

Ignoring Auri, Levi replied as eloquently as ever, "Bite. Me." He skidded to a halt on the incline, maneuvered around to her, then looked up at Rojas and clapped his hands once. Rojas tossed him the flashlight while he called for an ambulance.

"Levi," Auri said, visibly shaking.

"What the hell, Red?"

Sun kicked up enough dirt to bury them both when she tried to stop on the incline beside Levi.

"What part of crime scene is no one but me understanding?"

"Auri, baby, what happened?"

"I fell," she said. "And my bike came with me."

Levi shined the light. "Can you stand?"

"My foot is caught in the chain. Nothing is broken though. I'm not experiencing any nausea or extreme pain. I'm also not experiencing any dizziness or other signs of a concussion. I'm just tangled up. And there is a shooting pain in my ankle every time I try to move."

"Thank you for that assessment, Dr. Vicram," Sun said.

Levi shined the light on her ankle. "Ouch," he said. "We may have to cut this off you."

"With what?" Auri asked, panicking.

"Unless . . ." He studied it a bit more. "Can I try to lift this end up, Red?"

She nodded and took Sun's hand.

"If it hurts, tell me. I'll stop."

"Okay."

Sun kneeled closer to her. "Should I even ask what you're doing with a bike tangled around you in a ravine in the middle of the night?"

She pressed her lips together, then said meekly, "I had to apologize to Cruz."

"You couldn't text him?"

"He wasn't answering. I got worried."

"Auri," Sun admonished, but the girl drew in a sharp breath.

"There," Levi said, letting go of the bike. It slid the rest of the way down the ravine.

"You did it?" Auri asked, trying to sit up.

"Nah-uh." He pressed her back to the ground. "You stay where you are, Ricky Road Racer."

But she didn't. She threw her arms around his neck, shaking even harder.

"Where's that ambulance?" Sun shouted.

"On the way, boss," Rojas said. He'd found another flashlight.

"But for real," Auri said, talking into Levi's neck. "Dead body. Like two feet away."

"We'll worry about that in a minute," he said.

She let go. "I thought maybe whoever did it was still out here."

"Oh, baby." Sun pulled her into her arms.

"I have to take credit for this one," Levi said after shining a light on the half-covered body.

Sun heard the sirens getting closer. She put her hands over Auri's ears, fully aware she could still hear their conversation, but it offered Sun some consolation. "Is that your guy?"

He nodded. "That's him."

"You weren't kidding. He didn't even last two blocks."

"I never thought they'd dump him in the middle of town." He shined the light around the whole area. "He wasn't even dead when they tossed him. Look at all the blood."

"With friends like that."

"You guys know I can still hear you, right?" Auri asked.

Sun hugged her tighter, then looked up at Levi.

"I'm going to lift you up," he said to Auri. "If anything hurts, let me know."

"What's the plan?" Sun asked him.

He scanned the area. "I'm going to take her down and walk her to the railing. I can get her up from there."

Sun nodded. "Rojas, get Quince here to cordon off the area and call Albuquerque. We need another forensics team to process the scene."

"You got it, boss."

Levi lifted the lovebug of Sun's life into his arms. Auri wrapped herself around him as though he were a chocolate kiss and she was a piece of tinfoil.

Sun walked beside them, shining the light to help him maneuver the uneven ground.

"And wake up my parents!" she called over her shoulder.

Sun and Levi were watching the team from Albuquerque load the deceased man—naturally he had no ID on him—into the back of an ambulance to transport him to the OMI. They'd already been to urgent care with Auri, got her checked out, and sent her home, once again, with her grandparents. Maybe Sun was putting too much on them.

"Man," she said to Levi, "when you set out to kill a guy, you really throw yourself into the job."

"I try."

Her phone dinged with a text from Carver. She didn't even bother. It was almost three in the morning.

"That kid of yours is something else," Levi said.

"If that's your way of saying she's a trouble magnet, I agree."

"No more so than her mother." He said it with a lopsided grin that had nothing to do with the battered state of his face.

"True."

Auri had been beside herself at urgent care. "Grandma and Grandpa are going to be so mad."

"You don't think they have a right to be?" she asked as the nurse wrapped her sprained ankle.

She buried her face in her hands. "I keep screwing up. I just wanted to check on Cruz and—"

"Auri," Sun said, steeling herself. Her daughter needed to understand sneaking out would not be tolerated. Not in today's world. Hopefully the whole finding-a-dead-body thing would act as an extra layer of deterrent.

Auri's distress was killing Levi. He stood beside the divider curtain, arms crossed over his chest and working his jaw hard. A bigger sucker than even herself. Somehow that made her feel better.

"You purposely waited for them to go to bed before sneaking out. What does that imply?"

"Intent?" she asked from behind her cupped hands.

"Exactly. So what's going on?"

A ragged sob filtered through her fingers. "Cruz didn't pick up. I thought he might be in serious trouble with his dad. I wanted to explain to him that it was my fault. Since I was grounded for breaking and entering, I snuck out to go see him and apologize." She broke down into a fit of sobs. Getting her friends into trouble seemed to be the best punishment of all.

Still, there was more to it than that. It wasn't that Sun didn't believe her. She did. But there was something else going on. Now, however, was not the time to try to find out. Sun had to get back out to the crime scene. Her absence would give Auri some time to calm down. The fact that it would also give the inventive creature more time to come up with a better cover story did not escape her. But discipline could wait. Torment, however, could not.

"Auri, I'm just going to say this once."

She lowered her hands and looked at Sun, the tears glistening in her eyes like vise grips around Sun's heart.

Levi felt it, too. He shifted and dropped his gaze.

"When a young girl sneaks out to go see a boy in the middle

of the night, no matter how noble the reason, sometimes the boy's little friend—we'll call him Mr. Penis—wants to meet the girl's little friend—we'll call her Ms. Vagina."

"Oh, my God, Mom." She covered her face again.

And therein began the lesson as the nurse, who'd first regarded Sun with a shocked expression, struggled to suppress a smile. Others in the urgent care center gathered 'round to hear the timeless tales of Mr. Penis and Ms. Vagina. Because who wouldn't?

Well, besides Levi, who scrubbed his face and went for coffee.

When Sun finished with, "And that is why little girls never order nachos on a first date," she received a round of applause worthy of the greatest of thespians. "Finally, someone appreciates my talent."

"I'm filing for emaciation immediately."

"You do that, hon."

Sun turned and saw her parents standing in the doorway.

She stepped to them. "Do you think, and I know this is asking a lot, but do you think you could possibly keep your granddaughter from getting into any more trouble for the rest of the night?"

Her father shook his head. "I can't make any promises, Sheriff. Look who her mother is."

He had a point. They wheeled Auri out in a chair three times too big for her tiny body. Sun's chest tightened as the image replayed in her mind.

"No sign of Elliot?" she asked Levi when they went back out to the scene.

He shook his head. "He hasn't been back to the cabin."

"I get that he can take care of himself," she said, worry gnawing at her. She put a hand on his arm. "Levi, do you think they took him?"

He looked at her hand, then back at her. "No. He took off on his bike. And he had supplies. He was prepared. I'm sure Seabright had a contingency plan and Eli knew to go into hiding. I just don't know where."

"Can you find out?"

"I'll go back out in the morning and try to pick up his trail."

"Thank you. So, do you think the trauma of finding a dead body is enough of a punishment for the little vixen?" she asked, not sure why she was consulting Levi about parenting tactics.

"I do, but she doesn't need to know that. A few threats might go a long way."

"Oh, yeah? What kind of threats?"

"The usual. Cancel her cell service. Put a padlock on her bedroom door. Tell her the next dead body she's going to find will be Cruz De los Santos's."

She nodded. "Look at you, being all dadlike." She'd caught the tail end of a surprised expression a microsecond before he recovered. "You're amazing with Jimmy," she added, referring to how he was with his sister's kid. A kid who happened to be on the spectrum. It didn't stop Levi for a minute. "And with Auri." Honestly, the way he was with her astonished Sun to no end. "You'll make a great dad someday."

He regarded her for a long moment before commenting with an inscrutable, "You don't say."

Her phone rang before she could think up a comeback, which was too bad. She was great at comebacks.

She didn't recognize the number. "Sheriff Vicram."

A female voice, small and reminiscent of Auri's in the ravine, floated through the speaker. "Sunshine?"

"Speaking."

"Sunshine, it's Addison."

Sun's first thought was that Addison had Elliot with her. That he'd found his way home. But her voice was too thin. Too frightened, and alarm shot through her. "Addison, what's wrong?"

"It's Adam. My seven-year-old. He's"—her voice cracked—"he's missing."

Thirty minutes later, Sun and Levi pulled up to the Kent house in Santa Fe. The local police had the place surrounded and had flooded the area with lights.

Sun recognized several of the officers on duty as they ducked under the tape and strode into the house, making sure not to disturb the area.

Ronald Aranda, a detective she'd worked with for years, sat on a wingback across from Mr. and Mrs. Kent in the living room.

"I put him to bed at nine," Addison said, her voice breaking, "like I always do." She sobbed into a tissue. Mr. Kent sat beside her, but they did not touch. There was no comforting in either direction

"Did you hear anything?" Ronald asked.

"No. I—I didn't go to bed until late and went to check on him before I turned in. He was gone." She broke down.

Addison was dressed in jeans and a white button-down, sneakers, and a light jacket, none of which looked hastily thrown on. Meaning she'd still been wearing them at three in the morning.

Sun couldn't help but note that Mrs. Kent's anguish was more . . . genuine this time around? She'd cried when Elliot went missing, but Sun had always felt that she and Matthew were holding something back. She'd been devastated, but in a different way. This was as real as it got.

"Detective," she said to Ronald when she and Levi entered.

The detective stood and took her hand, genuinely pleased to see her. There was nobody better, in Sun's opinion. The Kents were in good hands.

Addison jumped up. "Sunshine." She rushed into Sunshine's arms while her husband, Matthew, looked on, his posture guarded, his expression pensive.

"What happened?" Sun asked.

Levi stood back and did as she'd asked him to do in the cruiser. He observed. Maybe he would see something she didn't.

"I went to check on him and he was gone," she repeated, this time leading Sun to Adam's bedroom.

Sun tossed Ronald an apologetic look over her shoulder; he shook his head and sat back down to talk to Matthew, basically giving Sun his okay. She was butting into his case, after all.

Levi followed them back. He tapped her shoulder and gestured toward the Kents' bedroom. A suitcase sat open on the bed as though she was packing it. Or repacking it.

"He was right here," Addison said, sweeping into Adam's room and gesturing toward a bed in the shape of a race car. "I put him to bed, and then I stayed up to get some work done. When I came back, he was gone."

The woman visibly shook, her pale face full of apprehension.

Sun took her hand to try to steady her. "I thought you guys were going to Albuquerque to stay with your mom?"

She tossed a furtive glance over her shoulder. "Matthew asked me to stay. Said we needed to work things out." She stepped forward and pleaded with her. "You have to find him, Sunshine."

Besides being utterly confused, considering her failed first attempt at finding a missing Kent child, Sun understood her grief, and her heart broke for the woman.

"Addison, Ronald Aranda is an excellent detective. Any interference from me would be frowned upon."

"Do you think I care?" she asked, "He can frown all he wants. You know us. You know me. I want you on this case."

"Okay, besides the fact that this is out of my jurisdiction, why would you want me, Addison? I never found Elliot. I never even got close."

Addison sank onto the bed. "You're wrong, Sunshine. You did find him. You almost ruined everything."

19

After a short period of recovery, Sun asked Addison to explain how she almost found Elliot when she'd always believed she'd never even come close.

"Somehow you connected the dots," she said, shaking her head. "Dots we never expected anyone to connect. You tracked Elliot and his bodyguard to a house near Tesuque."

Sun frowned. "No, I was wrong. There was no one there. That house had been vacant for weeks." Then she remembered the cabin. She turned to Levi. "The pot of beans?"

He lifted a shoulder.

"The house had a loaf of bread on the counter that had about two weeks' worth of mold on it. It was a setup?" When he shrugged again, she gaped at him, then turned back to Addison. "They had been there?"

"Not had. Were," she said. "They were in a hideout under the floorboards. You stood right over them. You came within seconds of catching them red-handed, Sunshine. A minute earlier and you would have."

Sun sat at a small desk chair, unable to believe it. While she was working to find the Kents' son, they were working to keep him hidden.

"Why?" she asked, even though her research on Matthew Kent's case told her pretty much everything she needed to know.

"We got a call," Addison began. "We don't know from who. A sympathetic party. She told us they were going to kidnap Elliot and hold him until Matthew turned over the money."

"The fifty million."

She nodded. "Or more. Who knows? But he swore he didn't have it. If he did, Sun, I never saw it. Matthew is an asshole. Don't get me wrong. And he deserved to go to prison for his part in what happened to all of those people, but he would never risk Elliot's life. He would've turned over the money."

"That's when you had Elliot kidnapped. Before the real bad guys could do it."

She nodded. "Matthew found a man willing to help us. I don't know how or where or who paid him. All I know is that we met Keith Seabright in a dark alley, literally. He explained what we needed to do. Things like, be sure to break the window from the outside. Knock some toys onto the floor. Pull the sheets to one side like the kidnapper dragged him out of his bed."

"He's thorough."

"And then . . ." A sob wrenched from her throat. "And then we just handed our baby over to him. A complete stranger." She covered her mouth with a hand as another sob racked her fragile shoulders.

"Did it work?" Sun asked. "Was it the Delmar family? Did they leave you alone after that?"

"After Matthew pointed the finger at them, they backed off. They didn't know who took him, either, and since they'd been planning to do it, I think the fact that Elliot was yanked out from under them made them take a step back."

Sun was very aware that Matthew pointed the finger at Antony Delmar. She'd investigated the family for weeks.

"And then?"

Addison drew in a deep breath. "Seabright stayed in the area. For us. For me. After a few weeks, we started to meet up so I could see Elliot in secret. My baby boy. I took every opportunity and probably too many chances, but I saw him every moment I could. I got pregnant right before Matthew's trial. I had Adam alone. After he got old enough to be curious about Elliot, old enough to ask questions, we told him the same thing Seabright told everyone else. That Elliot—Eli—was his sister's son."

Sun sat stunned. All those sleepless nights. All the anxiety and guilt and heartache. Their son's life was being threatened. They had to make it look good. But damn.

"It was only supposed to be for a little while," she continued. "He was supposed to miraculously be found. But Matthew swore the Delmars were waiting for him to slip up. That Elliot's life was still in danger."

Sun's brows slid together. "But if they were going to all that trouble to get the money from him, and Matthew swears he never had it—"

"Then where's the money," Addison finished for her, matter-of-fact. "I have asked Matthew that same thing for almost eight years. If I believed in magic, I'd say it vanished."

"How much of this does Elliot know?" Levi asked.

Addison blinked up at him. "You're Seabright's friend."

He gave her a half-hearted smile. "I used to think so."

"You are. He talks about you all the time. He admires what you did with your distillery." She stood. "Please don't let the fact that he never told you about Elliot bother you. We didn't tell anyone. Ever. Sunshine," she said, kneeling in front of her. "Even my own mother doesn't know." She winced. "She's going to hate me when she finds out the truth."

Sun suddenly felt better about being left out of the loop. She also detected a hint of shame in Addison's demeanor.

"To answer your question, Mr. Ravinder, Elliot knows everything. Seabright insisted. He would not lie to him. He's much too honorable. But it doesn't matter now. Seabright's in the hospital, Elliot is out there alone, and Adam is missing." She pleaded with Sun. "You're the only one who knows, Sunshine. Please find Adam."

Did the men scoping out the town take him? Did they work for the Delmar family? The family who insisted Matthew Kent stole their money? But if he had, why was Addison still driving the same beat-up minivan after all these years? Why was Addison having to work two jobs just to make ends meet?

Nothing added up.

"How is he?" Addison asked. She swallowed hard. "Seabright."

"You're in love with him."

She dropped her gaze, and whispered, "Yes."

"He's stable. That's all I know."

She nodded as fresh tears filled the space between her lashes.

"Is that why you're leaving your husband?"

She looked out the window. "I was going to leave Matthew before all of this started, eight years ago. Then he was arrested and we were thrust into the public eye and . . . and then everything with Elliot. Seabright has been a rock for me. And he grew to love my son as much as I do. Both of them. He would do anything for Elliot, including die for him."

"Do you think the men who attacked Seabright were after Elliot?"

"I don't know. But it's the only explanation, right? I mean, it has to be. But we don't have the money, Sunshine. What are they going to do to Adam when they demand it and we can't pay?"

Sun looked back at Levi who stood by the door with his arms crossed over his chest. He let his gaze slide past her and, with the barest hint of a nod, gestured for her to look.

The forensic team was coming down the hall toward them and they were about to be kicked out.

Sun turned and looked at one of the paintings on Adam's desk. A stick-figure family stood in front of a house with a yellow sun shining down on them. It was a mom and a dad and two boys. Across the youngest boy, written in a bold black marker, was the word *Sorry.*

Sun turned to stone, curbing her reaction. Schooling her features. She looked back to Addison. "I'll do everything I can, Addison. We may have a lead."

Addison's face brightened.

Sun bent her head closer as the team stepped inside. "Between you and me, yeah?"

She nodded.

"Don't even tell Matthew," she whispered.

"Sunshine, I stopped telling Matthew anything years ago. As far as I'm concerned, he got us into this mess by doing business with those people when he knew the deals were shady. He deserves nothing from me."

"Good for you. Call me if you hear anything."

Addison pulled her into a hug. "Thank you, Sunshine. Thank you."

"Don't thank me yet. I have a feeling our kidnapper is every bit as clever as the man who trained him."

Levi stayed close on her heels as they walked out of the house. Once they were out of earshot, he asked. "Did you see it?"

"I did."

They strode to her cruiser.

Once behind the wheel, she looked at Levi, more confused now than ever. "I don't get it. Why would Elliot take his own brother?"

"He's scared. There's more to this than meets the eye, and he is right at the center of it."

"I agree." She started the SUV and backed onto the narrow street.

"Sorry," he said, repeating the message on the painting.

She put it into drive. "Right. Not *I'm sorry.* Just *Sorry.* The same as the note at the Quick-Mart. It's like—" She slammed on the brakes well before the stop sign. Levi pitched forward, then raised a sexy, albeit bruised, brow at her. Thankfully, no one was behind them, because she sat there for a few seconds before explaining. "Sorry."

"Exactly," he said, clearly wondering about her.

When he didn't catch on, she repeated, "No, *Sorry.*"

She saw it the minute it dawned. "Wait, do you think—?"

"I do."

He sat back as realization washed over him. "Holy shit."

"You drive." She jumped out and played fire drill with Levi before climbing back in. He fastened his belt and pulled onto St. Francis while Sun did what she did best. She called in everyone.

Everyone.

Even with the painkillers the doctor gave her at urgent care, Auri couldn't sleep, and it was due to the worst, most selfish reason possible. She'd found a dead body and she had to tell someone. Namely Sybil and Cruz. And since her grandparents were insisting she stay home and miss a day of school—*the horror*—she couldn't tell them at said school as per her original plan.

Thus, she did the next best thing. She waited as long as she possibly could, a.k.a. six o'clock in the morning, and sent them both an *RU up yet?* text.

Sybil answered first with a saucy, *No. WTHeck?*

Cruz must've still been asleep. So Sybil would get to hear the news first. His loss.

Auri called her.

Sybil answered with a simple, "I told you I'm not up."

"Oh. My bad. I just thought you might want to know about the dead body I found."

"I'm up!"

Auri relayed the story about going over to Cruz's, falling into the ravine, dabbling in a little light bondage with her bike chain, and finding the body of the guy Levi killed. Sybil filled any empty airtime with a comical number of oohs and ahs.

"Was he, you know, bloated?" she asked.

"His hand was. That's really all I saw. I took a picture of it. It was very disturbing."

"You have to send it to me!"

"Are you sure?"

"Yes. How am I going to become a medical examiner if I can't study dead things?"

"True. Maybe when I become a detective, we'll end up working together."

"That would be amazing. We could be like Rizzoli and Isles!"

Auri laughed. "Totally."

"How's your ankle?"

"It's fine. Just a slight sprain. My pride hurts worse."

While she was busy talking to Sybil on the phone, Auri opened her laptop and saw a message from the cousin of the missing woman who stole the necklace.

"They're making you stay home?" Sybil asked, her voice turning whiny.

Auri chuckled. "Just today. They think I'm traumatized."

"You are. You can't *not* be."

"I don't know." She looked deep inside herself, but not too deep as she was a little scared of heights. "Maybe."

"Definitely."

She decided not to argue. "I'll let you go so you can get ready."

"Okay. Watch the soaps and fill me in."

"You got it." Auri hung up, then read Billy's message. Billy Press, the thirty-something car salesman from Amarillo who Auri believed to be Emily Press's cousin, had responded to her message faster than she thought he would.

Dear Aurora,

Thank you for writing. I could hardly believe it when I saw the picture you sent. I really think that's my cousin's necklace! And it's been found after all these years? My family is floored. I would love to chat and hear all about it. If it's

okay with your parents, can you give me a call? Any time,
day or night.

I look forward to hearing from you,
Billy

A part of Auri regretted sending that picture when she did, but now maybe the necklace would find its rightful owners.

But, again, what would happen to Mrs. Fairborn? Why would she still have it after all these years if she weren't the killer? What other explanation was there?

"You're up," her grandma said from her open door. She still wore the tattered turquoise robe Auri's mom teased her about mercilessly. The one that her grandmother demanded she be buried in because *its comfort transcends life itself.* Her words.

"I made bacon," she said.

"Why do you think I'm up?" Few things made her mouth water like the smell of bacon sizzling in the morning.

Auri once asked her mom why there wasn't bacon-scented perfume. She said there was. Bacon grease.

Auri tried it. It wasn't as appealing as she thought it would be.

"How are you feeling?" her grandma asked.

"I'm better. I'm sorry I snuck out, Grandma."

The woman sat on her bed and rubbed Auri's knee, careful to avoid her ankle. "Are you going to tell me what's going on?"

"What do you mean?"

"First you skip school and break into a friend of mine's home. Then you sneak out. Next thing you know, you'll be caught smoking behind the bleachers and playing chicken for pink slips on a dark deserted highway with a boy named Snake."

Auri scoffed. "Please. If I play chicken, it's not going to be with a boy named Snake. That's a horrible name for a car guy. His name will be Flash or Rocket or NOS-feratu. Get it? N-O-S-feratu?"

Her grandma smiled, but Auri could see the worry behind it. "You know you can talk to us about anything, right?"

"I know, Grandma. And I do have a question."

"Oh." She scooted farther onto the bed. "Ask away, peanut."

"Let's say that there is a sweet little old lady in town who used to be a, oh, I don't know, a serial killer of sorts."

Her grandma nodded her head in thought, playing along.

"And let's say, hypothetically, that she hasn't killed anyone in years."

"Okay, I'm with you."

"And everyone in town likes her."

"Mm-hm."

"And she's a little crazy but not in a dangerous way."

She stifled a grin. "Got it."

"It's just, would it matter if she were brought to justice? I mean, she doesn't have that much longer to live, right? So, would her going to prison for the rest of her life change anything?"

Her grandma sat back, her head bowed in thought. "I see where you're going with this."

"I was so dead set on bringing a serial killer to justice, I didn't even think about Mrs.—the woman in question. I mean, from what I can tell, she doesn't have a cruel bone in her body. If anything, she's too generous. And then Mom said that serial killers rarely stop of their own accord. Something or someone stops them." She hugged her pillow to her and sat back in frustration. "Maybe I'm wrong, Grandma. But I'm not." She pleaded with her. "I have irrefutable evidence."

"What kind of evidence?" she asked, suspiciously.

"I mean, I don't *have it* have it," she said, her voice rising a notch in panic. "I just know about it."

"I see. Well, could it have been anyone else? Perhaps another family member?"

"I thought of that, too, but she only had her husband and he went missing before the cases stopped. There was one more victim after his disappearance, the very man the police suspected did it, so her husband couldn't have done it. And Hercules Holmes was accused of murder and possibly killed because of one person's actions. Shouldn't his name be cleared? Shouldn't his family know that he wasn't a killer? That he was innocent?"

Her grandma drew in a deep breath and pressed a hand to Auri's chest. "I think all the answers you're searching for are in here, peanut."

"In my boobies?"

"Your heart, baby."

Auri deflated. "I was afraid you'd say that."

She laughed softly. "So, how many pieces?"

"Three." When the woman questioned her with a single skilled glance, she said, "Four." Her grandma got up to leave and was out the door when she shouted, "And a half!"

Her grandmother's laugh filtered toward her as Auri tapped the screen on her phone. She texted her mom to see how the case was going since her cruiser was already gone. She must've left super early.

She was just about to hop in the shower when a thought hit her. She sank back onto her bed and chewed on an already abused nail. What if there was a way to get the necklace back to Billy Press without getting Mrs. Fairborn thrown into prison? The woman couldn't go to jail. How would she ever learn to make a shiv out of her toothbrush if she didn't have any teeth left? How would she protect herself?

The answer was so simple. All Auri had to do was break the chain of custody. She would steal the necklace and tell her mom that she'd taken it when they first broke into Mrs. Fairborn's house, a lie that would never hold up in court. And if Mrs. Fairborn had a good lawyer, the necklace would never even be allowed in evidence, because Auri could've gotten it from a shack in Timbuktu for all anyone knew.

That settled it.

She went about making plans for the evening. One more time, then she'd never sneak out again. She had to get the necklace. Maybe Mrs. Fairborn wouldn't even notice it missing. Auri could return it to Billy Press and everyone would be happy.

She decided to call Billy and tell him her plan. If all went well, his family could have that necklace back in the next few weeks. She called him using video chat on Instagram.

He picked up immediately, but his screen was black. "Aurora?" he said.

"Yes. Is this Billy?"

"It is. Sorry about blank the screen. My camera is broken on my phone."

"Oh, that's okay. I just wanted to let you know that the necklace is safe and I know where it is."

"I can't believe this." He laughed, incredulous. "You don't know what this means to my family. We've wondered for so long what happened to Emily."

Unfortunately, she couldn't tell him the truth on that front. She would have to tread carefully, but he needed know the case would be solved. Just maybe not any time soon. "I've been looking into all the cases."

"All the cases?"

"Yes. Several people went missing from the area. Mostly travelers who stayed at a particular boardinghouse in Del Sol."

"You don't say."

"And I saw that necklace in what used to be the boardinghouse. I don't want to get your hopes up about finding out what happened to your cousin, but I think the person who ran the boardinghouse may have been killing travelers for their personal possessions."

"A boardinghouse, huh? And it's still there?"

"Well, no. It's not a boardinghouse anymore."

"Gotcha. But the necklace is inside the house now?"

Her pulse sped up. "Um, yes. I'm going to get it. But my mom's the sheriff."

"The sheriff?" he asked, seemingly alarmed.

"Yes. I'm going to get the necklace and give it to my mom. I'll tell her I found the necklace in the house and maybe they'll reopen the case." He didn't need to know she would purposely botch the chain of custody in the process and hopefully keep Mrs. Fairborn out of jail. "We can finally find out what happened to your—"

"Maybe we shouldn't bring your mom into this."

She blinked, taken aback. "I'm sorry?"

"I mean, you know how the law works. It could take years for my family to get back my cousin's things."

"But I have to tell her. How else will we find out what happened to Emily? And to the other victims? The families have a right to know what happened to their loved ones. Also, I think an innocent man was killed because of this case. His family needs to know he was falsely accused."

"Right." He laughed again. "Sorry, I didn't mean you should keep it a secret. Of course, we want to know what happened to Emily. That's our first priority."

"I'll let you know when I get the necklace."

"Thank you, Aurora. I appreciate this so much. My family is going to be over the moon."

"You're welcome." She hung up feeling slightly elated. At the same time, she felt like she'd just betrayed Mrs. Fairborn. She didn't know why. If the woman did kill those people, it was her own fault. And if she didn't, she had nothing to worry about. But what if her plan backfired and Mrs. Fairborn really did go to prison? Auri would just have to figure out a way to smuggle in a shiv.

20

Do you love your job? No.
But does it afford you the ability to go on lavish
vacations and buy anything you want? Also no.
And that's where we can help!
Stop in for a free portfolio consultation
and get 10% off your first psychic reading.
—SIGN AT DEL SOL BROKERAGE AND PSYCHIC READINGS

Sun and Levi didn't wait for backup. The minute the bright yellow orb crested the horizon, they headed out. They'd parked in a valley at the base of the Sangre de Cristos. It was going to be a long hike up to the mine.

They grabbed water and power bars from her emergency stash along with various supplies and a first-aid kit. Sun insisted on wearing the backpack, since she hadn't been hit by a truck as recently as he had, but he practically ripped it out of her hands and slid it over his shoulders despite her protests.

Men. Especially men who picked fights with Toyota Tundras.

"Thank you," Sun said, as they walked an overgrown trail.

"For?"

"I'm not sure I would've realized Elliot meant to write Sawry, as in the Sawry Silver Mine, without your prompting."

"You figured it out before I did, and without knowing how much Eli loves that mine."

"He loves the mine?"

"Seabright mentioned it a couple years ago."

"Either way, thank you."

He looked down at her, the trail wide enough at that point for them to walk side by side through the brush, and the appreciation she saw in his eyes went straight to her head. And other parts of her body. Like a margarita might. Or a hit of acid. Not that she'd ever done acid. Much.

She turned back to the trail. There was a time they could've gotten a vehicle up to the mine. It would've been rough, but it could've happened. Disuse and overgrowth put a stop to that, and while the mine had been boarded up for decades, kids still managed to find a way in. It rarely ended well.

Quincy and the gang were bringing ATVs, but the overgrowth would slow even those down, and Sun didn't want to wait.

"I don't care how much Elliot loves that mine, it's dangerous. And now he has a seven-year-old with him."

"He knows it like the back of his hand. He trains in there with Seabright."

"But Adam doesn't. And he's only seven. The pit has a way of sneaking up on you."

The pit was a massive hole deep in the mine and impossible to see until you were falling into it. It dropped thirty feet and led to another level. More than one kid had fallen into it over the years, despite it being boarded up. When a middle-school boy died after falling in a few years back, Sun's parents started a petition and tried to have it filled in with cement, but the city council dismissed it, arguing it would be impossible to get a cement truck up to the mine.

Difficult, yes. But not impossible. And worth the added cost, in Sun's opinion. She could hardly blame kids for their curiosity. She'd been one.

"By the way," Levi said after they'd been walking about forty minutes.

She liked walking with him. And driving with him. And watching him drive. "Yes?"

"We were followed."

She almost tripped but managed to keep her feet on solid ground. Staring straight ahead, she said, "Why didn't you tell me?"

"I wasn't positive."

"But you are now?"

He nodded.

"It has to be the Delmar family," she said. "There have been men stationed in town for a few days now. I'm certain they work for them. But they're still after Elliot? After all this time? They have to know Matthew Kent doesn't have the money."

He stayed silent for a long time, then said, "Revenge?"

A shiver raced up her spine. "Not on my watch. How do you know they're still following us?"

"They're keeping a watch with binoculars. Or a scope. The lens is reflecting in the trees off to the left."

"I'm thirsty," Sun said, turning toward him. She motioned for him to turn around.

He grinned down at her, his powerful frame like a mountain towering over her. When he didn't move, she rolled her eyes dramatically and walked around him, playing her part and taking the opportunity he'd provided to scan the distant tree line. A single lens flare reflected the sun then disappeared.

She fished a bottle of water out of the backpack and used the cover to depress the push-to-talk button on her mic clip.

"Zee, you there?"

"I'm here, boss."

"Your mom called. Your house is on fire. You need to go home immediately."

"Ten-four, boss. Thanks."

She reached down and turned the knob to change the channel from their standard to their tactical channel.

Zee came on almost immediately. "How many?"

"We don't know."

"We're coming up on your six," Quincy said.

"They left town early this morning," Rojas said, turning off his ATV. "Something got their attention."

"What time was this?" Sun asked.

"My guy at the front desk said they took off about three."

She glanced at Levi. "Right after Elliot took Adam?"

"That can't be a coincidence," he said.

"Sorry about this, guys. Hope you wore comfortable shoes." They would have to abandon the ATVs for the time being, but at least they'd almost caught up to her and Levi.

"Thank God I changed out of my heels," Quincy said.

She laughed softly and offered Levi the water bottle. "Signal when you have them in your sights. We'll distract them."

Zee came back. "You got it, boss."

Levi took a few shallow sips before eyeing her with a mixture of humor and interest. "I don't have any explosives on me."

After a pitying assessment, she tsked and said, "I thought all you Ravinder boys carried dynamite everywhere you went. How ever are we going to distract them now?"

The breathtaking grin he flashed her implied he had a few ideas.

She had to kickstart her heart to get it beating again. The things he could do to her with a single glance bordered on obscene. She looked around and sat on a fallen log, making the time-out sign with her hands. To an observer, it would look like she simply needed a break. Which she did. She hadn't slept in what felt like days.

He sat beside her and leaned against the tree behind them. Placing the backpack on the ground at their feet, he ferreted out a couple of power bars.

She took one and said nonchalantly, "I can't even imagine what my hair looks like at this point in my life."

"Hair has never been your strong suit," he said, a teasing sparkle in his eyes.

"Oh yeah? Well, brains have never been yours."

He chuckled and took a huge bite while she tried to come up with a legitimate distraction. Just something to keep their quarry's eyes trained on them.

"How about a fight?" she asked.

He shrugged. "Could work."

"Or," she said, excited, "I could slip and break my leg!"

"That might be hard to pull off."

"True." She took another bite.

Several minutes later, the radio clicked three times.

"That was fast."

"You thirsty?" Levi asked her.

She'd bent to stuff her wrapper into the backpack. When she straightened, she felt a firm hand wrap around the back of her skull. She looked up at him. He pulled her closer and lifted the bottle to her lips. The hard plastic of the rim pressed against them. Cool water filled her mouth.

She tried to swallow but a memory consumed her. Her breath caught and she coughed, but only slightly.

He lowered the bottle and licked his own lips as he studied hers. The image of her rescuer fifteen years ago, hood and shadows concealing his face, flashed in her mind. He held her the same way. An arm draped behind her back, supporting her. A large hand around her neck. The bottle at her lips, cool and wet against her hot mouth. A warmth spread throughout her body.

"What are you doing?" she asked, her voice whisper soft.

"There are only two things that will keep their attention focused on us while your team overtakes them. Either we fight or fuck."

She swallowed hard. "You're assuming they don't have a sniper rifle pointed at our heads as we speak."

"They clearly want the kid. Why would they blow their lead?"

"Fine. We fight."

His gaze traveled over her face. "Chickenshit."

She thought about arguing with him, but he did have a point. Desire glistened in his eyes as he looked down at her. He was either an incredible actor, or he was not wasting the opportunity, either.

"We should start fighting now," she said, her voice breathier than she'd planned.

"I'll follow your lead."

After another moment of considering his alternate plan, imagining her lips brushing across his, she stood to face him instead and railed, "What do you mean my hair has never been my strong suit? What's wrong with my hair?" She made a point to throw in some angry movements without exaggerating them too much. She had to sell it, not turn it into vaudeville.

He eased back. Took her in. Then did indeed follow her lead. Yet, unlike her, he stayed true to his character by offering no reaction whatsoever other than the barest hint of a smirk. He gestured toward the subject of their argument, a.k.a. the weakest point of her entire being apparently, and said, "It's just so blond."

She gaped at him. "It's too blond?"

"And nondescript."

"Excuse me?"

"And anemic."

He'd really thought about this. "Can hair even be anemic?"

"Apparently."

The humorous slant to his lips caused a momentary glitch in Sun's synaptic firings. She mentally rebooted, and asked, "Just what do you suggest I do about it?"

He lifted a shoulder. "I don't know. You never wear it down so it's hard to say."

She executed her best soap-opera spin and whirled away from him. It was a wonder Hollywood hadn't come knocking. "For your information, I'm a law enforcement officer. French braids are generally safer than ponytails or even buns, so I braid it." She spun back to him. "And you're one to talk. What exactly do you call that disaster?" She gestured toward his head of thick, dark auburn hair, the same hair she'd give her left kidney just to run her fingers through, and guessed, "The sasquatch?"

"Are you saying I need a trim?"

She stopped short in front of him and leaned in until they were nose-to-nose. "I'm saying you need a trim."

This was the most ridiculous argument she'd ever had. She should've come up with something better to argue about than hair, but a part of her did wonder if he really felt that way. Clearly, she needed to deep condition more often. Maybe give it a light tease.

He set the bottle aside and pinned her with a knowing look. "No," he said, his voice as deep and smooth as ever. "I do not really feel that way about your hair."

Holy crap. He could read her mind.

"Also no," he said.

She straightened. "No what?"

He stood to tower over her. "I cannot read your mind." *He really could.* When he lifted her chin and bent closer, their mouths almost touching, Sun was ninety-percent certain she ovulated. "Though I'd give anything for that ability."

A breathy laugh escaped her. "You'd rue the day. Trust me."

"Not likely." His gaze dropped to her mouth just as Quincy came over the radio.

"You two done?"

Sun pivoted away from Levi like she'd been caught in the act itself.

"Because we secured the men following you like five minutes ago."

She cleared her throat and pressed the talk button on her mic. "How many?"

"Two," Rojas said. "They supposedly don't know where the other guy is."

Quincy came back on, "We called in the staties to check out their hotel in case he stayed behind. They're coming out here, too. Hope that's okay."

"It's more than okay. Not sure what we can hold any of them on, but it's worth a shot to try to find out their end game. Did Zee have to shoot anyone?"

"Not today, boss," she said almost sadly. It was a joke. Sun saw firsthand what it did to her the last time she had to take down a perpetrator.

"You guys okay to get them back to the trailhead?"

"Ten-four on that," Quincy said.

"They're hog-tied, boss," Zee said. "I can stay on you. Watch your six, just in case."

Levi grabbed the backpack and Sun ripped it out of his hands. "Nah, stay on them, then hustle up with the ATVs when the state police get here."

"Ten-four."

With the stalkers out of the way, they could continue their journey to the boys and, hopefully, get some answers.

"I want a do-over," Levi said. After stuffing their water bottles into the backpack, he stole it once more and secured it on his shoulders. "I felt my performance lacked authenticity."

Unfortunately, Sun responded before giving it much thought. "I doubt your performances are ever found lacking, Mr. Ravinder." When her words sank in, she froze for a solid minute, then started forward, suddenly eager to be on her way.

Auri turned to the tapping on her window a microsecond after her grandmother left her room with her lunch tray. Finding dead bodies got her all kinds of special treatment. She'd give it five stars. Highly recommended.

She hobbled over and opened the window. "Cruz, what are you doing here?"

"Checking on you. I got your texts."

"Sorry. I just had to tell you about last night. Why aren't you in school?"

"Why aren't you in school?" he asked, his mouth pressed together on one side, forming a lopsided grin that made him so handsome, it hurt her heart.

"Either way, you will not believe what happened."

"You found a dead body," he said.

She frowned. "How did you know?"

"It's all over school."

"Of course it is. Come in." She stepped aside so he could scale the tower wall and enter her fortress of solitude. Also, mixing up fandoms was a specialty of hers.

"I can't, Auri. I have to respect your grandfather's wishes." He paused, his serious expression almost comical, then added, "And you. As a friend and as a woman, I have to respect you."

She offered him a look of bemusement before catching on. She rolled her eyes. "My grandpa is standing right behind me, isn't he?"

Cruz nodded.

"Can he hear me?"

He nodded again.

"That's what I meant, Cruz. Go to the front door and let my grandparents know you're here to see me. They won't mind." She turned to her grandfather who'd totally invaded her space bubble. "Right, Grandpa?"

His lashes narrowed on them. "I'm going to pretend I fell for that."

"Thanks, Grandpa!"

Cruz went around and was shown in the old-fashioned way, which was way easier on the shins. They lay on her bed, Auri under the covers and Cruz on top, and talked for the next hour nonstop.

"I'm going to confess everything," she said to him, "to Mrs. Fairborn. I'm going to tell her why we broke into her house, how it was all my idea, and how I was going to turn her in for being a maniacal serial killer." She hoped Cruz would understand. "I can't send her to prison, Cruz. She's too old."

"I don't think they would send her to a regular prison. Maybe they have one for the elderly that has a bingo palace."

"I'm not sure I want to take that chance. I do want to get that necklace, though. And I . . . I kind of need your help."

"I'm in."

"But I haven't—"

"I'm in."

"It'll be dangerous."

"I'm still in."

"And we'll have to wait until dark. We'll have a very narrow window. Basically, after my grandparents go to bed and before my mom gets home. She's working a big case."

"Still with ya."

"And Mrs. Fairborn could catch us and kill us. Clearly, she knows what she's doing."

"I'm still in, beautiful."

His compliment caused a rush of warmth a microsecond before reality sank in yet again. How could she risk Cruz's freedom? How could she be so selfish? And why would he agree to another one of her harebrained schemes without question? "Cruz, you're not listening."

The more she thought about it, the more panic took hold. But this was her best option. She would be appeasing the Press family while completely botching the investigation and keeping Mrs. Fairborn safe.

Still, she'd be putting Cruz at the center of it all. She'd opened the can of worms they were now swimming in. It was up to her to close it. She wouldn't need his lockpicking skills if she walked right up to Mrs. Fairborn's door and knocked. Once inside, she could excuse herself to go to the bathroom and grab the necklace.

"I'm pretty sure I am."

"You are?"

"Listening."

She fell back against her pillows. "Never mind. I can't get you into trouble again."

"Auri," he said, leaning over to brush his thumb across her bottom lip, "I'm in."

Relief washed over her. She really was selfish. "Thank you." She looked at the clock on her nightstand. "You know, sixth hour is starting soon. You're going to miss class."

"It's okay."

"You're in enough hot water with your dad, right? Did he make it home last night?"

"No, not yet. He had an emergency."

Auri had to wonder what kind of emergency a mechanic would have out of town, but her thoughts were interrupted when Sybil texted asking how she was doing.

"You answer," Cruz said. "I'm going to get you something to drink. You need to stay hydrated."

She smiled as he left and texted Sybil back. *I'm fine. Cruz is here.*

Oh, good. I was worried.

Why?

He hasn't been here all day. Thought maybe his dad killed him after all. LOL

Cruz said he heard at school about what happened last night.

IDK. Wasn't in any of his classes. It's all over FB tho. Maybe he saw it there.

That was strange. She texted back a quick *Maybe* then let her suspicions run wild. If Cruz hadn't gone to class, where did he go? And why did he lie to her about it?

21

Driver reported he swerved to miss a tree.
It was later discovered to be his air freshener.

—DEL SOL POLICE BLOTTER

Sun heard the ATVs coming up the mountain. It only took her and Levi another half-hour hike to get to the mine. She was surprised to hear her deputies coming so soon.

"The state cops must've been close," she said, panting as they studied the opening to the Sawry Silver Mine. Her lungs burned and her legs ached. Clearly she needed more cardio and less Oreo.

The entrance was boarded up with the words KEEP OUT plastered all over it. "They may as well post a sign that says, *Hey kids! Come on in! We dare you!*"

"They are kind of inviting trouble with all of this." He pulled away a board that hung loosely over one end of the opening. Dust billowed around him when it broke loose. "Here."

She walked over and looked inside. "It's very dark."

"Scared?" he asked, taking his flashlight off his belt. The flashlight right next to the hunting knife.

She scoffed, ducked inside, and took out her flashlight, too. The dank smell mixed with animal droppings took some getting used to.

Levi crawled in after her, his wide shoulders barely scraping through. He winced and groaned a little, favoring the left side of his rib cage.

"You know, if you get a punctured lung up here, your chances of survival are almost nonexistent."

"Thanks," he said, his voice strained.

"Let me have the backpack." She held out her hand.

"Please." He whacked it out of the way, then scraped past her into the mine.

Rude.

She followed, the underground cave so dark it seemed to absorb the light from their flashlights the deeper they went. The slits in the wood slats glowed when she looked back at the opening, but the light didn't reach far.

"How do you want to handle this?" he asked her.

"You're sure they're here?"

"I've been tracking them for the last two miles. Eli's dirt bike is tucked behind a copse of bushes about twenty feet from the opening."

"Do you think Adam came with his brother willingly?"

"I do. I don't think he would force him."

"I hope you're right."

"I am. If I remember correctly, the mine opens up to a chamber of sorts about a quarter mile in."

Sun spun in a circle, careful not to knock herself out. Parts of the rock ceiling dipped low when one least expected it. "I haven't been here since I was in high school."

"Who'd you come out here with?" he asked, ducking under a low boulder.

"Friends. Quincy and a few others."

"No romantic interludes?"

After an indelicate snort—not that any snort was delicate—she said, "Not unless you count the time Ryan Spalding tried to kiss me."

"Tried?"

"And failed. What about you? Any romantic rendezvous in a dark, cold, creepy mineshaft?"

"Nah. There are far easier places to get to."

Figured. She slipped but caught herself. Thankfully, he had taken the lead and missed her acrobatics. "What about with Crystal Meth?"

"I've never done meth. Here or anywhere else. Surely, you know that."

"I mean the girl, which, by the way: poor thing. Her parents suck."

"I gotta say, I really think they were oblivious."

"Nobody's that oblivious."

"And you brought her up because?"

"You guys were making out the night Seabright was attacked. Outside the bar."

He stopped and turned back to her. "Making out? Me and Crys?" The fact that he used her nickname so casually caused an unsettling in her stomach. "Where'd you get that from?"

"Crys."

"She told you that?"

She shined the light in his eyes. Mostly because she could. "Not in so many words. It was very much implied, however."

He frowned and tilted her flashlight downward. "We were just talking. She was asking for a job."

"I bet she was. I can only imagine the interview process."

He didn't say anything for a few seconds, then asked, "Is your opinion of me really so base?"

His indignation shocked her. And thrilled her. Not that she actually thought so low of him, but he was now one of the privileged. One of the elite with enough money to buy half the state. They thought differently than the rest of the world, however. She was glad to know money didn't change him. Or maybe it did, considering his tragic upbringing. His deplorable role models growing up.

"You're right. I'm sorry," she said, then squeezed past him, breathing in the earthy scent that wafted off his skin like a soft, alluring breeze, and headed farther inside the mineshaft. The ceiling dropped lower and lower and Levi had to duck down even more, putting a strain on his ribs if his breathing was any indication.

He put a hand on her shoulder to halt her and pointed. A couple dozen yards in front of them a soft light went out, while behind them, the ATV turned off. Its sound stopped its muffled echoing along the rock walls.

He twisted the lens on his flashlight. The color changed to a muted blue. Sun's didn't have that feature so she turned hers off altogether.

The floor was getting more uneven, the ceiling even lower, and the walls even tighter. Soon they would be on their hands and knees. "I forgot about this part," she said softly.

"For good reason. The walls are literally closing in on us."

She turned to him, panicked. "You're not claustrophobic, are you?"

He didn't say anything for a long moment and because she could barely see his face, she didn't know what he was thinking. Then he said softly, "I can see why Ryan Spalding tried to kiss you."

"Gross!" a kid shouted from deeper inside the mine.

They both startled and Sun almost knocked herself out on the rocky ceiling when she tried to straighten like the genius she was.

"That was so cheesy, Levi," the kid said before he made gagging sounds.

Levi covered her head with a hand to try to keep her from concussing herself, then chuckled as a kid carrying a lantern popped his head into the narrow tunnel.

"It gets better," he said. "Just keep coming. But only if you two stop making out."

Another kid, Adam, poked his head into the tunnel from the opposite side and giggled as he looked on.

The older boy motioned them forward, but Sun couldn't move. She could barely breathe. Elliot Kent, the boy she'd spent years trying to find, stood not fifteen feet away from her, as beautiful and healthy as ever.

If ever a dream had come true . . . She felt tears sting the backs of her eyes, the wave of emotion rising up within her unexpected and surprisingly strong.

"You okay, Shine?" Levi asked her softly.

She sank onto her knees and put both hands over her mouth.

"See?" Elliot said. "You shouldn't have kissed her. Now she's upset."

She made a sound that was half laugh and half sob before regaining her composure. She filled her lungs and nodded up to Levi.

He leaned closer and tucked a strand of hair that had escaped her braid over her ear.

She beamed at him, then duck-walked toward the boys to get past a particularly low part.

"Be careful of the tripwire connected to the claymore," Elliot said. When Sun stilled, he laughed. "Just kidding. I ran out of claymores a couple of months ago."

"That's too bad," she said, easing closer to the roomy chamber where she could finally stand.

She looked between the two boys. There would be no doubting Adam's parentage. He was the spitting image of his older brother. Smooth, pale skin. Thick, dark hair. Just enough baby fat to soften the strong features that would someday develop. It would be a sad day when that happened, because he was adorable.

"Elliot," she said, trying to keep her shit together. "And Adam. Do you remember me? We met at your house."

The younger boy smiled.

"I'm Sunshine."

"For real that's your name?" Adam asked.

"For real that's my name." She turned back to Elliot and did everything in her power to keep her expression neutral. "And I've been looking for you for a very, very long time."

"Why?" Adam asked her.

"She's stalking me," Elliot said to his little brother. "What can I say?"

He laughed and Elliot mussed his hair.

"Sorry," she whispered to him, remembering Adam didn't know Elliot was his long-lost brother.

"It's all good."

It took everything in her not to pull him into her arms. She didn't know if she could keep from stroking his hair and kissing his face, which would only scare him.

She looked around at the boys' encampment. They had pillows and blankets. Foodstuffs and water. They even had a small propane-powered cookstove. All the comforts of home.

After a quick scan, Sun remembered the chamber, though she'd only been to it once. It was called the cathedral because the shadows cast on the walls from the lamps made the rocks look like saints watching over the trespassers. She also remembered that off to the left was an alcove, another tunnel only a few feet long that led to the pit. No one dared go down. It was too deep and too dangerous, especially for non-climbers.

"Elliot," she began when a thought hit her. She turned to Levi. "There was only one."

He was busy introducing himself to Adam. "One what?"

"One ATV." She turned a confused expression back toward the main tunnel. "There should have been two. Quincy called for two."

He tensed. "Maybe Zee came back alone? Once they got the men following us to the trailhead?"

"No. She would've radioed ahead."

"Very good, Sheriff," a male voice said to her. But the first thing she saw come out of the tunnel was the barrel of an assault rifle.

Her hand immediately went to her duty weapon, but the intruder stopped her with a soft *tsk*.

"Really, Sunshine? Are you faster than a 5.56 steel jacket lead core?"

Elliot stepped closer to his brother, but the rifle swung toward him.

Instinct took hold. Sun moved in front of the boys as the bearer of the rifle eased into the lantern light.

She blinked in surprise. "Carver?" Her blind date from hell?

"You never texted me back," he said. The look he gave her expressed just how much he detested her. "I wouldn't." He gave Levi a sideways glance as though he were an idiot for even thinking about trying something.

Levi hadn't moved, but even Sun sensed the tension coiled in his muscles.

He motioned for Levi to get closer to the group. He did, strategically maneuvering in front of Adam as Carver scissor-walked toward the opening on the west wall, putting some distance between them.

"Look at you two. Willing to risk your lives all noble-like."

"What is this about, Carver?" Sun asked.

"See," he said, getting frustrated. "That's what I mean. You call yourself a sheriff, but you can't even figure out what's right in front of your face. There's a little thief among us." He leaned over and looked past her to Elliot, who'd eased his brother a little farther back. "Isn't that right?"

Sun took another step sideways, keeping her body between the gun and Elliot about the same time she realized Carver was shaking. Adrenaline tended to do that, but this seemed like more. He seemed paler than usual. Shinier, his skin caked with sweat and oil, like he was on something. That fact raised the stakes even higher. Negotiating with a perpetrator on drugs was always volatile.

"Your father is very upset with you," he said to Elliot, jabbing the gun in his direction. "But Seabright wouldn't let him near you when he got out of jail. Had no idea where the soldier was keeping you, so he sent me in to find out."

"Elliot's father sent you here?" Sun asked.

"Mmm," he said in answer. "I figured if I got Seabright out of the way, I could get to the kid."

"You hired those men at the bar?" Levi asked, his tone razor-sharp.

"I did."

"Sorry I had to kill one of them."

"No worries. I killed the other two."

"You killed them?" Sun asked, getting an answer to her immediate questions on how far was he willing to go. Rojas had called it. Man was a sociopath. "You tried to have Seabright killed because he wouldn't let his father near Elliot? But why? Why go to all that trouble?"

If looks could kill, he would've done her in as well. "Because somebody moved the money! Pay attention, Sunshine!" He looked around her again. "And there was only one person on the planet who knew where that money was, right *Eli*?"

"The money from the Ponzi scheme," Sun said as though confirming her suspicions. In reality, she was simply trying to keep him talking so she could come up with a plan. "His father had it the entire time."

"Little shit was only five, so his dad didn't expect him to understand what he was seeing when he buried that money. Much less remember where it was. But you did, didn't you?"

Sun glanced to the side and could see Elliot in her periphery. The color had drained from his face. Adam's as well. But both boys knew enough to stay quiet and absolutely still. Elliot reached out, took Adam's hand, and pulled him closer. At the same time, Levi closed the distance between Sun and himself to keep Adam covered.

Without taking his hands off the rifle, Carver lifted a shoulder and mopped his brow with his shirt sleeve.

"Are you okay, Carver?" Maybe she could appeal to his drug-addled side. "You don't look well."

"I'll be fine as soon as I get out of this fucking hole in the ground."

He was claustrophobic? Unfortunately, Sun didn't know if that would work for or against her. "You don't like confined spaces?" she asked him, pretending to care.

He didn't answer.

"Then I'm assuming you're not really in pest control, what with all the creeping under houses and squeezing into crawl spaces. On the count of three," she said as nonchalantly as possible.

"No," Levi said.

Carver was starting to panic. The whites of his eyes shined in the low light. His brows snapped together as he volleyed the gun between them.

"He'll take me out," she said. "I could very well survive the hit, especially this close. Through and through. You know that. Either way, it'll give you an opportunity to rush him."

A waxy grin slid across Carver's face. "This is going to be fun."

Levi shook his head. "Not on your life, beautiful. I'll rush him."

He mopped his brow with a sleeve again. "Shut. The. Fuck. Up."

"When I do, you put every round you have into his chest."

"I can't risk hitting you."

"Are you guys inbred?" Carver asked, astonished that they'd kept talking.

They both watched him like hawks waiting for their prey to flinch. To weaken. To lose focus for that tenth of a second it would take for them to make their move.

"You're stronger than I am," she said. "You'll have a better chance at overpowering him."

"That's it." He pointed the barrel at Levi's chest, and the world tilted under her feet. "How 'bout I just take him out of the equation altogether?"

Sun risked a glance. Adam had taken hold of Levi's T-shirt with his free hand, the fear on his face palpable. Elliot stood close behind her, but he was also almost as tall as she was. She wasn't as much of a barrier for him as Levi would have been. If she rushed Carver, Elliot could be shot instead of her. Or, more likely, the bullet would go right through her and into him.

She needed to divert the gunfire away from the boys and give Levi enough time to do the rushing. She would have to dive away from them.

"If you don't stop those wheels spinning in your brain, *Sheriff*, I'll kill the boys first."

"If you kill them, you won't know where the money is," she said.

"I only need one for that, sweet cheeks."

"Are you sure? How do you know Seabright didn't move the money himself? Elliot could have told him where to find it."

"I can work with that." He was having a hard time keeping the gun steady. Her chances of survival were multiplying by the second. "I'll kill you all and pay Seabright a visit in the hospital."

"He doesn't know where it is," Elliot said, trying to step around her.

She held him back.

"Only I know where it is and I'll never tell you."

"Problem solved," Carver said.

"On three," she said to Levi. Of course, she wasn't an idiot. She'd never really count. But Carver didn't need to know that. She dragged her palm across her duty weapon in preparation.

Levi lowered his head and watched Carver from underneath his thick lashes.

Carver scoffed at her. "Do you really think you stand a chance against an assault rifle?"

"I do." She tilted her head. "Not a particularly great one, but yeah. I think I have a decent chance."

"I think I have a better one." He stepped closer and aimed the gun at her chest point-blank.

He was really bad at this. He was far too close, for one thing. The small room probably had more to do with that than his bad-guy skills. She shouldn't be so quick to judge. But the claustrophobia? He should've thought this through before barreling into a mineshaft.

Sun tensed, preparing to make her move, when Zee's voice drifted toward them like a ghost in the darkness.

"I think I have the best chance of all." She eased forward into the light, the shadow from the tunnel sliding off her like water. She kept her rifle steady and leveled at Carver's head.

Quincy followed behind her, his sidearm drawn, his aim as steady as Zee's despite his heavy breathing. He knelt at her side, keeping the sites trained on the sociopath.

Both of them were covered in a fine sheen of sweat. They'd run. Something had alerted them to Carver's presence, and they'd run up the mountain instead of using the ATVs so they wouldn't tip him off.

"It's over, Carver." Sun raised a hand and showed him her palm, keeping her other one on her sidearm.

"You clearly don't know how talented I am with this gun. I once picked off a diplomat in a crowd of thousands in Russia at five hundred yards in high winds."

"You're an assassin?" she asked, appalled.

He lifted a shoulder.

"My parents set me up with an assassin?" She shook her head. "Why am I not surprised?"

He didn't fall for it.

"Actually," Elliot said from behind her, "if anyone pulls the trigger, the cave will explode."

She glanced over her shoulder in shock. "What? Why?"

"I opened the propane tank."

She looked down. Sure enough, he stood right by the propane tank hooked to the small cookstove and the smell of rotten eggs hit her.

"He's lying," Carver said.

She turned back to him. "Take a whiff, Carver. You pull that trigger, we all die."

She could see it in his eyes. The moment he made the decision. The microsecond he'd come to terms with the fact that he would just have to kill everyone there, including Elliot, and hope to make it out alive. He stood at the opening to the tunnel that led to the pit. It was too much to hope he'd fall into it. He could fire his rifle and dive into the next shaft, but the pit was farther in, if Sun's memory was correct. Carver could feasibly escape with his life. Maybe get to Seabright and attempt to torture the guy into telling him where the money was stashed.

Clearly, he didn't know Seabright.

Carver tightened his grip on the rifle and eased back into the adjoining tunnel. "Then I guess we all die," he said, squeezing his eyes shut for a fraction of a second as though trying to focus.

The claustrophobia was taking its toll. She imagined the walls were closing in on him. The edges of his vision were darkening. He was running out of time and he knew it.

Zee and Quincy exchanged glances, not sure of what to do. They couldn't fire, either.

Then again, if Carver did, would the explosion really kill them? Sun doubted there was enough gas in the air to get the job done. It would burn off instantly, but the propane tank could explode. The propane tank that was right beside the boys.

The fact that Carver had yet to pull the trigger gave Sun hope. He could have killed her easily before Zee and Quincy arrived, but he hesitated. Maybe not quite the world-renowned assassin he claimed to be.

Both Zee and Quincy looked to her for direction. She quickly dropped her gaze, then returned it to them, indicating the boys. They nodded. The minute Carver fired, they would protect them the best that they could while she and Levi tried to subdue her would-be ex.

Carver backed farther into the tunnel, putting more distance between them. Lessening her chances of success with each step.

Sun felt rather than saw the tension in Levi's muscles. They were coiled, ready to strike the moment she made her move.

Carver tightened his grip on the rifle, preparing to fire. She'd hoped for another blink. Another microsecond of freedom to up her chances of lunging toward him without getting a bullet through her heart, but even the sweat beading onto his lashes didn't elicit a response.

"You're forgetting one thing," she said, stalling when she realized he was actually aiming at the propane tank now. It would definitely explode. It would likely kill Elliot. Or Adam. Or Levi. She fought the fear that had a stranglehold on her throat and moved to block his line of sight.

The glare he cast her should've scorched her skin. "Do you honestly believe your skinny ass will stop this bullet?" A visible drop of sweat fell from his brow onto his lashes and the involuntary reflex was the opportunity she'd been waiting for.

She lunged.

The gun went off.

The cave erupted into a ball of fire.

The explosion echoed through the chamber so loudly, Sun thought her ears would bleed, but it did propel her forward. She rammed into Carver with everything she had, but it wasn't enough to take him down. He stumbled but kept his footing as they fought for the rifle.

Then she was airborne. She flew back and landed on the cavern floor. The air left her lungs in a pitiful whoosh.

Levi had dragged her off him so he could have Carver all to himself. Enraged, he wrapped a powerful arm around Carver's neck and dropped back, taking him to the ground. Their struggle lasted all of five seconds and Sun was worried he'd break his neck before Levi's choke hold began to take its toll.

Carver's kicks slowed. His face crimsoned and his shallow breaths came in short, choking wheezes. Sensing the inevitable, he raised the rifle and aimed it at Sun.

Their date must have gone so much worse than she'd thought.

She scrambled back, but the flash of a blade caught her gaze. Before she could order him to stop, Levi struck.

Two lightning-quick slices, as smooth and clean as a shark through water, and Carver's arm went limp. The rifle fell to the side and his eyes rounded in disbelief.

Sun scurried closer as Carver lost consciousness. She took the rifle out of his grasp and tossed it aside.

Levi let go and pushed the man off him as though disgusted. He'd sliced through the tendons under Carver's arm first, obliterating his ability to pull the trigger. In the process, he'd severed the man's brachial artery. Next he'd severed his femoral artery. So fast Sun barely saw it happen.

Carver's tactical khakis were soaked instantly, the blood-red pool spreading fast.

Sun pressed into Carver's wound and spared a quick glance over her shoulder for something to help stop the bleeding. The chamber was empty of children, thank God. Zee and Quincy had gotten the boys out, but Quincy eased back inside, his movements wary, his gun drawn.

"Sunshine?"

"Clear," she said loudly, then pointed to the boys' blankets. "Hand me one!" That was when she noticed the propane tank spewing a bright blue flame. It hadn't exploded.

Quincy hurried over and tried to turn the handle, but it was too hot. He grabbed a dirty T-shirt off the floor and twisted. The flame shut off. "The bullet bounced off," Quincy said, gesturing toward the scuff mark. "The spark must've set off the gas."

It must have. She'd been thrown from that direction. Not back, which was what would've happened if the gun had set it off. "Blanket."

Quincy grabbed one and rushed forward, handing it to her before giving her a doubtful look.

Levi straightened to his full height. "He's gone."

"I need your belt," she said, putting all of her weight into the task of suppressing the blood loss.

"Sun," Quincy said.

She looked at Carver's face. His eyes were open and his breathing had stopped.

Quincy bent to help her up. "He's gone, boss."

It all happened so fast, Sun sat stunned for a solid minute before she heard Elliot's voice.

"Is he dead?"

Sun hurried to cover Carver with the blanket, then let Quincy help her up. She rushed to the boys. "He is, honey. Are you guys okay?"

Zee had let them come back in. "Sorry, boss. They got away from me."

Sun summoned her best mommy frown and planted it on them. "I can't imagine how."

Elliot gave her a sheepish grin, but Adam's gaze was locked onto the body. They both had black residue on their faces and scorch marks on their T-shirts.

She knelt in front of them, turning them this way and that and lifting their shirts to get a better look. "Are you hurt? Were you burned?"

When she lifted Elliot's shirt where most of the scorching was, he grinned at his little brother. "What'd I tell you? Chicks dig me."

His skin was red. He was burned worse than his brother, but it wasn't nearly as bad as it could've been had the tank exploded.

Then she heard it. Someone else coming down the tunnel, but the newest visitor was having a hard time trying to navigate the narrow opening while running. All Sun heard was an occasional, "Son of a bitch," and a "What the fuck?"

After a few seconds, Rojas emerged, a little bloody but no worse for wear.

He skidded to a halt in the chamber, his sidearm drawn, and watched as Zee knelt to officially check Carver for a pulse, noting the time of death for the ME. He braced an arm on the cavern wall to catch his breath.

Sun no longer cared what her attentions would do to the boys. They would be traumatized regardless. She gathered them in her arms and hugged, making sure to avoid the scorched parts of their shirts. To her eternal joy, they hugged her back.

Adam visibly shook, but either Elliot was amazingly well-trained or he was in shock. He wasn't shaking at all, but he did hold on to her for dear life.

Then he turned and hugged Levi.

"What do you say we get you to your mom?" Sun said.

Adam nodded and wiped at his eyes.

She stood and nodded to Levi. "Thank you."

He didn't respond. He stared at her neck instead before walking closer and doing some checking of his own. "He got you."

"No. That's not my blood."

"It is."

Sun felt and realized the bullet had grazed her before ricocheting off the propane tank. "Oh." She drew her hand back for a look. "It's not bad. I'm fine."

The worried expression on his face confirmed he wasn't so sure. It left her warm and fuzzy inside, but she had to stay focused. She turned to Quincy. "How did you and Zee know Carver was up here?"

"Carver?" he asked, gaping at the assailant. "That was your date?"

"My parents set me up with an assassin."

"Told you," Rojas said, still panting. "Sociopath."

"If you didn't know he followed us up here, why did you run all that way?"

"We figured out that the third guy staking out the town wasn't at the hotel. We thought maybe he'd slipped past us on the trail."

A soft groan echoed off the rock walls around them.

Elliot cringed and looked at his brother. "He woke up."

"Excuse me?" Sun said.

"Thank goodness he didn't die," Adam said. "Mom would be so mad."

Elliot grabbed the charred lantern, eased around Carver's body, and ducked back through the alcove. "Careful," he said, stepping gingerly toward the edge of a very large, very dark hole bordered by a layer of rocks. He held the lantern over it and Adam shined a flashlight.

Sun, Levi, and Quincy looked over the edge. At the bottom of what looked like a mile-deep hole lay a man in a suit. He raised an arm against the light.

"Our third man?" Sun asked Quincy.

"I'd say so."

"And the money?" She looked at Elliot.

"Yeah, I moved it."

The man lay on a cushion of hundred-dollar bills. He laughed softly and called up to them. "I can think of worse ways to die."

A couple of the plastic-wrapped blocks of money had broken open and hundreds spilled out around him.

"Still," Sun said. "I know fifty million is a lot of money, but I didn't think it would be quite that voluminous."

"Try one hundred and fifty million," the man countered.

"Holy cow," Rojas said, leaning over the edge, shining his own light into the man's eyes. "You a cop?" he asked him.

"DEA."

"I suspected as much in town."

She stared at Rojas slack-jawed. How the hell did he know these things?

"DEA?" Adam asked. He punched his brother on the arm. "We are in so much trouble."

22

They would never have let her come. Auri knew that. Given the circumstances and what she'd already put Mrs. Fairborn through, her grandparents would never have let her come talk to the woman. She had no choice but to sneak out once again.

"This is the last time," she told Cruz when he picked her up down the block.

The impish grin he wore created a dimple on one cheek. "You know they're going to come in and check on you. They were checking on you every thirty minutes all day. And then they'll never let me see you again."

"Don't be silly. I told them I was going home to take a shower."

"A home that's thirty feet from their back door. They can check there, too."

"I turned on the water and cranked up the radio." When he gave her a less-than-convinced look, she added, "Really loud. And do you know how long it takes me to shower and get ready for bed?"

"Sadly, no."

"Oh." She felt heat rise up her neck. "Well, trust me. I just bought us an hour."

"What if something goes wrong and that hour turns into twenty to life?"

"What could possibly go wrong?" she asked. "We aren't breaking in this time. We're apologizing for breaking in, and while you distract her, I'll steal the necklace."

He nodded but kept the grin in place. He knew her too well.

She talked a good talk, but her nerves were frazzled and fried like her mom's hair that time she got a perm. Auri was not cut out for a life of crime, even one designed to benefit Mrs. Fairborn. Once Auri managed to snatch the necklace and get it back to the Press family, she was hanging up her black mustache for good. And then, after the elderly woman passed away, Auri would tell her mom where she really got the necklace from and prove the drifter, Hercules Holmes, innocent. At least, that was her plan.

They pulled onto Mrs. Fairborn's street and, just like before, parked down the block, just in case. "Maybe you should stay here," she said to Cruz. "I don't want to get you into any more trouble with your dad."

Something flashed across his face, but it was so fleeting, she missed the meaning behind it. "My dad's cool. It's okay."

She crossed her arms over her chest. "That's it, Cruz. What is going on?"

He draped his wrist over the steering wheel and looked out over the street. Only one side of the street was lined with houses. The other side was all forest and thick brush. He studied the orange moon that hung low over the treetops. "I'll explain later. I just want to spend every second possible with you while I can, Auri."

Alarm prickled over her skin. "What does that mean?"

"Let's just do this." His voice had thickened.

She scooted closer and put her hand on his arm. "Cruz?"

He dropped his head but kept his face averted.

She reached over and turned it toward her.

Tears glistened between his lashes.

"Cruz, what happened?"

He shook his head, and said, "Nothing important," before sliding out of the truck.

She scrambled after him.

He walked to the edge of the street and looked at the moon filtering through the trees.

Not sure if she should even try, she reached down and took his hand. He let her. His hand swallowed hers when he lifted it and ran his fingers over her knuckles.

Her stomach clenched in apprehension. She stepped in front of him and he slid an arm around her waist. "I'm not going to push you, Cruz. But please know you can tell me anything."

"I know. But if I tell you, it'll be real."

She nodded in understanding. "I get that. More than you can possibly know. If you say it out loud, the universe will hear you and the glass around you will shatter and everything will come crashing down."

"Exactly," he said, surprised. "And if I don't tell anyone, then I can keep living my life like nothing has changed." His breath hitched in his chest and Auri's squeezed tight around her heart.

She reached up and put a hand on his strong jaw. "Then don't tell me. Do what you do, Cruz. Put it in a poem and make it beautiful like you do everything else."

He swallowed hard and nodded. "I can try. And then you'll tell me exactly what happened on that cliff when you were a kid? How Mr. Ravinder helped you?"

"I can try."

A resigned smile spread across his face. "But first we have a necklace to steal."

"Think this'll work?" she asked, turning toward the woman's house.

"I think you can do anything you set your mind to."

She turned a surprised expression on him. "You have a lot

of faith in someone whose only goals in life are to befriend forest animals and create the perfect mocha latte."

They walked arm in arm to Mrs. Fairborn's front door, Auri giving part of her weight to Cruz. Her ankle was still a little sore. She knocked, then stepped back. As nervous as she was, this beat breaking and entering any day of the week.

"Maybe she's already in bed." She knocked softly again, then waited.

"She has had a busy few days," Cruz said. "What with her trying to stab a guy to death, running Mr. Ravinder over in her nonexistent truck, and then having to fess up to it all."

"It must've worn her out," Auri agreed with a giggle.

He looked down at her. "Try again tomorrow?"

"Yes, only we can go straight after school so I don't have to sneak out. I think I'm giving it up." They started back down the steps. "Hanging up my sneakers, so to speak. Get it?" she asked with a snort. "Sneakers?"

Cruz chuckled just as a crash sounded from inside Mrs. Fairborn's house. They looked at each other, then went back to the door. "Was that glass?" he asked.

Auri knocked and tried the doorknob. "Locked."

They peeked through the window but couldn't see much for the curtains.

"Cruz, she could've fallen."

"I agree. We need to check on her. Let's go around."

"Okay."

They hurried through the side gate and into her backyard. A backyard Auri was becoming very familiar with.

"It's unlocked," Cruz said, opening the back door and entering the mudroom.

The sound of someone tearing through the house, items falling and more glass shattering hit them. Cruz stopped her with an arm across her torso.

They heard a male voice, angry and volatile. "Where is it?"

Then the sound that broke Auri. Mrs. Fairborn crying. "I don't know. It was there."

"You are a lying bitch," he said.

Auri stood frozen, wanting to run to her but needing to call for help at the same time.

Cruz put his mouth to her ear, and whispered, "Run. Call the police."

"Wait, what are you going to do?"

"I'm just going to make sure he doesn't hurt her until the cops get here."

She nodded, but another thud sounded and Auri's feet moved before her brain told them to. Cruz's did, too. They rushed into her kitchen where Mrs. Fairborn sat tied to a chair. A man three times her size stood over her.

"Stop!" Auri shouted.

The man turned, his face the picture of rage.

Auri blinked. "You're . . . Are you Billy? Billy Press?"

"Aurora?" he asked, his face twisted in confusion.

"What are you doing?" Before he could answer, she rushed forward, pushed him out of the way, and knelt in front of Mrs. Fairborn. "Are you okay?" she asked, searching for a way to untie her.

The voice that traveled to her was tightly controlled, each word enunciated to precise calculations. "Where's the necklace?"

She turned and gaped up at him. "The necklace?" She started to point to the downstairs guest room, but something told her if she did, if she told him where to find the necklace, none of them would make it out of Mrs. Fairborn's house alive.

His fingers curled into two beefy fists in her periphery as he stared down at her, his face twisting in barely controlled rage.

"I—I gave it to my mother. I told you I would. She's the sheriff," she added, glancing at Cruz.

He stood a few feet away, his gaze locked onto an oblivious Billy.

She was about to signal for him to run when she found

herself airborne. She crashed into Mrs. Fairborn's glass hutch just as Cruz rushed the man. He delivered a powerful right hook. Then a left.

Billy didn't know what hit him. He stumbled back, stunned.

Cruz was an amazing fighter from what she'd been told, but Billy was twice his size. And angry. Cruz still knocked him to the ground. The guy didn't stand a chance until she saw him reach across the floor, his meaty fingers clawing for something.

Auri tried to get to her feet to help Cruz, but she couldn't move. Her feet wouldn't listen. Her arms lay motionless as blood leaked into her right eye. She could only watch as Billy sank a knife into Cruz's abdomen.

It went in so smoothly, it took Cruz a moment to realize what had happened. He looked down as Billy pulled out the knife and pushed it in again.

The surreal turn of events surprised Cruz just as much as it had Auri. He grabbed the blade when Billy pulled it out a second time, but it was slick with his blood. It sliced into his palm and slid free of his grasp before Billy sank it in a third time.

His movements were automatic. Like he was on autopilot as he plunged the knife in. Then his hand slipped off the slick handle. Just as the darkened edges of Auri's vision closed in on her, Cruz pulled out the knife himself and pressed a palm to his wounds as though trying to stop the bleeding.

Then she watched as Billy, almost in slow motion, reached up and took the knife away from him again. The world went black but she could hear Mrs. Fairborn's sobs.

Auri fought to get back to her, back to Cruz, but her lids were like anvils. She struggled to open them because she was floating then. She could feel it. Cool air rushed over her hot skin and consciousness danced just beyond her reach. She tried to grab it, but it inched away, taunting her like a schoolyard bully.

She heard labored breathing. Felt arms beneath her. Tasted the metallic tang of blood. The moon shifted into focus then disappeared, drowned out by red and blue lights so bright they blinded her. Then she heard footsteps and a young woman say her name before everything went black once again.

The state police brought the Kents up in an ATV that looked like a small truck. They had the coolest toys. She elbowed Quincy, then pointed. "I want one of those."

"I thought you said our budget was the size of your pinky."

"It is. Doesn't mean I can't want things."

"Oh. In that case, I want a service horse and a drone with a camera and a new radio because these things are older than my left ass cheek."

Sun watched as Addison, who proved surprisingly agile, jumped out of the ATV and ran to the boys across the rough terrain. She couldn't help but notice that Matthew seemed a little less enthusiastic. Addison hugged both of her boys and sobbed for several minutes.

Sun strolled closer. She hated to interrupt, but she needed a few answers so she could file her initial report. She looked across the mountain to a gorgeous orange moon rising over the horizon, then said, "I know it's getting late, but can I ask the boys some questions?"

Addison started to protest but changed her mind when she looked at Sun. "Of course. Thank you, Sunshine." She stood and hugged her, too.

Sun hugged back. It had been a long time coming. "Not at all," she said, stepping back. "It's your genius kid who sent us in the right direction." She grinned at him. "Sorry?"

He beamed at her. "I was hoping someone would catch onto that. It was my backup plan. When those men showed up at the convenience store, I knew I had to have a backup plan."

"Well, it worked. Levi and I figured it out." She looked across the clearing to where Levi stood talking to the DEA agent. They were loading the agent onto a stretcher to wait for the helicopter to airlift him to Albuquerque. It wasn't easy getting him out of the pit, especially since he'd fractured his tibia and dislocated a shoulder, but Elliot had a rope ladder and Sun had a lot of strong, young deputies.

And Levi. She had Levi.

The place was now crawling with representatives from practically every law enforcement agency in the western hemisphere. From the state police to the local PD, DEA, to the FBI. She half expected the CIA to show up. It was a lot of money. Enough to warrant bringing agents in by helicopter.

The DEA took Matthew Kent aside for questioning. They had already found evidence of his hiring Carver, an act of utter stupidity on his part. What kind of man sits on all that money, biding his time until he gets out of prison, only to leave a trail by hiring someone to find it? Not just someone, however. An assassin. How does one even find an assassin?

At least the DEA's involvement was easy to explain. The Delmar family were notorious. The Ponzi scheme was probably a side deal involving their money-laundering operations.

Normally, with that kind of money involved, Matthew Kent would never have made it out of prison. No one steals from an organized crime family and lives to tell the tale.

But that was probably the whole point. The fact that Kent knew the location of the money was the only thing keeping him alive. That's why he didn't tell his wife about it. They would hardly kill Kent before they found it, but they wouldn't hesitate to torture and kill his family.

Sun had so many questions she hardly knew where to start, so she decided to start small. She sank onto a boulder beside Elliot, and asked, "How did Agent Wilcox end up in the pit?"

He winced. "I didn't know he was a DEA guy."

"I didn't, either," she said.

"After what happened to Keith, after someone tried to kill him, I thought he was here to kill us, so we told him the money was in the pit and then pushed him in."

Figured. "Well, that's on him," she said with a grin. "I just can't figure out how he beat us here. How did he know where you were?"

"He said he saw the direction you were going, looked on a map, and found the mine. Then he went around you when you and Levi were kissing."

Addison's eyes rounded.

Sun's eyes rounded. "We were not kissing."

"He said you were."

Sun caved. "We just almost kissed, but it was all in the line of duty."

"That's not what he said."

Adam shook his head, agreeing with his brother. "That is not what he said."

Embarrassment surged through her, but why? They hadn't even kissed.

Elliot dropped his gaze. "It's all my fault, though. Everything." He swallowed hard and looked up at her. "I . . . I called them. The Delmar family. I told them I knew where the money was. I thought if they had it back, they would leave us alone and me and Mom and Adam and Keith could be a family."

Sun was only a little surprised he'd omitted his father.

"I just wanted us to be together."

"Oh, honey." Addison squeezed him tight. "I am so sorry."

"And I guess . . ." He chewed his bottom lip from over his mom's shoulder. "I guess a part of me wanted to punish Dad. That money was all he cared about. He would rather give up his own family than that stupid money. I *wanted* Mr. Delmar to have it. I know it's wrong, but—"

"Elliot," Sun said, brushing his hair across his brow, "you have every right to be angry, but I don't think that's why your father did it. Maybe he had a moment of weakness or maybe he'd been siphoning it for years, but once you do that to a family like the Delmars, there are no take backs. They would have killed him and possibly the whole family. Maybe as long as he had that money, he felt he was keeping you safe."

Elliot pressed his mouth together. "Thank you for saying that, but that's not exactly true."

Addison set him back. "What do you mean, honey?"

"Mom, Dad knew they couldn't kill him because he was the only one who knew where the money was. They couldn't get to him, because he'd already been arrested, so to get Dad to tell them where the money was, they were coming after us. You and me." His expression saddened. "Somehow, Dad found out. That's why he had me pretend kidnapped. I knew where the money was, too. He was worried I'd tell and he couldn't let that happen, so he had Keith take me and left you vulnerable."

"Sweetheart," she said, shaking her head.

"Dad handed you to them on a silver platter, Mom." His eyes glistened with unspent tears. It broke his heart to tell her the truth about her husband. "He didn't know the Delmars would stop harassing him once I was abducted and it was plastered all over the news. They were being watched too closely and it would raise too many suspicions."

"Elliot," Sun said, giving Addison a moment, "how do you know all of this?"

"Keith and I have been keeping an eye on things, mostly to make sure the Delmars didn't give the green light to go after Mom. He had someone on the inside. I think he's friends with that agent we pushed into the pit, but I can't be certain."

"We didn't know he was an agent, though," Adam said, wanting that made clear.

"But then Keith almost got killed and I realized it was my fault. Dad was getting out and I didn't want him to get the money he loved so much, so I called them and they tried to kill Keith to get to me."

"No, honey." Sun shook her head. "It wasn't your fault. Carver hired those men, not the Delmar family."

"And my dad hired Carver."

Addison's chin trembled as she fought back tears. "Why didn't Keith tell me any of this?"

"Mom," Elliot said, his expression stern, "we had to keep you safe. You and Adam."

"Oh, sweetheart." She hugged him again and wrapped an arm around Adam as well.

"You are the bravest kid I've ever met," Sun said to Elliot. "You stayed alive and kept your brother alive, too."

"Keith knew something was up when that guy tried to stab him at the gas station." His lower lip quivered. "That's when I told him what I did, but he didn't care. He wasn't even mad. And he didn't think it was the Delmar family, either. He went to meet his contact and said if he wasn't back by dawn to clear out and don't come back. He would find me." He wiped his eyes with the back of an arm. "I did, but then I got worried. I thought they would go after Mom and Adam. That's why I took him, and I was coming to get you, too, Mom, but Dad came home before I could get you." His shoulders slumped. "I had to leave you there. I'm sorry. I was going to come back."

"Elliot, why didn't you just come to us? Why leave the messages?"

He lifted a shoulder. "I knew Keith would get in trouble even though he didn't really kidnap me. And my mom. I just wanted you guys to find the money."

Addison covered her eyes with a hand as she hugged him. "I can't believe any of this is happening."

"Yep," Sun said, nodding. "You are definitely the bravest kid I've ever met."

A dubious frown slashed across his handsome face. He didn't believe her. She would just have to spend the next few days convincing him.

"You're Auri's mom," he said.

Surprise rocketed through her. "I am. Do you know my daughter?"

"Yeah. I see her at the lake during the summers. She's really nice."

"Nice?" Adam asked, wrinkling his nose at him. "You said you liked her butt."

Elliot slammed a hand over his brother's mouth and put him in a headlock. "He doesn't know what he's talking about."

"And her boobies," he said, his voice muffled.

A bright hot blush blossomed across Elliot's face. Oh, yeah. They were going to get along great.

"Wait, where was the money?" she asked. "Before you moved it? And how on earth did you get a hundred fifty million dollars up here?"

A calculating grin lifted one corner of his adorable mouth. "I'm sworn to secrecy."

She laughed.

"So," Adam said, his voice still muffled, "are we, like, brothers?"

Another helicopter flew overhead and news crews were beginning to show up.

"Sunny!"

Sun turned to see Quincy running up to her.

He skidded to a stop, not an easy task considering his size. "We have to go."

She shot to her feet. "If this is about Randy," she warned. That raccoon was a menace. When he put a hand on her shoulder, she sobered instantly. "Quincy," she said, the warning in her voice much sharper that time.

"It's Auri."

23

Donate blood today!
Please note: It must be your blood.
—SIGN AT DEL SOL URGENT CARE CENTER

Sun and Levi commandeered a ride into Albuquerque on the medevac with Agent Wilcox, making for a very tight squeeze with both a nurse and a paramedic also on board. Because Wilcox's life wasn't in immediate danger, the paramedic rode up front with the pilot.

Reception was so spotty, she didn't get much info from Salazar. All she knew for certain was that Auri was being airlifted to Pres with blunt force trauma to the head.

Sun's world turned upside down with the news. She hadn't eaten. Hadn't slept. Her adrenaline had reached new heights in several ways that day. She was running on fumes and yet she willed the helicopter to fly faster with every ounce of energy she had left.

Levi took her hand, his jaw hard set. He was just as worried as she was.

She had the pilot patch her through so she could call her parents from the helicopter, at first wondering where they were when all of this was happening, then suddenly worried they were hurt, too. But she could not blame them. She had a sneaking suspicion this was all Aurora Dawn Vicram.

Unable to hear half of what they said, she got the most important bits. They were fine. They were following the ambulance that was carrying Mrs. Fairborn. The kids should already be at the hospital.

"Mom, you guys have to calm down. You'll have a wreck. Why don't you meet Quincy when he gets to my cruiser and come down with him?"

"This is all our fault," her mother said, clearly in shock.

There was no getting through to them. Her only hope was for Quincy to hurry and try to catch up. Thankfully, Albuquerque traffic wasn't bad after nine. They should be fine. And, lest she forget, her dad was in military intelligence and drove missions all through the Middle East. Surely, he could handle a Tuesday night in Albuquerque.

With more than enough law enforcement officials at the mine, Sun ordered Zee and Rojas back to town to help Salazar with the crime scene. And yet another dead body. Del Sol seemed to have entered *The Twilight Zone*. Mid-season. And with ratings plummeting.

The DA was going to go ballistic. The mayor was going to kill her. Yet Sun couldn't find it in her to care. Her daughter could have died. She still could. Nothing else on Earth mattered.

She ordered Quincy back to her cruiser with her laptop and other essentials. Considering he had a mountain to get down, he could be in Albuquerque in a little over an hour if he double-timed it then drove at the speed of light. Thank God for emergency lights.

Auri and Cruz were still en route as the team at the medical center would've had to stabilize them before the flight. Sun and Levi were ordered to wait inside the building, but they refused. They saw to Agent Wilcox, then watched from the parking lot as the helicopter came in for a landing.

Sun ran to it the second it touched down and tried to talk to Cruz over the whir of the blades. Levi pulled her back so the staff could do their jobs, which made sense though she didn't appreciate his efforts in the least. They unloaded him just as a second helicopter crested the horizon.

He looked so pale, so ashen, Sun was reminded just how fragile life could be. He lay shirtless with a clear wrap covering his wounds. Three of them. Blood had pooled beneath the wrap, his normally flat abdomen distended with internal bleeding. Despite all this, he was fighting them. They were having a difficult time securing him.

Sun ran forward and took his hand, yelling over the sound. "Cruz! You're okay."

He looked at her and tried to focus, but she could tell he was struggling. His eyes rolled back and he pushed at their hands as they tried to get his arms back under the restraints.

"Where's Auri?" he asked, as though they'd taken her.

Sun brushed his hair out of his eyes and got close to him. Gave him something to focus on. "They have her, baby. She's right behind you."

That seemed to calm him. His pupils dilated as he looked at her. They hung the IV and rushed past her to get Cruz into surgery. Sun had been assured they'd called in their best surgeon.

They stood back and the first helicopter took off as another medical team rushed forward. The second helicopter touched down. They lifted Auri out and Sun's world fell away.

Auri's hair was caked with blood, her head wrapped in gauze, and her neck in a brace. Her arms were strapped down, her hands folded at her waist, and her face—her perfect face—was swollen and pale, punctuated with scrapes and bruises of all sizes and shapes.

Sun didn't realize she was falling until Levi caught her. Her bones had dissolved, and his solid arms clamped around her midsection, holding her upright. She watched as the team secured Auri's IV and rushed her inside.

Quincy flew into the parking lot, lights blazing, with Cyrus and Elaine Freyr right behind him. He'd caught up to them and escorted them all the way through town and to the hospital.

Levi and Sun followed the gurneys, but were stopped by a nurse who looked like she could handle herself in a wrestling tournament, and quickly shown to a waiting area.

"She has a subdural hematoma," someone in a lab coat said. Sun's mother cried out. Sun stood in shock. "We're going to have to operate, Sheriff. On both of them. Do we know where the boy's father is?"

"I'll try to get a hold of Chris," Quincy said, talking about Cruz's dad.

"Quincy, what happened?" Sun asked, staying him with a hand on his arm.

He sank into a chair. She followed. "As far as we can tell, the kids walked in on a robbery."

Sun blinked in confusion. "A robbery? At Mrs. Fairborn's?"

"I'm getting the footage from Salazar. She was first on the scene." Quincy's eyes were red-rimmed and Sun could tell he was barely holding it together as well. "It looks like Auri ran right into the middle of it. She tried to stop the suspect from hitting Mrs. Fairborn, so he hit her instead."

Sun's stomach clenched around shards of glass in response.

"All we know for certain is that Cruz and the suspect fought. Cruz won but he took one hell of a beating. According to Mrs. Fairborn, Cruz had the upper hand until the perp found a knife on the floor. He'd been tearing through her drawers. Clearing off her shelves. He was looking for something."

"Do we know what?"

"Not yet."

Sun nodded. "Have Zee go through Auri's cell phone and laptop. I want to know if anyone has threatened her in any way."

"You got it."

"Quincy," she said as he stood. He sank beside her again. "Thank you. For my parents. For everything."

"Of course, boss. I'm going to make some calls. Text me if they come out with an update." He squeezed her hand and took off.

They were in Pres, the same hospital as Seabright.

Levi scrubbed his face. He seemed to be in as much shock as she was, but he was also angry. With everyone and everything, including Sun. "Why would she rush into the middle of a robbery?" The accusing glare he cast her way knocked the breath from her lungs. "Haven't you taught her better?"

"Yes, I have." Her vision blurred. "At least, I thought I had. She's so hardheaded."

"She's you, Shine. You incarnate." He stood and stalked out the sliding glass doors, leaving her dumbfounded. Leaving her bereft. Leaving her. His words stung far more than she would've liked, and she fought a telltale quivering of her chin.

"Sun," her dad said, "if this is anyone's fault—"

"No, Dad. No." She held up an index finger to stop him. "This is not your fault."

Her mom shook her head. "No, it is."

"Mom, if that little redhead wants to do something, there is apparently nothing you or I can do about it. Once her mind is set, there's no stopping her."

"Levi is right," her dad said. "She is you incarnate. God help us all."

Sun sat stewing in all the ways she raised her daughter wrong. She wanted her to be independent, but not too independent. She wanted her to be strong and powerful and ready to take on the world, but had Sun given her too much freedom? She'd never had to worry about Auri. She got good grades. She had tons of friends. She was outgoing but not overbearing. She'd had some rough patches, like when she'd contemplated taking her own life when she was seven. But their lives had been so full since then.

Auri was bright, her intelligence off the charts, but Levi was right. Why would she rush into the middle of a robbery? Especially after everything Sun had taught her. Unless she didn't know Mrs. Fairborn was being robbed, which led to the inevitable question: why was she there in the first place?

So many unknowns her head hurt. Her dad brought her

a sandwich from vending and took one out to Levi. Sun was surprised. She thought Levi had left her there. Not the least bit hungry, she ended up devouring the whole sandwich nevertheless. Levi came back in, sat right beside her, and ate as well.

His eye was healing, but it almost looked worse than it had the day before. The bruises had spread and covered half his face. She reached up and touched the stubble on his jaw. He looked at her just as Quincy walked in.

"Salazar uploaded the dashcam and bodycam footage. She's sending it now." He handed her the laptop from her cruiser and sat on her other side.

Sun logged in and they first watched the dashcam footage. Salazar was responding to a call about suspicious activity in the area when something in the distance came into view. "What is that?" Sun asked, leaning closer.

As Salazar pulled forward, the image became clearer. It was Cruz, walking down the middle of the highway that turned into Main. Clearly in shock, he was carrying Auri in his arms. She lay draped over them, her head and limbs hanging limp.

Sun's hands shot to her mouth as she watched in horror.

He stumbled, caught himself, and took a couple more steps before he sank onto his knees, careful to keep Auri's head from hitting the pavement. He cradled her to his chest and waited as Salazar pulled to a stop in front of them.

Salazar called it in, ordered dispatch to send units from Las Vegas, and hurried out of the vehicle.

Even in the black-and-white image, Sun could see that Cruz's clothes were soaked in blood. He walked as far as he could before the blood loss became too much.

Salazar tried to ease Auri out of his arms, worried he would drop her, but he held fast. After a couple of minutes, his head lolled back, and she was finally able to convince him to lay Auri on the pavement, for her own safety, as another vehicle approached.

The driver got out and Salazar threw him a pair of gloves,

ordered him to get Cruz down and apply pressure to his abdo-men. The man, a local farmer, obeyed instantly, though Cruz was none too happy about it. He pointed to Mrs. Fairborn's house as the man tried to hold him down, as though telling them to go check on her. When another vehicle approached, Salazar did the same with them. And so on until she had half the town out there.

Once the ambulance and a unit from Las Vegas arrived, Sala-zar hurried to Mrs. Fairborn's house. The footage switched to her bodycam and Sun saw firsthand the wreckage that was once a home.

"What the hell?" she asked, her breath catching in her throat.

"He was definitely looking for something," Quincy said.

Levi took her hand as they watched. Salazar called out the door for another pedestrian to get a first responder to the house as she checked Mrs. Fairborn. The woman sat slumped in a chair. At her feet was an unconscious man, the floor beneath him a sea of blood.

"Intruder has no pulse," Salazar said into her mic before re-turning her attention to Mrs. Fairborn.

"Sunshine," her mother said, watching from Levi's other side. "What is going on?"

Sun unwelded her teeth to answer. "A missing persons case and a girl unwilling to accept defeat."

"Just like her mother," Levi said, his jaw just as tight.

She wanted to kiss him.

"She looks so tiny," her mom said, her nose red from blowing it so often.

They'd moved Auri from post-op into ICU, a cracker-box room with a glass wall and lots of equipment. Auri did look tiny in the bed, her small, willowy frame like a doll's. No, a fairy's. A fiery-haired fairy's. The kind that reveled in mischief. She defi-nitely fit the bill.

"We're getting a hotel," her dad said. "We'll be just down the street."

"Thanks, Dad." She kissed the man's cheek. He wrapped her tight.

Her mom took her turn. "Call if she wakes up before we get here tomorrow morning."

"Thanks, Mom. I will. But I doubt she'll wake up any time soon. They have her on the good stuff."

"Can we bring you anything?"

"No. I have my emergency stash in the cruiser."

"Okay, honey." She dabbed her eyes and smiled sadly as they left with a final wave.

Levi had been standing just outside the door. He came in and took the seat her father vacated.

The prognosis was good. The doctor said the swelling could have been much worse and it didn't seem like it would affect her memory or speech, but they wouldn't know for certain until she woke up. Even then, the true extent of her injuries could take months to uncover and her recovery could take even longer if indeed she didn't have permanent damage.

Sun made a mental note to call Hailey tomorrow so she could let Jimmy know, and to call Sybil's parents so they could break the news to her. At least she wasn't with them this time. Thank God for small miracles.

She sank into the chair and watched Levi watch Auri, his expression impossible to read, and she was dying to know what he was thinking.

Quincy snuck in and knocked softly. "Sun," he said.

She sat up and waved him in.

He seemed upset and she almost didn't want to hear what he had to say.

"Cruz is out of surgery."

She stood expectantly. "And?"

"It looks good. They think they got everything patched and cleaned out, so hopefully no infection. And he's strong. That'll help."

She put a hand over her heart. "Thank God."

"Sun, there's more."

Her brows slid together. "What?" It wasn't until that moment that she noticed the wetness shimmering in his eyes. "Quince?"

"Apparently," he said, his voice cracking, his expression full of sorrow, "his father had a stroke when they were camping near Angel Fire during spring break."

"What?" She thought back. "That was weeks ago. Is he okay?"

Sun knew Chris De los Santos, but Quincy had been friends with him. He covered his eyes and his breath hitched in his chest.

"Quincy, no."

"Cruz carried him more than two miles to their truck and took him to a hospital in Taos, but it was too late. He died before they got there."

"No."

Quincy broke. A sob escaped and his shoulders shook. He had to turn away. "They said it took them four hours to get Cruz to let go of him."

"No." The floodgates opened. "No wonder he wouldn't let Auri go," she said, covering her face with her hands. How much more could that kid take?

"He has no one," Quincy said.

"No, he has a grandfather, right? In Riley's Switch? He works construction with him in the summers."

Quincy shook his head. "That's who I've been talking to. When I couldn't get a hold of Chris, I called Philip, but Philip isn't his biological grandfather. He was Chris's foster dad." His voice cracked and Sun rubbed his back. "He helped with the cremation and asked Cruz to live with him, but Cruz said he wanted to stay with some friends until school let out. He told him he was staying with Chris's best friend."

"Who is that?"

"Me, apparently," he said right before he broke completely. He walked out, struggling to breathe.

Sun turned to Levi. He looked as astonished and heartbroken and crushed as Sun felt. She didn't know how close he and

Chris had been, but they'd been friends. She knew that much, because Levi was friends with all the cool people in town, and Chris De los Santos was one of the coolest.

He stood as though his body would no longer allow him to sit. She took one look at him, at the devastation etched into his face, and wanted nothing more than to console him. To make all of this go away. Instead, he strode past her as though worried he would break completely.

A nurse came in before she could go after him. Though he was Auri's critical-care nurse, Sun had asked him to find out what he could about Mrs. Fairborn. "They admitted Mrs. Fairborn for observation," he said, checking Auri's IV and taking some readings.

"Are you going to be right here for the next little bit?" she asked him.

"Absolutely. I won't leave this station if you need to grab something to eat."

"Actually, is there some place I could take a shower?"

"Sure thing, Sheriff."

Fifteen minutes later, Sun set her emergency bag on the closed toilet seat and combed through it until she found her toothbrush. The nurse found her a shower she could use down the hall from ICU, God bless him. The fragile threads holding her together were starting to fray. The seams ripping apart. The worn edges starting to show.

She brushed her teeth, then stepped into a shower so hot it would blister her skin. Why didn't Cruz say anything? How could the father of a minor in her town die and she not know about it? Shouldn't someone have let her know?

Cruz must have felt so alone. In turmoil and agony. And he had no one. The image of him refusing to let Auri go after having to let go of his father forever almost broke her. It stung her eyes and burned her throat.

The totality of the last several days hit her at once. She sank to the floor, as the scalding water rushed over her, and pressed both hands to her mouth to silence the sobs racking her body. And then she cried. Until her eyes swelled. Until her muscles ached. Until her stomach heaved. She cried until someone knocked on the door, the sound so soft she almost didn't hear it.

"I'll be out in a minute," she said a microsecond before she realized it could be someone with news of Auri.

She grabbed the towel they'd loaned her, wrapped it loosely around her body, then went to the door. Levi stood on the other side.

"Auri?"

He shook his head. "She's still asleep. You've been in here a while. I just wanted to make sure you were okay."

"Of course," she said between hiccups. She averted her face, suddenly self-conscious. She was a sheriff. She needed to start acting like one. "I'm almost done if you want the shower. You can use my emergency kit, though I don't have any clothes that will fit you."

He pushed his way in and closed the door behind them. "I'll wait in here."

"Oh. Okay. I'm almost finished." She stepped back into the shower and closed the curtain, realizing she hadn't even shampooed her hair yet. She held her breath while she lathered and rinsed to keep another sob from escaping, only allowing small gasps of air to enter her burning lungs.

He opened the curtain and, without hesitation, pulled her into his arms soaking wet. She didn't feel too bad about having a total meltdown in his arms. He cried, too. He held her tight enough for her to melt into him. And so she did.

24

Sunday's service will discuss which page of the
Bible explains how to turn water into wine.
Come early. Full house expected.
—SIGN AT DEL SOL CHURCH ON THE ROCKS

While Levi took his turn in the shower, Sun found a change of clothes for him thanks to a sympathetic admin and her magic key to a sparkling land called the gift shop. She worried he wouldn't want to wear what she got him, but he didn't really have a choice since his clothes were now soaking wet.

She always kept two different outfits in the back of her cruiser, business and super casual—a.k.a., comfy sweats and a tee—which was all they had in Levi's size as well: a pair of sweats and a T-shirt with a UNM Lobos emblem.

And thanks to Auri's ICU nurse, she also found him a clean pair of boxers and socks. She snuck them in while he showered, thought about peeking, then went back to ICU.

When she woke up in the wee hours of dawn two hours later, she found Levi's powerful frame slouched in the chair next to Auri's bed, his wide shoulders and long legs filling up half the room as the nurse worked around him.

The nurse smiled at her. "She's doing great, Sheriff," he said even though her uniform was in her duffel bag. "They're going to move her out of ICU in a bit."

Relief washed over her like cool water. "How about Cruz De los Santos?"

"He's two doors down if you want to see him. Though getting past his guardian angel might be difficult." He grinned at Levi. "Kind of like this one."

"Thank you."

"Any time. My shift ends in a few. It was really nice to meet you."

"You, too. Thank you so much for taking care of my kids."

He rewarded her with a bashful smile.

Sun stood and held Auri's hand for a while. Brushed her hair from her forehead. Marveled at the surreal creature she'd been given. Her face, though still pale, had a little more color. A soft blush blossomed over her lips and cheeks.

Sun glanced over at Levi. The man of her dreams was down for the count, his breathing soft and deep, his startlingly handsome face serene in slumber, so Sun peppered Auri's forehead with kisses then went to check on Cruz.

Sure enough, a guardian angel the size of an eighteen-wheeler sat between the door and Cruz's bed. His long legs were stretched out before him and one arm lay draped over Cruz's mattress. Still in his uniform, Quincy snored softly.

Sun eased around him to get to Cruz's side and for the second time that morning, relief washed over her. He looked much better as well.

He was such a handsome kid. Strong jaw. Full mouth. And the most perfectly shaped nose she'd ever seen. Sun knew exactly what Auri saw in him. But the thought of him all alone in the world once again threatened to shatter her. She fought off a crushing wave of emotion, leaned over, and placed a soft kiss on his cheek.

He stirred and his lashes fluttered. He opened his eyes to slits, as though that was all the energy he could muster. He was such a fighter for even trying.

She leaned close. "Hey, handsome. Thank you for saving my daughter's life."

One corner of his mouth rose weakly as his lids drifted shut again. He raised a hand toward her and she took it into both of hers. "Is she okay?"

"Thanks to you, yes."

Salazar got as much as she could from Mrs. Fairborn before they transported her to Albuquerque, so Sun knew the basics of what happened. Just not the hows or whys. She would need Cruz and Auri to fill in those blanks, though she had a pretty good idea.

"Cruz," she said, squeezing his hand, "I am so, so sorry about your dad."

Despite his eyes being closed, a tear pushed past his thick lashes moments before he slid back into oblivion.

Sun looked over. Quincy was watching her, his heavy-lidded gaze full of sorrow.

"Why don't you go home and get some rest," she said to him. "I'll keep an eye on this guy."

"It's okay, boss." He sat up in the chair and stretched. "I just need a toothbrush and I'm good to go."

"I think that can be arranged. I know where you can shower, too, if you want."

"I want."

She walked around to him and brushed a finger over his scruff.

He took her hand into his. "Is it that bad?"

"You're pretty wonderful, Quincy Lynn."

The look he gave her was full of suspicion. "All right. What'd I do?"

She chuckled softly and bent to kiss his cheek as well.

"Damn it. Am I fired? You're firing me, aren't you?"

"No," she said with a soft chuckle. "It's what you're about to do."

"Uh-oh."

"How would you like a roommate?"

An emotion born of panic and something akin to gut-wrenching terror flashed across his face, then he looked over at the unconscious kid beside him and calmed. "Will I get to order him around? Make him rake leaves and shit?"

"Of course."

"Then I'm in."

Sun knew it would be no walk in the park, unless it was one of those parks where all the kids hang out drinking beer they stole from their dad and smoking pot they stole from their mom, but she had faith in her BFF. He was amazing with Auri and Sun would be right there if he needed advice. Or a shoulder to cry on when he realized teens had their own form of logic that defied the conventions of all things in the known universe.

He'd be fine.

The staff managed to get Auri and Cruz assigned to rooms across the hall from one another once they got out of ICU. Auri would get transferred first, even though they probably wouldn't release Cruz until later that evening or possibly the next day.

But they were both still in ICU at seven that morning when Hailey walked in. She stopped short when she saw Levi, and her jaw fell open. She looked at Sun in a panic.

Thankfully, Hailey's brother was still asleep as she tiptoed backwards. Sun eased around him and took Hailey to the nurse's break room where the Jell-O was cheap and the coffee flowed free. She should know. She was on her eighth cup. In her defense, they were tiny cups.

Once they were out of Levi's line of sight, Hailey threw her arms around Sun. "I'm so sorry, honey," she said.

"I can't believe you're here," Sun said, thrilled to see her.

"I had to lie and say that I was Auri's aunt. Oh, my God, Sunshine. This is crazy. What happened?"

"I wish I knew. I have an idea, but I can't be certain until I interrogate the redhead. Under a thousand-watt lightbulb."

Hailey grinned sadly. "I'm just glad she and Cruz are okay. Is it true?"

"About his dad? Yes."

She covered her mouth with a hand. "That poor baby."

"Wait, how did you know?"

Hailey deadpanned her.

"Right. Small town." Sun couldn't let the depths of her sorrow take hold again. She was barely keeping her shit together as it was. "I was going to call you this morning so you could tell Jimmy."

She nodded. "I'll tell him later. He'll want to come up."

"Of course. They're moving her to a room in a little while. She would love to see him."

"And Levi?" Hailey wriggled her brows. "I notice he hasn't left your side."

A sheepish grin spread despite herself. "He hasn't left *Auri's* side."

"Auri's too. I just think he feels very differently about the two of you."

They giggled softly.

"Okay," Hailey said, "I'm going to head out before my brother wakes up and busts us."

"Oh, any news on the Clay Ravinder front?"

"No. There's another meeting soon, though. I'm sure of it."

"Be careful."

"You too. And give that beautiful girl a hug for me. And tell her I love her. And tell her Jimmy loves her. And we'll be up later. Oh, and see if she needs anything from home. Slippers. She'll probably need slippers. And toothpaste. Ask her if she needs toothpaste."

"Okay," Sun said with a soft laugh.

They hugged, and Sun reveled in the feel of it. Held it longer than she probably should have. She pulled back and noticed someone watching them from over Hailey's shoulder. While they'd moved out of Levi's line of sight, they'd walked directly into Quincy's. The man sat in the same chair, legs outstretched across the same floor, arm draped over the same bed, only this time his eyes were set ablaze by the two women he watched through the glass door.

"Oh, crap," Sun said.

Hailey spun around and gasped.

Quincy stood, checked on Cruz with a quick glance, then walked out of the main ICU area and toward them.

Sun searched her brain frantically for a logical explanation. No one knew she and Hailey were friends, and since Hailey was basically undercover, no one could know. It would be too dangerous for her. However, if she were to tell anyone, it would be the man walking toward them now. The one with the quizzical brow that framed a look of absolute astonishment.

Sun rolled her eyes. They were getting sloppy. First Auri. Now Quincy. The entire sting was crashing down around her.

Having found no explanation, her brain went into fight-or-flight mode. She turned to Hailey and railed, "And don't let me tell you again," she said, glaring at the blonde beside her. "You— you degenerate. You get out of here and don't come back. I don't want to ever—"

"Sun," Hailey said, pointing at the other blonde, the one standing so close Sun could feel the heat radiating off him.

She turned to him. "Quincy, thank goodness. I want you to arrest this . . . this—"

"Degenerate?" he offered.

"Yes. For trespassing."

"Degenerately?"

"Exactly." She poked Hailey on the shoulder. That'd show her.

"Sunshine," Hailey said, knowing when to give up the game long before Sun's brain did.

Sun slammed her lids shut, drew in a deep breath, then squared her shoulders. "Okay, this isn't what it looks like."

"Like you two are meeting in secret?"

Her jaw came loose from its hinges. She put it back, then said, "Well, of course that's what it looks like to the untrained eye."

"My eye is very trained."

And then, with the briefest, most ephemeral of flashes, something swept across his face. If Sun had blinked, she would have missed it. The glance. As though his pupils could not resist. The intake of breath. As though his lungs could not stop it. The softening of his features. As though his heart could not suppress its reaction.

Sun stood stunned for an eternity before she gaped at him.

"Hailey Ravinder?" she screeched, only really quietly because they were in a hospital. She stepped closer and spoke through clenched teeth. "That's who you've been pining over for months?"

"What?" He snorted. "No."

"Pining?" Hailey asked.

"After all this time, after everything we've been through, you think you can hide this from me?"

"Look who's talking." He gestured toward the two of them. "You two act like you're plotting to take over the world."

"We were discussing a town-wide rummage sale, for your information." *Now* her brain kicks in.

"Pining?" Hailey asked again, her gaze raking over Quincy like the break room was a desert and he was a sparkling oasis complete with lounge chairs and frou-frou drinks. The kind with tiny umbrellas, only there was nothing—and she would know— tiny about her chief deputy.

He cast his gaze down. "*Pining* is a strong word."

"For me?" She stepped closer.

He kicked at the floor with his boot.

Sun looked between the two, more than a little horrified. Not because they weren't perfect for each other. They kind of were. But because she didn't see it before.

When an electrifyingly romantic instrumental swept through the ICU over the loudspeakers—or in Sun's mind, either way— she decided to make her exit.

She walked to Auri's room in disbelief. Everyone was finding true love but her. Of course, she thought this as she rounded the corner and her gaze landed on the only man she'd ever really wanted. He sat with his back to her, holding Auri's hand.

"How is she?" her mother said, walking in behind her.

Levi turned and his gaze locked with Sun's as though he knew what she'd been thinking. Either that or her guilty conscience was projecting again. It did that.

"She's good, Mom. She hasn't woken up yet, but—"

"Mom?" Auri's tiny voice wafted to her.

Sun ran around the bed and took her other hand, carefully since that was the one with the IV.

Her bottom lip quivered. "Mom," she said, a soft sob escaping her.

Maybe it was a sign of the last couple of days or her guilty conscience projecting again, but Sun knew exactly what her daughter was thinking. "He's okay, Auri."

The look Auri gave her dissolved every bone in her body.

"He fought him off, sweetheart. Cruz was admitted with wounds, but he survived the surgery and is in ICU right down the hall."

Auri's gaze bounced between Sun and Levi, tears welling between her lashes before she broke down. Sun leaned in and hugged her for a very long time before Levi took over. It was a hard job. They took it in shifts. Her parents chipping in to cover when Sun and Levi needed a break. Even Quincy came in to lend a hand, cradling her to him until they came to transfer her. Each of them careful not to disturb her turban-like bandages.

They wheeled her to her room a little while later, the family following as though they were in a parade.

Quincy leaned close to her. "We need to talk."

She scowled at him. "I'll say. You have a lot of explaining to do."

"Me?" he asked, appalled.

She left it at that. All in all, it had been a very productive morning.

But it was about to get more productive. She had no choice.

Now that Auri was out of the woods, for the most part, she had to get back to Del Sol, even for just a few hours, to get on top of everything. Her parents would stay with Auri, but she needed the story before she went.

By noon, Auri was up and eating, a very good sign. Her head barely hurt from the submissive hemogoblin—her words—on the side of her head.

"Okay, bug bite," Sun said, sitting on the edge of her daughter's bed. "I need the truth, the whole truth, and nothing but the truth."

Elaine and Cyrus were in the room, too, as well as Levi and Quincy. They'd kicked the latter out of Cruz's room to clean the kid's wounds and change his bandages. Cruz had only awakened a couple of times but they were keeping him pretty medicated. According to the surgeon, the first forty-eight hours were crucial in the fight against sepsis, especially when the intestines had been punctured. The last thing they needed was Cruz fighting them again and ripping something inside.

Auri bit her lip. She wasn't 100 percent by any means, but she was definitely almost bright-eyed and bushy-tailed.

Levi sat on the other side of her bed. He took her hand. "I can leave, Red, if that will help."

She shook her head. "It doesn't matter. I almost got Cruz and Mrs. Fairborn killed. You'll find out eventually either way."

"Auri," Elaine said. "That's not true."

"It is, Grandma. I wish it weren't more than anything in the world, but it is. I just—" She looked at Sun. "I just wanted to be like my mom so bad." A wetness welled between her dark red lashes. "But I'm not. I never will be."

"Sweetheart, why would you say that?"

"You save people's lives. I just try to get them killed."

Levi reached out and wiped a tear streaming down her face. "How about you tell your mom what happened and let her decide if you two are alike or not? You might be surprised."

He was right. She did tend to put people in danger from time to time. But only if other people were in danger first. It was kind of her job.

"First, I was trying to prove that Mrs. Fairborn was a serial killer, then I was just trying to prove that the drifter accused of the crimes was innocent without getting Mrs. Fairborn sent to prison because she couldn't make a shank out of her toothbrush, then I just wanted to get the necklace back to its rightful owner, and then everything spun out of control."

No one spoke for a few minutes, so when Auri swallowed, it seemed really loud.

Sun came around first. "I thought we talked about how unlikely it was that Mrs. Fairborn was a serial killer."

"I know. I just thought you were wrong."

"And as far as proving the drifter innocent, that would be very difficult at this late stage."

"But not impossible," she argued. "Especially after you see all the things in Mrs. Fairborn's house. I even thought about asking her to write a confession letter that I could magically find after her untimely death to prove that Hercules Holmes was innocent."

"Wow," Sun's mom said, horrified. "You really thought this through."

She nodded. "But at the same time, I wanted to get the necklace back to its rightful owners since they seemed really upset about it."

"I read those articles, too, Auri," Sun said. "From what I remember, the family cared more about that necklace than they did their missing family member."

"I agree, but does that mean they don't deserve to get their things back? I mean, they said she stole the necklace before she ran off."

"And I'm guessing you told her cousin, Billy Press?"

Auri bit her lip as tears welled again. "I found him online and told him about the boardinghouse, but I didn't give him the name! I would never put Mrs. Fairborn in danger like that."

Sun squeezed her hand. "But you did, pumpkin. You almost got her killed. Not to mention Cruz."

"Sunny," Quincy said, admonishing her.

"Quince, she needs to hear the truth. She needs to realize there are consequences to her actions."

"She's right, Quincy," Auri said, her little chin trembling. "This is all my fault."

"That is not what I am saying," Sun said, enunciating each word. "You tried to do the right thing." She took hold of her quivering chin, softly guiding Auri's gaze back to her. "I am so proud of you for that. You said we aren't alike, but you're wrong. I have to make these kinds of decisions every day of my life. Is the risk worth the reward? Is whatever I'm trying to accomplish, whatever crime I'm trying to solve, worth the danger to me or my deputies? To the people who might get caught in the crossfire?"

"So then if it's too risky, you don't solve the crime?"

"No, honey. If it's too risky, I find another way. Take a different route. You had no way of knowing what Emily Press's cousin would do, but that's the problem. Why do you think people in law enforcement never give out any details during an active investigation?"

"Because it could hurt their case?"

"Often, yes, but also because others could use that information to their advantage. Again, the family was more upset about the necklace than they were about Emily. Something didn't add up and you knew that. In your gut."

Auri dropped her gaze as a pink hue blossomed across her cheeks. "I did."

"Okay, then. First, I'm putting alarms on your windows with a high-security surveillance system. No more sneaking out."

She shook her head. "You don't need to do that. It won't happen again.

"Regardless. And I'm putting an ankle bracelet on you with GPS and electroshock capabilities."

She swallowed hard. "Okay."

Sun wouldn't, of course. She didn't even know where to find an ankle bracelet with electroshock capabilities. "And that's just the beginning, hon."

"I know," she said with a sob, and Sun had to steel her heart. There had to be consequences. "For now, I want you to think about it and tell me what punishment you think you deserve."

"What if I can't?"

"I have faith." Sun knew that no one would be harder on Auri than she would herself. Maybe even a little too hard, but maybe that was what she needed. A harsh dose of reality.

After a fresh round of tears, Auri nodded in agreement.

It took a while but they finally got the whole story from her. It demolished Sun's heart to hear her daughter try to explain what it was like to find Mrs. Fairborn tied up. How she rushed in without even thinking, putting everyone in even greater danger. How she watched as the knife sank into Cruz's abdomen.

Sun decided right then and there the fiery minx learned her lesson in the hardest way possible. She would've given anything to protect her from it, too. Still, what she did could not go unpunished. Sun saw several thousand hours of community service in her future.

Possibly worse, for Sun anyway, she had to tell Auri about Cruz's father. Levi held the pixie for a long time while Sun stroked her hair, worried she'd broken her. They cried together and waited as they brought Cruz, barely conscious, to his room across the hall.

"What do I say to him, Mom?" she asked between sobs.

"Just be there for him, honey. That's all you can do."

Sun checked on her other stabbing victim, Keith Seabright. They'd downgraded his prognosis from *critical* to *serious but stable*. With that bit of good news, Sun had to get back to the office.

She took her parents aside before she left. "Okay, guys. She is connected to an IV. Her ass will show if she tries to make a run for it and that will mortify her. And she literally had brain surgery. Do you think you can keep her from sneaking out?" She had to ask.

The guilt on their faces was priceless.

"And I'm teasing you because you have to stop, too. This was not your fault. Any of it."

Her mom's expression told Sun she was not convinced. "We showed her the articles."

"No, she found those articles all on her own because she's a true-crime aficionado. You have no idea how many times I've had to drag her away from the Investigation Discovery channel. She knows more about hiding a body than I do."

"We're sorry either way, Sunny," her dad said. "If we could change what happened—"

"I would do it, too. And as many times as I've plotted your deaths for something that actually *was* your fault, this is not one of those times."

"You've plotted our deaths?" her mom asked.

"So many times."

"Like, how recently?"

"Remember Carver?" she asked, giving attitude.

"Oh, yeah." Her dad scratched his chin. "Our bad."

"Your bad?" she asked. "You set me up with a hitman and it's *your bad*?"

Her mom shrugged. "He seemed okay at the time."

She leaned in and kissed her cheek, then gave her dad a bear hug. "I'll be back as soon as I can."

She had to get to Del Sol to check on the progress of the Kent and the Fairborn cases. Billy Press's family was on the way from Amarillo, and they apparently wanted that damned necklace. They were about to be sorely disappointed. Sun decided right then and there to hold that thing in evidence as long as humanly possible. As soon as she could find it.

She promised to be back by nightfall and left Quincy in charge, only because he refused to leave. She took Levi with her. He had a business to run, after all, and he needed to get some rest that did not involve a plastic lounger that reclined about as much as a seat on a jetliner.

On the drive home, her mind spiraled in a thousand different directions. The irony was not lost on her. Kubrick Ravinder stabbed her rescuer fifteen years ago before her rescuer won control of the knife and slid it into Kubrick's chest.

And now Cruz. The saying that truth was stranger than fiction had never been more accurate.

Her thoughts, as they always did, eventually circled back to the man sitting beside her. The way he cared for Auri. The way he held Sun in the shower, completely unfazed by the fact that she was soaking him through. And the way he looked in the red T-shirt she bought one size too small, swearing it was all they had. It showed every muscle. Every dip and every curve. Every ounce of perfection.

Rojas called and snapped her out of her musings. The Bluetooth in her cruiser automatically picked it up and blasted the ringtone throughout the speakers. Levi had been just as lost in his thoughts as she was hers, but it was impossible for him not to hear the conversation.

"We got this, boss," Rojas said. "You do what you need to do. We have everything covered. Also, Randy set fire to the station."

"Damn it," she said, only half paying attention to him and more paying attention to the way Levi's biceps stretched the hem of the sleeve. "He didn't set off the suppression system, did he?"

"Only in the locker room."

"Okay, good. Who's Randy again?" She loved saying that. It was too bad Carver turned out to be an assassin and not a pest control technician. And that he was dead. She could've used him to trap the little guy.

Not thirty seconds after she ended her call with Rojas, her phone rang again.

"Hey, Sunny Girl," Royce Womack said.

"Hey yourself. What do you got?"

"So, you were right. My contact looked into one Mr. Carver Zuckerman. He wasn't so much a famous hitman as a wannabe famous hitman."

"Which, who doesn't want to be the top in their field?" she asked. "Goals, Womack. We all need them."

"We do at that. I did look into his Russian hit. It really happened, but it was by one of the most famous snipers in Russian history. Your guy has never even been out of the country."

"Ah, but maybe that was his genius. He was a hitman, after all. Surely he had multiple identities."

"Yeah, no. He was on absolutely no one's radar. How's the kid?"

"Better. Thank God. Thanks for looking into this, Royce."

"Any time. It looks like Matthew Kent is going away for a much longer stay than he'd planned now that his ties to the Delmars have been exposed and the money he had hidden all these years has been found."

"Good," she said, hoping Addison filed for divorce first thing that morning.

"How 'bout I buy you coffee again soon. We can watch the sunrise together."

She couldn't help but notice Levi tense just ever so slightly. "What's with this *again* crap? You haven't bought me coffee yet. I seem to remember someone forgetting his wallet last time."

He laughed and hung up.

"I thought he was retired," Levi said.

"He is. He just helps out when I need him."

"I know the feeling."

She couldn't argue that, but the way he said it, like she only called him when she needed help with a case. Not that he was wrong. She did only call him when she needed help with a case, but to call otherwise would imply they had a relationship of some kind. And the phone worked both ways. If he wanted to see her more often, he damned well knew where to find her. By the time she'd worked up the nerve to tell him that very thing, they were back at the station and thus Levi's truck.

He got out of the cruiser and turned toward her. The analytical once-over he gave her piqued her curiosity, especially when he said, "You can do better than Womack."

He closed the door before she could question him.

25

Levi's words threw her. Did he honestly think she and Womack were a thing? She loved the older man. Had for years. But not like she loved Levi. Because she did. She loved Levi.

The truth hit her hard. It was more than a schoolgirl crush and had been for years. Decades, probably.

Sun dwelled on that fact as she showered and changed into fresh clothes. The fact that her longtime affection for the man had turned into a deep and fervent love, almost desperate in its depth. Painful in its scope. It would be impossible to pinpoint an exact place or time it happened. Maybe it had always been the vibrant thing that it was today. Maybe she'd been in denial.

Nah.

After driving to her office, she suffered through an afternoon of briefings and interviews and paperwork, all punctuated with a constant barrage of texts to her parents to check up on the kids.

When she got back to the hospital room, she found her mom reading in a chair, her dad snoring on a built-in love seat, and her daughter gone.

"She snuck out?" she asked, appalled. She gaped at her mom. "Didn't we just talk about this?"

Her mom jumped to her feet, shushed her with an index finger over her mouth—Sun's, not hers—and led her across the hall. "We keep finding her like this," she whispered when Sun saw Auri curled up beside Cruz, careful not to put any weight on his wounds. Their arms were interlaced. Her face centimeters from his.

Sun felt like the Grinch when his heart started swelling painfully in his chest. "How is she?"

"A little dizzy, but no pain. She ate well, too, considering."

"Has it sunk in that they had to shave part of her head yet?"

"No. We're going to let her stay in denial as long as possible."

"And Cruz?"

"He only wakes up when the nurses come in and make Auri go to her own bed. He's delirious, starts fighting them until they finally let her come back just to calm him down."

Sun shook her head. "I never wanted this for her," she told her mom. "This intense of a relationship at so young an age."

"You can hardly blame her. You were the same way."

"What? I was never this intense when I dated. I don't think I ever fell in love. Not really."

"Because your love, your intensity, was focused elsewhere."

They'd known how she felt about Levi almost before she knew it herself.

"I got this, Mom. You two go home and get some rest."

"I'm only going to agree to this because your dad will pay for it dearly if he sleeps like that all night. But we'll be back in a few hours."

After they left, she sat on the recliner beside Auri. Cruz opened his eyes and looked at her over the girl in his arms.

She stood. "Hey, handsome. Do you need anything?"

His lids drifted shut as though he couldn't hold them open, but he fought and won, if only for a few minutes. He shook his head.

"I'm sorry, Sheriff," he whispered, his voice hoarse.

"For what, baby?"

"I tried to stop him."

"Cruz, you saved my daughter's life. And you almost paid for that with your own. I owe you everything."

He looked away, unconvinced.

"Cruz," she said softly, "why didn't you tell us about your dad?"

He pressed his mouth together, then said, "They would've taken me away. Probably would've sent me to my dad's foster dad in the Switch, but only if he had wanted me. He's getting too old to take in foster kids. Hasn't had any in years."

"And you're afraid you'll be a burden."

"I know I will be. Besides, it's really far away." He glanced at Auri's sleeping face, then looked away as though he didn't want Sun to know the real reason he wanted to stay. "If not, they'll send me to a children's home, most likely, and the closest is in Las Vegas."

"Well, I have an idea. I'm looking into it, okay?" She didn't want to promise him anything in case the state wouldn't allow Cruz to stay with Quincy.

He nodded. Just barely.

Unable to help herself, she brushed his hair off his brow. "No matter how this turns out, I am so sorry, Cruz. I can't imagine what you went through. How alone you must've felt." When a familiar wetness gathered between his lashes, she bent over the kids and kissed them both.

Auri, who'd been awake through the whole conversation because she squeezed Sun's hand thanking her, smiled sleepily.

When Sun woke up the next morning to the sound of nurses checking on the kids, she opened her eyes to the most beautiful sight in the world. Levi Ravinder on one side of the bed, dozing beside her daughter, and Quincy Cooper on the other, dozing beside Cruz. Auri was in bed with Cruz again, but they were about to kick her out to change his bandages.

Cruz was awake, his gaze heavy lidded but alert. He was studying Quincy, as though trying to figure him out. She'd often done the same.

Since the nurses were nanoseconds away from waking them up, Sun stood, walked over to Levi, and pressed her mouth to his. He was so darkly handsome, she had to steal a quick kiss before he woke up. Either women kissed him in his sleep often or he hadn't been asleep after all.

He returned the kiss immediately, going so far as to wrap a hand around the back of her neck and angle his head to deepen it. His tongue brushed softly against hers, causing a tremor low in her abdomen before she broke contact.

She leaned back to look at him. His whiskey-colored irises studied her as she gestured toward the nurses. "They need the redhead back in her own bed and you're in the way."

He offered her a single nod, stood to gather the pixie into his arms, and carried her across the hall to her own bed while Cruz looked on, gazing at her like she'd hung the moon. An emotion Sun understood all too well.

One of the younger nurses woke up Quincy, her eyes sparkling with interest. He smiled appreciatively.

Sun followed Levi. "I didn't know you were coming back."

"You didn't ask," he said, matter-of-fact.

She cast a worried glance over her shoulder at Cruz. "He has a hard road ahead of him."

Levi eased Auri onto her bed as though she were made of fine crystal. Or nitroglycerine. Either way.

"He'll have a lot to deal with," Sun continued. "Not only did he lose his dad, but he took a life. I'm worried what that will do to him."

After draping the blanket over Auri, Levi looked across the hall at Cruz. "We'll be here for him. Whatever it takes."

"I think he should talk to someone." When Levi nodded, she added, "Speaking of talking to someone, I thought I would have a chat with your friend, Keith Seabright."

"I saw him last night. He's doing a lot better."

"Good. I still need to have a chat."

"I don't think he remembers much."

"Yeah. I still need to chat."

She found Keith Seabright in a room two floors down. He was just as stunning in person as he was on video. Average height and lean. Wiry and strong. Still in military shape eight years after his honorable discharge. He looked like a child star from Hollywood who'd grown up even better looking than he was as a kid.

She introduced herself and got his side of the story firsthand. Levi had already told him what happened with Elliot and Adam, so he was up to date on current events.

"We've had an alarming amount of stabbings lately," she said to him afterwards.

He laughed but regretted it instantly.

She narrowed her eyes and watched him a long moment before saying, "I'd like you to stay in Del Sol."

"Is this a *don't leave town* kind of thing?" he asked, his voice hoarse and deep.

"No," she said with a soft chuckle. "This is an *I'm about to fill a lieutenant's position and I'll be down a deputy* kind of thing. There's an opening. I'd like you on my team."

Levi seemed just as surprised as Seabright at the proposition. Maybe more so.

"You don't even know me," he said.

"I've done my research. Ran a background. Talked to some of your COs. According to everyone who's ever met you, even Levi Ravinder—"

"Never heard of him."

"—you're kind of amazing."

"I never said amazing," Levi argued.

Seabright raised a brow. "Too late. No take backs."

"It's not a take back if I never said it."

"Here's how I see this working out," Sun said, interrupting the lover's quarrel.

He tucked a hand behind his head, slowly, each movement deliberate, and said, "This should be good."

"You marry Addison."

His brows shot up.

"You guys rent that house on Apollo Drive. The pretty one with the ivy?"

Levi nodded. "Oh, yeah. The Duran house."

"Exactly. Then you, Addison, and the boys move in, you go to police academy even though you could probably teach at it, and then you become my latest and greatest in sixteen weeks. Give or take."

"You've given this some thought."

"I have. I want you on my team. With your experience, I can hire you on as a sergeant."

"What if I say no?"

"Then I'll bring you in for kidnapping, you'll go to prison for the next thirty years, the boys will grow up without a father, and Addison will spend the next three decades visiting you in jail. But I hear conjugals are a reward unto themselves."

"Hmm," he hummed. "Can I sleep on it?"

"Sure." She stood to leave. "You have twenty-four hours. Also," she turned back to him, "thank you for keeping Elliot safe."

"From what I hear, I owe you the same thanks."

"Let's call it even. Twenty-four hours." She started to leave, then turned back to him. "I almost forgot. Elliot said you had a contact in the Delmar family. Was it Agent Wilcox?"

"I could tell you—"

"Yeah, yeah." She left to find Quincy waiting for her in the hall outside Seabright's room.

"I'm really beginning to question your recruiting techniques," he said.

"What?" she asked defensively. "They're effective."

"Right. Don't you think you're playing a dangerous game with Hailey's life? Have you met her uncle Clay?"

"Shhh," she shushed, leading him away from prying ears. "For your information, she came to me."

"Because she's innocent. She didn't know what she was getting herself into."

"Quincy, did she tell you what's going on?"

"No. She wouldn't tell me anything. But I can guess. Also, I can hardly talk around her, so it wasn't like we had an actual conversation after you left yesterday."

"Wow. How did I not pick up on your infatuation?"

"I'm not—" He gave up. "Does Ravinder know?"

"That you're in love with his sister?"

"No, about whatever's going on."

"Not that I'm aware of, but you know Levi."

He shrugged. "Not as well as you, obvs."

There was something terribly charming about a grown man using the word *obvs*, but she wasn't about to let him know that.

"Why am I just now learning about all of this?" he asked. "What is Clay Ravinder up to?"

"I didn't want to involve you until I knew what was going on for sure. And I still don't. Not exactly."

He crossed his arms in frustration. "Everyone was right about you growing up."

"When they said I had a sparkling personality and would probably be queen of the world someday?"

"When they voted you most likely to be institutionalized for inducing mass hysteria in children and small animals."

"Oh, yeah. I still have the sash."

Auri thought they would never leave. She loved her grandparents more than banana pudding with Nilla Wafers, which was saying a lot, but she had things to do. People to see. Apologies to give.

She texted Sybil, who'd bombarded her with texts after she'd heard what had happened, giving her the A-OK. Then she looked at Cruz as he slept. He lay on his back but his face was turned toward her. She lay pressed against his side, one arm under her head—the non–submissive hemogoblin side—and one over his chest. His ridiculously long lashes fanned across his cheeks like crescent moons. So. Not. Fair.

She rubbed her nose against his, and he raised his lashes. "I'm going to see her before my grandparents come back," she whispered.

He nodded sleepily. "I want to go."

She giggled. "You can't."

"They said they're going to get me up and walking today. May as well start now."

"Not on your life, Mr. De los Santos."

The bashful smile that spread across his face melted her. She wouldn't be surprised if her grandparents found her a mere puddle on the floor when they got back.

"Can you apologize for me, too?"

"Of course." She leaned forward and pressed her mouth to his. "And when I get back, we can talk if you want."

"About?"

She cupped his cheek in her hand. "When you're ready."

"If this is about the devil's doorbell, I was born ready."

She laughed softly and slipped out of bed. Pushing her IV stand wasn't as difficult as she thought it might be. She snuck past the nurse's station and got on the elevator, ignoring the few questioning glances that came her way.

She tapped on Mrs. Fairborn's door and eased inside to the sound of a moan. Alarm spurred her forward. She found the woman in bed, an arm thrown over her head, a drink in the other hand, and a horrible moan coming from her throat.

"Mrs. Fairborn!" Auri rushed up to her, dragging her IV stand and knocking it first into a chair and then into an important looking piece of equipment with lots of buttons and lights. "Are you okay? Can I get someone?"

"Oh, it's you, Aurora. No, I'm fine, sweetheart. I'm just really enjoying the service. Once they figure out I'm okay, they'll send me home. No one waits on me hand and foot at home anymore. All my servants left me when I never paid them. It's horrible."

She took a drink of her juice as though she were sipping a piña colada on the beach. Not that Auri had ever had a piña colada on a beach, or anywhere else for that matter, but someday hopefully.

"I wanted to apologize."

"For what, sweetheart? For saving my life?"

"No one told you?"

She gave her a patient smile.

Auri pressed her mouth together, trying to gather the courage to tell her the truth. After a couple of false starts, she finally fessed up in a lengthy soliloquy that bordered on Shakespearian. "I'm the one who told Billy Press the necklace was at your house. I mean, I didn't say your house specifically. I told him it was still at the old boardinghouse. He must've figured it out. I took a picture of it because I was going to use it to prove you were a serial killer a long time ago, then I changed my mind about exposing you for being a maniacal murderer because I don't want you to go to jail since you don't brush your teeth and I thought I would steal the necklace to botch the chain of custody and give it to my mom so she could get it back to the family, and then I thought maybe you could write a letter so that after you died people would know that the drifter Hercules Holmes was innocent all along."

"I see," Mrs. Fairborn said, her brows knitting in confusion.

"Anyway, none of that matters." She wanted to take Mrs. Fairborn's hand but didn't dare. The woman probably hated her. "It's my fault you were attacked. It's my fault you and Cruz almost died. He wants me to apologize for him, too, but he has nothing to apologize for. It was my idea. All of it. And I am so, so sorry, Mrs. Fairborn. I promise I will never almost get you killed again if it's the last thing I do."

The woman's pale face softened. "What if I told you I'm glad this happened."

Auri gaped at her.

"Well, not the getting attacked part or you and Cruz almost dying, but I'm glad you found those articles."

"You know about the articles?"

"Your grandparents told me. I've been silent too long, Aurora. People need to know the truth."

"The truth?"

"Yes. Elusive as it so often is. The last time I tried to tell it, I was intimidated into keeping my mouth shut. Threatened." Mrs. Fairborn held out her hand. Auri took it instantly, the elder woman's smooth skin like tissue paper between her hands. "No more. Women have been intimidated into silence for too long. When we get home and everything returns to normal, you come to my house and we'll chat. You can be my voice. You can tell the people what really happened all those years ago."

"You're not mad?"

"No, sweetheart."

"So, you're not going to kill me and bury me under your floorboards?"

A tinny cackle erupted from the woman that ended in a short fit of coughs. "Never," she said after she recovered.

Sheepish didn't even begin to describe how Auri felt. But there was still one thing bothering her above all else. "I don't understand, Mrs. Fairborn. Why was Billy so obsessed with that necklace? It's an antique ivory cameo, so it is valuable, but I looked them up. They aren't worth *that* much. Four thousand dollars? Maybe five? And the casing is just brass."

"Exactly." She poked her with a spindly finger, then pointed to her purse, a small fuchsia thing sitting on the overbed table.

Auri handed it to her then watched as she filtered through her belongings.

"And why did that girl's family make such a fuss about their niece running away with it? They were more concerned about this damned necklace," she said, lifting the necklace out of her purse, "than they were their own niece."

Auri gasped. "How did you get it?"

"I insisted the paramedics allow me to grab it when they brought me to the hospital."

"They let you take evidence from a crime scene?"

"I'm old, dear. You'd be amazed at what you can get away with when people think you're senile."

Auri's admiration increased tenfold.

She took Auri's hand and placed it on her palm. "I want you to take it."

Guilt assaulted her with such force, it paralyzed her lungs and stung her eyes. "I couldn't possibly, Mrs. Fairborn."

"I insist. You two saved my life."

"After we put it in danger."

She gave her a dismissive wave. "Tom-ay-to, tom-ah-to. I trust you to do the right thing and think about why that family cared so much about an ivory-and-brass necklace." She closed Auri's fingers around it and patted her hand.

Auri's curiosity got the better of her. "There has to be more to this."

"Precisely. I never figured it out. Maybe you can."

26

Beer: So much more than just a breakfast drink.
　　　　　—SIGN AT THE ROADHOUSE BAR AND GRILL

"Are you kidding me?" Sun walked in to find her parents frantically searching for her daughter. "You lost her again?"

They turned to her, frazzled and exasperated. Only Aurora Dawn could do that to them.

"You guys are fired."

A tiny voice floated to them from the doorway. "Hey, Grandma. Hey, Grandpa."

The queen of mischief hobbled in dragging her IV stand like a set of golf clubs.

"Auri," Elaine said, rushing to her and pulling her into her arms. Cyrus soon followed. "Where did you go?"

"For a walk."

Sun crossed her arms over her chest.

Auri caved like a cardboard roof during a rainstorm. "I went to apologize to Mrs. Fairborn."

"Auri," Sun scolded, helping her daughter into bed. "That poor woman doesn't need you traumatizing her anymore. Seeing her without her permission at this point borders on unethical, honey."

"But you're about to take her home. It was now or never. And she was moaning."

"I'm going to check on her. You stay."

Auri's tiny shoulders sagged but Sun didn't miss the reassuring smile she cast across the hall to Cruz. They must've been exonerated by Mrs. Fairborn, which would be a weight off her chest.

They were releasing Mrs. Fairborn that afternoon, and Sun offered to drive her home. It was the least she could do, all things considered. She threatened her parents one last time for good measure, then went in search of a serial killer.

"That girl of yours is clever," Mrs. Fairborn said after an hour of almost complete silence on the ride home. Mostly because she'd fallen asleep the instant they headed out of the parking lot.

"She is. Thank you."

"Oh, can you run me by the Swirls-n-Curls, honey? I need to grab a couple of things."

"Of course." They pulled in back and Mrs. Fairborn handed her a list. Sun laughed and went inside to gather the essentials, which were already bagged and waiting for her.

Next, they went to the grocery store, where Mrs. Fairborn only needed toilet paper and Dr Pepper, and would she mind? Then to the hardware supply store where she swore she needed three rolls of electrical tape. It wasn't until they ended up at the bait shop that Sun began to suspect the woman was leading her on a wild-goose chase, but to what end?

Sun couldn't help but wonder if she was afraid to go home. No one would blame her. Several members of the community cleaned the crime scene at her house after forensics finished. They even replaced a couple of broken windows, fixed a leaky faucet, and brought her some individually packaged home-cooked meals.

But she was still attacked in her home. Her sanctuary invaded. The one place she felt safe had been violated. Sun couldn't imagine how that felt.

"This is the very last stop," she promised.

"Mrs. Fairborn, is there somewhere else I can take you? You don't have to go home if you don't want to."

"Oh, no, honey. It's okay. I just have one more thing to get."

She blinked and looked out her windshield. "At The Angry Angler?"

"Yep."

"You going fly-fishing?"

"Better. Angry fly-fishing. I hear it's much more productive if you yell at the fish as you're pulling them in."

"I've heard that," Sun said with a snort.

Sun saw Quincy walking in the back.

She opened the door and hopped out. "Quince, wait up."

He turned. "Hey, boss." He gestured toward the fishing shop. "Got a call about a disturbance."

"Stay here, Mrs. Fairborn." She locked her doors before heading inside, her palm on her duty weapon.

Quincy knocked on the back door and tried the knob. "It's unlocked."

She nodded.

He opened the door and they slipped inside to an empty storeroom. After they headed up front and cleared the floor, they looked at each other. The sign on the locked front door read CLOSED.

"No one's here," Quincy said, right before they heard a crash.

"Does this place have a basement?" she asked.

They hurried to a set of stairs beside a bookcase, which were not easily visible or accessible. They drew their duty weapons.

"Sheriff's office!" Quincy said. "Show your hands!"

Sun followed him down a narrow set of stairs into a dark room just as the lights flared to life around them. She was blinded for a few vital seconds. When her vision adjusted, she looked around at a roomful of smiling faces.

She turned to Quince.

He turned to her. "What's going on?" he asked.

"I was about to ask you that same thing."

When she scanned the room again, she realized she knew every single person there, including Mrs. Fairborn, whom she'd just locked in her cruiser, and her parents. The same parents she'd just left in Albuquerque.

"Did you lose her again?" she asked them.

Her father grinned. "Don't worry about the peanut. She's in very good hands."

Sun took another sweep and saw Mayor Donna Lomas standing off to the side with her arms crossed over her chest and a satisfied smirk crinkling her mouth.

"You can put those away," she said, gesturing toward the guns.

They holstered their weapons, and Sun said, "Is this what I think it is?" Eleven of Del Sol's finest in the basement of an angler's shop. Because where else would they meet?

"You figured it out," the mayor said. "Thus, it was time."

"You figured what out?" Quincy asked her.

"That the mayor," Sun said, sharpening her gaze on her, "is a bona fide, card-carrying member of the Dangerous Daughters." That was the only explanation as to why Mayor Lomas would be so insistent that Sun figure out who they are. She had an ulterior motive, Sun just didn't know what it was.

"They're real?" he asked.

"They are. And I think I know why." She eyed Mrs. Fairborn, the only one sitting in one of many chairs strewn about the beautifully appointed room. "This is about the case Auri stumbled onto."

The twinkle in the older woman's eyes was infectious. "It is. I told you, that girl of yours is clever. How she found that Press boy is beyond me."

"The one who tried to kill you?" Quincy asked, his expression filled with horror. Then he frowned at the people standing around, smiling at him like they were part of a cult and he was this year's sacrifice at the Autumn Harvest Festival. "Would someone fill me in?"

"Absolutely." The mayor walked up to him and handed him a coin.

"Sordid?" He turned it over. "Son." He looked back at her. "Yeah, this doesn't clear anything up."

"Maybe this will," Mrs. Fairborn said. She stood, walked over to Sun, and handed her a coin as well.

While Quincy's was yellow gold, hers was rose gold and heavily worn, the words almost rubbed off completely. She read aloud, as well. "Daughter." She turned it over. "Dangerous." She smiled. "The crown, so to speak."

"That it is." She cackled and pointed to it. "Don't lose that. They're irreplaceable. This coin was made in 1937 by a German clockmaker who dabbled in rare coins and designed the official seal for the Royal House of Ezra."

Sun's mouth formed an O.

Mrs. Fairborn giggled. "Just kidding. About them being irreplaceable, that is. I've lost my coin twelve—"

"Thirteen," Elaine said.

"—thirteen times. But it is a pain in the ass to get them replaced. Just sayin'."

Sun looked around at what would be called the pillars of the community. Not necessarily those who were on the city council or who were in positions of authority. They were the farmers and the business owners. The custodians and the educators. Even the high school principal was there. And the second love of her life, Royce Womack.

She shook her head. "I have to admit, I had no idea about the sons."

"I'm Salacious," he said, a wicked grin spreading behind his scruffy beard.

"Why doesn't that surprise me?"

One by one they were introduced to the Dangerous Daughters and the Sordid Sons. Daughters like Dastardly and Diabolical and Devilish, a.k.a., her mother. And sons like Savage and Sinful and Scandalous, a.k.a., her father.

"We're being inducted," she said, feeling both humbled and profoundly underqualified.

These were the sons and daughters of Del Sol. People who were born and raised in the town and hadn't left for fifteen years like Sun did, though one, Rojas's tia Darlene, did live in Albuquerque for a few years before coming back into the fold. She was the Daughter Dastardly.

"If you accept," her mother said.

"And if we don't?" she asked.

"Well, you've already seen our faces, so we'd have to kill you."

"If you're taking Mrs. Fairborn's seat," Quincy said, looking at his coin, "whose seat am I taking?"

She'd wondered that herself.

Royce dropped his gaze. "Bo Britton, son. Your former lieutenant."

Bo, much beloved by the community, had died two weeks before Sun took over as sheriff. Quincy looked at the coin in his hand with a new respect.

Sun studied hers. "So, there's always a baker's dozen at any given time?"

"Yes," the mayor said. "Seven women and six men."

"And we're lucky to get that much," Royce said. "Mrs. Fairborn was very reluctant to let any man have a say in her secret club."

Mrs. Fairborn nodded. "The women will always have the final vote."

"Then we're missing one." Sun counted again.

"Sinister," the mayor confirmed. "While you are the reigning queen, so to speak, he would be—"

"The king?" she asked.

"More like the prince," Mrs. Fairborn said. "No one has more power in this group than the queen. He couldn't be here today, but he's already cast his vote."

"As we all have," her dad said.

An emotion she hadn't expected threatened to close her throat. She managed to get out two words: "I'm honored."

Quincy nodded, unable to speak himself.

Sun helped Mrs. Fairborn back to her chair and knelt in front of her. "This is a big day for you. Passing on the torch."

The woman nodded sadly. "More than fifty years I've been running this town. Well, the most important aspects of it."

"Why now?"

"I was waiting for you. Thought you'd never come back. Eventually, we realized we'd have to force your hand."

"You were involved with my parents' election tampering?"

"Involved? It was my idea."

Her parents laughed softly. "It was not her idea," her mom said.

"But why me?" she asked. "I'm honored. Don't get me wrong, but—"

"A butterfly and a hammer," the older woman said.

She and Quincy exchanged a quick glance, then asked simultaneously, "A butterfly and a hammer?"

She cackled. "You may not remember this, but when you were very young, I found you in the park cradling a pitiful little butterfly in your hands."

"King Henry," she said. She hadn't thought about him in years. "He was orange and black."

"Yes. Poor little guy had tattered wings and couldn't fly. Some boys were laughing and trying to kick it. And you, in all your five-year-old glory, stormed into the middle of their circle and ran them off. Then you picked up the butterfly, cradled it in your hands, and told me you were taking it to the vet."

"I remember. My mom wouldn't take it to the vet. She said they didn't treat insects."

Mrs. Fairborn nodded. "You were devastated. I'll never forget the look on your face when your mother told you it was going to die. So you took it home and cared for that poor thing day and night for almost two weeks because you wanted it to feel happy and safe for the rest of its life, no matter how long that would be."

"You never told me that story," Quince said.

"I'd forgotten about it."

"I didn't," Mrs. Fairborn said. "Your mother kept me up-dated. When it died, she was worried she was going to have to get you into grief counseling."

Sun smirked. "Figures."

"So where does the hammer come in?" Quince asked.

Mrs. Fairborn practically shimmied with mirth. "When I saw Little Miss Sunshine at the park right after the butterfly's passing, God rest its soul, she was carrying a hammer."

Sun frowned. "I don't remember this part."

"You stopped at the bench where I was sitting, pointed to the boys who'd been cruel to the butterfly, and told me you were go-ing to take out their kneecaps." She rocked back and clapped her hands, her laughter filling the room, her glee infectious.

Sun fought a sheepish grin.

"You almost pulled it off, too. I'd never seen boys run so fast in my life. If not for your mother capturing you mid-swing, your parents would've had several lawsuits on their hands."

Sun laughed, thinking back, then asked, "So that's why?"

The older woman leaned forward. "That was only the begin-ning. I've been watching you, Sunbeam." She tapped her temple. "You have all the fire and passion I once had. You're the one I want filling my shoes."

Sun took Mrs. Fairborn's hands into hers. "Thank you."

"How did all this get started?" Quincy asked. He brought around a chair for Sun and took one beside them. Everyone else did the same so they could hear the story once more. "The whole Dangerous Daughters thing."

"Like Sunny said. It started with the missing persons cases. It's so odd. It just doesn't seem like that long ago."

Sun leaned on her elbows and listened.

"Aurora was right. The people who went missing in the late fifties and early sixties, many of them anyway, had stayed with us at the boardinghouse. For almost a decade, travelers and the like just disappeared. Not many, mind you. Maybe one or two a year. Sometimes they'd leave some of their belongings. They'd head out at all hours and we wouldn't hear about the fact that they never made it to their destinations for weeks. Sometimes months, if at all."

Royce brought Mrs. Fairborn a cup of tea and put it on a side table.

"Thank you, Sheriff."

Sun smiled. Lots of people in town still called Royce "Sheriff." She loved it. If she could co-sheriff with anyone, it would be with that grizzly bear.

"But it was the Emily Press case that brought it all to the forefront. The papers got wind that she'd stolen a necklace, an old family heirloom, and was headed to Colorado to meet up with her beau when she disappeared."

"The necklace Billy Press was after?" Quincy asked.

"Yes, sir. That's when I first started to suspect. I found the necklace in the dresser of my husband, Mortimer. He said Miss Press forgot it when she took off, but I knew. Deep down, I knew he was killing those people for what little they had."

She took her cup into a shaky hand and sipped to calm herself, a haunted expression on her face. "He killed that sweet girl. He killed them all."

"I'm sorry," Quince said.

"Me too." Sun squeezed her hand. "I think this story should be told. The world needs to know who the real killer was."

"Oh, don't you worry about that. I have that rascally daughter of yours working on it."

Uh-oh. Not sure if that was a good thing or a bad one, Sun acquiesced with a nod.

"Mortimer didn't expect the firestorm he brought down on us. The family wanted that necklace back like the dickens. And, quite frankly, they were willing to move heaven and earth to get it. They had all kinds of investigators comb through this town and the whole area. We even had *gen-you-wine* Pinkertons in town."

"Wow," Quincy said. He'd wanted to become a Pinkerton at

one point. Allan Pinkerton had been a hero of his since he'd read about how the man saved Lincoln's life and helped with the Underground Railroad. "But I didn't think the necklace was worth that much."

"According to the family, it wasn't. Said they wanted it for sentimental reasons."

"You didn't buy it," Sun said.

"Not in the least. But my husband got it in his head it was worth a lot of money to them, so he was going to demand a ransom of sorts. In the meantime, the detectives began to realize that more than a handful of people who stayed at our boardinghouse went missing soon after. It did not look good."

"That's when you figured it out?"

"I confronted Mortimer about the killings before he could send his ransom demand." She took another sip. "Let's just say, Billy Press was not the first man to die in my kitchen."

Quincy and Sun both sat back in unison.

"You killed him?" Quincy asked.

"Yes and no. I told him I was going to tell the sheriff everything and, well, he flat did not want me to. Went to kill me with a toaster. When he grabbed it, I plugged it in real fast and he electrocuted himself." She shook her head. "I kept telling him to fix that old thing."

Sun covered her mouth and cleared her throat. It was horrific and hilarious at once.

"But with all the detectives running around, and now with Mortimer dead, I was afraid they'd think I was the killer. So, I buried him in the backyard, planted a cherry tree on top, and called it a day."

That time Quincy covered his mouth under the guise of deep thinking. He scrunched his brows together and everything.

Sun agreed. The image of Mrs. Fairborn hurrying to plug in a toaster to electrocute her husband was too much, but she and Quincy were now in one of those surreal situations where they were making an oath to a group of people that usually—but not always—had motivations and loyalties that lined up with the law. And they'd taken an oath to uphold said law, so what would happen when that was not the case? When one of those group decisions contradicted with their oath? What would they do then?

Mrs. Fairborn's actions were clearly self-defense. But one thing was certain: the next few months would be interesting. Sun had no doubt.

"As you may have guessed," Mrs. Fairborn continued, "I couldn't take it. The guilt was eating me alive. So, about a week after I planted Mortimer, I went to the sheriff, that old bastard Campbell Scott, and confessed everything." She cackled. "You should have seen the look on his face when I told him."

"He didn't think you could do it?"

"Oh, no. He knew I had it in me. I'd gone steady with him before I met Mortimer. The problem was, he was having an affair. He'd found himself a young filly on the side and I knew it. When he figured out I knew the truth and he could lose all that shiny money he'd married into, he told me I was mistaken about Mortimer being the killer. Said I was confused. Said I was—my favorite word—hysterical."

Ah. One of Sun's favorite words as well. *Not.*

"He told me they'd found the man responsible for the missing people over the years. Said a drifter by the name of Hercules Holmes had one of the missing men's wallets."

"Who was Hercules Holmes?" Quince asked.

"Just like he said. A drifter in the wrong place at the wrong time."

"But how would a man passing through town be responsible for all of those other people's deaths over the years? Didn't the detectives think of that?"

She shook her head. "They didn't much care. Once Hercules escaped the jail, their only lead was gone. They had nothing to go on and the family had no way of getting the necklace back. When they found Hercules dead two weeks later, the investigation fizzled."

"Did they ever find who killed him?"

"No. And it's funny how I was never brought up on charges myself. I guess Campbell figured if I stayed quiet, he'd stay quiet."

Sun gave her a dubious grin. "That doesn't much sound like you."

"It doesn't, does it? By that point, I'd had about enough of men and their handling of things around town. We were getting to be a bit of a tourist town, even back then, and I knew things needed to be handled right and corruption needed to be brought to a minimum, so I brought the Dangerous Daughters to life."

"And later the Sordid Sons," Cyrus said.

Sun looked up at her dad. So proud of him.

"Also, for the record, the fact that Sheriff Campbell Scott went missing himself a few months later had nothing to do with me."

Sun and Quincy exchanged glances and decided to let it go. For now.

"Wait," Sun said, thinking back to her research. "I thought the Dangerous Daughters was formed in the thirties after the mines shut down and a bunch of women were left undefended when the men went off to find work elsewhere."

Even the mayor was surprised by her question. "You really did your homework."

"Told you," Mrs. Fairborn said. She held out her hand and the mayor slapped a five into it. The older woman cackled again and stuffed it into her bra before turning back to them. "I suppose I should have said I brought the Dangerous Daughters *back* to life. My mother first started them when a group of men came in and tried to take over the town. And the women running it. There were about a dozen men. An outlaw gang called the Oxford Boys."

"Why?" the mayor asked.

"I think it had something to do with their shoes. All spit shined and fancy."

"Makes sense."

"And what's an outlaw gang to do when it finds a town full

of women all alone and defenseless?" When Sun only smiled, she said, "And that, my dear, is the true beginning of the Double Ds."

"Wow." Quincy sat back in thought.

"What happens now?" Sun asked. "We're just part of the gang?"

"You need to learn our mission statement and rules and swear to uphold them, but yeah. For the most part."

"Rules like?"

"Our main mission is to shift the balance from those suscep-tible to corruption, those with too much power, and even it out," her mother said.

Royce expanded on that. "And we cannot ever use our po-sition to gain power or favor for ourselves, to sway a vote on the city council for personal gain that does not benefit the whole town, for example."

"You're fighting basic human nature," Sun said thoughtfully. "Who wouldn't use their position to get a little extra parking at their business, if possible?"

"Which is why there are thirteen of us. We keep each other in line."

"Boy, do they," Ruby Moore, the woman with the affinity for baking cursed muffins, said with a roll of her eyes. "Don't even try to get special permission to hold a mass séance in the ceme-tery on All-Hallows Eve. You would've thought I was asking per-mission to kill my husband and bury his body in the backyard."

The mayor reminded her, "You did ask permission to kill your husband and bury his body in the backyard."

"I was joking." She glanced around. "It was a joke."

"Our system is far from perfect, Sunshine," Mrs. Fairborn said. "But it's the best we can make it and it's worked well for the past fifty-plus years."

Sun crossed her arms over her chest. "I think it's amazing, Mrs. Fairborn. What you've done."

"Does that mean you're in?"

She lifted a shoulder. "I'm in." Really, how could she not be?

"And you, Chief Deputy Cooper?" Cyrus asked Quincy.

"I was in the minute you gave me this coin." He admired it again and Sun laughed softly. He was like a chipmunk in fall.

They served a dinner for Mrs. Fairborn, all of her favorites, but Sun could tell she was getting tired.

She pulled her aside. "If you're ready to get some rest, I can take you home." The woman did just get out of the hospital, after all.

Was that what all of this was about? Did the sons and daughters choose today because they were worried about her? Or had today been the plan all along and the attack was just bad timing?

"I guess I am getting a little tired," Mrs. Fairborn said. She reached into her mammoth bag and handed a small tin to Sun. It was an antique sewing kit, the box rusted and the paint peeling. "This is for you. She who wears the crown . . ."

"Mrs. Fairborn, I am beyond honored to have been accepted into this organization, especially considering the limited seating, but the crown? For me to be Dangerous . . . I mean, the others have been here so much longer. They've put in the time and served the town."

"Sweetheart." She patted her arm. "I chose you as my successor over ten years ago."

Sun felt her eyes widen. "I don't understand."

"The way you handled . . . well, everything. I knew you were the one."

The abduction. Of course. "I hardly handled anything, Mrs. Fairborn. It happened. I just dealt with it the best way I knew how. If it weren't for my parents, I would've been lost."

"That's all any of us can do, love. But I disagree. I think, with or without your parents, you would've handled it all exactly the way you did. Not with anger or resentment, but with dignity and grace and, dare I say, a healthy dose of *fuck you*."

A bubble of laughter erupted from Sun's chest.

"You refused to let what happened stop you, to use it as a crutch, and you've only ever done right by that baby girl of yours."

"She's easy to do right by," Sun said, her appreciation boundless.

Mrs. Fairborn pushed the tin into her hands. "Like I said, she who wears the crown . . ."

Sun opened it. It was an assortment of odds and ends one might find at the bottom of a junk drawer. She rifled through it and brought out an old driver's license.

"Eugene Cosgrove," Mrs. Fairborn said. "Thirty-four years old. Steelworker from Pittsburgh. Headed to California for the American dream. Went missing November of '59."

She put it back and brought out a tortoiseshell comb.

"Virginia Bagwell. Fifty-four years old. Frontierswoman and explorer. Shot two men dead while helping to save a family in south Texas from a racially motivated attack. Went missing August of '63."

She placed it gently in the box and brought out a gold band.

"Martin Gallegos. Thirty-eight years old. Headed to California to look for work. Left behind a wife and six children. Went missing May of '61. His youngest son went on to head one of the most successful detective agencies in the Southwest."

She rubbed her fingertips over the tarnished gold, put it back, and pulled out a silver money clip.

"Darren Honeywell. He was an asshole."

She replaced the clip with a soft laugh and picked up a vial of perfume.

"Emily Press. Twenty-three years old. Took a necklace worth a couple hundred dollars at the time that was left to her specifically by her grandmother and ran from her abusive uncle. Went missing April of '65."

"You have all of these memorized," Sun said, astonished and heartbroken at the same time.

"It's all in my notes. All the people. All the families. I found Mortimer's trunk in the carriage house after he died. Took me years of research to figure out who some of them were. Three were drifters I could find nothing on. And two more are still unaccounted for. I thought maybe you could pick up where I left off." She handed Sun a file folder. The first page was a photo of the old-fashioned leather trunk.

"How do you know for sure there were twenty-three?"

She pointed to a strap on the top. "He kept a running tally. Notches in the top of the trunk. I could only find information on twenty-one. But the trunk and everything in it is yours. And Aurora's, of course. I have a feeling she would love to try to find the last two of my husband's victims. To be able to contact their families and let them know what happened to their loved ones."

"There are twenty-four notches," Sun said, counting again.

"Yeah, that last one is for Mortimer. Thought he'd like to see how it felt to have one's entire life reduced to a notch in a leather strap."

Sun studied the frail woman at her side. Marveled at her tenacity. "Have you contacted any of these families yet?"

"Nah. I don't figure they want to hear from the widow of the man who killed their loved ones. You can, though. I'm sure they would like answers, even sixty years later."

"You realize Auri is going to take this and run with it."

The older woman's eyes sparkled with warmth. "I'm counting on it."

A little while later, Quincy walked up to her as everyone sat around a table, an Arthurian round table made of thick wood and iron hardware, laughing and talking about Mrs. Fairborn and her antics. Her penchant for confessing to every crime ever committed came up often and lent itself to a lot of hearty laughter.

It was simply one of her quirks. How she coped with the horrors she'd endured, perhaps.

But the dinner, while very nice and nostalgic and heartfelt, saddened Sun to the depths of her soul. The entire town should be celebrating this woman's life. Not just the people in this room.

Quincy leaned closer and had clearly been thinking the same

thing. "This isn't enough," he said, sad himself. "After everything she's done."

"I agree." Then a thought hit her. "Hey, remember Gentleman Jack?"

He leveled a stoic expression on her. "What does the hamster you had when we were five have to do with anything?"

"You gave him a wonderful celebration of life when he died."

He thought back. "Oh, yeah. I did."

She decided to forgo reminding him how he cried over GJ for days. "Maybe we could do that for Mrs. Fairborn only while she's still with us. Like on her next birthday."

He brightened. "I could totally do that."

"Okay, it's next week."

"Oh, hell." His mind raced. "I have so much to do. I need to call the caterer. And get napkins ordered. And what about a champagne fountain?"

Oh, yeah. He clearly missed his calling. He stood to make some calls.

"You okay, Sunny?"

She turned to see her dad take a seat beside her. "I am. I'm so honored, Dad."

"But?"

"I'm just not sure I'm the girl for this."

"I have to be honest. I don't think Mrs. Fairborn has been wrong a day in her life."

"She married Mortimer."

"Touché."

She laughed, and then thought about what Rojas had said. "Can I ask you something completely unrelated?"

He took a swig of root beer as though it were a microbrew, and said, "Always."

"There's no delicate way of putting this, so here goes. Were you ever in prison?"

He'd been in the middle of downing the rest of his brewski

when she'd asked. He spit out the last swallow and proceeded to cough for the next five minutes. His face turned a sickly shade of purple and he gagged—a lot—repeating one sound over and over that reminded Sun of someone trying to start a chainsaw.

Clearly, she was on to something.

Her mother rushed over and took the opportunity to beat him senseless, asking if he needed water. Or CPR. Or Vicks VapoRub.

After another couple of minutes where he had to wave off all the expressions of concern surrounding him, he looked Sun square in the face, and said as calmly as a windless summer day, "No. Why do you ask?"

She blinked at him.

Her mother beat him on the back again for good measure.

He blinked at Sun.

"Okay, then," she said. "We'll circle back to that. For now, I'm going to go see if Levi wants to have sex with me."

It was her mother's turn to cough, only she coughed more delicately, and her gag sounded less like a chainsaw and more like the plumbing had backed up.

On the bright side, her dad got to beat her mom for a bit. Good times.

She pulled the tin box close to her chest, proof that this precious thing called life could be taken away with the snap of a finger. It was too short, and Sun had too many things she wanted to accomplish before her journey came to an end.

Having copious amounts of sex with the man of her dreams had been at the top of her bucket list for decades, and she wasn't getting any younger. Anything more would be pushing her luck, as they'd never really been on the same page about these things, but she would not go to her grave without having at least tried to have sex—real sex—with the man.

After her mother recovered, she cleared her throat, and said, "Thank God." She looked at her husband. "We can cancel that idiot Johnson boy."

"What idiot Johnson boy?"

Her mother opened her bag, took out a sheet of paper, and handed it to her.

Quincy, apparently having finished organizing Mrs. Fairborn's celebration of life, sat beside her and read over her shoulder. It was a list of names with the three at the top crossed out. Jay Johnson was next.

"You have a list?" she asked appalled. "You're just going down a list?"

"I like to be organized."

Quincy leaned over and pointed to a name.

"Joshua Ravinder?" she screeched. "You were going to set me up with Levi's cousin?"

Her mother pressed her mouth together. "It's a small town, honey. Our choices are limited."

Her dad patted her hand. "We didn't know how else to make you see the light."

"And what light would that be? The red one? Because you guys clearly shop at Pimps-R-Us."

Her mother pinched her lips tighter. "Don't be dramatic, dear. We had to make you realize that nobody else was right for you."

"Nobody else? You mean other than a hired assassin?"

"You're never going to let us live that down, are you?"

"Not in this lifetime."

Quincy put an arm around her shoulders and rocked her as she went through three of the five stages of grief.

27

Caller reported the little boy across the street
must've heard something he shouldn't have.
He keeps licking whipped cream off her cat.

—DEL SOL POLICE BLOTTER

"You're going to see Levi?" Auri asked when Sun called to check in on her way home. They had taken Cruz for some tests, and she was all alone in her hospital room. "He's been here all afternoon, but he left a little bit ago. He should be at his house in about fifteen."

"He was with you?"

"What do you smell like?"

"Tacos and disappointment."

"Mom."

"Cheesecake and loneliness."

"Mother."

"Xanax and the cold dark abyss of utter failure."

"Muh-ther. Men have a very strong sense of smell. He'll like you more if you smell good."

"Please. He's been sniffing moonshine his whole life. How good can his sense of smell be?" Just in case, she lifted her collar and took a whiff. Not bad. Could be worse. "Maybe I should shower first," she said, doubting herself now. "Even though," she added, recovering in the nick of time, "I am just going over there to go over what happened in the mine. We're being deposed in the morning."

"You have to get your stories straight?"

"There's nothing to get straight, sweetie."

"Yeah. Right. Okay. Wear pink."

"Auri."

"Guys like pink."

"I'll be at the hospital in a couple of hours. Quincy is on his way now. And your grandparents are getting a hotel."

"They're still sneaking around? The whole town knows about them."

"Love your face, bug."

"Love yours more."

Hailey Ravinder answered Sun's soft knock on the front door to the Ravinders' sprawling ranch house. The Ravinders used to live in squalor, their shacks, little better than tin cans, peppering the landscape. Levi started Dark River Shine and changed all of that. He'd taken them from the backwoods to Hollywood as his corn whiskey was very en vogue, a favorite among celebrities.

"Quincy Cooper?" Sun asked her, a wicked grin on her face. Yes, she was a twelve-year-old.

Hailey stepped over the threshold and eased the door closed. "What are you doing here?"

"I'm here to see your brother."

"Oh. Okay." She seemed to deflate.

"Are you disappointed?"

"No. Not at all."

Sun couldn't help but notice Hailey had curled her hair and applied a touch of mascara and blush. She really was a beauty. Though her party years did roughen the edges a bit, she would be called a looker in anyone's book.

Still, Hailey and Quincy? Her brain couldn't quite make the connection.

Hailey chewed on a nail. "Did he say anything about me?"

"He didn't give me a note to pass to you, if that's what you're wondering, but I do know he's going to be at the hospital for a while. All alone. With no one to talk to."

She smirked. "He'll have Auri and Cruz."

"Exactly. You know what it's like talking to teens. He'll lose what few marbles he has."

"Jimmy has been bugging me to go see her."

"See?" Look at her, all Cupidlike. "So, he's apparently been interested in you for a while."

"Why? Did he say something?"

"No. He won't tell me anything. My question is, how long have you been interested in him?"

She thought back. "Okay, do you remember when his shoulders got all wide and his biceps got all round and bumpy?"

Sun giggled.

"It was somewhere around there."

"So, a while ago."

"Yes. Unfortunately, every other girl in Del Sol noticed his transformation, too."

"I don't think he's interested in every other girl."

She wiggled her shoulders in delight, then said, "The dark lord just got back," referring to Levi. "He's in his room." She opened the door and gestured to the stairs behind her.

"And Clay?" Sun asked, worried about having to deal with their toxic uncle.

"He's at the plant."

"Good."

Sun took the stairs as Hailey went in search of her son. Having been inside the veritable mansion once before, she knew which door to knock on, but that knowledge didn't help her. No one answered. She tapped her knuckles on the thick wood again. Nothing. She just needed to give it a minute. Maybe he was on the phone or in the shower.

She looked around at the rich wood appointments, trying to

decide what to do. Levi had amazing taste. Everything about him was lush and hard and masculine. His truck. His house. His furniture.

Giving it one last go, she knocked again. Softly, at first, then harder. She had a job to do, damn it. She and Levi may not be destined for the altar, but they could have fun.

When he still didn't answer, she grew frustrated. She opened the door and stormed inside his massive bedroom, only to come face-to-face—well, twenty or so feet apart—with Levi Ravinder stepping out of the shower. He'd been in the middle of wrapping a towel around his waist. His dark, lean waist on which she could do her laundry if the zombie apocalypse ever happened and they lost power.

"Levi," she said, stopping short.

He let his gaze travel the length of her and her very pink summer blouse, which was so unlike her. She was going to kill Auri.

"Vicram." He finished securing the towel—damn it—and stepped into the bedroom.

"I didn't realize you were . . ." Humiliation surged through her. What had she been thinking? "You know what? I'll go. I just came by to—" She looked on a side table by the door where he'd clearly emptied his pockets as he came in. Keys, wallet, and a stack of hundreds any drug dealer would be proud of littered a decorative tray. But that wasn't what caught her attention. It was the coin. The gold coin that matched the one Quincy just got.

"You're Sinister."

"I've been called worse," he said from so close behind her she jumped. He reached past her and pushed the door closed.

She turned to see him towering over her. His skin still damp. His hair and lashes spiked with wetness. His full mouth framed by a day's worth of stubble.

"For or against?" she asked, her voice less confident than she'd hoped. When he raised a brow, she explained. "They said Sinister had already cast his vote. Did you vote for or against me?"

"The vote must be unanimous."

"Ah. I didn't know that."

"Then are you?" he asked.

"Am I what?"

He leaned closer until his mouth hovered at her ear. His warm breath fanned across her cheek, as he asked, "Are you Dangerous?"

After a twinge of arousal laced up her spine, she said, "Hardly. But if you mean, did I accept? Then, yes. We both did."

"Good." He went back to the bathroom to finish his routine.

She followed him, but only to the door.

"I didn't want my presence, or my membership, to sway your decision."

"For or against?" she repeated.

He smiled as he lathered the bottom half of his face with a shaving cream that smelled rich, like cologne. "Against, of course. I figured if you knew I was a Sordid Son, you'd run the other direction."

"You figured wrong. And here I thought you were good at complicated problems."

He stopped and studied her before raising his chin and gliding a razor up his neck, the deep bronze of his skin so at odds with the white of the foam.

Sun's world tilted just a little. That was about the sexiest thing she'd ever seen, and she'd seen a lot of sexy. Almost all of it revolved around Levi Ravinder in one form or another, but still.

His whiskey-colored irises sparkled in the low light. He shaved in the mirror and yet never took his gaze off her.

Of course, she didn't take her gaze off him, either. Fair was fair.

The bruises seemed to be fading, but as they did, a larger variety of vibrant colors surfaced. The subconjunctival hemorrhage in his left eye remained a dark, ominous red. And yet none of that did a thing to lessen his startling appeal. Surprisingly, the bruising on his body had faded much faster. She wondered how he felt, though. It still had to be tender. There was a reason people didn't enjoy getting hit by trucks.

"You are complicated, Vicram. I'll give you that." He flashed her a nuclear smile, his teeth as white as the foam.

She cleared her throat. "So, how is your evening going?"

"It could be better," he said, gliding the razor over his skin again.

"How so?"

"You could be naked."

Her breath caught in her throat. It was now or never, Vicram. Stop being a wuss. She lifted her chin and charged ahead. "What if I were?" When he arched a scythe-shaped brow, she asked, "What if I was standing in front of you right now, naked as the day I was born? What would you do?"

Without missing a beat, without a hint of hesitation, he said, "Ask for consent."

Wow, was that ever the right thing to say.

She loved everything about this man. Not just his physical appearance. It was him. Levi. The noble being she'd been in love with since she was a kid. He'd almost died saving his friend's life. He'd saved Auri's life. He'd come to Sun's rescue many times and in more ways than one. He'd brought his family out of the dark ages and given them something to be proud of. He was brilliant and clever and disarming.

He was still watching her as she fought for the courage to complete her mission.

She set her shoulders while he wiped the remnants of shaving cream off his jaw, the ritual ending far too soon in her opinion. After taking another moment to reconsider, she lifted her chin, and said, "Levi, the truth is . . ." Wait. What was the truth? Ah, yes. She bit down and glared at him. "The truth is, fuck you."

The corner of his mouth twitched.

"Fuck you and the horse you rode in on."

It inched heavenward. "What exactly did my horse do?"

"Life is too short and I'm in love with you. I have been since I was six. Maybe five. No, wait." She counted on her fingers, and said breathlessly, "Four-and-a-half. And I want to have a crap ton of sex before I get too old."

He pressed his mouth together and nodded, taking her offer into consideration.

"There. That's done. If you want to talk, you have my number."

She started to leave, but he said, "I just have one question."

"Okay." She turned back to him, fighting her flight response tooth and nail. The adrenaline dump was taking its toll. "That's certainly fair under the circumstances. What is it?"

"What do you consider too old to have sex?"

Oh. She hadn't thought that far ahead. "I don't know. Maybe ninety-three? Ninety-four?"

The grin that stole across his clean-shaven face was so stunning, it took her pupils a moment to adjust. "So, we have a little time."

"I suppose we do."

He walked up to her and put an elbow on one side of the doorjamb and a palm on the other, draping his arm across the opening. Then he ran his fingers through his wet hair, shook out his head, and gazed down at her.

The towel hung low on his hips, the evidence of his interest painfully obvious. One tug would be all it would take. But she was glued to his face. That gorgeous, rugged thing that had been the center of her dreams for so very, very long.

He leaned close again, brushed his lips along her cheek, and whispered in her ear three words she never thought she would hear from him. "Fuck you, too." He kept his mouth at her ear as fire surged throughout her body, and added, "And the broom you rode in on."

She leaned back. "Are you calling me a witch?"

He leaned forward. "How else do you explain it?" he asked, wrapping a large hand around her neck and pulling her closer. "You've bewitched me." He kissed the corner of her mouth. "You bewitched me the first time I saw you and no one else has ever measured up."

He pressed his warm body against hers, lifted her face, and looked down into her eyes. "There's only ever been you."

He lowered his mouth to hers. Ran his tongue along the seam of her lips until they parted. Dove in. Again he tasted like whiskey and butterscotch, and she wondered exactly what he was drinking that was so lovely.

His hands smoothed over her ass and he pulled her against him hard, then surprised her by lifting her into his arms. She wrapped hers around his neck, refusing to break the kiss, and heard the towel fall to the floor.

He pulled back. "I'm not sure we should be doing this."

"Why?"

"I think you're very fragile right now."

"Like a flower?" she asked.

"More like a bomb. Still, may I have your consent, Sunshine Vicram?"

"Yes. Yes. For the love of God, please fuck me."

Then she was on the bed. He eased on top of her, his biceps bunching with each carefully controlled movement. He smelled like soap and shaving cream. The scent only added to the euphoria she felt at finally having Levi Ravinder on top of her. Wanting her. Craving her. Well, if the growl he emitted was any indication. And she liked to think it was.

She sent her hands over his steely ass and pulled him against her. Her pink blouse had ridden up and his cock lay heavy on her exposed stomach. She pushed a hand between them and encircled it with her fingers. He stilled, his muscles contracting to the density of marble as she stroked him. First with small, hesitant strokes, then with longer ones.

"Fuck, Shine," he ground out as her confidence grew.

Before he could protest, she broke off the kiss and wiggled down between his legs until his cock was at her mouth. Magnificent. Hard. Flesh straining against the confines of its own skin.

She felt a rush of blood when she eased her lips around it. She teased the tip of his cock with the tip of her tongue, then took his ass into both hands and pulled. He slid into her.

"Fucking hell," he said when her teeth grazed the length of his erection, his voice hoarse, almost begging.

But she dug her fingernails into his ass to hold him inside her, to prevent him from unsheathing, and sucked. His breathing grew heavier. She slowly eased him out, then drew him back inside the warmth of her mouth, wrenching a groan from him.

The blood rushing just beneath the surface of his cock would suggest he was near orgasm, and that thought sent a scorching heat coiling in her abdomen. She felt the flood of her excitement between her legs as she slowly, painstakingly pumped him to climax. She wanted that for him. Wanted to be able to do that to him, as though it would be a coup, a notch in her Levi belt. At last.

But he reached down and wrapped a hand gently around her jaw to stop her. "Wait," he said breathlessly. "I'm going to come if you don't stop."

He pulled out of her, and she grinned up at him, still straddled above her.

"That was the general idea."

He reached behind her head, grabbed the sheet she was lying on, and jerked her back up like she weighed nothing. A wicked grin slid across his startlingly handsome face. "My turn."

Taking both wrists into one of his hands, he locked them above her head and ran his free hand over her stomach before undoing the buttons on her blouse. With one hand. She was impressed. And light-headed.

Cool air rushed over her skin when he laid the shirt open. He stopped to look at her, his eyes shimmering with interest. Her bra hooked in front. One more magic trick and it fell open, too. Her breasts spilled out, his large hand catching one. He caressed it. Massaged it before he bent his head and suckled the nipple. Whatever he was doing with his tongue caused the most incredible tremors of pleasure to quake inside her.

"What the hell?" she asked, trying to figure out his technique. "How are you . . ." Her voice trailed off as she felt the promise of an orgasm flourish between her legs, the heat pooling in her abdomen astonishing. "I've never . . . ," she said between gasps. "This is . . . new."

He released her nipple only to transfer his scorching mouth to the other. It was like an invisible thread had been pulled taut between her nipples and her clit, and every time he sucked—so softly she ached—and flicked his tongue—so sweetly she writhed—it strummed and vibrated, drawing the orgasm closer and closer.

She parted her legs involuntarily. He took that as a cue to unfasten her jeans and send his hand down the front of them. Still sucking, he dipped two fingers inside her, causing her to clench around them, then pulled out and circled her clit, her own wetness slickening his fingertips.

He worked hard, bringing her to the brink then pulling her back, for several long minutes.

"Levi, please," she begged, parting her legs further.

After climbing onto his knees, he peeled off first her jeans, then her panties. He slid them down her legs with meticulous care, caressing each inch of her skin as he did so.

She threw back her head and reveled in his touch. His kisses between her knees. His tongue sliding up her thighs.

She heard the sound of foil tearing and lifted her head to watch like a voyeur. She bit her bottom lip as he rolled the condom onto his hard cock. He was sculpted to absolute perfection, the hills and valleys creating the most alluring play of shadow and light all over his lean body. His large hand finished the task, and then he stroked himself. Once. Twice.

Blood rushed into her clit. It swelled and pulsed and pleaded for release. He could have taken her sweetly. He could have covered her body with his and placed tiny, hot kisses on the corners of her mouth as he slid gently inside her.

But he was done with sweetly, apparently. He grabbed her hips and pulled her ass onto him, guiding her cunt onto his cock. He slid in with ease and she arched her back to draw him deeper, the sensations swirling inside her like blistering molten lava. She took every inch of him over and over as he milked the orgasm. His strokes grew shorter and faster, coaxing the sweet sting closer.

And then it happened. Pleasure spiked inside her, surging deep and hot and sharp. It spilled out and flooded every cell in her body. She clamped down on him and he came with a guttural growl, his chest heaving, his muscles contracting as he slammed into her.

After a moment, he collapsed and rolled to the side, but her orgasm was still there, on the edge of the precipice. The wave still rocking her, it had never fully subsided.

She grabbed his hand and pushed it between her legs. She had no idea what his reaction was, because her body was too busy trying to come again.

He pressed his fingers inside her and scraped a palm over her clit. His mouth was at her ear, his warm breath "Come on," he said. "One more."

Then he drew a nipple into his mouth as his fingers pumped in and out of her. The wave swelled, built momentum a second time, but when he shoved her legs apart and drew her clit into his mouth, sucking softly, it exploded inside her. She grabbed hand-fuls of hair as he circled his tongue around her clit. Helping her ride the wave. Easing her back to Earth.

"Oh, my God," she said when she could talk again. "That has never happened to me."

He kissed her clitoris and took up a position next to her again, the length of his body pressed against hers the very definition of heaven. "Which part?" he asked.

"All of the parts. I've never . . . I haven't experienced an or-gasm from a man. And so far, you are two for two."

"Are you kidding?" he asked, surprised.

"Not at all."

"What did you do? You know, when you were with some-one?"

"It's called faking it. I took a class," she said, teasing.

"Hell, if you faked it this time, you deserve an Academy Award. You're good."

She grinned at him. "Nobody's that good. I'm sorry, I'm just . . . shocked. I didn't know it could be like that."

"You know sex is all in the mind."

"Maybe so, but it felt much closer to my clit."

"Holy fuck, you're sexy." He buried his face in her hair.

She was sexy? Had he looked in the mirror? Like ever?

The fact that she'd just had sex with Levi Ravinder was not lost on her. It was like a dam inside her had broken and elation spilled out, flooding every cell in her body. She would wonder about what this meant long-term later. For now, she only had one question: when would they get to do it again?

28

Free belly rubs with exam!
(Sorry, pets only. And Levi Ravinder.)
—SIGN AT DEL SOL VETERINARY CLINIC

A little while later, Sun lay in his arms. Levi Ravinder's arms. "What is this?" he asked, lifting up the key she had on a chain necklace around her neck.

"Oh." She took it and tried to tuck it under the sheets. "It's nothing."

He propped himself up on an elbow and brought it out again. Held it between his fingers. Flipped it over and over. "Is this what I think it is?"

When they were kids, the Ravinders had been harassing her one summer afternoon. Hailey, who back then hated Sun with the fiery passion of, well, the sun, ripped off the chain she'd had around her neck, the one with the key to her house, and tossed it down Levi's shorts.

It was the day everything was truly solidified for her. She fell in love. Because while the Ravinder cousins were hooting and hollering, Levi took out the key himself, fixed the chain, and put it back around her neck.

She learned that day what Levi was really made of, despite his crude upbringing.

"It's just a key," she said, trying to take it from him.

He took a closer look at the smiley face she'd engraved into it as a kid. "Is this the key from—"

"That day? Yes." She snatched it back. "It's my good luck charm. Everyone needs a good luck charm."

"You're right." He bent and brushed his mouth over her jaw and down her neck.

"Do you have one?"

"Yes," he said, absently, focused on more productive things.

"Really? What is it?"

He leaned back, the whiskey in his irises glistening, and said, "You, Shine. It's always been you."

Her heart swelled. Why had it taken them so long? She had so many questions. So many doubts, but she'd never doubted her feelings for him.

"Now, hush." He bent again and made his way to a breast. A breast that betrayed her instantly by tightening under his touch. Then he started doing that thing with his tongue again, and her fingers clenched in his hair.

By the time he rolled on top and slid inside her, the pleasure in her core peaked almost instantly. He sucked a breath in through his teeth, then covered her mouth with his as though staking his claim. It was a claim she gladly relinquished.

Perhaps it was the angle of the light.

Levi had stood and was wrapping the towel around his waist again when she noticed them. His skin was so tight against his flesh, they were hard to see, but there on the left side of his lower abdomen were three indents. Three distinct scars. Three straight lines, each one about an inch in length.

Three knife wounds.

Her mind rushed into the past as a flood tide of memories flashed bright and hot. Two men fought in a downpour, but she couldn't focus. Why couldn't she focus? Was she hurt? Drugged? She couldn't tell who the men were beyond the fact that one was young, just a boy, and one was older. Should she root for one or fear both?

The icy rain sliced into her flesh and chilled her bones and yet she was on fire. Hot and cold warred for her attention as the men struggled.

Her mind plucked a fact out of hindsight, a truth she didn't know back then. One of the fighters was Kubrick Ravinder, the man who'd abducted her fifteen years ago. And the other one . . . he had to be Wynn. Kubrick's brother. Because he'd rescued her.

But he didn't have the scar on his wrist when she interviewed him in prison. Her rescuer had been bleeding from his wrist when he gave her water in his truck. A defensive wound, deep and ugly. A wound Wynn didn't have. And yet the DNA test came back positive. It had to be Wynn.

Another memory ripped her from the present and dragged her into the past. They fought hard and Kubrick got her rescuer down. He wedged a knee into his throat, baring his teeth like an animal.

She could barely see past the rain, but she heard him when he said, "You're gonna learn what it means to be a Ravinder, boy."

Her rescuer scissor-hooked him and slammed him onto the ground. He was fast. Faster than Kubrick. And young. He scrambled on top of the older man before Kubrick could recover. From there, he began punching the older man in the face. Over and over. Pummeling him until he hovered in and out of consciousness. Then the kid did the same thing Kubrick had done to him. He lifted his knee onto the man's throat and pressed his weight into his larynx.

Her rescuer was so focused on his mission, on crushing the man's windpipe, that he missed the knife until it slid into his side. Sun realized she had to have known which one to root for even back then, because despite her disoriented state, fear washed over her. He kept the pressure on the man's throat regardless, as though completely unaware he'd just been stabbed. Kubrick pulled the knife out and slid it into her rescuer again.

That time he stopped. Leaned back. Looked at the knife protruding from his gut as though in disbelief. Kubrick pulled it out again and the boy grabbed hold of his abdomen just as the older man slid it in a third time. It sliced into the boy's wrist as well as punctured his midsection.

When Kubrick slid out the knife to repeat the heinous act a fourth time, the boy moved so fast, Sun's mind didn't register it until he held the knife perpendicular to Kubrick's chest. Right over where his heart should have been if he'd had one.

Kubrick looked at him, hatred twisting his face as the boy rose onto his knees, pressed a palm to the hilt, and shifted all of his weight forward.

It sank into Kubrick's chest in one smooth thrust. Kubrick stopped moving instantly, but he was still alive as he looked at his opponent, his face the picture of shock.

The boy kept his weight on the knife, waiting it out, his face mere centimeters from Kubrick's. It couldn't have been more than fifteen seconds, maybe as little as ten before Kubrick's gaze slid past the boy and into oblivion.

He rolled off the older man, lay flat on his back for a couple more seconds, then stumbled to her, clutching his side. She looked up, tried to see through the shadows created by the hood, but the rain pelting her face made it impossible. Until one perfectly timed flash of lightning set the area ablaze with light. And in that briefest of moments, she saw him. His perfect face. His sculpted mouth. His strong brow.

Levi.

Her rescuer.

"What are you hungry for?"

She heard his voice from far away, but she was trapped in the past as he lifted her into his arms and stumbled forward. She was so wet he could hardly hold on. He fell to one knee, lifted her again, and charged forward just as she lost her battle with the encroaching darkness.

"I happen to make a mean fajita."

Sun clawed her way back to the present. Tried to focus on the question. Tried to school her features. But the past kept tumbling around in her mind. She couldn't get her footing.

"Hey," he said, concern softening his face. "You okay?" He reached up and brushed something off her face. A tear?

She took the opportunity to look at his wrist. A scar, straight and deep, cut across the top side, probably to the bone, and she couldn't believe the knife didn't slice through an artery or sever a tendon.

He was there. If he wasn't a part of the abduction scheme, why not tell her he rescued her? Why keep that a secret? And how did Wynn's blood get on Kubrick's jacket?

She tried to focus through the darkening edges of her vision.

"Vicram?" he said, growing wary.

"Yes." She snapped out of it the best she could. "I, um, I have to get to the hospital. I told Auri I'd be there hours ago." She hurried and gathered her clothes, throwing on the blouse braless when she couldn't locate the damned thing.

He looked around confused, as though trying to figure out what had triggered the change in her behavior. She didn't give him time to ask. She ran out of there so fast, she left a cloud of dust in her wake. At least it felt that way.

Once she was safely ensconced inside her cruiser, she threw it into reverse, peeled out, and called her lifeline.

She remembered heavy breathing, but not hers. Hers was shallow. Barely enough to form a wisp of smoke on the frigid air. She remembered a heartbeat racing in her ear, but not hers. Hers was weak. Barely enough to push the blood to and from her heart. She remembered a warmth around her, but not hers. She was ice and the warmth was doing its darnedest to keep her from freezing to death. She curled into it, begging for more.

He stumbled again, jostling her against him as he lifted her into the vehicle. Then he stepped back. Tried to catch his breath.

Dropped to one knee and clutched his side, doubling over. But she wanted him closer because she was falling again. She didn't want to lose him.

"Quincy," she said into the phone as she tore down Levi's long drive. "Where are you?"

A hand held the back of her head while another pushed a water bottle against her lips. A soft whisper encouraged her to drink. Water flooded her mouth, causing her to choke. She coughed, her stomach muscles writhing and constricting until she vomited.

She remembered the clear liquid soaking into his jacket, onto her pants, and running over the seat of a truck. Mortified, she tried to wipe it off but her limbs were filled with cement. Impossible to lift. And again she fell.

"I'm at the hospital," Quincy said. "What's wrong? Where are you?"

The overhead lights blinded her. She felt his warmth again. Heard the heartbeats in his chest. He called out. "Nurse!" But she couldn't figure out why he was calling for a nurse in his truck.

No, not his truck. Too sterile. Too bright.

His warmth evaporated and the blinding lights overhead rushed past her. People's faces popped in and out of her vision, all of them talking to her, but she was falling again. She reached out for him.

"Did you get a name?" someone asked.

"No. He took off. He looked hurt."

He was gone.

Sun pressed the phone to her ear with a shoulder as she took the turn out of Levi's drive too fast. Her tires spun and dirt billowed in her headlights. "I'll be there in an hour," she said, then hung up as her world spun in circles around her.

Auri and Cruz were asleep when she got to the hospital. Her parents had gone back to the hotel, and Quincy sat in the room scrolling through his phone. He shot to his feet when she walked in, questioning her with a single look.

"It was him," she said, breathless from running and panicking and freaking out. "It was Levi. He fought with Kubrick. He got stabbed. He killed him and took me to the hospital and never said anything. After all these years, why wouldn't he tell me?"

Quincy shook his head and led her out of the room. "That's not possible. The DNA test. It was Wynn's blood on Kubrick's jacket," he said as they walked toward the elevators.

"Where are we going?" she asked, oblivious.

"Coffee. Unless you want something stronger."

"I want something stronger."

They ended up at a bar on Central named after a tenacious frontierswoman and performer in the 1800s.

"It makes no sense," he said, his brows knitting in confusion.

"They're related," Sun said, throwing back a shot of one of Levi's creations, a butterscotch-flavored moonshine called Warm Butter Moon. It scorched her throat and she coughed before tapping the bar for another.

"I've never said anything out loud, but just an FYI, you don't handle your liquor nearly as well as you think you do."

"I know. I promise to take this one slower." It was hot and sweet and delicious, much like its creator.

"And it doesn't matter. The test would've told us if it was a relation or the real deal, and Wynn is the real deal."

"It was him, Quince." She ended up downing the drink after all. After another cough, she breathed cool air into her burning lungs, and said, "I remember. Only bits and pieces, but I remember." She tapped the bar again. The bartender, a woman with rich brown hair and the most incredible gold irises Sun had ever seen, poured her another, but not before raising a quizzical brow.

Sun nodded and the woman poured, albeit reluctantly.

"You do realize that shit is a hundred proof," Quincy said.

Again, just like its creator.

When she ignored him, he looked at the bartender. "What do you think?" he asked her.

She grinned, forming the most charming dimples at the

corners of her mouth, and said, "In my limited experience, it always boils down to one, unmitigated fact. People lie."

Quincy nodded. "And there you go."

The bartender winked at him, then went to take another order at the end of the bar. It was a good thing, because next time Sun spoke, she did so with a slight slur. "I agree. People lie. Tests don't."

"Sun, you and I both know those tests aren't foolproof and human error is a real thing, even in the world of forensics."

"Especially in the world of forensics. It was odd, though," she said, thinking back. "I'd sent those samples in months ago. True, I held on to them for too long, but it still took longer to get the results than I'd expected."

"You didn't get the results."

"Yes, I did."

"No. You never got them. You had to call the DPS for the results. And they just happened to be ready on the day you called?"

Sun took a sip of the warm liquid, her thoughts tumbling around in her brain like dice on a craps table. "On the day after we visited Wynn Ravinder in Arizona?"

"What's the common denominator?"

"Nancy is a good friend of mine," she said.

"Okay, who's Nancy and what does she have to do with this case?"

"Nancy works at DPS. She ran the labs for this case."

He leaned back in his chair. "As my mentor would say, when you've eliminated all the impossible crap, whatever crap remains, however improbable that crap may be, must be the true crap." He turned to her. "I'm paraphrasing."

She breathed through a head rush as though she were in labor and practicing Lamaze. Then she frowned at him. "I thought Allan Pinkerton was your mentor."

"He's my hero. Sherlock is my mentor."

"I want a fictional character as a mentor."

"I think Minnie Mouse is still available."

"Okay," she said, hopping off the stool, "I'm tired and I'm angry and I have a lot to process."

"Clues?"

"No, carbs. I have a lot of carbs to process. I had a weak moment on the way over."

"I hope you don't think you're driving."

"Nope." She tossed him her keys. "You are. We need to get to Santa Fe."

He pouted. "I drank, too."

"You took, like, three sips."

"I'm being punished for not being a lush?"

"How is catching bad guys punishment?"

A sheepish grin slid across his handsome face. "Good point."

29

If one day when you're famous
people will say things like,
"I used to work with her" or
"We were Facebook friends" or
"I'm not surprised she used an axe,"
book an appointment with us immediately.
　　　　—SIGN AT DEL SOL MENTAL HEALTH RESOURCES

An hour later, Quincy dropped Sun off at an old friend's house and she found herself in the woman's living room, drinking a glass of chardonnay and reminiscing about the good old days. Not that Nancy was home yet, but Sun could wait. And she did.

When she heard the keys jingle in the lock at the door, she put the glass aside and watched as the woman stepped inside her dark house. She flipped on the light to the living room, turned, and saw Sun.

"Oh, my God!" she said, throwing a hand over her heart. "Sunshine? What the hell? You scared the shit out of me."

"Hey, Nance. Long time."

The woman, a tall strawberry blond with a wide smile and huge brown eyes, put down her bag and grew wary. Glancing around like she half expected a team of law enforcement officers to emerge from the darkness and arrest her, she asked warily, "How'd you get in here?"

Sun lifted the key. "You still keep it in the same place. And you still keep late hours, I see."

Nancy slipped off her heels, looked at the open bottle of wine, and took a glass out of the cabinet. She walked over and poured herself a couple of ounces, her hand shaking, clinking the bottle against the rim on the delicate glass.

"To what do I owe the pleasure?" she asked Sun.

"More like, to whom," Sun said. "Two names. Wynn. Ravinder."

Nancy pulled her lips tight through her teeth as she studied her wine. "The man whose DNA was on that jacket?"

"The very one."

She shook out of her thoughts. "I don't have the file here. What did you need to know?"

"How he did it."

"I only run the tests, Sun. You know that."

"No, right. I know. I'm just wondering how he got you to alter it for him."

She said nothing for a very long time, then downed the drink in one gulp before pouring another one.

Sun took that as a sign of guilt. "I believe the words you're searching for are, 'He blackmailed me.' Or 'He threatened me.' Or, hell, even, 'He coerced me to do his bidding by discovering my weakness for Oreos and offering me a year's supply.' Anything but, 'I did it because I love him.' That's just a little too cliché."

She kept her gaze downcast. "I do love him."

"Oh, my God, Nancy." Sun scrubbed her face with her fingertips and stood to look out a plate glass window, the stunning view of Santa Fe at night lost on her, her fury too great to appreciate it.

Her friend had always been a hot mess, but altering DNA evidence? Every single test she'd ever run would now be questioned. Every person convicted on evidence she processed would be thrown out. People guilty of murder and rape and molestation and trafficking . . . any number of felons would now have to be retried or released altogether.

What Sun was about to do was beyond unethical, but she could not allow that to happen. Not if she could help it. She had to know.

"Don't worry, Sun," Nancy said, her voice breaking. "He doesn't love me back."

"How many?"

"You don't understand. He saved my brother's life in Arizona. They were going to kill him."

"How many cases, Nance? How many did you tamper with?"

"Just this one, I swear. You've met my brother. Kevin wouldn't be alive today if not for Wynn."

"He's a shot caller, Nance. Your brother probably wasn't even in any real danger. It was most likely a setup to get you under his thumb. To save you for a rainy day."

"No, this happened years ago. And then we started writing." She looked away. "Well, I wrote him mostly. He never asked me for anything until now."

"That's how they work. C'mon, Nancy. You can't be this naïve."

When she didn't respond, Sun did the only thing she could do in this situation. "Tomorrow morning, you're going to resign."

A look of absolute panic hijacked her face. "I—I can't."

"You will or I'll turn you over to SFPD. All of your cases . . . It'll be a mess, and you know it."

She raised her chin. "It'll be your word against mine."

"Nancy, don't make me do this." She brought out her phone. "I've recorded this whole conversation. You'll be arrested."

"Then arrest me. I can't quit." Her expression was one of both fear and desperation. It suddenly made sense.

"Who else has you in their pocket?"

Her fingers tightened around her glass. "Someone a lot scarier than you."

"You just told me you hadn't altered any other tests."

"I haven't." She stepped closer, pleading. "I swear to God, Sun. He just—I just do a couple of side jobs for him from time to time. Off the books. That's all."

What kind of side jobs would a lab rat in forensics do? "Who?"

Wetness gathered between her lashes. "If I tell you, I'll be dead by morning."

"I can protect you."

She scoffed. "You can't even protect yourself."

"Nancy, you're putting me in a very bad position."

She put her glass down. "You do what you have to do, Sunshine."

One thing was for certain. She was going to have to look into Nancy's situation further. But for now . . . "I want the analysis you falsified destroyed immediately."

She nodded. "Of course."

"Then you and I are going to talk." Sun walked up to her and lowered her voice, hopefully hampering anyone who might be listening. "And just for the record, I can be scary, too."

Nancy nodded again, her hands twisting into knots.

Sun texted her parents to let them know she would be late getting to the hospital the next morning. Auri was getting out and she needed them there. They wanted to keep Cruz another couple of days, much to Auri's distress.

She stepped out of her cruiser into the blinding light of the New Mexico sun. She'd gotten exactly three seconds of sleep, which could explain her vampiric aversion to the bright orb in the sky.

"What's wrong?" Quincy asked her.

"It's daylight."

Quincy scanned the blue above them. "I believe this is the kind of daylight they call *broad*."

She ran through every scenario possible last night about why Levi kept the truth from her. The law enforcement officer in her came to one disturbing conclusion: he was in on it from the beginning. But if so, why? And what happened?

He was just a kid, himself. Well, young anyway. He was only twenty when it happened. Had Kubrick tricked him into helping with the abduction somehow? If so, what event led to their falling out and subsequent fight to the death? And what in the bloody heck did Wynn have to do with any of it? Had he been involved as well? Was it a family affair?

Her brain had swelled in her skull with all the questions rolling around in there. On a quest for answers, she and Quincy found themselves at the state pen in Santa Fe. The DA had pulled it off. He'd gotten Wynn Ravinder transferred to New Mexico, and he'd done it in record time.

"I think I should go this one alone," she said to Quince. "Wynn may talk more openly to me if you aren't there."

"That's what you get for thinking, boss."

She shook her head. "Don't make me pull rank."

"Don't make me pull hair. It's not very manly but it's effective."

They were shown to an office with stacks of files as tall as Quincy on the desk.

"He just came in last night," an intake specialist said, rifling through the items on his desk for a file. He found what he was looking for and sat at his computer.

"Yes. Wynn Ravinder. He has quite the record." He gave them a thorough inspection. "This must be really important to have gotten him transferred this fast," he said, fishing.

"It is," she said, not biting.

"I'll have the sergeant bring him up."

She tugged at the collar of her uniform as they waited in a small room much like the one in Arizona, only New Mexico clearly didn't have quite the money they did. The metal table had been painted about a hundred times, each layer showing a different shade of the same neutral colors.

"Apple," Wynn said when they brought him in. He eyed

Quincy, then returned his attention to Sun. "You got my message."

"Nope. No message."

He seemed surprised. "Then why are you here so soon?"

"Questions."

"Lots of questions," Quincy added.

Suspicion narrowed his lids. "That's going to have to wait. You have to get to Ravinder."

She frowned. "You are Ravinder."

"I'm not *the* Ravinder. I'm not Levi."

She'd always found it fascinating how all the other Ravinders called Levi by their last name.

"Did you get my message or not?"

"No," she said. The edge in his voice alarmed her, but she needed to stay focused. "Look, we got you transferred to get answers. It's time to pay up."

"That can wait. You need to get to him immediately. I thought that was why you were here."

"I have a feeling you're going to be getting a message soon, as well. From Nancy Danforth?" She stood and leaned over the table. "You lied."

"Nancy?" he asked. He sat back in his chair, his silence confirmation.

"How did you get her to falsify the DNA test?"

He licked his lips. "We don't have time for this."

"And why? Why confess to a killing you didn't do?"

He worked his scruffy jaw in frustration. "I answer your questions, then you get to Ravinder?"

"Yes."

"Fine. Get rid of the hulk."

Sun turned to him.

"This again?" Quincy asked. When she didn't respond, he made a grand show of standing, his annoyance evident in every sharp move he made. He knocked on the door to be let out and exited with the same enthusiastic performance.

After the door closed, she refocused on Wynn. "You confessed to a murder you didn't commit."

"Doesn't matter."

"You didn't do it," she reiterated.

"Doesn't matter who did it, apple blossom. You get to solve the case. I go down for the killing. Everyone is happy."

"That's not how the law works."

"Listen. Just because I didn't kill Brick doesn't mean I haven't killed." He leaned closer. "How did you figure it out?"

"I remembered."

"Oh, son of a bitch. That must've sucked."

"You have no idea." Her exhaustion, her devastation, was catching up to her. She rubbed her eyes. "I don't want to play games anymore."

"That's too bad."

She had to be honest with him. There was a part of Wynn Ravinder that was noble. She could tell by the way he reacted to her. He tried to put up a front, but for some reason a part of him truly cared for her. Now to find out how much sway that part had.

She studied her hands, and said, "I'm in love with him."

He crossed his arms over his chest and watched her.

"I've been in love with him since I was a kid. I'm pretty sure my very first memory is of Levi Ravinder doing jumps on a Huffy. I think the fireworks bursting and sparkling around him were my imagination, but the rest was all him. And then last night, it all came back to me in a rush." She blinked through the tears, unable to believe she was losing it like that in front of an inmate. "It was him."

"Finally," he said, tilting his head to one side. "I thought you'd never show yourself."

"Wynn, why was he there? Why do you know so much about what happened that night?"

He released a heavy sigh, resigned to telling her the truth. He put his elbows on the table and clasped his hands. "When I heard what Brick was up to, I was working a job in Colorado."

She sniffed, and asked, "Hitman?"

"Close. Logger."

"Ah."

"It was over and done by the time I got to town. When I found him that night, he was delirious. Bleeding to death in his bed. Refusing to tell me what happened. Swearing he'd be fine. He just needed to sleep it off." He chuckled softly.

It took her a moment to realize he was talking about Levi. She stilled, hanging on his every word.

"His sheets were soaked with blood, and this was hours after he got you to the hospital."

His words crushed her and it took everything in her to maintain her composure. "Why didn't he go to a hospital?"

"Too many questions, apple. But I had no choice. I had to risk it. I wrapped him up the best I could and took him to an emergency room."

"But there were no stabbing victims admitted into any of the local hospitals."

"I drove him into Albuquerque. That was the biggest risk. I was scared shitless he was going to bleed to death on the way there. Took him to Southside. Admitted him under a false name. Then I whisked him out of there as soon as I could after surgery."

The image of Levi almost bleeding to death made her queasy.

He saddened as he thought back. "He was in a bad way. Told me everything in his drugged state. Well, most everything." He grinned up at her. "There were never any ropes, were there?"

Her test. She shook her head. "No. Chains. I only remember chains. And possibly duct tape."

"Clever girl."

She shrugged. "Hardly. It took me fifteen years to figure this out."

"Brain injuries tend to do that. I went back and buried the body in a shallow grave, but I figure the animals got to him anyway."

"They did. Not all of him, of course. And the knife?"

"I have it. Like I said."

"Are you going to tell me where?"

"In due time."

"Was he—" She could hardly believe she was asking this. Did she really want the truth? "Was he a part of it?"

The look he gave her was filled with almost as much sympathy as dubiousness. "You know the answer to that as well as I do."

"No, I know. I just thought maybe Kubrick had coerced him or forced him somehow."

"Apple, when have you ever known Levi Ravinder to be forced into anything he didn't want to do?"

"Then why not just tell me? After all these years, why keep it a secret?"

"Who the hell knows?" He raked a hand through his shoulder-length blond hair. "Pride? Self-preservation?"

She bit her bottom lip. "He could've died saving my life and I would never have known."

He studied her a long moment. "Do you have any idea what it would've done to him if you'd died?"

His question surprised her.

"He would've never gotten over it. He would not be the same man you see today. Besides, you helped."

"I helped what?"

"You helped him win the fight that night."

The snort that escaped her expressed her feelings on the subject beautifully, but she elaborated anyway. "Wynn, I literally lay there and watched as Levi was stabbed over and over. I couldn't have been more useless if I were made of hair gel."

"When Brick was abducting you, I guess he'd drugged you, but you fought back regardless. You bit his hand. That's how Levi figured it out. He knew you were missing, saw Brick's hand, and put two and two together. In a way, apple, you aided in your own rescue."

She remembered Brick's yell when he was taking her from

her truck. Blood on his hand. But she didn't remember biting him. "I thought he hurt it on the truck somehow."

"You bit him. You clamped down so hard, you literally took a chunk out it. It weakened him. Made it possible for Levi to wrest the knife away."

"He told you that?"

"He did. Again, he was high as a kite, but he rarely lies either way."

"Wait a minute," she said, when it dawned on her. "All those confessions muddying the waters. That was you."

"A few, yeah. Not all. What can I say? The man is loved."

"The man is almost worshiped, truth be known. And why do you keep calling me apple?"

He laughed softly. "You don't remember? You stole apples out of my tree one summer. I chased your ass for a half a mile, at which point you turned and threw a half-eaten Granny Smith at me."

"That was you?"

"God, you could run. I've called you apple blossom ever since. Just not to your face."

"When are you going to tell me where the knife is?"

"When I see the girl."

Her lids slammed shut. She had put it off long enough. Time for the ten-thousand-dollar question. "Why do you want to see her?"

"Because I've heard she looks like her grandmother."

Her lungs seized and turned to cement. "You aren't talking about my mother, are you?"

The corners of his eyes crinkled as he studied her. "She was a lot like you, apple. Strong. Beautiful. Fiercely protective of her family."

"You were in love with her."

"Body and soul."

She sobered with the knowledge that Wynn had been in love with his sister-in-law. With Levi's mother. "You're telling me Levi is Auri's father."

"You know he is," he said, his voice dripping with sympathy.

She took a long moment to process his words. To let them and their implications sink in. "You just said he wasn't a part of it."

"I don't understand. What does your abduction have to do with Levi being Auri's father?"

"Because that's when it happened. I woke up pregnant."

"You woke up with retrograde amnesia."

"True, but I've remembered a lot since then. Almost everything."

"Clearly, you haven't. That could explain why Levi hasn't told you the truth. Maybe he's waiting for you to remember. And a little sad you haven't. According to him, that night was *everything*. His word. One night you're underneath him with skin as soft as an ocean breeze—again, his words—and the next you're gone."

The emotion simmering beneath the surface bubbled up and boiled over. All these years, the answer was right in front of her. How did she not guess the truth? Was it denial? Or just sheer stupidity?

She'd gone for so long believing she'd been violated. Raped by a monster. And she'd never wanted Auri to feel less-than because of it. Because of something beyond her control.

"Does he know?" she asked, her chin trembling. "That he's Auri's father?" The words seemed foreign. Surreal. Before Wynn could answer, however, she did it for him. "Of course, he knows. He loves her so much."

"She's yours, apple." He reached up and brushed the wetness off her cheek. "He would love her either way."

That wrenched the sob building inside her chest right out of it. She didn't care. Screw policy. Screw procedure. Screw the rules. She stood, walked around the table, and threw her arms around him. He'd stood as well, anticipating her break from reality, and hugged her right back. Astonishingly, he let her cry and slobber on him like a lost puppy and didn't seem to care in the least.

After another eon of emotional instability, she stood at arm's length, and said, "Wait, what did you mean I have to get to Ravinder? What message were you talking about?"

Humor sparkled in his eyes. "Oh, now you want to know?"

A sheepish smile crept across her face. "Yes."

He waited a beat, looked down into her eyes, and said, "Clay is going to take him out."

30

*Celebrating the fact that you don't
have enough friends for an intervention?
First drink is on the house!*

—SIGN AT THE ROADHOUSE BAR AND GRILL

They sat at the table again, one on each side, genuine worry lining Wynn's rugged face. "He's working with a man named Redding."

She took out a notepad. "Yes. Del Sol's former sheriff. How do you know these things from prison?" she asked, amazed.

"Connections."

"Names?"

"Not on your life."

"Okay then. Well, I've been aware of Clay and Redding for a while. They're planning something."

Wynn nodded. "Clay wants the business Ravinder spent the last fifteen years building from the ground up. He brought our family out of the dark ages, and Clay can't stand it."

"From what I hear, he also wants to be inducted into the Southern Mafia again."

"The Southern Mafia isn't quite the well-oiled machine you might think it is. It's basically a few pockets of the criminally clueless, and half of those are now beholden to crime families a little farther south."

"Tucson?"

"Mexico," he said with a smile. "Among others."

"Okay. But what does Redding hope to get out of it? What's his endgame? Besides my badge."

"Your badge?" he asked, surprised.

"Yes. He very much wants this badge back."

A darkness came over him at the thought. "That would make trafficking easier."

"So, for his influence as an officer of the law? To make it easier to move drugs?"

"Maybe. I'll have to look into it."

"And Nancy Danforth?"

"Hey," he said, showing his palms, "she came to me."

"Really?" Sun said, doubt in every drawn-out syllable.

"I'm not quite the evil ne'er-do-well you imagine me to be, apple."

She kind of believed him. Kind of. And Nancy always was a bit of a sheep. "Someone else is pulling her strings. Someone powerful. She's afraid of him."

"Who?"

"I'd love the answer to that as well." She closed her notepad. "You look into Redding. I'll look into Danforth. Does Levi know he's in danger?"

"That kid." He stood and checked out his reflection in the observation mirror. Smoothed his blond goatee. "Still thinks he's invincible. You just need to buy me some time. A week. Two at the most."

"What does that mean? How am I going to buy you time?"

"Get him into hiding. I'll take care of the rest."

She stood and walked to him. "Wynn, I can't condone violence, even for a good cause."

He turned to her. "And you don't have to, apple. I'll get you the evidence to arrest Clay on the spot. I just need two weeks to do it. In the meantime, you have to get my nephew to safety."

"And just how am I going to do that? You know he's not just going to lay low because I ask him to."

"Take him on a romantic getaway."

After she ran out on him without an explanation? Not likely. "I've just had three violent attacks in my town. Well, one was in a mine. And multiple stabbings. Not to mention all the dead bodies." Her gaze slid past him. "So many dead bodies." She bounced back. "I can't leave."

"Then you have only one option left." He lifted a brow. "But he's not going to like it."

"He's been lying to me for the last fifteen years. Let's hear it."

After she and Wynn came up with a plan to keep his nephew safe, she offered him her best grave expression. "Who was his partner?" she asked, worried it really was Wynn. "Now that I know how my daughter came about."

He tilted his head in a sheepish shrug. "There was never a partner. It was all Kubrick."

She nodded, then knocked on the door.

The CO stepped aside and Quincy came into view. Brows drawn in a severe line. Arms crossed over his chest.

The door didn't have a window like the one in Arizona. He couldn't see inside the room, so he stood on the other side, a tad on edge if his expression were any indication.

"You okay?" he asked, peering past her to the inmate at her back.

But she was more than okay. Her world had just changed. She tackled him, throwing her arms around his neck.

"Okay, then," he said, patting her back and, Sun was certain, questioning Wynn from over her shoulder.

"Right this way," the CO said to them, ready to lead them out.

She let go of Quince and threw her arms around the guard's neck, too. He let her, though he didn't hug back so much as pat the top of her shoulder. Gingerly.

She was so happy. Mostly because he didn't tase her.

She stood back and scanned the area to see how much of a fool she was making of herself. The large room had several tables, and a handful of COs and administrators looked on, witnesses if the guard decided to file a sexual harassment lawsuit. A few inmates were there as well, one doing paperwork and one cleaning the tables. Probably a trustee who had earned the right to help in other areas of the prison.

As one of the officials came forward, determined to put a stop to whatever was going on, Quincy stepped in front of him and held up a hand, politely requesting a moment.

She turned and pushed her luck as far as she possibly could by giving Wynn another quick hug, then she faced the wrath of Quincy.

"We have to go save the dark lord's life," she said, utilizing Hailey's pet name for her brother. She gave Quincy a warning lift of her left brow. "He's going to be very, very angry."

Auri could hardly blame him for breaking out. Cruz. He escaped from Presbyterian Hospital a few hours after they released her. It also happened to be the day before his father's birthday.

"I can't let him spend his birthday in that box," he'd said when they were lying in bed, which sounded worse than it was. She was already dressed in clothes her grandma had brought for the trip home.

Her mom was signing the discharge papers while her grandparents gathered her things. The nurse had brought a cart to take all the flowers to the car. Her room had been filled with them. Cruz's room was empty. Not a single vase or potted plant and only one get-well card her grandparents had bought and had everyone sign.

Auri forced it out of her mind. The town loved him. She knew that. But did they understand what he'd done? How he'd saved her life? How he'd saved Mrs. Fairborn's?

They lay nose-to-nose, his handsome face and previously ashen pallor back to normal. And yet the sadness that consumed him was like an anvil on her chest, cutting off her air supply.

"My dad hated confined spaces," he said, his eyes glistening with tears he refused to shed.

"And now he's in a cardboard box." He bit out the words from between a clenched jaw. "Like his life didn't matter. Like all he was worth was a piece of corrugated paper."

She'd cupped his cheek. "Cruz, no one believes that. Everyone loved your father."

How he had kept his father's death a secret still boggled Auri's mind. He'd been working nights on the cars that were in his dad's shop before he died, then he would have people pick them up, telling them his dad was running errands. He'd be right back if they wanted to wait.

They never did.

The authorities still didn't know what to do with Cruz. His nonbiological grandfather was coming from Riley's Switch the next day. When Auri thought about it, she panicked. The thought of him moving killed her.

"I'll never see you again," he'd told Auri.

"Of course, you will," she lied. She knew how these things worked. She'd watched her mother pine after Levi for years. Now they're back and her mom and Levi still hadn't hooked up. Sometimes it didn't matter how much you loved someone. "Besides, you may not want to see me after this."

He inched back to get a better look at her. "Why would you say that?"

She bit her lip, and admitted, "My head."

"Your what?"

"It's lopsided."

"It's what?"

"My head is lopsided."

"That's so weird," he said, astonished. "I love lopsided heads."

"Really?"

He took her hand into his. "Really." He looked down and uncurled her fingers to see the necklace she had clasped in them. "What do you think of this?"

"That's just it. I don't know what to think. I've tried to look for engravings or markings, but there's nothing."

He took it from her, and said with a teasing grin, "Let me look."

"Okay, but there's simply nothing unusual about it."

He studied it closely as she studied him. What she wouldn't do for his eyelashes. "My dad was super into this stuff."

"What stuff?"

"Clocks and watches. He loved the mechanics and detail."

"Like in the carving?"

"Exactly." He showed her a part of the woman's hair where a ribbon held it back. "Look closely around the edges of that bow."

She did. "It seems a little more indented than the other lines. Deeper."

"Because it is." He pushed on the bow, but nothing happened. "I need something sharp."

"I used to be sharp," she said sadly.

He laughed.

"Oh! How about this?" She brought a tongue depressor out of the pocket of her sweater.

"Do I want to know why you have that?"

"It's grape flavored."

"Ah." He broke it to create a point and pressed it onto the bow. "This might work."

"What's it supposed to do exactly?" She imagined a music box inside the brass setting that played when someone pressed the button, but when he said, "This," and held it out to her, she sucked in a soft breath of air.

The cameo clicked and swung open to reveal a secret chamber. "No way."

"Way," he said, just as astonished. He tried to sit up but gave up with a wince.

"Here." She took it and brought out an aged piece of paper.

"What is it?"

She unfolded it carefully and screwed up her face. "It's . . . mineral rights?"

"Okay," he said, just as confused.

Her mother walked in with a smile. "Hey, you two."

"Mom, look!" She handed the paper to her mother. "I knew it. I knew there was more to that necklace. Mrs. Fairborn knew, too. But Cruz figured it out! We have to tell Mrs. Fairborn."

Her mom took the paper and read it over. She was wearing her usual black uniform and had pushed her sunglasses to the top of her head, holding locks of hair back that had come loose from her French braid. She was so pretty. Auri had always thought so, but she seemed to get prettier as she grew more and more elderly and decrepit.

"Auri, this is big," her mom said.

"Really?"

"Didn't you say Emily was a poor relation of the Press family?"

"Yes. A cousin. The family said that was why she stole the necklace."

"I don't think so. Mrs. Fairborn said Emily's grandmother left her that necklace in her will and, I'm assuming, what was inside. These are the mineral rights to the Press land in Texas."

"So, like, salt and stuff?" Cruz asked.

"Not really. These refer specifically to fluid mineral rights." She looked at them. "Guys, this means that Emily owned the oil rights to the Press land. Those oil wells make millions a year. Clearly, her side of the family never knew."

"Does this mean they're rich?"

"It could. And this is definitely worth killing over to keep secret."

"Billy was never after the necklace," Cruz said.

"But what was inside," Auri finished.

"Good work, guys. I can't wait to dig deeper into this."

"Me too. I found out Emily had a little brother but, again, they were very poor. I can't find anything else about him."

Her mom beamed at her. "We'll find them, bug. We'll make

sure this gets into the right hands. How are you guys doing?" She asked them both but she looked at Cruz.

He seemed to withdraw again. "I'm feeling better, thank you, Sheriff."

"I'm so glad. Quincy will be here later today."

He let go of Auri's hand and turned toward her mom. "It's okay. He doesn't have to come."

"Cruz," she admonished. "You're part of our family. He'll be here. We're going to figure this out."

He nodded, clearly unconvinced.

"I'll be back later, too. We'll talk about it then. You ready, bug?"

A pang of anxiety cramped her stomach. She leaned over and kissed his cheek before letting her mother lead her out. She missed him the minute she got to the elevator.

They had pizza and cake at home, and she was in the middle of begging her mom to let her go back with her when the phone rang.

"He did what?" her mom asked. "Okay. Okay, we'll be on the lookout here." When she hung up, she gave Auri her best mom look.

"What'd I do?" she asked. "I had a submissive hemogoblin. It's not my fault."

"Cruz escaped."

She stood and the floor spun but only a little. "Mom, we have to find him. He got stabbed."

"Yes, bug, I remember. Did he tell you he was going to leave?"

"No." She thought back and guilt washed over her. "But I think I know where he's going."

"Be careful," her mom said an hour later as they hiked up the Bear Hollow Trail to Rosita Peak. It wasn't far, but they knew he was there. Her mom's friend, Royce Womack, had driven out and checked as her deputies checked Cruz's house and a couple other possibilities. His dad's truck was parked at the trailhead.

"Did he tell you he was coming here?" her mom asked.

"No. But his mom's ashes were spread here." She fought the trembling her chin. "If he pulled any stitches, I swear, Mom, I'm going to kill him."

"I know. He's hurting, baby."

Tears welled in her eyes again. Every time she thought about what Cruz was going through, how alone in the world he was, her chest hurt and the waterworks started again.

"I'm sorry." Sun squeezed the hand she was holding to keep Auri steady. "I know you understand."

"I can't fully, but I can imagine."

"Even with your submissive hemogoblin?"

She drew in a deep breath. "I'm saying it wrong, aren't I?"

"Not at all." She cast a sideways glance to Auri's other escort up the trail, Quincy Cooper. She was definitely saying it wrong.

"How did he get his dad's truck?" she asked, dropping the whole thing but vowing to research submissive hemogoblins later. "How did he even get back to Del Sol from Albuquerque?"

"Uber."

"Wow."

"Apparently, he was determined," Quincy said. He took out a flashlight and lit the way. The sun was going down quick.

Her grandparents came up behind them then. "Grandma, Grandpa, what are you guys doing here?" Cruz must've been in more trouble than she thought if her grandparents were getting involved.

"We're here for you and Cruz, peanut," her grandpa said.

"Here for us?"

Before they could explain, they crested Rosita Peak and Auri saw the most beautiful sight she'd ever seen. Cruz standing on a massive rock formation with the sun setting just beyond. He was silhouetted by the bright pinks and oranges splashed across the sky.

"Cruz!" Auri said. She tried to run to him, but Quincy held her back.

Her mom eased forward. "Cruz, honey, how about you step away from that ledge?"

Auri hadn't even considered that. Her heart leapt into her throat when she realized how close he was. He wore old jeans and a loose T-shirt and he was shivering. He was shivering and wounded and in pain and Auri's heart shattered.

He turned back and looked over his shoulder. "He can't spend his birthday in a box."

"Cruz," Auri said, fighting Quincy.

"Can we come up?" her mom asked.

He lifted a shoulder and nodded.

Her mom gave Quincy the go-ahead and they climbed the rocks together. A few feet in front of him was a chain-link barrier no more than four feet high. If he were going to jump, he would have to climb over it first.

Auri put her arm on his shoulder. He held the box in both hands as if it were a precious thing. His cheeks were wet and dirty and his hair mussed. He just seemed so lost.

Her mom stood on the other side of her and Quincy on the other side of Cruz.

Cruz held out his elbow like he wanted her to wrap her arm in his, so she did. The lump in her throat grew bigger as he opened the box and gave his dad to the wind. He fought for control as a sob racked his body. Quincy wiped his eyes with one hand and she could hear her grandma weeping softly below them.

He put the lid on the box and reached into his jeans. "I did what you said. I wrote a poem."

"Cruz, he would've loved that."

But he handed her the folded piece of paper. "Would you mind?"

Did he want her to read it aloud? She stood confused until he stepped out of her embrace and eased closer to the barrier. She realized what he was doing.

She opened the paper and, with the help of Quincy's flashlight, read the first line as Cruz signed it almost bashfully for his dad.

"If you can hear now, Dad, don't let it worry you." Her voice broke, but she continued. "The sound of happiness is summer rain as it falls on the porch. The sound of joy is the pop and hiss of a soda can opening. The sound of excitement is paper crumpling on Christmas morning."

His signing wasn't dramatic or sensational or boisterous. It just was. It was his message to his dad. A private thing made public, but still a private thing.

"The sound of serenity," she continued through her constricted throat, "is an ocean wave rushing onto sand. The sound of sorrow is a sparrow singing to her lost mate. The sound of regret because things were left unsaid is thunder rumbling in the distance. It's half-spoken words. And sometimes it's no sound at all. But the sound of love is the loudest. It's the sound of my heartbeat every time I think of you."

Auri had to stop and catch her breath. Her mom sniffed beside her and rubbed her back. Cruz waited, his head down, for her to finish.

"If you can hear now, Dad, I hope you hear me talk to you sometimes and I hope you like my voice, because if you can hear now, Dad, my voice will be all of those things, and everything else you ever taught me. Thank you."

He signed, *thank you*, looking at the ground because he could hardly stand on his own anymore. Quincy rushed forward and wrapped an arm around him to take his weight as, one by one, lights started flickering in the mountains around them.

Auri watched and realized they were candles being lit in the distance. And then closer, down the mountain around them, a curtain of glimmering lights, casting a soft glow.

"Cruz," she said, pointing.

He wiped his eyes and looked out over the canyon at the hundreds of candles being lit in honor of his father. He took her hand and began sobbing in earnest on Quincy's shoulder. Quincy hugged him and cried, too. They pulled her mom into their huddle, then Quincy lifted Cruz into his arms.

"I can walk," he said in protest, though it was a weak one.

Quincy shook his head. "I gotcha, kid."

Her mom led them down the trail with the flashlight as Auri took one last look into the canyon. Levi stood a little farther down. He looked up at her, smiled sadly, then turned and headed back to his truck.

Quincy took Cruz to his house to grab his things, the basic necessities, insisting he stay with him. Auri's mom promised to sort it out, telling him he could stay with Quincy as long as he could put up with a man with a bacon tattoo.

"Hailey has offered her home, too," Quincy said. "If you would feel more comfortable there. To be honest, half the town has offered. You can pretty much take your pick of places to crash."

That seemed to surprise her mom, but she nodded. It would make sense for Cruz to stay with Hailey. They certainly had the room, and she had Jimmy. Either way, Cruz wasn't going anywhere anytime soon.

31

If that annoying knock is coming
from the motor and not the trunk,
stop by for a free checkup.

—SIGN AT GARY'S GARAGE

She rode with Deputy Tricia Salazar on the way to the Ravinder compound. The young deputy seemed nervous, and Sun couldn't imagine why.

"Everything okay, Salazar?"

"Of course," she said, a little too quickly. She had the chubbiest cheeks Sun had ever seen. And the biggest eyes. That combination made people underestimate her. Question her intelligence, which Sun had learned firsthand was a mistake. "Absolutely."

"But?" Sun asked.

She drove through the picturesque Sangre de Cristos with both hands on the wheel, gripping it perhaps a little too tight. "It's just, well, I'm not on the schedule for next week."

"Yes, I know," Sun said absently. Her stomach had been churning for hours thinking about their plan. Hers and Wynn's. They'd spoken on the phone twice already. Whoever Wynn had on the inside only knew that Clay and Redding were making a move soon.

Her life had turned into *The Godfather* when she wasn't looking. Secret assassinations. Familial coups. Brother pitted against brother. And in the middle of it all, the real seat of power. The enigmatic nephew. Now Sun just had to save the man's life without losing him forever.

Salazar squared her shoulders, and asked, "Am I fired, boss?"

Sun frowned at her. "Not that I know of, and since I'm the sheriff, I think I'd know."

"Oh." That brought her motors to a full stop. She thought a moment, then asked, "Are you forcing me to use my vacation time? Because I don't need it. I have paperwork piling up as we speak."

"Salazar, the day you have paperwork piling up will be the day I'm elected president of the Hair Club for Men."

"I meant after this. I'll have, you know, paperwork."

"Ah."

"Did I do something wrong, boss?"

Sun caved. She couldn't torture her any longer. "Wrong? Not at all." She reached over and lifted the mic off her radio. "This is Sheriff Vicram. I'd like to take this opportunity to announce the promotion of Deputy Tricia Salazar to lieutenant, the preferment to take place immediately if she accepts." She glanced at the deputy whose eyes, unbelievably, got bigger. "You'll need to take the test, which is why I scheduled you some free time to study. There's one in two weeks."

She opened her mouth to talk but then just left it there. Open.

"Deputy Salazar," she continued into the mic, "do you accept this promotion and promise to serve it and the Del Sol County Sheriff's Office to the best of your abilities?"

She handed her the mic. After a moment, the young deputy depressed the talk button. "Thank you, Sheriff. I do."

Zee was the first to congratulate her, with a hearty, "Booyah, Salazar. Congrats."

"Booyah, Lieutenant," Rojas said next. "Can I get a better parking spot?"

Quincy came on next with, "What happened to radio silence?" Smart-ass. "Booyah, Salazar. I look forward to passing you the buck."

Sun took the mic. "You already pass the buck to her, Chief Deputy. That's kind of like your thing."

"That's a 10–4, Sheriff. Just making sure you were paying attention."

They were coming up Levi's drive. "Showtime," she said, to silence the troops. Then she looked at a young deputy in serious threat of going into shock. Or crying. It could go either way. "You good with this, Salazar?"

She swallowed hard. "I am, boss. I'm—I'm honored. Thank you."

"Thank *you*," she said. "The way you handled the situation with Mrs. Fairborn? You took charge and saved those kids' lives. I've never been more impressed with an officer than I was with you. Nor more grateful."

Her chin trembled, and she said again, "Thank you, boss."

Sun nodded and drew in a deep breath as they pulled up to Levi's front door. Showtime indeed.

Surrounded by her troops, she steeled her nerves and knocked on the thick wooden door.

Levi opened it armed with a dish towel and a faint yet deadsexy smile. Her chest tightened as his gaze slid past her. It landed on the deputies in accompaniment and the smile faded.

"Levant Ravinder?" she said, only a slight wobble in her voice.

He pressed his mouth together and dropped his gaze to the towel.

"You are under arrest for the murder of Kubrick Farwell Ravinder."

He dried his hands, then tossed the towel on a side table and let her lead them behind his back as she read him his rights, the width of his shoulders making the cuffs even more uncomfortable.

"Do you understand these rights as I have said them to you?"

He raised his chin a visible notch and kept his gaze locked straight ahead, refusing to look at her.

Clay Ravinder, a stocky man with mousy brown hair and the

kind of scruff that was more hillbilly than sexy, moseyed out like he owned the place. The place that Levi had built with his own two hands. Where Clay lived free of charge because they shared the same last name.

"Knew that would catch up to you, boy," he said to Levi, the level of gloating sickening to Sun. Not that she would expect any less. He picked up the dish towel Levi had discarded and pretended to dry his hands with it.

Sun could see Clay's mind working. Whatever he'd planned to do to *take Levi out* would have to wait, but clearly he didn't mind. He saw this as an opportunity to seize control of the distillery, Sun had no doubt.

Hailey rushed onto the porch as they led Levi away. She glared at Sun, her face twisting in anger. "You," she said, and for a moment Sun didn't know if she was acting or not. "He saved your life and this is how you repay him?"

She charged forward, her nails protracted like a cat's claws. Quincy grabbed her and held her back, but she fought him like a rabid banshee.

Sun cast a worried glance to him. He was supposed to fill her in.

He bit back a curse. "If you don't calm down, ma'am, I will arrest you."

"You just try it." She twisted and turned until Quincy had no choice but to drag her to his cruiser kicking and screaming. He and the officers loaded them both into the back of his SUV and watched as Clay closed the front door to the Ravinder estate softly behind them.

Hailey continued to scream profanities. Levi stared straight ahead, reminding Sun of the calm before the storm.

"How'd we do?" Quince asked her when she walked up to him.

"That woman missed her calling."

He grinned. "She's a firecracker."

Sun laughed, hiding her face in case Clay was watching.

"And dare I say," Quincy said, daring, "that the man sitting in the back of my cruiser is a tad miffed."

"You think?"

"Maybe we should've, I don't know, filled him in on the plan?"

"He would never have gone along with it. He would've wanted to deal with Clay on his own. No telling how that would've ended up. Lest you forget, I'm trying to keep the man alive *and* out of prison. *And*. Not *or*."

"That's not going to be easy. He's even more stubborn than you are."

Ignoring his statement, Sun asked, "What about Jimmy?"

"He's with Auri and your parents. They're meeting us at the cabin later."

"Good. I just need him safe."

"Yeah, about that, are you sure you know what you're doing?"

Sun pressed her mouth to one side in a noncommittal shrug as she looked at the hard lines on the face of the man she loved more than a good bottle of chardonnay. And that was saying a lot. "Ask me tomorrow when he's had time to cool off."

"Sunbeam," he said, sucking air in through his teeth, "I don't think there's enough ice in the world that would have him cooled off by tomorrow, but you keep believing that." He climbed into his car amidst a bombardment of language so colorful, her new lieutenant blushed. Then Quince winked at Sun. "Denial is a glorious thing."

It was. It really was.

By the time they got to the cabin, Levi had figured out it was a ploy, probably because Hailey calmed down and explained what was going on. According to Quincy, Levi didn't seem to care.

"If I only had one word to describe him," Quincy said when Sun entered the rustic garage, "it would be homicidal."

Levi was still in the back seat. Still cuffed. Still livid by the hard set of his jaw.

"You left him in there?" Sun had driven to the cabin at a

slower pace and taken a few side roads to make sure they weren't being followed.

"I am not unlocking those cuffs until he calms down," Quincy said.

"You're bigger than he is."

He snorted. "Yeah. Like that would matter."

He was right. Skill trumped body weight most of the time, and few were more skilled than the man sitting in the back seat of Quincy's cruiser.

"I tried talking to him," Hailey said. "He's impossible once he gets like this. Best to just let him cool down."

Which was not likely to happen until they uncuffed him. It was a vicious cycle.

Sun scanned the site. They'd chosen that particular cabin not only because of its seclusion, but also because it had an attached garage, a rarity in the cabin world. It was important no one see them going from house to vehicle. The team had no idea how many minions Clay and Redding had on their payroll who could be watching at any given time.

The cabin belonged to a friend of her dad's who was summering in the Hamptons.

"People really do that?" she'd asked her dad when they'd come up with the plan.

"'Parently."

Quincy had stocked it with the essentials earlier. God only knew what he considered essential, but it should be enough to get them through the next week or so while Wynn tried to ascertain exactly what Clay's plan was. How and when they were going to make the attempt on Levi's life.

The mere thought weakened Sun's knees. She would arrest him a million times if it meant keeping him safe, so he could just be furious.

"Okay, thanks, guys. I'll uncuff him."

Quincy held up a hand. "I don't know if that's a good idea, boss."

But Hailey had a little more faith in her. "I think she's got this, Deputy."

He grinned down at her. "It's Chief Deputy, actually."

She wiggled her shoulders in a soft shiver, her excitement betraying her like a cat flicking its tail. It was no wonder Quincy had volunteered his services as personal bodyguard and put Salazar on Cruz duty. Passing the buck already.

Sun opened the back door of Quincy's cruiser and scooted onto the seat beside Levi. He'd now had the cuffs on for over half an hour. Behind his back, no less. He could not possibly be comfortable. But he didn't look at her. Didn't ask to have them removed. Didn't move a muscle.

Oh, yeah. He was pissed.

Oddly enough, she didn't care. She studied the profile of the man beside her. The man she'd loved since the beginning of time, so it seemed. The feelings that had threatened to overwhelm her when she was fake-arresting him—when she was leading his large hands behind his back, his sinewy forearms constricting, his jaw hardening—resurfaced.

A wave of emotion she hadn't expected swept over her. The last few days of her life had taken its toll. Not only with Auri and Cruz and even Mrs. Fairborn and the whole secret society thing, but to learn the truth after so long. To learn that Auri had been conceived not out of hatred or deviance, but out of love. A love that had endured for almost three decades. To learn that her rescuer was none other than the man of her dreams. That, like Cruz with Auri, he'd almost died protecting her.

Since ethics didn't seem to be her thing anyway, Sun twisted around in the seat, eased a leg over his, and straddled him.

He turned his head to the side, but only slightly, as her breasts brushed against him. A day's worth of growth covered his strong jaw. Framed his perfect face. Showcased his full, sculpted mouth. She lifted her fingers to it, unable to resist.

At least he didn't tell her to get off. Maybe he was just racking up points for the assault charges, but she didn't think so.

"You can be mad at me forever, Levi Ravinder." She brushed them over his five-o'clock. "You can curse me and hate me and never talk to me again, but know this." She slid her index finger down the bridge of his refined nose. "I will always do whatever it takes to keep you safe. And I will always love you."

The images that had flashed in her mind two nights ago when she saw his scars made an impromptu appearance. Levi fighting Kubrick in the rain. Stumbling toward her. Carrying her to the truck. Forcing water into her burning mouth. Levi hurt. Covered in blood. Doubling over in pain.

Levi dying. Lying in his bed, literally bleeding to death. Because of her. Because he saved her.

And almost eight years later, he'd saved Auri as well.

"You've said that before," he said, his tone ice cold. "Two hours later, you ran out on me."

"Speaking of which . . ." She leaned back against the cage and crossed her arms over her chest. "I remembered." She gestured to his abdomen. "I remembered. It all came back to me. Well, most of it." Once again, emotion welled inside her and thickened her voice for a moment. "You saved me," she said when she recovered. "You . . . you fought Kubrick. You wer stabbed and still you fought."

Realization dawned on his face and he bit down. "The scars."

"Yes, the scars, Levi. Why would you keep that from me?"

He scoffed, and said through gritted teeth, "Wynn." He said his uncle's name as though he were already conjuring a plan to get back at him. She almost felt bad for the guy.

"Yes, Wynn. But why not you? Why keep this from me all these years?"

The look he gave her would've melted a lesser woman. Apparently, that included her. She melted on the spot at the turmoil in his expression.

"What was I supposed to say, Vicram? 'Oh, hey, you were raped. Yeah, a Ravinder did it. Better luck next time.' I didn't *want* you to remember. To associate something that horrible with my family. With me."

She let that sink in, then asked, "When did you figure out I wasn't?"

"Wasn't what?"

"Raped."

A stillness settled over him, and she could tell his calmness reflected only what was on the surface. Underneath, his heart and mind were like thoroughbreds racing to an invisible finish line.

"I know that you know, Levi. You have to know."

His dark irises glittered, wary and guarded. "Know what?"

Had it really come to this? Was she going to have to force him to acknowledge the truth? She took his gorgeous face into both of her hands, and said softly, "You know Auri is yours."

Acknowledgments

Thank you, dear reader, for choosing to accompany me in the further adventures of Sunshine and Auri Vicram! These books have been an absolute joy to write—a dream come true, really—but I certainly didn't do it alone. So many people helped with this book, and they all have my undying gratitude. The following is only a partial list.

First, I must thank my amazing editor, Alexandra Sehulster, who spent almost as much time editing this book as I did writing it. I handed her what we in the biz call a *hot mess* and she made it pretty. And sparkly. And, you know, readable. Thank you for the hours and hours you put into this project. I am beyond grateful.

Thank you to the most amazing agent on the planet, Alexandra Machinist, a star so bright, I am honored to be in her orbit.

And to Josie Freedman, my incredible film agent who I can't wait to meet face-to-face. It will happen! I know it!

Thank you to Trayce Layne, my continuity editor, beta reader, research assistant, shoulder. . . . Here's to all of the hats you wear so beautifully!

And to copyeditor Ed Chapman. Sunshine would not shine nearly as brightly without your expertise. (Someday, in the distant—very distant—future, I will learn the difference between rack and wrack.)

Thank you to Jeffe Kennedy for hanging with me all day, every day, until I wrote *The End.* (Metaphorically.) I love Zooming with you! (Non-metaphorically.)

Thanks to everyone at St. Martin's Press, Macmillan Audio, ICM Partners, and Piatkus for everything you do. You're the wizards behind the curtain who fill people's lives with happiness.

And thank you to the insanely talented Lorelei King! Eeeep! I'm so thrilled you're bringing Sunshine and the gang to life and I hope we get to work together for decades to come.

Thank you to my Netterly for being the Netterly Nette that you are. My Danerly for having that incredible Danerly brain of yours. And my Kinter Pot Pie for the blatant borrowing of your identity. It had to be done.

Thank you to my early readers, Jeffe, Dana, Wendy, Jessica, Yennifer, and Ursula, for your input and profound advice. I promise to stop using *gorgeous* so often, but for now, you are all gorgeous creatures and I'm so grateful for you.

Thank you to my family. You know who you are. There is no escape.

Thank you to my GRIMLETS!!! You are the best Grimlets a girl could ask for. Sometimes we writers get stuck on the simplest things. Thanks for unsticking me, especially the lovely Brianna Cowles who may recognize a line from the book, since she wrote it.

And thank you, again, dear readers! I hope you're enjoying Sunshine as much as I'm enjoying writing her. Here's to your health and happiness in the coming years!

Donita Massey-Privett

New York Times and *USA Today* bestselling author DARYNDA JONES won a Golden Heart and a RITA for her manuscript *First Grave on the Right*. A born storyteller, she grew up spinning tales of dashing damsels and heroes in distress for any unfortunate soul who happened by, annoying man and beast alike. Darynda lives in the Land of Enchantment, also known as New Mexico, with her husband and two beautiful sons, the Mighty, Mighty Jones Boys.